Cecilia by Frances Burney

or MEMOIRS OF AN HEIRESS

Volume II of III

Frances Burney was born on June 13th, 1752 in Lynn Regis (now King's Lynn). By the age of 8 Frances had still not learned the alphabet and couldn't read. She now began a period of self-education, which included devouring the family library and to begin her own 'scribblings', these journal writings would document her life and cover the next 72 years.

Her journal writing was accepted but writing novels was frowned upon by her family and friends. Feeling that she had been improper, she burnt her first manuscript, The History of Caroline Evelyn, which she had written in secret.

It was only in 1778 with the anonymous publication of Evelina that her talents were available to the wider world. She was now a published and admired author.

Despite this success and that of her second novel, Cecilia, in 1785, Frances travelled to the court of King George III and Queen Charlotte and was offered the post of "Keeper of the Robes". Frances hesitated. She had no wish to be separated from her family, nor to anything that would restrict her time in writing. But, unmarried at 34, she felt obliged to accept and thought that improved social status and income might allow her greater freedom to write.

The years at Court were fruitful but took a toll on her health, writing and relationships and in 1790 she prevailed upon her father to request her release from service. He was successful.

The ideals of the French Revolution had brought support from many English literates for the ideals of equality and social justice. Frances quickly became attached to General Alexandre D'Arblay, an artillery officer who had fled to England. In spite of the objections of her father they were married on July 28th, 1793.

On December 18th, 1794, Frances gave birth to their only child, a son, Alexander.

Frances's third novel, Camilla, in 1796 earned her £2000 and was enough for them to build a house in Westhumble; Camilla Cottage.

In 1801 D'Arblay was offered service with the government of Napoleon in France, and in 1802 Frances and her son followed him to Paris, where they expected to remain for a year. The outbreak of the war between France and England meant their stay extended for ten years.

In August 1810 Frances developed breast cancer and underwent a mastectomy performed by "7 men in black". Frances was later able to write about the operation in detail, being conscious through most of it, anesthetics not yet being in use.

With the death of D'Arblay, in 1818, of cancer, Frances moved to London to be near her son. Tragically he died in 1837. Frances, in her last years, was by now retired but entertained many visits from younger members of the Burney family, who gathered to listen to her fascinating accounts and her talents for imitating the people she described.

Frances Burney died on January 6th, 1840.

Index of Contents

BOOK V

CHAPTER I

A ROUT.

The day at length arrived of which the evening and the entrance of company were, for the first time, as eagerly wished by Cecilia as by her dissipated host and hostess. No expence and no pains had been spared to render this long projected entertainment splendid and elegant; it was to begin with a concert, which was to be followed by a ball, and succeeded by a supper.

Cecilia, though unusually anxious about her own affairs, was not so engrossed by them as to behold with indifference a scene of such unjustifiable extravagance; it contributed to render her thoughtful and uneasy, and to deprive her of all mental power of participating in the gaiety of the assembly. Mr Arnott was yet more deeply affected by the mad folly of the scheme, and received from the whole evening no other satisfaction than that which a look of sympathetic concern from Cecilia occasionally afforded him.

Till nine o'clock no company appeared, except Sir Robert Floyer, who stayed from dinner time, and Mr Morrice, who having received an invitation for the evening, was so much delighted with the permission to again enter the house, that he made use of it between six and seven o'clock, and before the family had left the dining parlour. He apologized with the utmost humility to Cecilia for the unfortunate accident at the Pantheon; but as to her it had been productive of nothing but pleasure, by exciting in young Delvile the most flattering alarm for her safety, she found no great difficulty in according him her pardon.

Among those who came in the first crowd was Mr Monckton, who, had he been equally unconscious of sinister views, would in following his own inclination, have been as early in his attendance as Mr Morrice; but who, to obviate all suspicious remarks, conformed to the fashionable tardiness of the times.

Cecilia's chief apprehension for the evening was that Sir Robert Floyer would ask her to dance with him, which she could not refuse without sitting still during the ball, nor accept, after the reports she knew to be spread, without seeming to give a public sanction to them. To Mr Monckton therefore, innocently considering him as a married man and her old friend, she frankly told her distress, adding, by way of excuse for the hint, that the partners were to be changed every two dances.

Mr Monckton, though his principal study was carefully to avoid all public gallantry or assiduity towards Cecilia, had not the forbearance to resist this intimation, and therefore she had the pleasure of telling Sir Robert, when he asked the honour of her hand for the two first dances, that she was already engaged.

She then expected that he would immediately secure her for the two following; but, to her great joy, he was so much piqued by the evident pleasure with which she announced her engagement, that he proudly walked away without adding another word.

Much satisfied with this arrangement, and not without hopes that, if she was at liberty when he arrived, she might be applied to by young Delvile, she now endeavoured to procure herself a place in the music room.

This, with some difficulty, she effected; but though there was an excellent concert, in which several capital performers played and sung, she found it impossible to hear a note, as she chanced to be seated just by Miss Leeson, and two other young ladies, who were paying one another compliments upon their dress and their looks, settling to dance in the same cotillon, guessing who would begin the minuets, and wondering there were not more gentlemen. Yet, in the midst of this unmeaning conversation, of which she remarked that Miss Leeson bore the principal part, not one of them failed, from time to time, to exclaim with great rapture "What sweet music!—" "Oh! how charming!" "Did you ever hear any thing so delightful?—"

"Ah," said Cecilia to Mr Gosport, who now approached her, "but for your explanatory observations, how much would the sudden loquacity of this supercilious lady, whom I had imagined all but dumb, have perplext me!"

"Those who are most silent to strangers," answered Mr Gosport, "commonly talk most fluently to their intimates, for they are deeply in arrears, and eager to pay off their debts. Miss Leeson now is in her proper set, and therefore appears in her natural character; and the poor girl's joy in being able to utter all the nothings she has painfully hoarded while separated from her coterie, gives to her now the wild transport of a bird just let loose from a cage. I rejoice to see the little creature at liberty, for what can be so melancholy as a forced appearance of thinking, where there are no materials for such an occupation?"

Soon after, Miss Larolles, who was laughing immoderately, contrived to crowd herself into their party, calling out to them, "O you have had the greatest loss in the world! if you had but been in the next room just now!—there's the drollest figure there you can conceive; enough to frighten one to look at him." And presently she added "O Lord, if you stoop a little this way, you may see him!"

Then followed a general tittering, accompanied with exclamations of "Lord, what a fright!" "It's enough to kill one with laughing to look at him!" "Did you ever see such a horrid creature in your life?" And soon after, one of them screamed out "O Lord, see!—he's grinning at Miss Beverley!"

Cecilia then turned her head towards the door, and there, to her own as well as her neighbours' amazement, she perceived Mr Briggs! who, in order to look about him at his ease, was standing upon a chair, from which, having singled her out, he was regarding her with a facetious smirk, which, when it caught her eye, was converted into a familiar nod.

She returned his salutation, but was not much charmed to observe, that presently descending from his exalted post, which had moved the wonder and risibility of all the company, he made a motion to approach her; for which purpose, regardless of either ladies or gentlemen in his way, he sturdily pushed forward, with the same unconcerned hardiness he would have forced himself through a crowd in the street; and taking not the smallest notice of their frowns, supplications that he would stand still, and exclamations of "Pray, Sir!"—"Lord, how troublesome!" and "Sir, I do assure you here's no room!" he fairly and adroitly elbowed them from him till he reached her seat; and then, with a waggish grin, he looked round, to show he had got the better, and to see whom he had discomposed.

When he had enjoyed this triumph, he turned to Cecilia, and chucking her under the chin, said "Well, my little duck, how goes it? got to you at last; squeezed my way; would not be nicked; warrant I'll mob with the best of them! Look here! all in a heat!—hot as the dog days."

And then, to the utter consternation of the company, he took off his wig to wipe his head! which occasioned such universal horror, that all who were near the door escaped into other, apartments, while those who were too much enclosed, for flight, with one accord turned away their heads.

Captain Aresby, being applied to by some of the ladies to remonstrate upon this unexampled behaviour, advanced to him, and said, "I am quite abimé, Sir, to incommode you, but the commands of the ladies are insuperable. Give me leave, Sir, to entreat that you would put on your wig."

"My wig?" cried he, "ay, ay, shall in a moment, only want to wipe my head first."

"I am quite assommé, Sir," returned the Captain, "to disturb you, but I must really hint you don't comprehend me; the ladies are extremely inconvenienced by these sort of sights, and we make it a principle they should never be accablées with them."

"Anan!" cried Mr Briggs, staring.

"I say, Sir," replied the Captain, "the ladies are quite au desespoir that you will not cover your head."

"What for?" cried he, "what's the matter with my head? ne'er a man here got a better! very good stuff in it; won't change it with ne'er a one of you!"

And then, half unconscious of the offence he had given, and half angry at the rebuke he had received, he leisurely compleated his design, and again put on his wig, settling it to his face with as much composure as if he had performed the operation in his own dressing-room.

The Captain, having gained his point, walked away, making, however, various grimaces of disgust, and whispering from side to side "he's the most petrifying fellow I ever was obsedé by!"

Mr Briggs then, with much derision, and sundry distortions of countenance, listened to an Italian song; after which, he bustled back to the outer apartment, in search of Cecilia, who, ashamed of seeming a party in the disturbance he had excited, had taken the opportunity of his dispute with the Captain, to run into the next room; where, however, he presently found her, while she was giving an account to Mr Gosport of her connection with him, to which Morrice, ever curious and eager to know what was going forward, was also listening.

"Ah, little chick!" cried he, "got to you again! soon out jostle those jemmy sparks! But where's the supper? see nothing of the supper! Time to go to bed,—suppose there is none; all a take in; nothing but a little piping."

"Supper, Sir?" cried Cecilia; "the Concert is not over yet. Was supper mentioned in your card of invitation?"

"Ay, to be sure, should not have come else. Don't visit often; always costs money. Wish I had not come now; wore a hole in my shoe; hardly a crack in it before."

"Why you did not walk, Sir?"

"Did, did; why not? Might as well have stayed away though; daubed my best coat, like to have spoilt it."

"So much the better for the taylors, Sir," said Morrice, pertly, "for then you must have another."

"Another! what for? ha'n't had this seven years; just as good as new."

"I hope," said Cecilia, "you had not another fall?"

"Worse, worse; like to have lost my bundle."

"What bundle, Sir?"

"Best coat and waistcoat; brought 'em in my handkerchief, purpose to save them. When will Master Harrel do as much?"

"But had you no apprehensions, Sir," said Mr Gosport drily, "that the handkerchief would be the sooner worn out for having a knot tied in it?"

"Took care of that, tied it slack. Met an unlucky boy; little dog gave it a pluck; knot slipt; coat and waistcoat popt out."

"But what became of the boy, Sir?" cried Morrice, "I hope he got off?"

"Could not run for laughing; caught him in a minute; gave him something to laugh for; drubbed him soundly."

"O poor fellow!" cried Morrice with a loud hallow, "I am really sorry for him. But pray, Sir, what became of your best coat and waistcoat while you gave him this drubbing? did you leave them in the dirt?"

"No, Mr Nincompoop," answered Briggs angrily, "I put them on a stall."

"That was a perilous expedient, Sir," said Mr Gosport, "and I should fear might be attended with ill consequences, for the owner of the stall would be apt to expect some little douçeur. How did you manage, Sir?"

"Bought a halfpenny worth of apples. Serve for supper to-morrow night."

"But how, Sir, did you get your cloaths dried, or cleaned?"

"Went to an alehouse; cost me half a pint."

"And pray, Sir," cried Morrice, "where, at last, did you make your toilette?"

"Sha'n't tell, sha'n't tell; ask no more questions. What signifies where a man slips on a coat and waist-coat?"

"Why, Sir, this will prove an expensive expedition to you," said Mr Gosport, very gravely; "Have you cast up what it may cost you?"

"More than it's worth, more than it's worth," answered he pettishly "ha'n't laid out so much in pleasure these five years."

"Ha! ha!" cried Morrice, hallowing aloud, "why it can't be more than sixpence in all!"

"Sixpence?" repeated he scornfully, "if you don't know the value of sixpence, you'll never be worth fivepence three farthings. How do think got rich, hay?—by wearing fine coats, and frizzling my pate? No, no; Master Harrel for that! ask him if he'll cast an account with me!—never knew a man worth a penny with such a coat as that on."

Morrice again laughed, and again Mr Briggs reproved him; and Cecilia, taking advantage of the squabble, stole back to the music-room. Here, in a few minutes, Mrs Panton, a lady who frequently visited at the house, approached Cecilia, followed by a gentleman, whom she had never before seen, but who was so evidently charmed with her, that he had looked at no other object since his entrance into the house. Mrs Panton, presenting him to her by the name of Mr Marriot, told her he had begged her intercession for the honour of her hand in the two first dances; and the moment she answered that she was already engaged, the same request was made for the two following. Cecilia had then no excuse, and was therefore obliged to accept him.

The hope she had entertained in the early part of the evening, was already almost wholly extinguished; Delvile appeared not! though her eye watched the entrance of every new visitor, and her vexation made her believe that he alone, of all the town, was absent.

When the Concert was over, the company joined promiscuously for chat and refreshments before the ball; and Mr Gosport advanced to Cecilia, to relate a ridiculous dispute which had just passed between Mr Briggs and Morrice.

"You, Mr Gosport," said Cecilia, "who seem to make the minutiae of absurd characters your study, can explain to me, perhaps, why Mr Briggs seems to have as much pleasure in proclaiming his meanness, as in boasting his wealth?"

"Because," answered Mr Gosport, "he knows them, in his own affairs, to be so nearly allied, that but for practising the one, he had never possessed the other; ignorant, therefore, of all discrimination,—except, indeed, of pounds, shillings and pence!—he supposes them necessarily inseparable, because with him they were united. What you, however, call meanness, he thinks wisdom, and recollects, therefore, not with shame but with triumph, the various little arts and subterfuges by which his coffers have been filled."

Here Lord Ernolf, concluding Cecilia still disengaged from seeing her only discourse with Mr Gosport and Mr Monckton, one of them was old enough to be her father, and the other was a married man, advanced, and presenting to her Lord Derford, his son, a youth not yet of age, solicited for him the honour of her hand as his partner.

Cecilia, having a double excuse, easily declined this proposal; Lord Ernolf, however, was too earnest to be repulsed, and told her he should again try his interest when her two present engagements were fulfilled. Hopeless, now, of young Delvile, she heard this intimation with indifference; and was accompanying Mr Monckton into the ballroom, when Miss Larolles, flying towards her with an air of infinite eagerness, caught her hand, and said in a whisper "pray let me wish you joy!"

"Certainly!" said Cecilia, "but pray let me ask you of what?"

"O Lord, now," answered she, "I am sure you know what I mean; but you must know I have a prodigious monstrous great favour to beg of you; now pray don't refuse me; I assure you if you do, I shall be so mortified you've no notion."

"Well, what is it?"

"Nothing but to let me be one of your bride maids. I assure you I shall take it as the greatest favour in the world."

"My bride maid!" cried Cecilia; "but do you not think the bridegroom himself will be rather offended to find a bridesmaid appointed, before he is even thought of?"

"O pray, now," cried she, "don't be ill-natured, for if you are, you've no idea how I shall be disappointed. Only conceive what happened to me three weeks ago! you must know I was invited to Miss Clinton's wedding, and so I made up a new dress on purpose, in a very particular sort of shape, quite of my own invention, and it had the sweetest effect you can conceive; well, and when the time came, do you know her mother happened to die! Never any thing was so excessive unlucky, for now she won't be married this half year, and my dress will be quite old and yellow; for it's all white, and the most beautiful thing you ever saw in your life."

"Upon my word you are very obliging!" cried Cecilia laughing; "and pray do you make interest regularly round with all your female acquaintance to be married upon this occasion, or am I the only one you think this distress will work upon?"

"Now how excessive teazing!" cried Miss Larolles, "when you know so well what I mean, and when all the town knows as well as myself."

Cecilia then seriously enquired whether she had really any meaning at all.

"Lord yes," answered she, "you know I mean about Sir Robert Floyer; for I'm told you've quite refused Lord Derford."

"And are you also told that I have accepted Sir Robert Floyer?"

"O dear yes!—the jewels are bought, and the equipages are built; it's quite a settled thing, I know very well."

Cecilia then very gravely began an attempt to undeceive her; but the dancing beginning also at the same time, she stayed not to hear her, hurrying, with a beating heart, to the place of action. Mr Monckton and his fair partner then followed, mutually exclaiming against Mr Harrel's impenetrable conduct; of which Cecilia, however, in a short time ceased wholly to think, for as soon as the first cotillon was over, she perceived young Delvile just walking into the room.

Surprise, pleasure and confusion assailed her all at once; she had entirely given up her expectation of seeing him, and an absence so determined had led her to conclude he had pursuits which ought to make her join in wishing it lengthened; but now he appeared, that conclusion, with the fears that gave rise to it, vanished; and she regretted nothing but the unfortunate succession of engagements which would prevent her dancing with him at all, and probably keep off all conversation with him till supper time.

She soon, however, perceived a change in his air and behaviour that extremely astonished her; he looked grave and thoughtful, saluted her at a distance, shewed no sign of any intention to approach her, regarded the dancing and dancers as a public spectacle in which he had no chance of personal interest, and seemed wholly altered, not merely with respect to her, but to himself, as his former eagerness for her society was not more abated than [his] former general gaiety.

She had no time, however, for comments, as she was presently called to the second cotillon; but the confused and unpleasant ideas which, without waiting for time or reflection, crowded upon her imagination on observing his behaviour, were not more depressing to herself, than obvious to her partner; Mr Monckton by the change in her countenance first perceived the entrance of young Delvile, and by her apparent emotion and uneasiness, readily penetrated into the state of her mind; he was confirmed that her affections were engaged; he saw, too, that she was doubtful with what return.

The grief with which he made the first discovery, was somewhat lessened by the hopes he conceived from, the second; yet the evening was to him as painful as to Cecilia, since he now knew that whatever prosperity' might ultimately attend his address and assiduity, her heart was not her own to bestow; and that even were he sure of young Delvile's indifference, and actually at liberty to make proposals for himself, the time of being first in her esteem was at an end, and the long-earned good opinion which he had hoped would have ripened into affection, might now be wholly undermined by the sudden impression of a lively stranger, without trouble to himself, and perhaps without pleasure!

Reflections such as these wholly embittered the delight he had promised himself from dancing with her, and took from him all power to combat the anxiety with which she was seized; when the second cotillon, therefore, was over, instead of following her to a seat, or taking the privilege of his present situation to converse with her, the jealousy rising in his breast robbed him of all satisfaction, and gave to him no other desire than to judge its justice by watching her motions at a distance.

Mean while Cecilia, inattentive whether he accompanied or quitted her proceeded to the first vacant seat. Young Delvile was standing near it, and, in a short time, but rather as if he could not avoid than as if he wished it, he came to enquire how she did.

The simplest question, in the then situation of her mind, was sufficient to confuse her, and though she answered, she hardly knew what he had asked. A minute's recollection, however, restored an apparent composure, and she talked to him of Mrs Delvile, with her usual partial regard for that lady, and with an earnest endeavour to seem unconscious of any alteration in his behaviour.

Yet, to him, even this trifling and general conversation was evidently painful, and he looked relieved by the approach of Sir Robert Floyer, who soon after joined them.

At this time a young lady who was sitting by Cecilia, called to a servant who was passing, for a glass of lemonade; Cecilia desired he would bring her one also; but Delvile, not sorry to break off the discourse, said he would himself be her cup-bearer, and for that purpose went away.

A moment after, the servant returned with some lemonade to Cecilia's neighbour, and Sir Robert, taking a glass from him, brought it to Cecilia at the very instant young Delvile came with another.

"I think I am before hand with you, Sir," said the insolent Baronet.

"No, Sir," answered young Delvile, "I think we were both in together; Miss Beverley, however, is steward of the race, and we must submit to her decision."

"Well, madam," cried Sir Robert, "here we stand, waiting your pleasure. Which is to be the happy man!"

"Each, I hope," answered Cecilia, with admirable presence of mind, "since I expect no less than that you will both do me the honour of drinking my health."

This little contrivance, which saved her alike from shewing favour or giving offence, could not but be applauded by both parties; and while they obeyed her orders, she took a third glass herself from the servant.

While this was passing, Mr Briggs, again perceiving her, stumpt hastily towards her, calling out "Ah ha! my duck! what's that? got something nice? Come here, my lad, taste it myself."

He then took a glass, but having only put it to his mouth, made a wry face, and returned it, saying "Bad! bad! poor punch indeed!—not a drop of rum in it!

"So much the better, Sir," cried Morrice, who diverted himself by following him, "for then you see the master of the house spares in something, and you said he spared in nothing."

"Don't spare in fools!" returned Mr Briggs, "keeps them in plenty."

"No, Sir, nor in any out of the way characters," answered Morrice.

"So much the worse," cried Briggs, "so much the worse! Eat him out of house and home; won't leave him a rag to his back nor a penny in his pocket. Never mind 'em, my little duck; mind none of your guardians but me; t'other two a'n't worth a rush."

Cecilia, somewhat ashamed of this speech, looked towards young Delvile, in whom it occasioned the first smile she had seen that evening.

"Been looking about for you!" continued Briggs, nodding sagaciously; "believe I've found one will do. Guess what I mean;—£100,0000—hay?—what say to that? any thing better at the west end of the town?"

"£100,000!" cried Morrice, "and pray, Sir, who may this be?"

"Not you, Mr jackanapes! sure of that. A'n't quite positive he'll have you, neither. Think he will, though."

"Pray; Sir, what age is he?" cried the never daunted Morrice.

"Why about—let's see—don't know, never heard,—what signifies?"

"But, Sir, he's an old man, I suppose, by being so rich?"

"Old? no, no such thing; about my own standing."

"What, Sir, and do you propose him for an husband to Miss Beverley?"

"Why not? know ever a one warmer? think Master Harrel will get her a better? or t'other old Don, in the grand square?"

"If you please, Sir," cried Cecilia hastily, "we will talk of this matter another time."

"No, pray," cried young Delvile, who could not forbear laughing, "let it be discussed now."

"Hate 'em," continued Mr Briggs, "hate 'em both! one spending more than he's worth, cheated and over-reached by fools, running into gaol to please a parcel of knaves; t'other counting nothing but uncles and grandfathers, dealing out fine names instead of cash, casting up more cousins than guineas—"

Again Cecilia endeavoured to silence him, but, only chucking her under the chin, he went on, "Ay, ay, my little duck, never mind 'em; one of 'em i'n't worth a penny, and t'other has nothing in his pockets but lists of the defunct. What good will come of that? would not give twopence a dozen for 'em! A poor set of grandees, with nothing but a tie-wig for their portions!"

Cecilia, unable to bear this harangue in the presence of young Delvile, who, however, laughed it off with a very good grace, arose with an intention to retreat, which being perceived by Sir Robert Floyer, who had attended to this dialogue with haughty contempt, he came forward, and said, "now then, madam, may I have the honour of your hand?"

"No, Sir," answered Cecilia, "I am engaged."

"Engaged again?" cried he, with the air of a man who thought himself much injured.

"Glad of it, glad of it!" said Mr Briggs; "served very right! have nothing to say to him, my chick!"

"Why not, Sir?" cried Sir Robert, with an imperious look.

"Sha'n't have her, sha'n't have her! can tell you that; won't consent; know you of old."

"And what do you know of me, pray Sir?"

"No good, no good; nothing to say to you; found fault with my nose! ha'n't forgot it."

At this moment Mr Marriot came to claim his partner, who, very willing to quit this scene of wrangling and vulgarity, immediately attended him. Miss Larolles, again flying up to her, said "O my dear, we are all expiring to know who that creature is! I never saw such a horrid fright in my life!"

Cecilia was beginning to satisfy her, but some more young ladies coming up to join in the request, she endeavoured to pass on; "O but," cried Miss Larolles, detaining her, "do pray stop, for I've something to tell you that's so monstrous you've no idea. Do you know Mr Meadows has not danced at all! and he's been standing with Mr Sawyer, and looking on all the time, and whispering and laughing so you've no notion. However, I assure you, I'm excessive glad he did not ask me, for all I have been sitting still all this time, for I had a great deal rather sit still, I assure you; only I'm sorry I put on this dress, for any thing would have done just to look on in that stupid manner."

Here Mr Meadows sauntered towards them; and all the young ladies began playing with their fans, and turning their heads another way, to disguise the expectations his approach awakened; and Miss Larolles, in a hasty whisper to Cecilia, cried, "Pray don't take any notice of what I said, for if he should happen to ask me, I can't well refuse him, you know, for if I do, he'll be so excessive affronted you can't think."

Mr Meadows then, mixing in the little group, began, with sundry grimaces, to exclaim "how intolerably hot it is! there's no such thing as breathing. How can anybody think of dancing! I am amazed Mr Harrel has not a ventilator in this room. Don't you think it would be a great improvement?"

This speech, though particularly addressed to no one, received immediately an assenting answer from all the young ladies.

Then, turning to Miss Larolles, "Don't you dance?" he said.

"Me?" cried she, embarrassed, "yes, I believe so,—really I don't know,—I a'n't quite determined."

"O, do dance!" cried he, stretching himself and yawning, "it always gives me spirits to see you."

Then, turning suddenly to Cecilia, without any previous ceremony of renewing his acquaintance, either by speaking or bowing, he abruptly said "Do you love dancing, ma'am?"

"Yes, Sir, extremely well."

"I'm very glad to hear it. You have one thing, then, to soften existence."

"Do you dislike it yourself?"

"What dancing? Oh dreadful! how it was ever adopted in a civilized country I cannot find out; 'tis certainly a Barbarian exercise, and of savage origin. Don't you think so, Miss Larolles?"

"Lord no," cried Miss Larolles, "I assure you I like it better than any thing; I know nothing so delightful, I declare I dare say I could not live without it; I should be so stupid you can't conceive."

"Why I remember," said Mr Marriot, "when Mr Meadows was always dancing himself. Have you forgot, Sir, when you used to wish the night would last for ever, that you might dance without ceasing?"

Mr Meadows, who was now intently surveying a painting that was over the chimney-piece, seemed not to hear this question, but presently called out "I am amazed Mr Harrel can suffer such a picture as this to be in his house. I hate a portrait, 'tis so wearisome looking at a thing that is doing nothing!"

"Do you like historical pictures, Sir, any better?"

"O no, I detest them! views of battles, murders, and death! Shocking! shocking!—I shrink from them with horror!"

"Perhaps you are fond of landscapes?"

"By no means! Green trees and fat cows! what do they tell one? I hate every thing that is insipid."

"Your toleration, then," said Cecilia, "will not be very extensive."

"No," said he, yawning, "one can tolerate nothing! one's patience is wholly exhausted by the total tediousness of every thing one sees, and every body one talks with. Don't you find it so, ma'am?"

"Sometimes!" said Cecilia, rather archly.

"You are right, ma'am, extremely right; one does not know what in the world to do with one's self. At home, one is killed with meditation, abroad, one is overpowered by ceremony; no possibility of finding ease or comfort. You never go into public, I think, ma'am?"

"Why not to be much marked, I find!" said Cecilia, laughing.

"O, I beg your pardon! I believe I saw you one evening at Almack's; I really beg your pardon, but I had quite forgot it."

"Lord, Mr Meadows," said Miss Larolles, "don't you know you are meaning the Pantheon? only conceive how you forget things!"

"The Pantheon, was it? I never know one of those places from another. I heartily wish they were all abolished; I hate public places. 'Tis terrible to be under the same roof with a set of people who would care nothing if they saw one expiring!"

"You are, at least, then, fond of the society of your friends?"

"O no! to be worn out by seeing always the same faces!—one is sick to death of friends; nothing makes one so melancholy."

Cecilia now went to join the dancers, and Mr Meadows, turning to Miss Larolles, said, "Pray don't let me keep you from dancing; I am afraid you'll lose your place."

"No," cried she, bridling, "I sha'n't dance at all."

"How cruel!" cried he, yawning, "when you know how it exhilarates me to see you! Don't you think this room is very close? I must go and try another atmosphere,—But I hope you will relent, and dance?"

And then, stretching his arms as if half asleep, he sauntered into the next room, where he flung himself upon a sofa till the ball was over.

The new partner of Cecilia, who was a wealthy, but very simple young man, used his utmost efforts to entertain and oblige her, and, flattered by the warmth of his own desire, he fancied that he succeeded; though, in a state of such suspence and anxiety, a man of brighter talents had failed.

At the end of the two dances, Lord Ernolf again attempted to engage her for his son, but she now excused herself from dancing any more, and sat quietly as a spectatress till the rest of the company gave over. Mr Marriot, however, would not quit her, and she was compelled to support with him a trifling conversation, which, though irksome to herself, to him, who had not seen her in her happier hour, was delightful.

She expected every instant to be again joined by young Delvile, but the expectation was disappointed; he came not; she concluded he was in another apartment; the company was summoned to supper, she then thought it impossible to miss him; but, after waiting and looking for him in vain, she found he had already left the house.

The rest of the evening she scarce knew what passed, for she attended to nothing; Mr Monckton might watch, and Mr Briggs might exhort her, Sir Robert might display his insolence, or Mr Marriot his gallantry,—all was equally indifferent, and equally unheeded; and before half the company left the house, she retired to her own room.

She spent the night in the utmost disturbance; the occurrences of the evening with respect to young Delvile she looked upon as decisive; if his absence had chagrined her, his presence had still more shocked her, since, while she was left to conjecture, though she had fears she had hopes, and though all she saw was gloomy, all she expected was pleasant; but they had now met, and those expectations proved fallacious. She knew not, indeed, how to account for the strangeness of his conduct; but in seeing it was strange, she was convinced it was unfavourable; he had evidently avoided her while it was in his power, and when, at last, he was obliged to meet her, he was formal, distant, and reserved.

The more she recollected and dwelt upon the difference of his behaviour in their preceding meeting, the more angry as well as amazed she became at the change, and though she still concluded the pursuit of some other object occasioned it, she could find no excuse for his fickleness if that pursuit was recent, nor for his caprice if it was anterior.

CHAPTER II

A BROAD HINT.

The next day Cecilia, to drive Delvile a little from her thoughts, which she now no longer wished him to occupy, again made a visit to Miss Belfield, whose society afforded her more consolation than any other she could procure.

She found her employed in packing up, and preparing to remove to another lodging, for her brother, she said, was so much better, that he did not think it right to continue in so disgraceful a situation.

She talked with her accustomed openness of her affairs, and the interest which Cecilia involuntarily took in them, contributed to lessen her vexation in thinking of her own. "The generous friend of my brother," said she, "who, though but a new acquaintance to him, has courted him in all his sorrows, when every body else forsook him, has brought him at last into a better way of thinking. He says there is a gentleman whose son is soon going abroad, who he is almost sure will like my brother vastly, and in another week, he is to be introduced to him. And so, if my mother can but reconcile herself to parting with him, perhaps we may all do well again."

"Your mother," said Cecilia, "when he is gone, will better know the value of the blessing she has left in her daughter."

"O no, madam, no; she is wrapt up in him, and cares nothing for all the world besides. It was always so, and we have all of us been used to it. But we have had a sad scene since you were so kind as to come last; for when she told him what you had done, he was almost out of his senses with anger that we had acquainted you with his distress, and he said it was publishing his misery, and undoing whatever his friend or himself could do, for it was making him ashamed to appear in the world, even when his affairs might be better. But I told him again and again that you had as much sweetness as goodness, and instead of hurting his reputation, would do him nothing but credit."

"I am sorry," said Cecilia, "Mrs Belfield mentioned the circumstance at all; it would have been better, for many reasons, that he should not have heard of it."

"She hoped it would please him," answered Miss Belfield, "however, he made us both promise we would take no such step in future, for he said we were not reduced to so much indigence, whatever he was; and that as to our accepting money from other people, that we might save up our own for him, it would be answering no purpose, for he should think himself a monster to make use of it."

"And what said your mother?"

"Why she gave him a great many promises that she would never vex him about it again; and indeed, much as I know we are obliged to you, madam, and gratefully as I am sure I would lay down my life to serve you, I am very glad in this case that my brother has found it out. For though I so much wish him to do something for himself, and not to be so proud, and live in a manner he has no right to do, I think, for all that, that it is a great disgrace to my' poor father's honest memory, to have us turn beggars after his death, when he left us all so well provided for, if we had but known how to be satisfied."

"There is a natural rectitude in your heart," said Cecilia, "that the ablest casuists could not mend."

She then enquired whither they were removing, and Miss Belfield told her to Portland Street, Oxford Road, where they were to have two apartments up two pair of stairs, and the use of a very good parlour, in which her brother might see his friends. "And this," added she, "is a luxury for which nobody can blame him, because if he has not the appearance of a decent home, no gentleman will employ him."

The Padington house, she said, was already let, and her mother was determined not to hire another, but still to live as penuriously as possible, in order, notwithstanding his remonstrances, to save all she could of her income for her son.

Here the conversation was interrupted by the entrance of Mrs Belfield, who very familiarly said she came to tell Cecilia they were all in the wrong box in letting her son know of the £10 bank note, "for," continued she, "he has a pride that would grace a duke, and he thinks nothing of his hardships, so long as nobody knows of them. So another time we must manage things better, and when we do him any good, not let him know a word of the matter. We'll settle it all among ourselves, and one day or other he'll be glad enough to thank us."

Cecilia, who saw Miss Belfield colour with shame at the freedom of this hint, now arose to depart; but Mrs Belfield begged her not to go so soon, and pressed her with such urgency to again sit down, that she was obliged to comply.

She then began a warm commendation of her son, lavishly praising all his good qualities, and exalting even his defects, concluding with saying "But, ma'am, for all he's such a complete gentleman, and for all he's made so much of, he was so diffident, I could not get him to call and thank you for the present you made him, though, when he went his last airing, I almost knelt to him to do it. But, with all his merit, he wants as much encouragement as a lady, for I can tell you it is not a little will do for him."

Cecilia, amazed at this extraordinary speech, looked from the mother to the daughter in order to discover its meaning, which, however, was soon rendered plainer by what followed.

"But pray now, ma'am, don't think him the more ungrateful for his shyness, for young ladies so high in the world as you are, must go pretty good lengths before a young man will get courage to speak to them. And though I have told my son over and over that the ladies never like a man the worse for being a little bold, he's so much down in the mouth that it has no effect upon him. But it all comes of his being brought up at the university, for that makes him think he knows better than I can tell him. And so, to be sure, he does. However, for all that, it is a hard thing upon a mother to find all she says goes just for nothing. But I hope you'll excuse him, ma'am, for it's nothing in the world but his over-modesty."

Cecilia now stared with a look of so much astonishment and displeasure, that Mrs Belfield, suspecting she had gone rather too far, added "I beg you won't take what I've said amiss, ma'am, for we mothers of families are more used to speak out than maiden ladies. And I should not have said so much, but only I was afraid you would misconstrue my son's backwardness, and so that he might be flung out of your favour at last, and all for nothing but having too much respect for you."

"O dear mother!" cried Miss Belfield, whose face was the colour of scarlet, "pray!"—

"What's the matter now?" cried Mrs Belfield; "you are as shy as your brother; and if we are all to be so, when are we to come to an understanding?"

"Not immediately, I believe indeed," said Cecilia, rising, "but that we may not plunge deeper in our mistakes, I will for the present take my leave."

"No, ma'am," cried Mrs Belfield, stopping her, "pray don't go yet, for I've got a great many things I want to talk to you about. In the first place, ma'am, pray what is your opinion of this scheme for sending my son abroad into foreign parts? I don't know what you may think of it, but as to me, it half drives me out of my senses to have him taken away from me at last in that unnatural manner. And I'm sure, ma'am, if you would only put in a word against it, I dare say he would give it up without a demur."

"Me?" cried Cecilia, disengaging herself from her hold, "No, madam, you must apply to those friends who better understand his affairs, and who would have a deeper interest in detaining him."

"Lack a day!" cried Mrs Belfield, with scarcely smothered vexation, "how hard it is to make these grand young ladies come to reason! As to my son's other friends, what good will it do for him to mind what they say? who can expect him to give up his journey, without knowing what amends he shall get for it?"

"You must settle this matter with him at your leisure," said Cecilia, "I cannot now stay another moment."

Mrs Belfield, again finding she had been too precipitate, tried to draw back, saying "Pray, ma'am, don't let what I have mentioned go against my son in your good opinion, for he knows no more of it than the furthest person in the world, as my daughter can testify for as to shyness, he's just as shy as a lady himself; so what good he ever got at the University, as to the matter of making his fortune, it's what I never could discover. However, I dare say he knows best; though when all comes to all, if I was to speak my mind, I think he's made but a poor hand of it."

Cecilia, who only through compassion to the blushing Henrietta forbore repressing this forwardness more seriously, merely answered Mrs Belfield by wishing her good morning; but, while she was taking a kinder leave of her timid daughter, the mother added "As to the present, ma'am, you was so kind to make us, Henny can witness for me every penny of it shall go to my son."

"I rather meant it," said Cecilia, "for your daughter; but if it is of use to any body, my purpose is sufficiently answered."

Mrs Belfield again pressed her to sit down, but she would not again listen to her, coldly saying "I am sorry you troubled Mr Belfield with any mention of what passed between his sister and me, but should you speak of it again, I beg you will explain to him that he had no concern in that little transaction, which belonged wholly to ourselves."

She then hastened down stairs, followed, however, by Mrs Belfield, making awkward excuses for what she had said, intermixed with frequent hints that she knew all the time she was in the right.

This little incident, which convinced Cecilia Mrs Belfield was firmly persuaded she was in love with her son, gave her much uneasiness; she feared the son himself might entertain the same notion, and thought it most probable the daughter also had imbibed it, though but for the forward vulgarity of the sanguine mother, their opinions might long have remained concealed. Her benevolence towards them, notwithstanding its purity, must now therefore cease to be exerted; nor could she even visit Miss Belfield, since prudence, and a regard for her own character, seemed immediately to prohibit all commerce with the family.

"And thus difficult," cried she, "is the blameless use of riches, though; all who want them, think nothing so easy as their disposal! This family I have so much wished to serve, I may at last only have injured, since the disappointment of their higher expectations, may render all smaller benefits contemptible. And thus this unfortunate misconstruction of my good offices, robs them of a useful assistant, and deprives me at the same time of an amiable companion."

As soon as she returned home, she had a letter put into her hand which came from Mr Marriot, whose servant had twice called for an answer in the short time she had been absent.

This letter contained a most passionate avowal of the impression she had made on his heart the preceding evening, and an angry complaint that Mr Harrel had refused to hear his proposals. He entreated her permission to wait upon her for only five minutes, and concluded with the most fervent professions of respect and admiration.

The precipitancy of this declaration served merely to confirm the opinion she had already conceived of the weakness of his understanding; but the obstinacy of Mr Harrel irritated and distressed her, though weary of expostulating with so hopeless a subject, whom neither reason nor gratitude could turn from his own purposes, she was obliged to submit to his management, and was well content, in the present instance, to affirm his decree. She therefore wrote a concise answer to her new admirer, in the usual form of civil rejection.

CHAPTER III

AN ACCOMMODATION.

Cecilia was informed the next morning that a young woman begged to speak with her, and upon sending for her up stairs, she saw, to her great surprise, Miss Belfield.

She came in fear and trembling, sent, she said, by her mother, to entreat her pardon for what had passed the preceding day; "But I know, madam," she added, "you cannot pardon it, and therefore all that I mean to do is to clear my brother from any share in what was said, for indeed he has too much sense to harbour any such presumption; and to thank you with a most grateful heart for all the goodness you have shewn us."

And then, modestly courtsying, she would have returned home; but Cecilia, much touched by her gentleness, took her hand, and kindly reviving her by assurances of esteem, entreated that she would lengthen her stay.

"How good is this, madam," said she, "after having so much reason to think so ill of me and of all of us I tried all in my power to undeceive my mother, or at least to keep her quiet; but she was so much persuaded she was right, that she never would listen to me, and always said, did I suppose it was for me you condescended to come so often?"

"Yes," answered Cecilia, "most undoubtedly; had I not known you, however well I might have wished your brother, I should certainly not have visited at his house. But I am very happy to hear the mistake had spread no further."

"No indeed, madam, I never once thought of it; and as to my brother, when my mother only hinted it to him, he was quite angry. But though I don't mean to vindicate what has happened, you will not, I hope, be displeased if I say my mother is much more pardonable than she seems to be, for the same mistake she made with you, she would have been as apt to have made with a princess; it was not, therefore, from any want of respect, but merely from thinking my brother might marry as high as he pleased, and believing no lady would refuse him, if he would but have the courage to speak."

Cecilia assured her she would think no more of the error, but told her that to avoid its renewal, she must decline calling upon her again till her brother was gone. She begged therefore to see her in Portman-square whenever she had leisure, repeatedly assuring her of her good opinion and regard, and of the pleasure with which she should seize every opportunity of shewing them.

Delighted by a reception so kind, Miss Belfield remained with her all the morning; and when at last she was obliged to leave her, she was but too happy in being solicited to repeat her visit.

She suffered one day only to elapse before she shewed her readiness to accept the friendship that was offered her; and Cecilia, much pleased by this eagerness, redoubled her efforts to oblige and to serve her.

From this time, hardly a day passed in which she did not call in Portman-square, where nothing in her reception was omitted that could contribute to her contentment. Cecilia was glad to employ her mind in any way that related not to Delvile, whom she now earnestly endeavoured to think of no more, denying herself even the pleasure of talking of him with Miss Belfield, by the name of her brother's noble friend.

During this time she devised various methods, all too delicate to give even the shadow of offence, for making both useful and ornamental presents to her new favourite, with whom she grew daily more satisfied, and to whom she purposed hereafter offering a residence in her own house.

The trial of intimacy, so difficult to the ablest to stand, and from which even the most faultless are so rarely acquitted, Miss Belfield sustained with honour. Cecilia found her artless, ingenuous, and affectionate; her understanding was good, though no pains had been taken to improve it; her disposition though ardent was soft, and her mind seemed informed by intuitive integrity.

She communicated to Cecilia all the affairs of her family, disguising from her neither distress nor meanness, and seeking to palliate nothing but the grosser parts of the character of her mother. She seemed equally ready to make known to her even the most chosen secrets of her own bosom, for that such she had was evident, from a frequent appearance of absence and uneasiness which she took but little trouble to conceal. Cecilia, however, trusted not herself, in the present critical situation of her own mind, with any enquiries that might lead to a subject she was conscious she ought not to dwell upon; a short time, she hoped, would totally remove her suspence; but as she had much less reason to expect good than evil, she made it her immediate study to prepare for the worst, and therefore carefully avoided all discourse that by nourishing her tenderness, might weaken her resolution.

While thus, in friendly conversation and virtuous forbearance, passed gravely, but not unhappily, the time of Cecilia, the rest of the house was very differently employed; feasting, revelling, amusements of all sorts were pursued with more eagerness than ever, and the alarm which so lately threatened their destruction, seemed now merely to heighten the avidity with which they were sought. Yet never was the disunion of happiness and diversion more striking and obvious; Mr Harrel, in spite of his natural levity, was seized from time to time with fits of horror that embittered his gayest moments, and cast a cloud upon all his enjoyments. Always an enemy to solitude, he now found it wholly insupportable, and ran into company of any sort, less from a hope of finding entertainment, than from a dread of spending half an hour by himself.

Cecilia, who saw that his rapacity for pleasure encreased with his uneasiness, once more ventured to speak with his lady upon the subject of reformation; counselling her to take advantage of his present apparent discontent, which showed at least some sensibility of his situation, in order to point out to him the necessity of an immediate inspection into his affairs, which, with a total change in his way of life, was her only chance for snatching him from the dismal despondency into which he was sinking.

Mrs Harrel declared herself unequal to following this advice, and said that her whole study was to find Mr Harrel amusement, for he was grown so ill-humoured and petulant she quite feared being alone with him.

The house therefore now was more crowded than ever, and nothing but dissipation was thought of. Among those who upon this plan were courted to it, the foremost was Mr Morrice, who, from a peculiar talent of uniting servility of conduct with gaiety of speech, made himself at once so agreeable and useful in the family, that in a short time they fancied it impossible to live without him. And Morrice, though his first view in obtaining admittance had been the cultivation of his acquaintance with Cecilia, was perfectly satisfied with the turn that matters had taken, since his utmost vanity had never led him to entertain any matrimonial hopes with her, and he thought his fortune as likely to profit from the civility of her friends as of herself. For Morrice, however flighty, and wild, had always at heart the study of his own interest; and though from a giddy forwardness of disposition he often gave offence, his meaning and his serious attention was not the less directed to the advancement of his own affairs; he formed no connection from which he hoped not some benefit, and he considered the acquaintance and friendship of his superiors in no other light than that of procuring him sooner or later recommendations to new clients.

Sir Robert Floyer also was more frequent than ever in his visits, and Mr Harrel, notwithstanding the remonstrances of Cecilia, contrived every possible opportunity of giving him access to her. Mrs Harrel herself, though hitherto neutral, now pleaded his cause with earnestness; and Mr Arnott, who had been her former refuge from this persecution, grew so serious and so tender in his devoirs, that unable any longer to doubt the sentiments she had inspired, she was compelled even with him to be guarded and distant.

She now with daily concern looked back to the sacrifice she had made to the worthless and ungrateful Mr Harrel, and was sometimes tempted to immediately chuse another guardian, and leave his house for ever; yet the delicacy of her disposition was averse to any step that might publicly expose him, and her early regard for his wife would not suffer her to put it in execution.

These circumstances contributed strongly to encrease her intimacy with Miss Belfield; she now never saw Mrs Delvile, whom alone she preferred to her, and from the troublesome assiduity of Sir Robert, scarce ever met Mr Monckton but in his presence; she found, therefore, no resource against teazing and vexation, but what was afforded her by the conversation of the amiable Henrietta.

CHAPTER IV

A DETECTION.

A fortnight had now elapsed in which Cecilia had had no sort of communication with the Delviles, whom equally from pride and from prudence she forbore to seek for herself, when one morning, while she was sitting with Miss Belfield, her maid told her that young Mr Delvile was in the drawing-room, and begged the honour of seeing her for a few moments.

Cecilia, though she started and changed colour with surprize at this message, was unconscious she did either, from the yet greater surprize she received by the behaviour of Miss Belfield, who hastily arising, exclaimed "Good God, Mr Delvile!—do you know Mr Delvile, madam?—does Mr Delvile visit at this house?"

"Sometimes; not often," answered Cecilia; "but why?"

"I don't know,—nothing, madam,—I only asked by accident, I believe,—but it's very—it's extremely—I did not know"—and colouring violently, she again sat down.

An apprehension the most painful now took possession of Cecilia, and absorbed in thought, she continued for some minutes silent and immoveable.

From this state she was awakened by her maid, who asked if she chose to have her gloves.

Cecilia, taking them from her without speaking, left the room, and not daring to stop for enquiry or consideration, hastened down stairs; but when she entered the apartment where young Delvile was waiting for her, all utterance seemed denied her, and she courtsied without saying a word.

Struck with the look and uncommon manner of her entrance, he became in a moment as much disturbed as herself, pouring forth a thousand unnecessary and embarrassed apologies for his visit, and so totally forgetting even the reason why he made it, that he had taken his leave and was departing before he recollected it. He then turned back, forcing a laugh at his own absence of mind, and told her he had only called to acquaint her, that the commands with which she had honoured him were now obeyed, and, he hoped, to her satisfaction.

Cecilia, who knew not she had ever given him any, waited his further explanation; and he then informed her he had that very morning introduced Mr Belfield to the Earl of Vannelt, who had already heard him very advantageously spoken of by some gentlemen to whom he had been known at the University, and who was so much pleased with him upon this first interview, that he meant, after a few enquiries, which could not but turn out to his credit, to commit his eldest son to his trust in making the tour of Europe.

Cecilia thanked him for her share in the trouble he had taken in this transaction; and then asked if Mrs Delvile continued well.

"Yes," answered he, with a smile half reproachful, "as well as one who having ever hoped your favour, can easily be after finding that hope disappointed. But much as she has taught her son, there is one lesson she might perhaps learn from him;—to fly, not seek, those dangerous indulgences of which the deprivation is the loss of peace!"

He then bowed, and made his exit.

This unexpected reproof, and the yet more unexpected compliment that accompanied it, in both which more seemed meant than met the ear, encreased the perturbation into which Cecilia had already been thrown. It occurred to her that under the sanction of his mother's name, he had taken an opportunity of making an apology for his own conduct; yet why avoiding her society, if to that he alluded, should be flying a dangerous indulgence, she could not understand, since he had so little reason to fear any repulse in continuing to seek it.

Sorry, however, for the abrupt manner in which she had left Miss Belfield, she lost not a moment in hastening back to her; but when she came into the room, she found her employed in looking out of the window, her eye following some object with such earnestness of attention, that she perceived not her return.

Cecilia, who could not doubt the motive of her curiosity, had no great difficulty in forbearing to offer her any interruption. She drew her head back in a few minutes, and casting it upwards, with her hands clasped, softly whispered, "Heaven ever shield and bless him! and O may he never feel such pain as I do!"

She then again looked out, but soon drawing herself in, said, in the same soft accents, "Oh why art thou gone! sweetest and noblest of men! why might I not see thee longer, when, under heaven, there is no other blessing I wish for!"

A sigh which at these words escaped Cecilia made her start and turn towards the door; the deepest blushes overspread the cheeks of both as their eyes met each other, and while Miss Belfield trembled in every limb at the discovery she had made, Cecilia herself was hardly able to stand.

A painful and most embarrassed silence succeeded, which was only broken by Miss Belfield's bursting into tears.

Cecilia, extremely moved, forgot for a moment her own interest in what was passing, and tenderly approaching, embraced her with the utmost kindness; but still she spoke not, fearing to make an enquiry, from dreading to hear any explanation.

Miss Belfield, soothed by her softness, clung about her, and hiding her face in her arms, sobbed out, "Ah madam! who ought to be unhappy if befriended by you! if I could help it, I would love nobody else in almost the whole world. But you must let me leave you now, and to-morrow I will tell you every thing."

Cecilia, who had no wish for making any opposition, embraced her again, and suffered her quietly to depart.

Her own mind was now in a state of the utmost confusion. The rectitude of her heart and the soundness of her judgment had hitherto guarded her both from error and blame, and, except during her recent suspence, had preserved her tranquility inviolate; but her commerce with the world had been small and confined, and her actions had had little reference but to herself. The case was now altered; and she was suddenly in a conjuncture of all others the most delicate, that of accidentally discovering a rival in a favourite friend.

The fondness she had conceived for Miss Belfield, and the sincerity of her intentions as well as promises to serve her, made the detection of this secret peculiarly cruel; she had lately felt no pleasure but in her society, and looked forward to much future comfort from the continuance of her regard, and from their constantly living together; but now this was no longer even to be desired, since the utter annihilation of the wishes of both, by young Delvile's being disposed of to a third person, could alone render eligible their dwelling under the same roof.

Her pity, however, for Miss Belfield was almost wholly unallayed by jealousy; she harboured not any suspicion that she was loved by young Delvile, whose aspiring spirit led her infinitely more to fear some higher rival, than to believe he bestowed even a thought upon the poor Henrietta; but still she wished with the utmost ardour to know the length of their acquaintance, how often they had met, when they had conversed, what notice he had taken of her, and how so dangerous a preference had invaded her heart.

But though this curiosity was both natural and powerful, her principal concern was the arrangement of her own conduct; the next day Miss Belfield was to tell her every thing by a voluntary promise; but she doubted if she had any right to accept such a confidence. Miss Belfield, she was sure, knew not she was interested in the tale, since she had not even imagined that Delvile was known to her. She might hope, therefore, not only for advice but assistance, and fancy that while she reposed her secret in the bosom of a friend, she secured herself her best offices and best wishes for ever.

Would she obtain them? no; the most romantic generosity would revolt from such a demand, for however precarious was her own chance with young Delvile, Miss Belfield she was sure could not have any; neither her birth nor education fitted her for his rank in life, and even were both unexceptionable, the smallness of her fortune, as Mr Monckton had instructed her, would be an obstacle insurmountable.

Would it not be a kind of treachery to gather from her every thing, yet aid her in nothing? to take advantage of her unsuspicious openness in order to learn all that related to one whom she yet hoped would belong ultimately to herself, and gratify an interested curiosity at the expence of a candour not more simple than amiable? "No," cried Cecilia, "arts that I could never forgive, I never will practice; this sweet, but unhappy girl shall tell me nothing; betrayed already by the tenderness of her own heart, she shall at least suffer no further from any duplicity in mine. If, indeed, Mr Delvile, as I suspect, is engaged elsewhere, I will make this gentle Henrietta the object of my future solicitude; the sympathy of our situations will not then divide but unite us, and I will take her to my bosom, hear all her sorrows, and calm her troubled spirit by participating in her sensibility. But if, on the contrary, this mystery ends more happily for myself, if Mr Delvile has now no other engagement, and hereafter clears his conduct to my satisfaction, I will not be accessory to loading her future recollection with the shame of a confidence she then cannot but repent, nor with an injury to her delicacy that may wound it for ever."

She determined, therefore, carefully to avoid the subject for the present, since she could offer no advice for which she might not, hereafter, be suspected of selfish motives; but yet, from a real regard to the tender-hearted girl, to give all the tacit discouragement that was in her power, to a passion which she firmly believed would be productive of nothing but misery.

Once, from the frankness natural to her disposition, she thought not merely of receiving but returning her confidence; her better judgment, however, soon led her from so hazardous a plan, which could only have exposed them both to a romantic humiliation, by which, in the end, their mutual expectations might prove sources of mutual distrust.

When Miss Belfield, therefore, the next morning, her air unusually timid, and her whole face covered with blushes, made her visit, Cecilia, not seeming to notice her confusion, told her she was very sorry she was obliged to go out herself, and contrived, under various pretences, to keep her maid in the room. Miss Belfield, supposing this to be accidental, rejoiced in her imaginary reprieve, and soon recovered her usual chearfulness; and Cecilia, who really meant to call upon Mrs Delvile, borrowed Mrs Harrel's carriage, and set down her artless young friend at her new lodgings in Portland-street, before she proceeded to St James's-square, talking the whole time upon matters of utter indifference.

CHAPTER V

A SARCASM.

The reproach which Cecilia had received from young Delvile in the name of his mother, determined her upon making this visit; for though, in her present uncertainty, she wished only to see that family when sought by themselves, she was yet desirous to avoid all appearance of singularity, lest any suspicions should be raised of her sentiments.

Mrs Delvile received her with a cold civility that chilled and afflicted her; she found her seriously offended by her long absence, and now for the first time perceived that haughtiness of character which hitherto she had thought only given to her by the calumny of envy; for though her displeasure was undisguised, she deigned not to make any reproaches, evidently shewing that her disappointment in the loss of her society, was embittered by a proud regret for the kindness she believed she had thrown away. But though she scrupulously forbore the smallest complaint, she failed not from time to time to cast out reflections upon fickleness and caprice the most satirical and pointed.

Cecilia, who could not possibly avow the motives of her behaviour, ventured not to offer any apology for her apparent negligence; but, hitherto accustomed to the most distinguished kindness, a change to so much bitterness shocked and overpowered her, and she sat almost wholly silent, and hardly able to look up.

Lady Honoria Pemberton, a daughter of the Duke of Derwent, now came into the room, and afforded her some relief by the sprightliness of her conversation. This young lady, who was a relation of the Delviles, and of a character the most airy and unthinking, ran on during her whole visit in a vein of fashionable scandal, with a levity that the censures of Mrs Delvile, though by no means spared, had no power to [controul]; and, after having completely ransacked the topics of the day, she turned suddenly to Cecilia, with whom during her residence in St James's-square she had made some acquaintance, and said, "So I hear, Miss Beverley, that after half the town has given you to Sir Robert Floyer, and the other half to my Lord Derford, you intend, without regarding one side or the other, to disappoint them both, and give yourself to Mr Marriot."

"Me? no, indeed," answered Cecilia, "your ladyship has been much misinformed."

"I hope so," said Mrs Delvile, "for Mr Marriot, by all I ever heard of him, seems to have but one recommendation, and that the last Miss Beverley ought to value, a good estate."

Cecilia, secretly delighted by a speech which she could not resist flattering herself had reference to her son, now a little revived, and endeavoured to bear some part in the conversation.

"Everybody one meets," cried Lady Honoria, "disposes of Miss Beverley to some new person; yet the common opinion is that Sir Robert Floyer will be the man. But upon my word, for my own part, I cannot conjecture how she will manage among them, for Mr Marriot declares he's determined he won't be refused, and Sir Robert vows that he'll never give her up. So we none of us know how it will end; but I am vastly glad she keeps them so long in suspence."

"If there is any suspence," said Cecilia, "I am at least sure it must be wilful. But why should your ladyship rejoice in it?"

"O, because it helps to torment them, and keeps something going forward. Besides, we are all looking in the news-papers every day, to see when they'll fight another duel for you."

"Another?" cried Cecilia; "indeed they have never yet fought any for me."

"O, I beg your pardon," answered her ladyship, "Sir Robert, you know, fought one for you in the beginning of the winter, with that Irish fortune-hunter who affronted you at the Opera."

"Irish fortune-hunter?" repeated Cecilia, "how strangely has that quarrel been misrepresented! In the first place, I never was affronted at the Opera at all, and in the second, if your Ladyship means Mr Belfield, I question if he ever was in Ireland in his life."

"Well," cried Lady Honoria, "he might come from Scotland, for aught I know, but somewhere he certainly came from; and they tell me he is wounded terribly, and Sir Robert has had all his things packed up this month, that in case he should die, he may go abroad in a moment."

"And pray where, Lady Honoria," cried Mrs Delvile, "do you contrive to pick up all this rattle?"

"O, I don't know; everybody tells me something, so I put it all together as well as I can. But I could acquaint you with a stranger piece of news than any you have heard yet."

"And what is that?"

"O, if I let you know it, you'll tell your son."

"No indeed," said Mrs Delvile laughing, "I shall probably forget it myself."

She then made some further difficulty, and Cecilia, uncertain if she was meant to be a party in the communication, strolled to a window; where, however, as Lady Honoria did not lower her voice, she heard her say "Why you must know I am told he keeps a mistress somewhere in Oxford-Road. They say she's mighty pretty; I should like vastly to see her."

The consternation of Cecilia at this intelligence would certainly have betrayed all she so much wished to conceal, had not her fortunate removal to the window guarded her from observation. She kept her post, fearing to look round, but was much pleased when Mrs Delvile, with great indignation answered "I am sorry, Lady Honoria, you can find any amusement in listening to such idle scandal, which those who tell will never respect you for hearing. In times less daring in slander, the character of Mortimer would have proved to him a shield from all injurious aspersions; yet who shall wonder he could not escape, and who shall contemn the inventors of calumny, if Lady Honoria Pemberton condescends to be entertained with it?"

"Dear Mrs Delvile," cried Lady Honoria, giddily, "you take me too seriously."

"And dear Lady Honoria," said Mrs Delvile, "I would it were possible to make you take yourself seriously; for could you once see with clearness and precision how much you lower your own dignity, while you stoop to depreciate that of others, the very subjects that now make your diversion, would then, far more properly, move your resentment."

"Ay but, dear madam," cried Lady Honoria, "if that were the case, I should be quite perfect, and then you and I should never quarrel, and I don't know what we should do for conversation."

And with these words, hastily shaking hands with her, she took leave.

"Such conversation," said Mrs Delvile when she was gone, "as results from the mixture of fruitless admonition with incorrigible levity, would be indeed more honoured in the breach than the observance. But levity is so much the fashionable characteristic of the present age, that a gay young girl who, like Lady Honoria Pemberton, rules the friends by whom she ought to be ruled, had little chance of escaping it."

"She seems so open, however, to reproof," said Cecilia, "that I should hope in a short time she may also be open to conviction."

"No," answered Mrs Delvile, "I have no hope of her at all. I once took much pains with her; but I soon found that the easiness with which she hears of her faults, is only another effect of the levity with which she commits them. But if the young are never tired of erring in conduct, neither are the older in erring in judgment; the fallibility of mine I have indeed very lately experienced."

Cecilia, who strongly felt the poignancy of this sarcasm, and whose constant and unaffected value of Mrs Delvile by no means deserved it, was again silenced, and again most cruelly depressed; nor could she secretly forbear repining that at the very moment she found herself threatened with a necessity of foregoing the society of her new favourite, Miss Belfield, the woman in the whole world whom she most wished to have for her friend, from an unhappy mistake was ready to relinquish her. Grieved to be thus fallen in her esteem, and shocked that she could offer no justification, after a short and thoughtful pause, she gravely arose to take leave.

Mrs Delvile then told her that if she had any business to transact with Mr Delvile, she advised her to acquaint him with it soon, as the whole family left town in a few days.

This was a new and severe blow to Cecilia, who sorrowfully repeated "In a few days, madam?"

"Yes," answered Mrs Delvile, "I hope you intend to be much concerned?"

"Ah madam!" cried Cecilia, who could no longer preserve her quietness, "if you knew but half the respect I bear you, but half the sincerity with which I value and revere you, all protestations would be useless, for all accusations would be over!"

Mrs Delvile, at once surprised and softened by the warmth of this declaration, instantly took her hand, and said "They shall now, and for ever be over, if it pains you to hear them. I concluded that what I said would be a matter of indifference to you, or all my displeasure would immediately have been satisfied, when once I had intimated that your absence had excited it."

"That I have excited it at all," answered Cecilia, "gives me indeed the severest uneasiness; but believe me, madam, however unfortunately appearances maybe against me, I have always had the highest sense of the kindness with which you have honoured me, and never has there been the smallest abatement in the veneration, gratitude, and affection I have inviolably borne you."

"You see, then," said Mrs Delvile with a smile, "that where reproof takes any effect, it is not received; with that easiness you were just now admiring; on the contrary, where a concession is made without pain, it is also made without meaning, for it is not in human nature to project any amendment without a secret repugnance. That here, however, you should differ from Lady Honoria Pemberton, who can wonder, when you are superior to all comparison with her in every thing?"

"Will you then," said Cecilia, "accept my apology, and forgive me?"

"I will do more," said Mrs Delvile laughing, "I will forgive you without an apology; for the truth is I have heard none! But come," continued she, perceiving Cecilia much abashed by this comment, "I will enquire no more about the matter; I am glad to receive my young friend again, and even half ashamed, deserving as she is, to say how glad!"

She then embraced her affectionately, and owned she had been more mortified by her fancied desertion than she had been willing to own even to herself, repeatedly assuring her that for many years she had not made any acquaintance she so much wished to cultivate, nor enjoyed any society from which she had derived so much pleasure.

Cecilia, whose eyes glistened with modest joy, while her heart beat quick with revived expectation, in listening to an effusion of praise so infinitely grateful to her, found little difficulty in returning her friendly professions, and, in a few minutes, was not merely reconciled, but more firmly united with her than ever.

Mrs Delvile insisted upon keeping her to dinner, and Cecilia, but too happy in her earnestness, readily agreed to send Mrs Harrel an excuse.

Neither of the Mr Delviles spent the day at home, and nothing, therefore, disturbed or interrupted those glowing and delightful sensations which spring from a cordial renewal of friendship and kindness. The report, indeed, of Lady Honoria Pemberton gave her some uneasiness, yet the flighty character of that lady, and Mrs Delvile's reply to it, soon made her drive it from her mind.

She returned home early in the evening, as other company was expected, and she had not changed her dress since the morning; but she first made a promise to see Mrs Delvile some part of every day during the short time that she meant to remain in town.

CHAPTER VI

A SURMISE.

The next morning opened with another scene; Mrs Harrel ran into Cecilia's room before breakfast, and acquainted her that Mr Harrel had not been at home all night.

The consternation with which she heard this account she instantly endeavoured to dissipate, in order to soften the apprehension with which it was communicated; Mrs Harrel, however, was extremely uneasy, and sent all the town over to make enquiries, but without receiving any intelligence.

Cecilia, unwilling to leave her in a state of such alarm, wrote an excuse to Mrs Delvile, that she might continue with her till some information was procured. A subject also of such immediate concern, was sufficient apology for avoiding any particular conversation with Miss Belfield, who called, as usual, about noon, and whose susceptible heart was much affected by the evident disturbance in which she found Cecilia.

The whole day passed, and no news arrived; but, greatly to her astonishment, Mrs Harrel in the evening prepared for going to an assembly! yet declaring at the same time it was extremely disagreeable to her, only she was afraid, if she stayed away, every body would suppose something was the matter.

Who then at last, thought Cecilia, are half so much the slaves of the world as the gay and the dissipated? Those who work for hire, have at least their hours of rest, those who labour for subsistence are at liberty when subsistence is procured; but those who toil to please the vain and the idle, undertake a task which can never be finished, however scrupulously all private peace, and all internal comfort, may be sacrificed in reality to the folly of saving appearances!

Losing, however, the motive for which she had given up her own engagement, she now sent for her chair, in order to spend an hour or two with Mrs Delvile. The servants, as they conducted her up stairs, said they would call their lady; and in entering the drawing-room she saw, reading and alone, young Delvile.

He seemed much surprised, but received her with the utmost respect, apologizing for the absence of his mother, whom he said had understood she was not to see her till the next day, and had left him to write letters now, that she might then be at liberty.

Cecilia in return made excuses for her seeming inconsistency; after which, for some time, all conversation dropt.

The silence was at length broken by young Delvile's saying "Mr Belfield's merit has not been thrown away upon Lord Vannelt; he has heard an excellent character of him from all his former acquaintance, and is now fitting up an apartment for him in his own house till his son begins his tour."

Cecilia said she was very happy in hearing such intelligence; and then again they were both silent.

"You have seen," said young Delvile, after this second pause, "Mr Belfield's sister?"

Cecilia, not without changing colour, answered "Yes, Sir."

"She is very amiable," he continued, "too amiable, indeed, for her situation, since her relations, her brother alone excepted, are all utterly unworthy of her."

He stopt; but Cecilia made no answer, and he presently added "Perhaps you do not think her amiable?—you may have seen more of her, and know something to her disadvantage?"

"O no!" cried Cecilia, with a forced alacrity, "but only I was thinking that—did you say you knew all her relations?"

"No," he answered, "but when I have been with Mr Belfield, some of them have called upon him."

Again they were both silent; and then Cecilia, ashamed of her apparent backwardness to give praise, compelled herself to say, "Miss Belfield is indeed a very sweet girl, and I wish—" she stopt, not well knowing herself what she meant to add.

"I have been greatly pleased," said he, after waiting some time to hear if she would finish her speech, "by being informed of your goodness to her, and I think she seems equally to require and to deserve it. I doubt not you will extend it to her when she is deprived of her brother, for then will be the time that by doing her most service, it will reflect on yourself most honour."

Cecilia, confounded by this recommendation, faintly answered "Certainly,—whatever is in my power,—I shall be very glad—"

And just then Mrs Delvile made her appearance, and during the mutual apologies that followed, her son left the room. Cecilia, glad of any pretence to leave it also, insisted upon giving no interruption to Mrs Delvile's letter writing, and having promised to spend all the next day with her, hurried back to her chair.

The reflections that followed her thither were by no means the most soothing; she began now to apprehend that the pity she had bestowed upon Miss Belfield, Miss Belfield in a short time might bestow upon her; at any other time, his recommendation would merely have served to confirm her opinion of his benevolence, but in her present state of anxiety and uncertainty, every thing gave birth to conjecture, and had power to alarm her. He had behaved to her of late with the strangest coldness and distance,—his praise of Henrietta had been ready and animated,—Henrietta she knew adored him, and she knew not with what reason,—but an involuntary suspicion arose in her mind, that the partiality she had herself once excited, was now transferred to that little dreaded, but not less dangerous rival.

Yet, if such was the case, what was to become either of the pride or the interest of his family? Would his relations ever pardon an alliance stimulated neither by rank nor riches? would Mr Delvile, who hardly ever spoke but to the high-born, without seeming to think his dignity somewhat injured, deign to receive for a daughter-in-law the child of a citizen and tradesman? would Mrs Delvile herself, little less elevated in her notions, though infinitely softer in her manners, ever condescend to acknowledge her? Cecilia's own birth and connections, superior as they were to those of Miss Belfield, were even openly disdained by Mr Delvile, and all her expectations of being received into his family were founded upon the largeness of her fortune, in favour of which the brevity of her genealogy might perhaps pass unnoticed. But what was the chance of Miss Belfield, who neither had ancestors to boast, nor wealth to allure?

This thought, however, awakened all the generosity of her soul; "If," cried she, "the advantages I possess are merely those of riches, how little should I be flattered by any appearance of preference! and how ill can I judge with what sincerity it may be offered! happier in that case is the lowly Henrietta, who to poverty may attribute neglect, but who can only be sought and caressed from motives of purest regard. She loves Mr Delvile, loves him with the most artless affection;—perhaps, too, he loves her in return,—why else his solicitude to know my opinion of her, and why so sudden his alarm when he thought it unfavourable? Perhaps he means to marry her, and to sacrifice to her innocence and her attractions all plans of ambition, and all views of aggrandizement;—thrice happy Henrietta, if such is thy prospect of felicity! to have inspired a passion so disinterested, may humble the most insolent of thy superiors, and teach even the wealthiest to envy thee!"

CHAPTER VII

A BOLD STROKE.

When Cecilia returned home, she heard with much concern that no tidings of Mr Harrel had yet been obtained. His lady, who did not stay out late, was now very seriously frightened, and entreated Cecilia to sit up with her till some news could be procured; she sent also for her brother, and they all three, in trembling expectation of what was to ensue, passed the whole night in watching.

At six o'clock in the morning, Mr Arnott besought his sister and Cecilia to take some rest, promising to go out himself to every place where Mr Harrel was known to resort, and not to return without bringing some account of him.

Mrs Harrel, whose feelings were not very acute, finding the persuasions of her brother were seconded by her own fatigue, consented to follow his advice, and desired him to begin his search immediately.

A few moments after he was gone, while Mrs Harrel and Cecilia were upon the stairs, they were startled by a violent knocking at the door; Cecilia, prepared for some calamity, hurried her friend back to the drawing-room, and then flying out of it again to enquire who entered, saw to her equal surprize and relief, Mr Harrel himself.

She ran back with the welcome information, and he instantly followed her; Mrs Harrel eagerly told him of her fright, and Cecilia expressed her pleasure at his return; but the satisfaction of neither was of long duration.

He came into the room with a look of fierceness the most terrifying, his hat on, and his arms folded. He made no answer to what they said, but pushed back the door with his foot, and flung himself upon a sofa.

Cecilia would now have withdrawn, but Mrs Harrel caught her hand to prevent her. They continued some minutes in this situation, and then Mr Harrel, suddenly rising, called-out "Have you any thing to pack up?"

"Pack up?" repeated Mrs Harrel, "Lord bless me, for what?"

"I am going abroad," he answered; "I shall set off to-morrow."

"Abroad?" cried she, bursting into tears, "I am sure I hope not!"

"Hope nothing!" returned he, in a voice of rage; and then, with a dreadful oath, he ordered her to leave him and pack up.

Mrs Harrel, wholly unused to such treatment, was frightened into violent hysterics; of which, however, he took no notice, but swearing at her for a fool who had been the cause of his ruin, he left the room.

Cecilia, though she instantly rang the bell, and hastened to her assistance, was so much shocked by this unexpected brutality, that she scarcely knew how to act, or what to order. Mrs Harrel, however, soon recovered, and Cecilia accompanied her to her own apartment, where she stayed, and endeavoured to sooth her till Mr Arnott returned.

The terrible state in which Mr Harrel had at last come home was immediately communicated to him, and his sister entreated him to use all his influence that the scheme for going abroad might be deferred, at least, if not wholly given up.

Fearfully he went on the embassy, but speedily, and with a look wholly dismayed, he returned. Mr Harrel, he said, told him that he had contracted a larger debt of honour than he had any means to raise, and as he could not appear till it was paid, he was obliged to quit the kingdom without delay.

"Oh brother!" cried Mrs Harrel, "and can you suffer us to go?"

"Alas, my dear sister," answered he, "what can I do to prevent it? and who, if I too am ruined, will in future help you?"

Mrs Harrel then wept bitterly, nor could the gentle Mr Arnott, forbear, while he tried to comfort her, mixing his own tears with those of his beloved sister; but Cecilia, whose reason was stronger, and whose justice was offended, felt other sensations; and leaving Mrs Harrel to the care of her brother, whose tenderness she infinitely compassionated, she retreated into her own room. Not, however, to rest; the dreadful situation of the family made her forget she wanted it, but to deliberate upon what course she ought herself to pursue.

She determined without any hesitation against accompanying them in their flight, as the irreparable injury she was convinced she had already done her fortune, was more than sufficient to satisfy the most romantic ideas of friendship and humanity; but her own place of abode must now immediately be changed, and her choice rested only between Mr Delvile and Mr Briggs.

Important as were the obstacles which opposed her residence at Mr Delvile's, all that belonged to inclination and to happiness encouraged it; while with respect to Mr Briggs, though the objections were lighter, there was not a single allurement. Yet whenever the suspicion recurred to her that Miss Belfield was beloved by young Delvile, she resolved at all events to avoid him; but when better hopes intervened, and represented that his enquiries were probably accidental, the wish of being finally acquainted with his sentiments, made nothing so desirable as an intercourse more frequent.

Such still was her irresolution, when she received a message from Mr Arnott to entreat the honour of seeing her. She immediately went down stairs, and found him in the utmost distress, "O Miss Beverley," he cried, "what can I do for my sister! what can I possibly devise to relieve her affliction!"

"Indeed I know not!" said Cecilia, "but the utter impracticability of preparing her for this blow, obviously as it has long been impending, makes it now fall so heavily I wish much to assist her,—but a debt so unjustifiably contracted—"

"O madam," interrupted he, "imagine not I sent to you with so treacherous a view as to involve you in our misery; far too unworthily has your generosity already been abused. I only wish to consult with you what I can do for my sister."

Cecilia, after some little consideration, proposed that Mrs Harrel should still be left in England, and under their joint care.

"Alas!" cried he, "I have already made that proposal, but Mr Harrel will not go without her, though his whole behaviour is so totally altered, that I fear to trust her with him."

"Who is there, then, that has more weight with him?" said Cecilia, "shall we send for Sir Robert Floyer to second our request?"

To this Mr Arnott assented, forgetting in his apprehension of losing his sister, the pain he should suffer from the interference of his rival.

The Baronet presently arrived, and Cecilia, not chusing to apply to him herself, left him with Mr Arnott, and waited for intelligence in the library.

In about an hour after, Mrs Harrel ran into the room, her tears dried up, and out of breath with joy, and called out "My dearest friend, my fate is now all in your hands, and I am sure you will not refuse to make me happy."

"What is it I can do for you?" cried Cecilia, dreading some impracticable proposal; "ask me not, I beseech you, what I cannot perform!"

"No, no," answered she, "What I ask requires nothing but good nature; Sir Robert Floyer has been begging Mr Harrel to leave me behind, and he has promised to comply, upon condition you will hasten your marriage, and take me into your own house."

"My marriage!" cried the astonished Cecilia.

Here they were joined by Mr Harrel himself, who repeated the same offer.

"You both amaze and shock me!" cried Cecilia, "what is it you mean, and why do you talk to me so wildly?"

"Miss Beverley," cried Mr Harrel, "it is high time now to give up this reserve, and trifle no longer with a gentleman so unexceptionable as Sir Robert Floyer. The whole town has long acknowledged him as your husband, and you are every where regarded as his bride, a little frankness, therefore, in accepting him, will not only bind him to you for ever, but do credit to the generosity of your character."

At that moment Sir Robert himself burst into the room, and seizing one of her hands, while both of them were uplifted in mute amazement, he pressed it to his lips, poured forth a volley of such compliments as he had never before prevailed with himself to utter, and confidently entreated her to complete his long-attended happiness without the cruelty of further delay.

Cecilia, almost petrified by the excess of her surprise, at an attack so violent, so bold, and apparently so sanguine, was for some time scarce able to speak or to defend herself; but when Sir Robert, presuming on her silence, said she had made him the happiest of men, she indignantly drew back her hand, and with a look of displeasure that required little explanation, would have walked out of the room; when Mr Harrel, in a tone of bitterness and disappointment, called out "Is this lady-like tyranny then never to end?" And Sir Robert, impatiently following her, said "And is my suspense to endure for ever? After so many months' attendance—"

"This, indeed, is something too much," said Cecilia, turning back, "You have been kept, Sir, in no suspense; the whole tenor of my conduct has uniformly declared the same disapprobation I at present avow, and which my letter, at least, must have put beyond all doubt."

"Harrel," exclaimed Sir Robert, "did not you tell me—"

"Pho, Pho," cried Harrel, "what signifies calling upon me? I never saw in Miss Beverley any disapprobation beyond what it is customary for young ladies of a sentimental turn to shew; and every body knows that where a gentleman is allowed to pay his devoirs for any length of time, no lady intends to use him very severely."

"And can you, Mr Harrel," said Cecilia, "after such conversations as have passed between us, persevere in this wilful misapprehension? But it is vain to debate where all reasoning is disregarded, or to make any protestations where even rejection is received as a favour."

And then, with an air of disdain, she insisted upon passing them, and went to her own room.

Mrs Harrel, however, still followed, and clinging round her, still supplicated her pity and compliance.

"What infatuation is this!" cried Cecilia, "is it possible that you, too, can suppose I ever mean to accept Sir Robert?"

"To be sure I do," answered she, "for Mr Harrel has told me a thousand times, that however you played the prude, you would be his at last."

Cecilia, though doubly irritated against Mr Harrel, was now appeased with his lady, whose mistake, however ill-founded, offered an excuse for her behaviour; but she assured her in the strongest terms that her repugnance to the Baronet was unalterable, yet told her she might claim from her every good office that was not wholly unreasonable.

These were words of slender comfort to Mrs Harrel, who well knew that her wishes and reason had but little affinity, and she soon, therefore, left the room.

Cecilia then resolved to go instantly to Mrs Delvile, acquaint her with the necessity of her removal, and make her decision whither, according to the manner in which her intelligence should be received.

She sent, therefore, to order a chair, and was already in the hall, when she was stopt by the entrance of Mr Monckton, who, addressing her with a look of haste and earnestness, said, "I will not ask whither you are going so early, or upon what errand, for I must beg a moment's audience, be your business what it may."

Cecilia then accompanied him to the deserted breakfast room, which none but the servants had this morning entered, and there, grasping her hand, he said, "Miss Beverley, you must fly this house directly! it is the region of disorder and licentiousness, and unfit to contain you."

She assured him she was that moment preparing to quit it, but begged he would explain himself.

"I have taken care," he answered, "for some time past, to be well informed of all the proceedings of Mr Harrel; and the intelligence I procured this morning is of the most alarming nature. I find he spent the night before the last entirely at a gaming table, where, intoxicated by a run of good luck, he passed the whole of the next day in rioting with his profligate intimates, and last night, returning again to his favourite amusement, he not only lost all he had gained, but much more than he could pay. Doubt not, therefore, but you will be called upon to assist him; he still considers you as his resource in times of danger, and while he knows you are under his roof, he will always believe himself secure."

"Every thing indeed conspires," said Cecilia, more shocked than surprised at this account, "to make it necessary I should quit his house; yet I do not think he has at present any further expectations from me, as he came into the room this morning not merely without speaking to me, but behaved with a brutality to Mrs Harrel that he must be certain would give me disgust. It shewed me, indeed, a new part of his character, for ill as I have long thought of him, I did not suspect he could be guilty of such unmanly cruelty."

"The character of a gamester," said Mr Monckton, "depends solely upon his luck; his disposition varies with every throw of the dice, and he is airy, gay and good humoured, or sour, morose and savage, neither from nature nor from principle, but wholly by the caprice of chance."

Cecilia then related to him the scene in which she had just been engaged with Sir Robert Floyer.

"This," cried he, "is a manoeuvre I have been some time expecting; but Mr Harrel, though artful and selfish, is by no means deep. The plan he had formed would have succeeded with some women, and he therefore concluded it would with all. So many of your sex have been subdued by perseverance, and so many have been conquered by boldness, that he supposed when he united two such powerful besiegers in the person of a Baronet, he should vanquish all obstacles. By assuring you that the world thought the marriage already settled, he hoped to surprise you into believing there was no help for it, and by the suddenness and vehemence of the attack, to frighten and hurry you into compliance. His own wife, he knew, might have been managed thus with ease, and so, probably, might his sister, and his mother, and his cousin, for in love matters, or what are so called, women in general are, readily duped. He discerned not the superiority of your understanding to tricks so shallow and impertinent, nor the firmness of your mind in maintaining its own independence. No doubt but he was amply to have been rewarded for his assistance, and probably had you this morning been propitious, the Baronet in return was to have cleared him from his present difficulty."

"Even in my own mind," said Cecilia, "I can no longer defend him, for he could never have been so eager to promote the interest of Sir Robert, in the present terrible situation of his own affairs, had he not been stimulated by some secret motives. His schemes and his artifices, however, will now be utterly lost upon me, since your warning and advice, aided by my own suffering experience of the inutility of all I can do for him, will effectually guard me from all his future attempts."

"Rest no security upon yourself," said Mr Monckton, "since you have no knowledge of the many tricks and inventions by which you may yet be plundered. Perhaps he may beg permission to reside in your house in Suffolk, or desire an annuity for his wife, or chuse to receive your first rents when you come of age; and whatever he may fix upon, his dagger and his bowl will not fail to procure him. A heart so liberal as yours can only be guarded by flight. You were going, you said, when I came,—and whither?"

"To—to St James's-square," answered she, with a deep blush.

"Indeed!—is young Delvile, then, going abroad?"

"Abroad?—no,—I believe not."

"Nay, I only imagined it from your chusing to reside in his house."

"I do not chuse it," cried Cecilia, with quickness, "but is not any thing preferable to dwelling with Mr Briggs?"

"Certainly," said Mr Monckton coolly, "nor should I have supposed he had any chance with you, had I not hitherto observed that your convenience has always been sacrificed to your sense of propriety."

Cecilia, touched by praise so full of censure, and earnest to vindicate her delicacy, after an internal struggle, which Mr Monckton was too subtle to interrupt, protested she would go instantly to Mr Briggs, and see if it were possible to be settled in his house, before she made any attempt to fix herself elsewhere.

"And when?" said Mr Monckton.

"I don't know," answered she, with some hesitation, "perhaps this afternoon."

"Why not this morning?"

"I can go out no where this morning; I must stay with Mrs Harrel."

"You thought otherwise when I came, you were then content to leave her."

Cecilia's alacrity, however, for changing her abode, was now at an end, and she would fain have been left quietly to re-consider her plans; but Mr Monckton urged so strongly the danger of her lengthened stay in the house of so designing a man as Mr Harrel, that he prevailed with her to quit it without delay, and had himself the satisfaction of handing her to her chair.

CHAPTER VIII

Mr Briggs was at home, and Cecilia instantly and briefly informed him that it was inconvenient for her to live any longer at Mr Harrel's, and that if she could be accommodated at his house, she should be glad to reside with him during the rest of her minority.

"Shall, shall," cried he, extremely pleased, "take you with all my heart. Warrant Master Harrel's made a good penny of you. Not a bit the better for dressing so fine; many a rogue in a gold lace hat."

Cecilia begged to know what apartments he could spare for her.

"Take you up stairs," cried he, "shew you a place for a queen."

He then led her up stairs, and took her to a room entirely dark, and so close for want of air that she could hardly breathe in it. She retreated to the landing-place till he had opened the shutters, and then saw an apartment the most forlorn she had ever beheld, containing no other furniture than a ragged stuff bed, two worn-out rush-bottomed chairs, an old wooden box, and a bit of broken glass which was fastened to the wall by two bent nails.

"See here, my little chick," cried he, "everything ready! and a box for your gimcracks into the bargain."

"You don't mean this place for me, Sir!" cried Cecilia, staring.

"Do, do;" cried he, "a deal nicer by and by. Only wants a little furbishing; soon put to rights. Never sweep a room out of use; only wears out brooms for nothing."

"But, Sir, can I not have an apartment on the first floor?"

"No, no, something else to do with it; belongs to the club; secrets in all things! Make this do well enough. Come again next week; wear quite a new face. Nothing wanting but a table; pick you up one at a broker's."

"But I am obliged, Sir, to leave Mr Harrel's house directly."

"Well, well, make shift without a table at first; no great matter if you ha'n't one at all, nothing particular to do with it. Want another blanket, though. Know where to get one; a very good broker hard by. Understand how to deal with him! A close dog, but warm."

"I have also two servants, Sir," said Cecilia.

"Won't have 'em! Sha'n't come! Eat me out of house and home."

"Whatever they eat, Sir," answered she, "will be wholly at my expence, as will everything else that belongs to them."

"Better get rid of them; hate servants; all a pack of rogues; think of nothing but stuffing and guzzling."

Then opening another door, "See here," he cried, "my own room just by; snug as a church!"

Cecilia, following him into it, lost a great part of her surprise at the praise he had lavished upon that which he destined for herself, by perceiving that his own was yet more scantily furnished, having nothing in it but a miserable bed without any curtains, and a large chest, which, while it contained his clothes, sufficed both for table and chair.

"What are doing here?" cried he angrily, to a maid who was making the bed, "can't you take more care? beat 'out all the feathers, see! two on the ground; nothing but waste and extravagance! never mind how soon a man's ruined. Come to want, you slut, see that, come to want!"

"I can never want more than I do here," said the girl, "so that's one comfort."

Cecilia now began to repent she had made known the purport of her visit, for she found it would be utterly impossible to accommodate either her mind or her person to a residence such as was here to be obtained and she only wished Mr Monckton had been present, that he might himself be convinced of the impracticability of his scheme. Her whole business, therefore, now, was to retract her offer, and escape from the house.

"I see, Sir," said she, when he turned from his servant, "that I cannot be received here without inconvenience, and therefore I will make some new arrangement in my plan."

"No, no," cried he, "like to have you, 'tis but fair, all in our turn; won't be choroused; Master Harrel's had his share. Sorry could not get you that sweetheart! would not bite; soon find out another; never fret."

"But there are so many things with which I cannot possibly dispense," said Cecilia, "that I am certain my removing hither would occasion you far more trouble than you at present foresee."

"No, no; get all in order soon; go about myself; know how to bid; understand trap; always go shabby; no making a bargain in a good coat. Look sharp at the goods; say they won't do; come away; send somebody else for 'em. Never go twice myself; nothing got cheap if one seems to have a hankering."

"But I am sure it is not possible," said Cecilia, hurrying down stairs, "that my room, and one for each of my servants, should be ready in time."

"Yes, yes," cried he, following her, "ready in a trice. Make a little shift at first; double the blanket till we get another; lie with the maid a night or two; never stand for a trifle."

And, when she was seated in her chair, the whole time disclaiming her intention of returning, he only pinched her cheek with a facetious smirk, and said, "By, by, little duck; come again soon. Warrant I'll have the room ready. Sha'n't half know it again; make it as smart as a carrot."

And then she left the house; fully satisfied that no one could blame her refusing to inhabit it, and much less chagrined than she was willing to suppose herself, in finding she had now no resource but in the Delviles.

Yet, in her serious reflections, she could not but think herself strangely unfortunate that the guardian with whom alone it seemed proper for her to reside, should by parsimony, vulgarity, and meanness, render riches contemptible, prosperity unavailing, and economy odious; and that the choice of her uncle should thus unhappily have fallen upon the lowest and most wretched of misers, in a city abounding with opulence, hospitality, and splendour, and of which the principal inhabitants, long eminent for their wealth and their probity, were now almost universally rising in elegance and liberality.

CHAPTER IX

A DECLARATION.

Cecilia's next progress, therefore, was to St James's-square, whither she went in the utmost anxiety, from her uncertainty of the reception with which her proposal would meet.

The servants informed her that Mr and Mrs Delvile were at breakfast, and that the Duke of Derwent and his two daughters were with them.

Before such witnesses to relate the reasons of her leaving the Harmless was impossible; and from such a party to send for Mrs Delvile, would, by her stately guardian, be deemed an indecorum unpardonable. She was obliged, therefore, to return to Portman-square, in order to open her cause in a letter to Mrs Delvile.

Mr Arnott, flying instantly to meet her, called out, "O madam, what alarm has your absence occasioned! My sister believed she should see you no more, Mr Harrel feared a premature discovery of his purposed retreat, and we have all been under the cruellest apprehensions lest you meant not to come back."

"I am sorry I spoke not with you before I went out," said Cecilia, accompanying him to the library, "but I thought you were all too much occupied to miss me. I have been, indeed, preparing for a removal, but I meant not to leave your sister without bidding her adieu, nor, indeed, to quit any part of the family with so little ceremony. Is Mr Harrel still firm to his last plan?"

"I fear so! I have tried what is possible to dissuade him, and my poor sister has wept without ceasing. Indeed, if she will take no consolation, I believe I shall do what she pleases, for I cannot bear the sight of her in such distress."

"You are too generous, and too good!" said Cecilia, "and I know not how, while flying from danger myself, to forbear counselling you to avoid it also."

"Ah madam!" cried he, "the greatest danger for me is what I have now no power to run from!"

Cecilia, though she could not but understand him, felt not the less his friend for knowing him the humblest of her admirers; and as she saw the threatening ruin to which his too great tenderness exposed him, she kindly said "Mr Arnott, I will speak, to you without reserve. It is not difficult to see that the destruction which awaits Mr Harrel, is ready also to ensnare his brother-in-law; but let not that blindness to the future which we have so often lamented for him, hereafter be lamented for yourself. Till his present connections are broken, and his way of living is changed, nothing can be done for him, and whatever you were to advance, would merely be sunk at the gaming table. Reserve, therefore, your liberality till it may indeed be of service to him, for believe me, at present, his mind is as much injured as his fortune."

"And is it possible, madam," said Mr Arnott, in an accent of surprize and delight, "that you can deign to be interested in what may become of me! and that my sharing or escaping the ruin of this house is not wholly indifferent to you?"

"Certainly not," answered Cecilia; "as the brother of my earliest friend, I can never be insensible to your welfare."

"Ah madam!" cried he, "as her brother!—Oh that there were any other tie!—"

"Think a little," said Cecilia, preparing to quit the room, "of what I have mentioned, and, for your sister's sake, be firm now, if you would be kind hereafter."

"I will be any and every thing," cried he, "that Miss Beverley will command."

Cecilia, fearful of any misinterpretation, then came back, and gravely said, "No, Sir, be ruled only by your own judgment; or, should my advice have any weight with you, remember it is given from the most disinterested motives, and with no other view than that of securing your power to be of service to your sister."

"For that sister's sake, then, have the goodness to hear my situation, and honour me with further directions."

"You will make me fear to speak," said Cecilia, "if you give so much consequence to my opinion. I have seen, however, nothing in your conduct I have ever wished changed, except too little attention to your own interest and affairs."

"Ah!" cried he, "with what rapture should I hear those words, could I but imagine—"

"Come, come," said Cecilia, smiling, "no digression! You called me back to talk of your sister; if you change your subject, perhaps you may lose your auditor."

"I would not, madam, for the world encroach upon your goodness; the favour I have found has indeed always exceeded my expectations, as it has always surpassed my desert; yet has it never blinded me to my own unworthiness. Do not, then, fear to indulge me with your conversation; I shall draw from it no inference but of pity, and though pity from Miss Beverley is the sweetest balm to my heart, it shall never seduce me to the encouragement of higher hopes."

Cecilia had long had reason to expect such a declaration, yet she heard it with unaffected concern, and looking at him with the utmost gentleness, said "Mr Arnott, your regard does me honour, and, were it somewhat more rational, would give me pleasure; take, then, from it what is more than I wish or merit, and, while you preserve the rest, be assured it will be faithfully returned."

"Your rejection is so mild," cried he, "that I, who had no hope of acceptance, find relief in having at last told my sufferings. Could I but continue to see you every day, and to be blest with your conversation, I think I should be happy, and I am sure I should be grateful."

"You are already," answered she, shaking her head, and moving towards the door, "infringing the conditions upon which our friendship is to be founded."

"Do not go, madam," he cried, "till I have done what you have just promised to permit, acquainted you with my situation, and been honoured with your advice. I must own to you, then, that £5000, which I had in the stocks, as well as a considerable sum in a banker's hands, I have parted with, as I now find for ever but I have no heart for refusal, nor would my sister at this moment be thus distressed, but that I have nothing more to give without I cut down my trees, or sell some farm, since all I was worth, except my landed property, is already gone. What, therefore, I can now do to save Mr Harrel from this desperate expedition I know not."

"I am sorry," said Cecilia, "to speak with severity of one so nearly connected with you, yet, suffer me to ask, why should he be saved from it at all? and what is there he can at present do better? Has not he long been threatened with every evil that is now arrived? have we not both warned him, and have not the clamours of his creditors assailed him? yet what has been the consequence? he has not submitted to the smallest change in his way of life, he has not denied himself a single indulgence, nor spared any expence, nor thought of any reformation. Luxury has followed luxury, and he has only grown fonder of extravagance, as extravagance has become more dangerous. Till the present storm, therefore, blows over, leave him to his fate, and when a calm succeeds, I will myself, for the sake of Priscilla, aid you to save what is possible of the wreck."

"All you say, madam, is as wise as it is good, and now I am acquainted with your opinion, I will wholly new model myself upon it, and grow as steady against all attacks as hitherto I have been yielding."

Cecilia was then retiring; but again detaining her, he said "You spoke, madam, of a removal, and indeed it is high time you should quit this scene; yet I hope you intend not to go till to-morrow, as Mr Harrel has declared your leaving him sooner will be his destruction."

"Heaven forbid," said Cecilia, "for I mean to be gone with all the speed in my power."

"Mr Harrel," answered he, "did not explain himself; but I believe he apprehends your deserting his house at this critical time, will raise a suspicion of his own design of going abroad, and make his creditors interfere to prevent him."

"To what a wretched state," cried Cecilia, "has he reduced himself! I will not, however, be the voluntary instrument of his disgrace; and if you think my stay is so material to his security, I will continue here till to-morrow morning."

Mr Arnott almost wept his thanks for this concession, and Cecilia, happy in making it to him instead of Mr Harrel, then went to her own room, and wrote the following letter to Mrs Delvile.

To the Hon. Mrs Delvile, St James's-square.

PORTMAN SQUARE, June 12.

DEAR MADAM,—I am willing to hope you have been rather surprised that I have not sooner availed myself of the permission with which you yesterday honoured me of spending this whole day with you, but, unfortunately for myself, I am prevented waiting upon you even for any part of it. Do not, however, think me now ungrateful if I stay away, nor to-morrow impertinent, if I venture to enquire whether that apartment which you had once the goodness to appropriate to my use, may then again be spared for me! The accidents which have prompted this strange request will, I trust, be sufficient apology for the liberty I take in making it, when I have the honour to see you, and acquaint you what they are.—I am, with the utmost respect, Dear Madam, your most obedient humble servant, CECILIA BEVERLEY.

She would not have been thus concise, had not the caution of Mr Arnott made her fear, in the present perilous situation of affairs, to trust the secret of Mr Harrel to paper.

The following answer was returned her from Mrs Delvile;—

To Miss Beverley, Portman-square.

The accidents you mention are not, I hope, of a very serious nature, since I shall find difficulty insurmountable in trying to lament them, if they are productive of a lengthened visit from my dear Miss Beverley to her Faithful humble servant, AUGUSTA DELVILE.

Cecilia, charmed with this note, could now no longer forbear looking forward to brighter prospects, flattering herself that once under the roof of Mrs Delvile, she must necessarily be happy, let the engagements or behaviour of her son be what they might.

CHAPTER X

A GAMESTER'S CONSCIENCE.

From this soothing prospect, Cecilia was presently disturbed by Mrs Harrel's maid, who came to entreat she would hasten to her lady, whom she feared was going into fits.

Cecilia flew to her immediately, and found her in the most violent affliction. She used every kind effort in her power to quiet and console her, but it was not without the utmost difficulty she could sob out the cause of this fresh sorrow, which indeed was not trifling. Mr Harrel, she said, had told her he could not possibly raise money even for his travelling expences, without risking a discovery of his project, and being seized by his creditors; he had therefore charged her, through her brother or her friend, to procure for him £3000, as less would not suffice to maintain them while abroad, and he knew no method by which he could have any remittances without danger. And, when she hesitated in her compliance, he furiously accused her of having brought on all this distress by her negligence and want of management, and declared that if she did not get the money, she would only be served as she merited by starving in a foreign gaol, which he swore would be the fate of them both.

The horror and indignation with which Cecilia heard this account were unspeakable. She saw evidently that she was again to be played upon by terror and distress, and the cautions and opinions of Mr Monckton no longer appeared overstrained; one year's income was already demanded, the annuity and the country house might next be required; she rejoiced, however, that thus wisely forewarned, she was not liable to surprise, and she determined, be their entreaties or representations what they might, to be immovably steady in her purpose of leaving them the next morning.

Yet she could not but grieve at suffering the whole burthen of this clamorous imposition to fall upon the soft-hearted Mr Arnott, whose inability to resist solicitation made him so unequal to sustaining its weight; but when Mrs Harrel was again able to go on with her account, she heard, to her infinite surprise, that all application to her brother had proved fruitless. "He will not hear me," continued Mrs Harrel, "and he never was deaf to me before! so now I have lost my only and last resource, my brother himself gives me up, and there is no one else upon earth who will assist me!"

"With pleasure, with readiness, with joy," cried Cecilia, "should you find assistance from me, were it to you alone it were given; but to supply fuel for the very fire that is consuming you—no, no, my whole heart is hardened against gaming and gamesters, and neither now nor ever will I suffer any consideration to soften me in their favour."

Mrs Harrel only answered by tears and lamentations; and Cecilia, whose justice shut not out compassion, having now declared her purposed firmness, again attempted to sooth her, entreating her not to give way to such immoderate grief, since better prospects might arise from the very gloom now before her, and a short time spent in solitude and oeconomy, might enable her to return to her native land with recovered happiness.

"No, I shall never return!" cried she, weeping, "I shall die, I shall break my heart before I have been banished a month! Oh Miss Beverley, how happy are you! able to stay where you please,—rich,—rolling in wealth which you do not want,—of which had we but one year's income only, all this misery would be over, and we might stay in our dear, dear, country!"

Cecilia, struck by a hint that so nearly bordered upon reproach, and offended by seeing the impossibility of ever doing enough, while anything remained to be done, forbore not without difficulty enquiring what next was expected from her, and whether any part of her fortune might be guarded, without giving room for some censure! but the deep affliction of Mrs Harrel soon removed her resentment, and scarcely thinking her, while in a state of such wretchedness, answerable for what she said, after a little recollection, she mildly replied "As affluence is all comparative, you may at present think I have more than my share; but the time is only this moment past, when your own situation seemed as subject to the envy of others as mine may be now. My future destiny is yet undetermined, and the occasion I may have for my fortune is unknown to myself; but whether I possess it in peace or in turbulence, whether it proves to me a blessing or an injury, so long as I can call it my own, I shall always remember with alacrity the claim upon that and upon me which early friendship has so justly given Mrs Harrel. Yet permit me, at the same time, to add, that I do not hold myself so entirely independent as you may probably suppose me. I have not, it is true, any Relations to call me to account, but respect for their memory supplies the place of their authority, and I cannot, in the distribution of the fortune which has devolved to me, forbear sometimes considering how they would have wished it should be spent, and always remembering that what was acquired by industry and labour, should never be dissipated in idleness and vanity. Forgive me for thus speaking to the point; you will not find me less friendly to yourself, for this frankness with respect to your situation."

Tears were again the only answer of Mrs Harrel; yet Cecilia, who pitied the weakness of her mind, stayed by her with the most patient kindness till the servants announced dinner. She then declared she would not go down stairs; but Cecilia so strongly represented the danger of awakening suspicion in the servants, that she at last prevailed with her to make her appearance.

Mr Harrel was already in the parlour, and enquiring for Mr Arnott, but was told by the servants he had sent word he had another engagement. Sir Robert Floyer also kept away, and, for the first time since her arrival in town, Cecilia dined with no other company than the master and mistress of the house.

Mrs Harrel could eat nothing; Cecilia, merely to avoid creating surprise in the servants, forbore following her example; but Mr Harrel ate much as usual, talked all dinner-time, was extremely civil to Cecilia, and discovered not by his manners the least alteration in his affairs.

When the servants were gone, he desired his wife to step for a moment with him into the library. They soon returned, and then Mr Harrel, after walking in a disordered manner about the room, rang the bell, and ordered his hat and cane, and as he took them, said "If this fails—" and, stopping short, without speaking to his wife, or even bowing to Cecilia, he hastily went out of the house.

Mrs Harrel told Cecilia that he had merely called her to know the event of her two petitions, and had heard her double failure in total silence. Whither he was now gone it was not easy to conjecture, nor what was the new resource which he still seemed to think worth trying; but the manner of his quitting the house, and the threat implied by if this fails, contributed not to lessen the grief of Mrs Harrel, and gave to Cecilia herself the utmost alarm.

They continued together till tea-time, the servants having been ordered to admit no company. Mr Harrel himself then returned, and returned, to the amazement of Cecilia, accompanied by Mr Marriot.

He presented that young man to both the ladies as a gentleman whose acquaintance and friendship he was very desirous to cultivate. Mrs Harrel, too much absorbed in her own affairs to care about any other, saw his entrance with a momentary surprise, and then thought of it no more; but it was not so with Cecilia, whose better understanding led her to deeper reflection.

Even the visits of Mr Marriot but a few weeks since Mr Harrel had prohibited, yet he now introduced him into his house with particular distinction; he came back too himself in admirable spirits, enlivened in his countenance, and restored to his good humour. A change so extraordinary both in conduct and disposition convinced her that some change no less extra-ordinary of circumstance must previously have happened; what that might be it was not possible for her to divine, but the lessons she had received from Mr Monckton led her to suspicions of the darkest kind.

Every part of his behaviour served still further to confirm them; he was civil even to excess to Mr Marriot; he gave orders aloud not to be at home to Sir Robert Floyer; he made his court to Cecilia with unusual assiduity, and he took every method in his power to procure opportunity to her admirer of addressing and approaching her.

The young man, who seemed enamoured even to madness, could scarce refrain not merely from prostration to the object of his passion, but to Mr Harrel himself for permitting him to see her. Cecilia, who not without some concern perceived a fondness so fruitless, and who knew not by what arts or with what views Mr Harrel might think proper to encourage it, determined to take all the means that were in her own power towards giving it immediate control. She behaved, therefore, with the utmost reserve, and the moment tea was over, though earnestly entreated to remain with them, she retired to her own room, without making any other apology than coldly saying she could not stay.

In about an hour Mrs Harrel ran up stairs to her.

"Oh Miss Beverley," she cried, "a little respite is now granted me! Mr Harrel says he shall stay another day; he says, too, one single thousand pound would now make him a new man."

Cecilia returned no answer; she conjectured some new deceit was in agitation to raise money, and she feared Mr Marriot was the next dupe to be played upon. Mrs Harrel, therefore, with a look of the utmost disappointment, left her, saying she would send for her brother, and once more try if he had yet any remaining regard for her.

Cecilia rested quiet till eleven o'clock, when she was summoned to supper; she found Mr Marriot still the only guest, and that Mr Arnott made not his appearance.

She now resolved to publish her resolution of going the next morning to St James's-square. As soon, therefore, as the servants withdrew, she enquired of Mr Harrel if he had any commands with Mr or Mrs Delvile, as she should see them the next morning, and purposed to spend some time with them.

Mr Harrel, with a look of much alarm, asked if she meant the whole day.

Many days, she answered, and probably some months.

Mrs Harrel exclaimed her surprise aloud, and Mr Harrel looked aghast; while his new young friend cast upon him a glance of reproach and resentment, which fully convinced Cecilia he imagined he had procured himself a title to an easiness of intercourse and frequency of meeting which this intelligence destroyed. Cecilia, thinking after all that had passed, no other ceremony on her part was necessary but that of simply speaking her intention, then arose and returned to her own room.

She acquainted her maid that she was going to make a visit to Mrs Delvile, and gave her directions about packing up her clothes, and sending for a man in the morning to take care of her books.

This employment was soon interrupted by the entrance of Mrs Harrel, who desiring to speak with her alone, when the maid was gone, said "O Miss Beverley, can you indeed be so barbarous as to leave me?"

"I entreat you, Mrs Harrel," answered Cecilia, "to save both yourself and me any further discussions. I have delayed this removal very long, and I can now delay it no longer."

Mrs Harrel then flung herself upon a chair in the bitterest sorrow, declaring she was utterly undone; that Mr Harrel had declared he could not stay even an hour in England if she was not in his house; that he had already had a violent quarrel with Mr Marriot upon the subject; and that her brother, though she had sent him the most earnest entreaties, would not come near her.

Cecilia, tired of vain attempts to offer comfort, now urged the warmest expostulations against her opposition, strongly representing the real necessity of her going abroad, and the unpardonable weakness of wishing to continue such a life as she now led, adding debt to debt, and hoarding distress upon distress.

Mrs Harrel then, though rather from compulsion than conviction, declared she would agree to go, if she had not a dread of ill usage; but Mr Harrel, she said, had behaved to her with the utmost brutality, calling her the cause of his ruin, and threatening that if she procured not this thousand pound before the ensuing evening, she should be treated as she deserved for her extravagance and folly.

"Does he think, then," said Cecilia with the utmost indignation, "that I am to be frightened through your fears into what compliances he pleases?"

"O no," cried Mrs Harrel, "no; his expectations are all from my brother. He surely thought that when I supplicated and pleaded to him, he would do what I wished, for so he always did formerly, and so once again I am sure he would do now, could I but make him come to me, and tell him how I am used, and tell him that if Mr Harrel takes me abroad in this humour, I verily think in his rage he will half murder me."

Cecilia, who well knew she was herself the real cause of Mr Arnott's resistance, now felt her resolution waver, internally reproaching herself with the sufferings of his sister; alarmed, however, for her own constancy, she earnestly besought Mrs Harrel to go and compose herself for the night, and promised to deliberate what could be done for her before morning.

Mrs Harrel complied; but scarce was her own rest more broken than that of Cecilia, who, though extremely fatigued with a whole night's watching, was so perturbed in her mind she could not close her eyes. Mrs Harrel was her earliest, and had once been her dearest friend; she had deprived her by her own advice of her customary refuge in her brother; to refuse, therefore, assistance to her seemed cruelty, though to deny it to Mr Harrel was justice; she endeavoured, therefore, to make a compromise between her judgment and compassion, by resolving that though she would grant nothing further to Mr Harrel while he remained in London, she would contribute from time to time both to his necessities and comfort, when once he was established elsewhere upon some plan of prudence and economy.

CHAPTER XI

A PERSECUTION.

The next morning by five o'clock Mrs Harrel came into Cecilia's room to know the result of her deliberation; and Cecilia, with that graceful readiness which accompanied all her kind offices, instantly assured her the thousand pound should be her own, if she would consent to seek some quiet retreat, and receive it in small sums, of fifty or one hundred pounds at a time, which should be carefully transmitted, and which, by being delivered to herself, might secure better treatment from Mr Harrel, and be a motive to revive his care and affection.

She flew, much delighted, with this proposal to her husband; but presently, and with a dejected look, returning, said Mr Harrel protested he could not possibly set out without first receiving the money. "I shall go myself, therefore," said she, "to my brother after breakfast, for he will not, I see, unkind as he is grown, come to me; and if I do not succeed with him, I believe I shall never come back!"

To this Cecilia, offended and disappointed, answered "I am sorry for Mr Arnott, but for myself I have done!"

Mrs Harrel then left her, and she arose to make immediate preparations for her removal to St James's-square, whither, with all the speed in her power, she sent her books, her trunks, and all that belonged to her.

When she was summoned down stairs, she found, for the first time, Mr Harrel breakfasting at the same table with his wife; they seemed mutually out of humour and comfortless, nothing hardly was spoken, and little was swallowed; Mr Harrel, however, was civil, but his wife was totally silent, and Cecilia the whole time was planning how to take her leave.

When the tea things were removed, Mr Harrel said, "You have not, I hope, Miss Beverley, quite determined upon this strange scheme?"

"Indeed I have, Sir," she answered, "and already I have sent my clothes."

At this information he seemed thunderstruck; but, after somewhat recovering, said with much bitterness, "Well, madam, at least may I request you will stay here till the evening?"

"No, Sir," answered she coolly, "I am going instantly."

"And will you not," said he, with yet greater asperity, "amuse yourself first with seeing bailiffs take possession of my house, and your friend Priscilla follow me to jail?"

"Good God, Mr Harrel!" exclaimed Cecilia, with uplifted hands, "is this a question, is this behaviour I have merited!"

"O no!" cried he with quickness, "should I once think that way—" then rising and striking his forehead, he walked about the room.

Mrs Harrel arose too, and weeping violently went away.

"Will you at least," said Cecilia, when she was gone, "till your affairs are settled, leave Priscilla with me? When I go into my own house, she shall accompany me, and mean time Mr Arnott's I am sure will gladly be open to her."

"No, no," answered he, "she deserves no such indulgence; she has not any reason to complain, she has been as negligent, as profuse, as expensive as myself; she has practised neither oeconomy nor self-denial, she has neither thought of me nor my affairs, nor is she now afflicted at any thing but the loss of that affluence she has done her best towards diminishing.

"All recrimination," said Cecilia, "were vain, or what might not Mrs Harrel urge in return! but let us not enlarge upon so ungrateful a subject, the wisest and the happiest scheme now were mutually and kindly to console each other."

"Consolation and kindness," cried he, with abruptness, "are out of the question. I have ordered a post chaise to be here at night, and if till then you will stay, I will promise to release you without further petition if not, eternal destruction be my portion if I live to see the scene which your removal will occasion!"

"My removal," cried Cecilia, shuddering, "good heaven, and how can my removal be of such dreadful consequence?"

"Ask me not," cried he, fiercely, "questions or reasons now; the crisis is at hand, and you will soon, happen what may, know all; mean time what I have said is a fact, and immutable; and you must hasten my end, or give me a chance for avoiding it, as you think fit. I scarce care at this instant which way you decide; remember, however, all I ask of you is to defer your departure; what else I have to hope is from Mr Arnott."

He then left the room.

Cecilia now was again a coward! In vain she called to her support the advice, the prophesies, the cautions of Mr Monckton, in vain she recollected the impositions she had already seen practised, for neither the warnings of her counsellor, nor the lessons of her own experience, were proofs against the terrors which threats so desperate inspired; and though more than once she determined to fly at all events from a tyranny he had so little right to usurp, the mere remembrance of the words if you stay not till night I will not live, robbed her of all courage; and however long she had prepared herself for this very attack, when the moment arrived, its power over her mind was too strong for resistance.

While this conflict between fear and resolution was still undecided, her servant brought her the following letter from Mr Arnott.

To Miss Beverley, Portman-square.

June 13th, 1779.

MADAM,—Determined to obey those commands which you had the goodness to honour me with, I have absented myself from town till Mr Harrel is settled; for though I am as sensible of your wisdom as of your beauty, I find myself too weak to bear the distress of my unhappy sister, and therefore I run from the sight, nor shall any letter or message follow me, unless it comes from Miss Beverley herself, lest she should in future refuse the only favour I dare presume to solicit, that of sometimes deigning to honour with her directions, the most humble and devoted of her servants, J. ARNOTT.

In the midst of her apprehensions for herself and her own interest, Cecilia could not forbear rejoicing that Mr Arnott, at least, had escaped the present storm; yet she was certain it would fall the more heavily upon herself; and dreaded the sight of Mrs Harrel after the shock which this flight would occasion.

Her expectations were but too quickly fulfilled; Mrs Harrel in a short time after rushed wildly into the room, calling out "My brother is gone! he has left me for ever! Oh save me, Miss Beverley, save me from abuse and insult!" And she wept with so much violence she could utter nothing more.

Cecilia, quite tortured by this persecution, faintly asked what she could do for her?

"Send," cried she, "to my brother, and beseech him not to abandon me! send to him, and conjure him to advance this thousand pound!—the chaise is already ordered,—Mr Harrel is fixed upon going,—yet he says without that money we must both starve in a strange land,—O send to my cruel brother! he has left word that nothing must follow him that does not come from you."

"For the world, then," cried Cecilia, "would I not baffle his discretion! indeed you must submit to your fate, indeed Mrs Harrel you must endeavour to bear it better."

Mrs Harrel, shedding a flood of tears, declared she would try to follow her advice, but again besought her in the utmost agony to send after her brother, protesting she did not think even her life would be safe in making so long a journey with Mr Harrel in his present state of mind; his character, she said, was totally changed, his gaiety, good humour, and sprightliness were turned into roughness and moroseness, and, since his great losses at play, he was grown so fierce and furious, that to oppose him even in a trifle, rendered him quite outrageous in passion.

Cecilia, though truly concerned, and almost melted, yet refused to interfere with Mr Arnott, and even thought it but justice to acknowledge she had advised his retreat.

"And can you have been so cruel?" cried Mrs Harrel, with still increasing violence of sorrow, "to rob me of my only friend, to deprive me of my Brother's affection, at the very time I am forced out of the kingdom, with a husband who is ready to murder me, and who says he hates the sight of me, and all because I cannot get him this fatal, fatal money!—O Miss Beverley, how could I have thought to have had such an office from you?"

Cecilia was beginning a justification, when a message came from Mr Harrel, desiring to see his wife immediately.

Mrs Harrel, in great terror, cast herself at Cecilia's feet, and clinging to her knees, called out "I dare not go to him! I dare not go to him! he wants to know my success, and when he hears my brother is run away, I am sure he will kill me!—Oh Miss Beverley, how could you send him away? how could you be so inhuman as to leave me to the rage of Mr Harrel?"

Cecilia, distressed and trembling herself, conjured her to rise and be consoled; but Mrs Harrel, weak and frightened, could only weep and supplicate; "I don't ask you," she cried, "to give the money yourself, but only to send for my brother, that he may protect me, and beg Mr Harrel not to treat me so cruelly,—consider but what a long, long journey I am going to make! consider how often you used to say you would love me for ever! consider you have robbed me of the tenderest brother in the world!—Oh Miss Beverley, send for him back, or be a sister to me yourself, and let not your poor Priscilla leave her native land without help or pity!"

Cecilia, wholly overcome, now knelt too, and embracing her with tears, said "Oh Priscilla, plead and reproach no more! what you wish shall be yours,—I will send for your brother,—I will do what you please!"

"Now you are my friend indeed!" cried Mrs Harrel, "let me but see my brother, and his heart will yield to my distress, and he will soften Mr Harrel by giving his unhappy sister this parting bounty."

Cecilia then took a pen in her hand to write to Mr Arnott; but struck almost in the same moment with a notion of treachery in calling him from a retreat which her own counsel made him seek, professedly to expose him to a supplication which from his present situation might lead him to ruin, she hastily flung it from her, and exclaimed "No, excellent Mr Arnott, I will not so unworthily betray you!"

"And can you, Miss Beverley, can you at last," cried Mrs Harrel, "be so barbarous as to retract?"

"No, my poor Priscilla," answered Cecilia, "I cannot so cruelly disappoint you; my pity shall however make no sufferer but myself,—I cannot send for Mr Arnott,—from me you must have the money, and may it answer the purpose for which it is given, and restore to you the tenderness of your husband, and the peace of your own heart!"

Priscilla, scarce waiting to thank her, flew with this intelligence to Mr Harrel; who with the same impetuosity, scarce waiting to say he was glad of it, ran himself to bring the Jew from whom the money was to be procured. Every thing was soon settled, Cecilia had no time for retracting, and repentance they had not the delicacy to regard; again, therefore, she signed her name for paying the principal and interest of another 1000l. within ten days after she was of age; and having taken the money, she accompanied Mr and Mrs Harrel into another room. Presenting it then with an affecting solemnity to Mrs Harrel, "accept, Priscilla," she cried, "this irrefragable mark of the sincerity of my friendship; but suffer me at the same time to tell you, it is the last to so considerable an amount I ever mean to offer; receive it, therefore, with kindness, but use it with discretion."

She then embraced her, and eager now to avoid acknowledgment, as before she had been to escape importunities, she left them together.

The soothing recompense of succouring benevolence, followed not this gift, nor made amends for this loss; perplexity and uneasiness, regret and resentment, accompanied the donation, and rested upon her mind; she feared she had done wrong; she was certain Mr Monckton would blame her; he knew not the persecution she suffered, nor would he make any allowance for the threats which alarmed, or the intreaties which melted her.

Far other had been her feelings at the generosity she exerted for the Hills; no doubts then tormented her, and no repentance embittered her beneficence. Their worth was without suspicion, and their misfortunes were not of their own seeking; the post in which they had been stationed they had never deserted, and the poverty into which they had sunk was accidental and unavoidable.

But here, every evil had been wantonly incurred by vanity and licentiousness, and shamelessly followed by injustice and fraud; the disturbance of her mind only increased by reflection, for when the rights of the creditors with their injuries occurred to her, she enquired of herself by what title or equity, she had so liberally assisted Mr Harrel in eluding their claims, and flying the punishment which the law would inflict.

Startled by this consideration, she most severely reproached herself for a compliance of which she had so lightly weighed the consequences, and thought with the utmost dismay, that while she had flattered herself she was merely indulging the dictates of humanity, she might perhaps be accused by the world as an abettor of guile and injustice.

"And yet," she continued, "whom can I essentially have injured but myself? would his creditors have been benefitted by my refusal? had I braved the execution of his dreadful threat, and quitted his house before I was wrought upon to assist him, would his suicide have lessened their losses, or secured their demands? even if he had no intention but to intimidate me, who will be wronged by my enabling him to go abroad, or who would be better paid were he seized and confined? All that remains of his shattered fortune may still be claimed, though I have saved him from a lingering imprisonment, desperate for himself and his wife, and useless for those he has plundered."

And thus, now soothed by the purity of her intentions, and now uneasy from the rectitude of her principles, she alternately rejoiced and repined at what she had done.

At dinner Mr Harrel was all civility and good humour. He warmly thanked Cecilia for the kindness she had shewn him, and gaily added, "You should be absolved from all the mischief you may do for a twelvemonth to come, in reward for the preservation from mischief which you have this day effected."

"The preservation," said Cecilia, "will I hope be for many days. But tell me, sir, exactly, at what time I may acquaint Mrs Delvile I shall wait upon her?"

"Perhaps," he answered, "by eight o'clock; perhaps by nine; you will not mind half an hour?"

"Certainly not;" she answered, unwilling by disputing about a trifle to diminish his satisfaction in her assistance. She wrote, therefore, another note to Mrs Delvile, desiring she would not expect her till near ten o'clock, and promising to account and apologize for these seeming caprices when she had the honour of seeing her.

The rest of the afternoon she spent wholly in exhorting Mrs Harrel to shew more fortitude, and conjuring her to study nothing while abroad but oeconomy, prudence and housewifery; a lesson how hard for the thoughtless and negligent Priscilla! she heard the advice with repugnance, and only answered it with helpless complaints that she knew not how to spend less money than she had always done.

After tea, Mr Harrel, still in high spirits, went out, entreating Cecilia to stay with Priscilla till his return, which he promised should be early.

Nine o'clock, however, came, and he did not appear; Cecilia then grew anxious to keep her appointment with Mrs Delvile; but ten o'clock also came, and still Mr Harrel was absent.

She then determined to wait no longer, and rang her bell for her servant and chair; but when Mrs Harrel desired to be informed the moment that Mr Harrel returned, the man said he had been come home more than half an hour.

Much surprised, she enquired where he was.

"In his own room, madam, and gave orders not to be disturbed."

Cecilia, who was not much pleased at this account, was easily persuaded to stay a few minutes longer; and, fearing some new evil, she was going to send him a message, by way of knowing how he was employed, when he came himself into the room.

"Well, ladies," he cried in a hurrying manner, "who is for Vauxhall?"

"Vauxhall!" repeated Mrs Harrel, while Cecilia, staring, perceived in his face a look of perturbation that extremely alarmed her.

"Come, come," he cried, "we have no time to lose. A hackney coach will serve us; we won't wait for our own."

"Have you then given up going abroad?" said Mrs Harrel.

"No, no; where can we go from half so well? let us live while we live! I have ordered a chaise to be in waiting there. Come, let's be gone."

"First," said Cecilia, "let me wish you both good night."

"Will you not go with me?" cried Mrs Harrel, "how can I go to Vauxhall alone?"

"You are not alone," answered she; "but if I go, how am I to return?"

"She shall return with you," cried Mr Harrel, "if you desire it; you shall return together."

Mrs Harrel, starting up in rapture, called out "Oh Mr Harrel, will you indeed leave me in England?"

"Yes," answered he reproachfully, "if you will make a better friend than you have made a wife, and if Miss Beverley is content to take charge of you."

"What can all this mean?" exclaimed Cecilia, "is it possible you can be serious? Are you really going yourself, and will you suffer Mrs Harrel to remain?"

"I am," he answered, "and I will."

Then ringing the bell, he ordered a hackney coach.

Mrs Harrel was scarce able to breathe for extacy, nor Cecilia for amazement; while Mr Harrel, attending to neither of them, walked for some time silently about the room.

"But how," cried Cecilia at last, "can I possibly go? Mrs Delvile must already be astonished at my delay, and if I disappoint her again she will hardly receive me."

"O make not any difficulties," cried Mrs Harrel in an agony; "if Mr Harrel will let me stay, sure you will not be so cruel as to oppose him?"

"But why," said Cecilia, "should either of us go to Vauxhall? surely that is no place for a parting so melancholy."

A servant then came in, and said the hackney coach was at the door.

Mr Harrel, starting at the sound, called out, "come, what do we wait for? if we go not immediately, we may be prevented."

Cecilia then again wished them good night, protesting she could fail Mrs Delvile no longer.

Mrs Harrel, half wild at this refusal, conjured her in the most frantic manner, to give way, exclaiming, "Oh cruel! cruel! to deny me this last request! I will kneel to you day and night," sinking upon the ground before her, "and I will serve you as the humblest of your slaves, if you will but be kind in this last instance, and save me from banishment and misery!"

"Oh rise, Mrs Harrel," cried Cecilia, ashamed of her prostration, and shocked by her vehemence, "rise and let me rest!—it is painful to me to refuse, but to comply for ever in defiance of my judgment—Oh Mrs Harrel, I know no longer what is kind or what is cruel, nor have I known for some time past right from wrong, nor good from evil!"

"Come," cried Mr Harrel impetuously, "I wait not another minute!"

"Leave her then with me!" said Cecilia, "I will perform my promise, Mr Arnott will I am sure hold his to be sacred, she shall now go with him, she shall hereafter come to me,—leave her but behind, and depend upon our care."

"No, no," cried he, with quickness, "I must take care of her myself. I shall not carry her abroad with me, but the only legacy I can leave her, is a warning which I hope she will remember for ever. You, however, need not go."

"What," cried Mrs Harrel, "leave me at Vauxhall, and yet leave me alone?"

"What of that?" cried he with fierceness, "do you not desire to be left? have you any regard for me? or for any thing upon earth but yourself! cease these vain clamours, and come, I insist upon it, this moment."

And then, with a violent oath, he declared he would be detained no longer, and approached in great rage to seize her; Mrs Harrel shrieked aloud, and the terrified Cecilia exclaimed, "If indeed you are to part to-night, part not thus dreadfully!—rise, Mrs Harrel, and comply!—be reconciled, be kind to her, Mr Harrel!—and I will go with her myself,—we will all go together!"

"And why," cried Mr Harrel, more gently yet with the utmost emotion, "why should you go!—you want no warning! you need no terror!—better far had you fly us, and my wife when I am set out may find you."

Mrs Harrel, however, suffered her not to recede; and Cecilia, though half distracted by the scenes of horror and perplexity in which she was perpetually engaged, ordered her servant to acquaint Mrs Delvile she was again compelled to defer waiting upon her.

Mr Harrel then hurried them both into the coach, which he directed to Vauxhall.

"Pray write to me when you are landed," said Mrs Harrel, who now released from her personal apprehensions, began to feel some for her husband.

He made not any answer. She then asked to what part of France he meant to go; but still he did not reply; and when she urged him by a third question, he told her in a rage to torment him no more.

During the rest of the ride not another word was said; Mrs Harrel wept, her husband guarded a gloomy silence, and Cecilia most unpleasantly passed her time between anxious suspicions of some new scheme, and a terrified wonder in what all these transactions would terminate.

CHAPTER XII

A MAN OF BUSINESS.

When they entered Vauxhall, Mr Harrel endeavoured to dismiss his moroseness, and affecting his usual gaiety, struggled to recover his spirits; but the effort was vain, he could neither talk nor look like himself, and though from time to time he resumed his air of wonted levity, he could not support it, but drooped and hung his head in evident despondency.

He made them take several turns in the midst of the company, and walked so fast that they could hardly keep pace with him, as if he hoped by exercise to restore his vivacity; but every attempt failed, he sunk and grew sadder, and muttering between his teeth "this is not to be borne!" he hastily called to a waiter to bring him a bottle of champagne.

Of this he drank glass after glass, notwithstanding Cecilia, as Mrs Harrel had not courage to speak, entreated him to forbear. He seemed, however, not to hear her; but when he had drunk what he thought necessary to revive him, he conveyed them into an unfrequented part of the garden, and as soon as they were out of sight of all but a few stragglers, he suddenly stopt, and, in great agitation, said, "my chaise will soon be ready, and I shall take of you a long farewell!—all my affairs are unpropitious to my speedy return;—the wine is now mounting into my head, and perhaps I may not be able to say much by and by. I fear I have been cruel to you, Priscilla, and I begin to wish I had spared you this parting scene; yet let it not be banished your remembrance, but think of it when you are tempted to such mad folly as has ruined us."

Mrs Harrel wept too much to make any answer; and turning from her to Cecilia, "Oh Madam," he cried, "to you, indeed, I dare not speak! I have used you most unworthily, but I pay for it all! I ask you not to pity or forgive me, I know it is impossible you should do either."

"No," cried the softened Cecilia, "it is not impossible, I do both at this moment, and I hope—"

"Do not hope," interrupted he, "be not so angelic, for I cannot bear it! benevolence like yours should have fallen into worthier hands. But come, let us return to the company. My head grows giddy, but my heart is still heavy; I must make them more fit companions for each other."

He would then have hurried them back; but Cecilia, endeavouring to stop him, said "You do not mean, I hope, to call for more wine?"

"Why not?" cried he, with affected spirit, "what, shall we not be merry before we part? Yes, we will all be merry, for if we are not, how shall we part at all?—Oh not without a struggle!—" Then, stopping, he paused a moment, and casting off the mask of levity, said in accents the most solemn "I commit this packet to you," giving a sealed parcel to Cecilia; "had I written it later, its contents had been kinder to my wife, for now the hour of separation approaches, ill will and resentment subside. Poor Priscilla!—I am sorry—but you will succour her, I am sure you will,—Oh had I known you myself before this infatuation—bright pattern of all goodness!—but I was devoted,—a ruined wretch before ever you entered my house; unworthy to be saved, unworthy that virtues such as yours should dwell under the same roof with me! But come,—come now, or my resolution will waver, and I shall not go at last."

"But what is this packet?" cried Cecilia, "and why do you give it to me?"

"No matter, no matter, you will know by and by;—the chaise waits, and I must gather courage to be gone."

He then pressed forward, answering neither to remonstrance nor intreaty from his frightened companions.

The moment they returned to the covered walk, they were met by Mr Marriot; Mr Harrel, starting, endeavoured to pass him; but when he approached, and said "you have sent, Sir, no answer to my letter!" he stopt, and in a tone of forced politeness, said, "No, Sir, but I shall answer it to-morrow, and to-night I hope you will do me the honour of supping with me."

Mr Marriot, looking openly at Cecilia as his inducement, though evidently regarding himself as an injured man, hesitated a moment, yet accepted the invitation.

"To supper?" cried Mrs Harrel, "what here?"

"To supper?" repeated Cecilia, "and how are we to get home?"

"Think not of that these two hours," answered he; "come, let us look for a box."

Cecilia then grew quite urgent with him to give up a scheme which must keep them so late, and Mrs Harrel repeatedly exclaimed "Indeed people will think it very odd to see us here without any party;" but he heeded them not, and perceiving at some distance Mr Morrice, he called out to him to find them a box; for the evening was very pleasant, and the gardens were so much crowded that no accommodation was unseized.

"Sir," cried Morrice, with his usual readiness, "I'll get you one if I turn out ten old Aldermen sucking custards."

Just after he was gone, a fat, sleek, vulgar-looking man, dressed in a bright purple coat, with a deep red waistcoat, and a wig bulging far from his head with small round curls, while his plump face and person announced plenty and good living, and an air of defiance spoke the fullness of his purse, strutted boldly up to Mr Harrel, and accosting him in a manner that shewed some diffidence of his reception, but none of his right, said "Sir your humble servant." And made a bow first to him, and then to the ladies.

"Sir yours," replied Mr Harrel scornfully, and without touching his hat he walked quickly on.

His fat acquaintance, who seemed but little disposed to be offended with impunity, instantly replaced his hat on his head, and with a look that implied I'll fit you for this! put his hands to his sides, and following him, said "Sir, I must make bold to beg the favour of exchanging a few words with you."

"Ay, Sir," answered Mr Harrel, "come to me to-morrow, and you shall exchange as many as you please."

"Nothing like the time present, Sir," answered the man; "as for to-morrow, I believe it intends to come no more; for I have heard of it any time these three years. I mean no reflections, Sir, but let every man have his right. That's what I say, and that's my notion of things."

Mr Harrel, with a violent execration, asked what he meant by dunning him at such a place as Vauxhall?

"One place, Sir," he replied, "is as good as another place; for so as what one does is good, 'tis no matter for where it may be. A man of business never wants a counter if he can meet with a joint-stool. For my part, I'm all for a clear conscience, and no bills without receipts to them."

"And if you were all for broken bones," cried Mr Harrel, angrily, "I would oblige you with them without delay."

"Sir," cried the man, equally provoked, "this is talking quite out of character, for as to broken bones, there's ne'er a person in all England, gentle nor simple, can say he's a right to break mine, for I'm not a person of that sort, but a man of as good property as another man; and there's ne'er a customer I have in the world that's more his own man than myself."

"Lord bless me, Mr Hobson," cried Mrs Harrel, "don't follow us in this manner! If we meet any of our acquaintance they'll think us half crazy."

"Ma'am," answered Mr Hobson, again taking off his hat, "if I'm treated with proper respect, no man will behave more generous than myself; but if I'm affronted, all I can say is, it may go harder with some folks than they think for."

Here a little mean-looking man, very thin, and almost bent double with perpetual cringing, came up to Mr Hobson, and pulling him by the sleeve, whispered, yet loud enough to be heard, "It's surprizeable to me, Mr Hobson, you can behave so out of the way! For my part, perhaps I've as much my due as another person, but I dares to say I shall have it when it's convenient, and I'd scorn for to mislest a gentleman when he's taking his pleasure."

"Lord bless me," cried Mrs Harrel, "what shall we do now? here's all Mr Harrel's creditors coming upon us!"

"Do?" cried Mr Harrel, re-assuming an air of gaiety, "why give them all a supper, to be sure. Come, gentlemen, will you favour me with your company to supper?"

"Sir," answered Mr Hobson, somewhat softened by this unexpected invitation, "I've supped this hour and more, and had my glass too, for I'm as willing to spend my money as another man; only what I say is this, I don't chuse to be cheated, for that's losing one's substance, and getting no credit; however, as to drinking another glass, or such a matter as that, I'll do it with all the pleasure in life."

"And as to me," said the other man, whose name was Simkins, and whose head almost touched the ground by the profoundness of his reverence, "I can't upon no account think of taking the liberty; but if I may just stand without, I'll make bold to go so far as just for to drink my humble duty to the ladies in a cup of cyder."

"Are you mad, Mr Harrel, are you mad!" cried his wife, "to think of asking such people as these to supper? what will every body say? suppose any of our acquaintance should see us? I am sure I shall die with shame."

"Mad!" repeated he, "no, not mad but merry. O ho, Mr Morrice, why have you been so long? what have you done for us?"

"Why Sir," answered Morrice, returning with a look somewhat less elated than he had set out, "the gardens are so full, there is not a box to be had; but I hope we shall get one for all that; for I observed one of the best boxes in the garden, just to the right there, with nobody in it but that gentleman who made me spill the tea-pot at the Pantheon. So I made an apology, and told him the case; but he only said humph? and hay? so then I told it all over again, but he served me just the same, for he never seems to hear what one says till one's just done, and then he begins to recollect one's speaking to him; however, though I repeated it all over and over again, I could get nothing from him but just that humph? and hay? but he is so remarkably absent, that I dare say if we all go and sit down round him, he won't know a word of the matter."

"Won't he?" cried Mr Harrel, "have at him, then!"

And he followed Mr Morrice, though Cecilia, who now half suspected that all was to end in a mere idle frolic, warmly joined her remonstrances to those of Mrs Harrel, which were made with the utmost, but with fruitless earnestness.

Mr Meadows, who was seated in the middle of the box, was lolloping upon the table with his customary ease, and picking his teeth with his usual inattention to all about him. The intrusion, however, of so large a party, seemed to threaten his insensibility with unavoidable disturbance; though imagining they meant but to look in at the box, and pass on, he made not at their first approach any alteration in his attitude or employment.

"See, ladies," cried the officious Morrice, "I told you there was room; and I am sure this gentleman will be very happy to make way for you, if it's only out of good-nature to the waiters, as he is neither eating nor drinking, nor doing any thing at all. So if you two ladies will go in at that side, Mr Harrel and that other gentleman," pointing to Mr Marriot, "may go to the other, and then I'll sit by the ladies here, and those other two gentlemen—"

Here Mr Meadows, raising himself from his reclining posture, and staring Morrice in the face, gravely said, "What's all this, Sir!"

Morrice, who expected to have arranged the whole party without a question, and who understood so little of modish airs as to suspect neither affectation nor trick in the absence of mind and indolence of manners which he observed in Mr Meadows, was utterly amazed by this interrogatory, and staring himself in return, said, "Sir, you seemed so thoughtful—I did not think—I did not suppose you would have taken any notice of just a person or two coming into the box."

"Did not you, Sir?" said Mr Meadows very coldly, "why then now you do, perhaps you'll be so obliging as to let me have my own box to myself."

And then again he returned to his favourite position.

"Certainly, Sir," said Morrice, bowing; "I am sure I did not mean to disturb you; for you seemed so lost in thought, that I'm sure I did not much believe you would have seen us."

"Why Sir," said Mr Hobson, strutting forward, "if I may speak my opinion, I should think, as you happen to be quite alone, a little agreeable company would be no such bad thing. At least that's my notion."

"And if I might take the liberty," said the smooth tongued Mr Simkins, "for to put in a word, I should think the best way would be, if the gentleman has no peticklar objection, for me just to stand somewhere hereabouts, and so, when he's had what he's a mind to, be ready for to pop in at one side, as he comes out at the t'other; for if one does not look pretty 'cute such a full night as this, a box is whipt away before one knows where one is."

"No, no, no," cried Mrs Harrel impatiently, "let us neither sup in this box nor in any other; let us go away entirely."

"Indeed we must! indeed we ought!" cried Cecilia; "it is utterly improper we should stay; pray let us be gone immediately."

Mr Harrel paid not the least regard to these requests; but Mr Meadows, who could no longer seem unconscious of what passed, did himself so much violence as to arise, and ask if the ladies would be seated.

"I said so!" cried Morrice triumphantly, "I was sure there was no gentleman but would be happy to accommodate two such ladies!"

The ladies, however, far from happy in being so accommodated, again tried their utmost influence in persuading Mr Harrel to give up this scheme; but he would not hear them, he insisted upon their going into the box, and, extending the privilege which Mr Meadows had given, he invited without ceremony the whole party to follow.

Mr Meadows, though he seemed to think this a very extraordinary encroachment, had already made such an effort from his general languor in the repulse he had given to Morrice, that he could exert himself no further; but after looking around him with mingled vacancy and contempt, he again seated himself, and suffered Morrice to do the honours without more opposition. Morrice, but too happy in the office, placed Cecilia next to Mr Meadows, and would have made Mr Marriot her other neighbour, but she insisted upon not being parted from Mrs Harrel, and therefore, as he chose to sit also by that lady himself, Mr Marriot was obliged to follow Mr Harrel to the other side of the box; Mr Hobson, without further invitation, placed himself comfortably in one of the corners, and Mr Simkins, who stood modestly for some time in another, finding the further encouragement for which he waited was not likely to arrive, dropt quietly into his seat without it.

Supper was now ordered, and while it was preparing Mr Harrel sat totally silent; but Mr Meadows thought proper to force himself to talk with Cecilia, though she could well have dispensed with such an exertion of his politeness.

"Do you like this place, ma'am?"

"Indeed I hardly know,—I never was here before."

"No wonder! the only surprise is that any body can come to it at all. To see a set of people walking after nothing! strolling about without view or object! 'tis strange! don't you think so, ma'am?"

"Yes,—I believe so," said Cecilia, scarce hearing him.

"O it gives me the vapours, the horrors," cried he, "to see what poor creatures we all are! taking pleasure even from the privation of it! forcing ourselves into exercise and toil, when we might at least have the indulgence of sitting still and reposing!"

"Lord, Sir," cried Morrice, "don't you like walking?"

"Walking?" cried he, "I know nothing so humiliating; to see a rational being in such mechanical motion! with no knowledge upon what principles he proceeds, but plodding on, one foot before another, without even any consciousness which is first, or how either—"

"Sir," interrupted Mr Hobson, "I hope you won't take it amiss if I make bold to tell my opinion, for my way is this, let every man speak his maxim! But what I say as to this matter, is this, if a man must always be stopping to consider what foot he is standing upon, he had need have little to do, being the right does as well as the left, and the left as well as the right. And that, Sir, I think is a fair argument."

Mr Meadows deigned no other answer to this speech than a look of contempt.

"I fancy, Sir," said Morrice, "you are fond of riding, for all your good horsemen like nothing else."

"Riding!" exclaimed Mr Meadows, "Oh barbarous! Wrestling and boxing are polite arts to it! trusting to the discretion of an animal less intellectual than ourselves! a sudden spring may break all our limbs, a stumble may fracture our sculls! And what is the inducement? to get melted with heat, killed with fatigue, and covered with dust! miserable infatuation!—Do you love riding, ma'am?"

"Yes, very well, Sir."

"I am glad to hear it," cried he, with a vacant smile; "you are quite right; I am entirely of your opinion."

Mr Simkins now, with a look of much perplexity, yet rising and bowing, said "I don't mean, Sir, to be so rude as to put in my oar, but if I did not take you wrong, I'm sure just now I thought you seemed for to make no great 'count of riding, and yet now, all of the sudden, one would think you was a speaking up for it!"

"Why, Sir," cried Morrice, "if you neither like riding nor walking, you can have no pleasure at all but only in sitting."

"Sitting!" repeated Mr Meadows, with a yawn, "O worse and worse! it dispirits me to death! it robs me of all fire and life! it weakens circulation, and destroys elasticity."

"Pray then, Sir," said Morrice, "do you like any better to stand?"

"To stand? O intolerable! the most unmeaning thing in the world! one had better be made a mummy!"

"Why then, pray Sir," said Mr Hobson, "let me ask the favour of you to tell us what it is you do like?"

Mr Meadows, though he stared him full in the face, began picking his teeth without making any answer.

"You see, Mr Hobson," said Mr Simkins, "the gentleman has no mind for to tell you; but if I may take the liberty just to put in, I think if he neither likes walking, nor riding, nor sitting, nor standing, I take it he likes nothing."

"Well, Sir," said Morrice, "but here comes supper, and I hope you will like that. Pray Sir, may I help you to a bit of this ham?"

Mr Meadows, not seeming to hear him, suddenly, and with an air of extreme weariness, arose, and without speaking to anybody, abruptly made his way out of the box. — Mr Harrel now, starting from the gloomy reverie into which he had sunk, undertook to do the honours of the table, insisting with much violence upon helping every body, calling for more provisions, and struggling to appear in high spirits and good humour.

In a few minutes Captain Aresby, who was passing by the box, stopt to make his compliments to Mrs Harrel and Cecilia.

"What a concourse!" he cried, casting up his eyes with an expression of half-dying fatigue, "are you not accablé? for my part, I hardly respire. I have really hardly ever had the honour of being so obsedé before."

"We can make very good room, Sir," said Morrice, "if you chuse to come in."

"Yes," said Mr Simkins, obsequiously standing up, "I am sure the gentleman will be very welcome to take my place, for I did not mean for to sit down, only just to look agreeable."

"By no means, Sir," answered the Captain; "I shall be quite au desespoir if I derange any body."

"Sir," said Mr Hobson, "I don't offer you my place, because I take it for granted if you had a mind to come in, you would not stand upon ceremony; for what I say is, let every man speak his mind, and then we shall all know how to conduct ourselves. That's my way, and let any man tell me a better!"

The Captain, after looking at him with a surprise not wholly unmixt with horror, turned from him without making any answer, and said to Cecilia, "And how long, ma'am, have you tried this petrifying place?"

"An hour,—two hours, I believe," she answered.

"Really? and nobody here! assez de monde, but nobody here! a blank partout!"

"Sir," said Mr Simkins, getting out of the box that he might bow with more facility, "I humbly crave pardon for the liberty, but if I understood right, you said something of a blank? pray, Sir, if I may be so free, has there been any thing of the nature of a lottery, or a raffle, in the garden? or the like of that?"

"Sir!" said the Captain, regarding him from head to foot, "I am quite assommé that I cannot comprehend your allusion."

"Sir, I ask pardon," said the man, bowing still lower, "I only thought if in case it should not be above half a crown, or such a matter as that, I might perhaps stretch a point once in a way."

The Captain, more and more amazed, stared at him again, but not thinking it necessary to take any further notice of him, he enquired of Cecilia if she meant to stay late.

"I hope not," she replied, "I have already stayed later than I wished to do."

"Really!" said he, with an unmeaning smile, "Well, that is as horrid a thing as I have the malheur to know. For my part, I make it a principle not to stay long in these semi-barbarous places, for after a certain time, they bore me to that degree I am quite abimé. I shall, however, do mon possible to have the honour of seeing you again."

And then, with a smile of yet greater insipidity, he protested he was reduced to despair in leaving her, and walked on.

"Pray, ma'am, if I may be so bold," said Mr Hobson, "what countryman may that gentleman be?"

"An Englishman, I suppose, Sir," said Cecilia.

"An Englishman, ma'am!" said Mr Hobson, "why I could not understand one word in ten that came out of his mouth."

"Why indeed," said Mr Simkins, "he has a mighty peticklar way of speaking, for I'm sure I thought I could have sworn he said something of a blank, or to that amount, but I could make nothing of it when I come to ask him about it."

"Let every man speak to be understood," cried Mr Hobson, "that's my notion of things; for as to all those fine words that nobody can make out, I hold them to be of no use. Suppose a man was to talk in that manner when he's doing business, what would be the upshot? who'd understand what he meant? Well, that's the proof; what i'n't fit for business, i'n't of no value; that's my way of judging, and that's what I go upon."

"He said some other things," rejoined Mr Simkins, "that I could not make out very clear, only I had no mind to ask any more questions, for fear of his answering me something I should not understand; but as well as I could make it out, I thought I heard him say there was nobody here! what he could mean by that, I can't pretend for to guess, for I'm sure the garden is so stock full, that if there was to come many more, I don't know where they could cram 'em."

"I took notice of it at the time," said Mr Hobson, "for it i'n't many things are lost upon me; and, to tell you the truth, I thought he had been making pretty free with his bottle, by his seeing no better."

"Bottle!" cried Mr Harrel, "a most excellent hint, Mr Hobson! come! let us all make free with the bottle!"

He then called for more wine, and insisted that every body should pledge him. Mr Marriot and Mr Morrice made not any objection, and Mr Hobson and Mr Simkins consented with much delight.

Mr Harrel now grew extremely unruly, the wine he had already drunk being thus powerfully aided; and his next project was to make his wife and Cecilia follow his example. Cecilia, more incensed than ever to see no preparation made for his departure, and all possible pains taken to unfit him for setting out, refused him with equal firmness and displeasure, and lamented, with the bitterest self-reproaches, the consent which had been forced from her to be present at a scene of such disorder; but Mrs Harrel would have opposed him in vain, had not his attention been called off to another object. This was Sir Robert Floyer, who perceiving the party at some distance, no sooner observed Mr Marriot in such company, than advancing to the box with an air of rage and defiance, he told Mr Harrel he had something to say to him.

"Ay," cried Harrel, "say to me? and so have I to say to you! Come amongst us and be merry! Here, make room, make way! Sit close, my friends!"

Sir Robert, who now saw he was in no situation to be reasoned with, stood for a moment silent; and then, looking round the box, and observing Messrs Hobson and Simkins, he exclaimed aloud "Why what queer party have you got into? who the d—-l have you picked up here?"

Mr Hobson, who, to the importance of lately acquired wealth, now added the courage of newly drunk Champagne, stoutly kept his ground, without seeming at all conscious he was included in this interrogation; but Mr Simkins, who had still his way to make in the world, and whose habitual servility would have resisted a larger draught, was easily intimidated; he again, therefore stood up, and with the most cringing respect offered the Baronet his place; who, taking neither of the offer nor offerer the smallest notice, still stood opposite to Mr Harrel, waiting for some explanation.

Mr Harrel, however, who now grew really incapable of giving any, only repeated his invitation that he would make one among them.

"One among you?" cried he, angrily, and pointing to Mr Hobson, "why you don't fancy I'll sit down with a bricklayer?"

"A bricklayer?" said Mr Harrel, "ay, sure, and a hosier too; sit down, Mr Simkins, keep your place, man!"

Mr Simkins most thankfully bowed; but Mr Hobson, who could no longer avoid feeling the personality of this reflection, boldly answered, "Sir, you may sit down with a worse man any day in the week! I have done nothing I'm ashamed of, and no man can say to me why did you so? I don't tell you, Sir, what I'm worth; no one has a right to ask; I only say three times five is fifteen! that's all."

"Why what the d——l, you impudent fellow," cried the haughty Baronet, "you don't presume to mutter, do you?"

"Sir," answered Mr Hobson, very hotly, "I sha'n't put up with abuse from no man! I've got a fair character in the world, and wherewithal to live by my own liking. And what I have is my own, and all I say is, let every one say the same, for that's the way to fear no man, and face the d——l."

"What do you mean by that, fellow?" cried Sir Robert.

"Fellow, Sir! this is talking no how. Do you think a man of substance, that's got above the world, is to be treated like a little scrubby apprentice? Let every man have his own, that's always my way of thinking; and this I can say for myself, I have as good a right to shew my head where I please as ever a member of parliament in all England; and I wish every body here could say as much."

Sir Robert, fury starting into his eyes, was beginning an answer; but Mrs Harrel with terror, and Cecilia with dignity, calling upon them both to forbear, the Baronet desired Morrice to relinquish his place to him, and seating himself next to Mrs Harrel, gave over the contest.

Meanwhile Mr Simkins, hoping to ingratiate himself with the company, advanced to Mr Hobson, already cooled by finding himself unanswered, and reproachfully said "Mr Hobson, if I may make so free, I must needs be bold to say I am quite ashamed of you! a person of your standing and credit for to talk so disrespectful! as if a gentleman had not a right to take a little pleasure, because he just happens to owe you a little matters of money; fie, fie, Mr Hobson! I did not expect you to behave so despiseable!"

"Despiseable!" answered Mr Hobson, "I'd scorn as much to do anything despiseable as yourself, or any thing misbecoming of a gentleman; and as to coming to such a place as this may be, why I have no objection to it. All I stand to is this, let every man have his due; for as to taking a little pleasure, here I am, as one may say, doing the same myself; but where's the harm of that? who's a right to call a man to account that's clear of the world? Not that I mean to boast, nor nothing like it, but, as I said before; five times five is fifteen; [Footnote; I hardly know whether the authoress has here forgotten her arithmetic, or intentionally suffered Mr Hobson to forget his, from the effects of champagne.—Ed.]—that's my calculation."

Mr Harrel, who, during this debate, had still continued drinking, regardless of all opposition from his wife and Cecilia, now grew more and more turbulent; he insisted that Mr Simkins should return to his seat, ordered him another bumper of champagne, and saying he had not half company enough to raise his spirits, desired Morrice to go and invite more.

Morrice, always ready to promote a frolic, most chearfully consented; but when Cecilia, in a low voice, supplicated him to bring no one back, with still more readiness he made signs that he understood and would obey her.

Mr Harrel then began to sing, and in so noisy and riotous a manner, that nobody approached the box without stopping to stare at him; and those who were new to such scenes, not contented with merely looking in, stationed themselves at some distance before it, to observe what was passing, and to contemplate with envy and admiration an appearance of mirth and enjoyment which they attributed to happiness and pleasure! Mrs Harrel, shocked to be seen in such mixed company, grew every instant more restless and miserable; and Cecilia, half distracted to think how they were to get home, had passed all her time in making secret vows that if once again she was delivered from Mr Harrel she would never see him more.

Sir Robert Floyer perceiving their mutual uneasiness, proposed to escort them home himself; and Cecilia, notwithstanding her aversion to him, was listening to the scheme, when Mr Marriot, who had been evidently provoked and disconcerted since the junction of the Baronet, suspecting what was passing, offered his services also, and in a tone of voice that did not promise a very quiet acquiescence in a refusal.

Cecilia, who, too easily, in their looks, saw all the eagerness of rivalry, now dreaded the consequence of her decision, and therefore declined the assistance of either; but her distress was unspeakable, as there was not one person in the party to whose care she could commit herself, though the behaviour of Mr Harrel, which every moment grew more disorderly, rendered the necessity of quitting him urgent and uncontroulable.

When Morrice returned, stopping in the midst of his loud and violent singing, he vehemently demanded what company he had brought him?

"None at all, sir," answered Morrice, looking significantly at Cecilia; "I have really been so unlucky as not to meet with any body who had a mind to come."

"Why then," answered he, starting up, "I will seek some for myself." "O no, pray, Mr Harrel, bring nobody else," cried his wife. "Hear us in pity," cried Cecilia, "and distress us no further."

"Distress you?" cried he, with quickness, "what shall I not bring you those pretty girls? Yes, one more glass, and I will teach you to welcome them."

And he poured out another bumper.

"This is so insupportable!" cried Cecilia, rising, "[that] I can remain here no longer."

"This is cruel indeed," cried Mrs. Harrel, bursting into tears; "did you only bring me here to insult me?"

"No!" cried he, suddenly embracing her, "by this parting kiss!" then wildly jumping upon his seat, he leapt over the table, and was out of sight in an instant.

Amazement seized all who remained; Mrs Harrel and Cecilia, indeed, doubted not but he was actually gone to the chaise he had ordered; but the manner of his departure affrighted them, and his preceding behaviour had made them cease to expect it; Mrs Harrel, leaning upon Cecilia, continued to weep, while she, confounded and alarmed, scarce knew whether she should stay and console her, or fly after Mr Harrel, whom she feared had incapacitated himself from finding his chaise, by the very method he had taken to gather courage for seeking it.

This, however, was but the apprehension of a moment; another and a far more horrible one drove it from her imagination; for scarcely had Mr Harrel quitted the box and their sight, before their ears were suddenly struck with the report of a pistol.

Mrs Harrel gave a loud scream, which was involuntarily echoed by, Cecilia; everybody arose, some with officious zeal to serve the ladies, and others to hasten to the spot whence the dreadful sound proceeded.

Sir Robert Floyer again offered his services in conducting them home; but they could listen to no such proposal; Cecilia, with difficulty refrained from rushing out herself to discover what was passing; but her dread of being followed by Mrs Harrel prevented her; they both, therefore, waited, expecting every instant some intelligence, as all but the Baronet and Mr Marriot were now gone to seek it.

Nobody, however, returned; and their terrors encreased every moment; Mrs Harrel wanted to run out herself, but Cecilia, conjuring her to keep still, begged Mr Marriot to bring them some account. Mr Marriot, like the messengers who had preceded him, came not back; an instant seemed an age, and Sir Robert Floyer was also entreated to procure information.

Mrs Harrel and Cecilia were now left to themselves, and their horror was too great for speech or motion; they stood close to each other, listening to every sound and receiving every possible addition to their alarm, by the general confusion which they observed in the gardens, in which, though both gentlemen and waiters were running to and fro, not a creature was walking, and all amusement seemed forgotten.

From this dreadful state they were at length removed, though not relieved, by the sight of a waiter, who, as he was passing shewed himself almost covered with blood! Mrs Harrel vehemently called after him, demanding whence it came? "From the gentleman, ma'am," answered he in haste, "that has shot himself," and then ran on.

Mrs Harrel uttered a piercing scream, and sunk on the ground; for Cecilia, shuddering with horror, lost all her own strength, and could no longer lend her any support.

So great at this time was the general confusion of the place, that for some minutes their particular distress was unknown, and their situation unnoticed; till at length an elderly gentleman came up to the box, and humanely offered his assistance.

Cecilia, pointing to her unfortunate friend, who had not fallen into a fainting fit, but merely from weakness and terror, accepted his help in raising her. She was lifted up, however, without the smallest effort on her own part, and was only kept upon her seat by being held there by the stranger, for Cecilia, whose whole frame was shaking, tried in vain to sustain her.

This gentleman, from the violence of their distress, began now to suspect its motive, and addressing himself to Cecilia, said, "I am afraid, madam, this unfortunate gentleman was some Relation to you?"

Neither of them spoke, but their silence was sufficiently expressive.

"It is pity, madam," he continued, "that some friend can't order him out of the crowd, and have him kept quiet till a surgeon can be brought."

"A surgeon!" exclaimed Cecilia, recovering from one surprize by the effect of another; "is it then possible he may be saved?"

And without waiting to have her question answered, she ran out of the box herself, flying wildly about the garden, and calling for help as she flew, till she found the house by the entrance; and then, going up to the bar, "Is a surgeon sent for?" she exclaimed, "let a surgeon be fetched instantly!" "A surgeon, ma'am," she was answered, "is not the gentleman dead?" "No, no, no!" she cried; "he must be brought in; let some careful people go and bring him in." Nor would she quit the bar, till two or three waiters were called, and received her orders. And then, eager to see them executed herself, she ran, fearless of being alone, and without thought of being lost, towards the fatal spot whither the crowd guided her. She could not, indeed, have been more secure from insult or molestation if surrounded by twenty guards; for the scene of desperation and horror which many had witnessed, and of which all had heard the signal, engrossed the universal attention, and took, even from the most idle and licentious, all spirit for gallantry and amusement.

Here, while making vain attempts to penetrate through the multitude, that she might see and herself judge the actual situation of Mr Harrel, and give, if yet there was room for hope, such orders as would best conduce to his safety and recovery, she was met by Mr Marriot, who entreated her not to press forward to a sight which he had found too shocking for himself, and insisted upon protecting her through the crowd.

"If he is alive," cried she, refusing his aid, "and if there is any chance he may be saved, no sight shall be too shocking to deter me from seeing him properly attended."

"All attendance," answered he, "will be in vain; he is not indeed, yet dead, but his recovery is impossible. There is a surgeon with him already; one who happened to be in the gardens, and he told me himself that the wound was inevitably mortal."

Cecilia, though greatly disappointed, still determined to make way to him, that she might herself enquire if, in his last moments, there was any thing he wished to communicate, or desired to have done; but, as she struggled to proceed, she was next met and stopt by Sir Robert Floyer, who, forcing her back, acquainted her that all was over!

The shock with which she received this account, though unmixed with any tenderness of regret, and resulting merely from general humanity, was yet so violent as almost to overpower her. Mr Harrel, indeed, had forfeited all right to her esteem, and the unfeeling selfishness of his whole behaviour had long provoked her resentment and excited her disgust; yet a catastrophe so dreadful, and from which she had herself made such efforts to rescue him, filled her with so much horror, that, turning extremely sick, she was obliged to be supported to the nearest box, and stop there for hartshorn and water.

A few minutes, however, sufficed to divest her of all care for herself, in the concern with which she recollected the situation of Mrs Harrel; she hastened, therefore, back to her, attended by the Baronet and Mr Marriot, and found her still leaning upon the stranger, and weeping aloud.

The fatal news had already reached her; and though all affection between Mr Harrel and herself had mutually subsided from the first two or three months of their marriage, a conclusion so horrible to all connection between them could not be heard without sorrow and distress. Her temper, too, naturally soft, retained not resentment, and Mr Harrel, now separated from her for ever, was only remembered as the Mr Harrel who first won her heart.

Neither pains nor tenderness were spared on the part of Cecilia to console her; who finding her utterly incapable either of acting or directing for herself, and knowing her at all times to be extremely helpless, now summoned to her own aid all the strength of mind she possessed, and determined upon this melancholy occasion, both to think and act for her widowed friend to the utmost stretch of her abilities and power.

As soon, therefore, as the first effusions of her grief were over, she prevailed with her to go to the house, where she was humanely offered the use of a quiet room till she should be better able to set off for town. Cecilia, having seen her thus safely lodged, begged Mr Marriot to stay with her, and then, accompanied by the Baronet, returned herself to the bar, and desiring the footman who had attended them to be called, sent him instantly to his late master, and proceeded next with great presence of mind, to inquire further into the particulars of what had passed, and to consult upon what was immediately to be done with the deceased; for she thought it neither decent nor right to leave to chance or to strangers the last duties which could be paid him.

He had lingered, she found, about a quarter of an hour, but in a condition too dreadful for description, quite speechless, and, by all that could be judged, out of his senses; yet so distorted with pain, and wounded so desperately beyond any power of relief, that the surgeon, who every instant expected his death, said it would not be merely useless but inhuman, to remove him till he had breathed his last. He died, therefore, in the arms of this gentleman and a waiter.

"A waiter!" cried Cecilia, reproachfully looking at Sir Robert, "and was there no friend who for the few poor moments that remained had patience to support him?"

"Where would be the good," said Sir Robert, "of supporting a man in his last agonies?"

This unfeeling speech she attempted not to answer, but, suffering neither her dislike to him, nor her scruples for herself, to interfere with the present occasion, she desired to have his advice what was now best to be done.

Undertaker's men must immediately, he said, be sent for, to remove the body.

She then gave orders for that purpose, which were instantly executed.

Whither the body was to go was the next question; Cecilia wished the removal to be directly to the townhouse, but Sir Robert told her it must be carried to the nearest undertaker's, and kept there till it could be conveyed to town in a coffin.

For this, also, in the name of Mrs Harrel, she gave directions. And then addressing herself to Sir Robert, "You will now Sir, I hope," she said, "return to the fatal spot, and watch by your late unfortunate friend till the proper people arrive to take charge of him?"

"And what good will that do?" cried he; "had I not better watch by you?"

"It will do good," answered she, with some severity, "to decency and to humanity; and surely you cannot refuse to see who is with him, and in what situation he lies, and whether he has met, from the strangers with whom he was left, the tenderness and care which his friends ought to have paid him."

"Will you promise, then," he answered, "not to go away till I come back? for I have no great ambition to sacrifice the living for the dead."

"I will promise nothing, Sir," said she, shocked at his callous insensibility; "but if you refuse this last poor office, I must apply elsewhere; and firmly I believe there is no other I can ask who will a moment hesitate in complying."

She then went back to Mrs Harrel, leaving, however, an impression upon the mind of Sir Robert, that made him no longer dare dispute her commands.

Her next solicitude was how they should return to town; they had no equipage of their own, and the only servant who came with them was employed in performing the last duties for his deceased master. Her first intention was to order a hackney coach, but the deplorable state of Mrs Harrel made it almost impossible she could take the sole care of her, and the lateness of the night, and their distance from home, gave her a dread invincible to going so far without some guard or assistant. Mr Marriot earnestly desired to have the honour of conveying them to Portman-square in his own carriage, and notwithstanding there were many objections to such a proposal, the humanity of his behaviour upon the present occasion, and the evident veneration which accompanied his passion, joined to her encreasing aversion to the Baronet, from whom she could not endure to receive the smallest obligation, determined her, after much perplexity and hesitation, to accept his offer.

She begged him, therefore, to immediately order his coach, and, happy to obey her, he went out with that design; but, instantly coming back, told her, in a low voice, that they must wait some time longer, as the Undertaker's people were then entering the garden, and if they stayed not till the removal had taken place, Mrs Harrel might be shocked with the sight of some of the men, or perhaps even meet the dead body.

Cecilia, thanking him for this considerate precaution, readily agreed to defer setting out; devoting, mean time, all her attention to Mrs Harrel, whose sorrow, though violent, forbad not consolation. But before the garden was cleared, and the carriage ordered, Sir Robert returned; saying to Cecilia, with an air of parading obedience which seemed to claim some applause, "Miss Beverley, your commands have been executed."

Cecilia made not any answer, and he presently added, "Whenever you chuse to go I will order up my coach."

"My coach, Sir," said Mr Marriot, "will be ordered when the ladies are ready, and I hope to have the honour myself of conducting them to town."

"No, Sir," cried the Baronet, "that can never be; my long acquaintance with Mrs Harrel gives me a prior right to attend her, and I can by no means suffer any other person to rob me of it."

"I have nothing," said Mr Marriot, "to say to that, Sir, but Miss Beverley herself has done me the honour to consent to make use of my carriage."

"Miss Beverley, I think," said Sir Robert, extremely piqued, "can never have sent me out of the way in order to execute her own commands, merely to deprive me of the pleasure of attending her and Mrs Harrel home."

Cecilia, somewhat alarmed, now sought to lessen the favour of her decision, though she adhered to it without wavering.

"My intention," said she, "was not to confer, but to receive an obligation; and I had hoped, while Mr. Marriot assisted us, Sir Robert would be far more humanely employed in taking charge of what we cannot superintend, and yet are infinitely more anxious should not be neglected."

"That," said Sir Robert, "is all done; and I hope, therefore, after sending me upon such an errand, you don't mean to refuse me the pleasure of seeing you to town?"

"Sir Robert," said Cecilia, greatly displeased, "I cannot argue with you now; I have already settled my plan, and I am not at leisure to re-consider it."

Sir Robert bit his lips for a moment in angry silence; but not enduring to lose the victory to a young rival he despised, he presently said, "If I must talk no more about it to you, madam, I must at least beg leave to talk of it to this gentleman, and take the liberty to represent to him—"

Cecilia now, dreading how his speech might be answered, prevented its being finished, and with an air of the most spirited dignity, said, "Is it possible, sir, that at a time such as this, you should not be wholly indifferent to a matter so frivolous? little indeed will be the pleasure which our society can afford! your dispute however, has given it some importance, and therefore Mr Marriot must accept my thanks for his civility, and excuse me for retracting my consent."

Supplications and remonstrances were, however, still poured upon her from both, and the danger, the impossibility that two ladies could go to town alone, in a hackney coach, and without even a servant, at near four o'clock in the morning, they mutually urged, vehemently entreating that she would run no such hazard.

Cecilia was far other than insensible to these representations; the danger, indeed, appeared to her so formidable, that her inclination the whole time opposed her refusal; yet her repugnance to giving way to the overbearing Baronet, and her fear of his resentment if she listened to Mr Marriot, forced her to be steady, since she saw that her preference would prove the signal of a quarrel.

Inattentive, therefore, to their joint persecution, she again deliberated by what possible method she could get home in safety; but unable to devise any, she at last resolved to make enquiries of the people in the bar, who had been extremely humane and civil, whether they could assist or counsel her. She therefore desired the two gentlemen to take care of Mrs Harrel, to which neither dared dissent, as both could not refuse, and hastily arising, went out of the room; but great indeed was her surprize when, as she was walking up to the bar, she was addressed by young Delvile!

Approaching her with that air of gravity and distance which of late he had assumed in her presence, he was beginning some speech about his mother; but the instant the sound of his voice reached Cecilia, she joyfully clasped her hands, and eagerly exclaimed, "Mr Delvile!—O now we are safe!—this is fortunate indeed!"

"Safe, Madam," cried he astonished, "yes I hope so!—has any thing endangered your safety?"

"O no matter for danger," cried she, "we will now trust ourselves with you, and I am sure you will protect us."

"Protect you!" repeated he again, and with warmth, "yes, while I live!—but what is the matter?—why are you so pale?—are you ill?—are you frightened?—what is the matter?"

And losing all coldness and reserve, with the utmost earnestness he begged her to explain herself.

"Do you not know," cried she, "what has happened? Can you be here and not have heard it?"

"Heard what?" cried he, "I am but this moment arrived; my mother grew uneasy that she did not see you, she sent to your house, and was told that you were not returned from Vauxhall; some other circumstances also alarmed her, and therefore, late as it was, I came hither myself. The instant I entered this place, I saw you here. This is all my history; tell me now yours. Where is your party? where are Mr and Mrs Harrel?—Why are you alone?"

"O ask not!" cried she, "I cannot tell you!—take us but under your care, and you will soon know all."

She then hurried from him, and returning to Mrs Harrel, said she had now a conveyance at once safe and proper, and begged her to rise and come away.

The gentlemen, however, rose first, each of them declaring he would himself attend them.

"No," said Cecilia, steadily, "that trouble will now be superfluous; Mrs Delvile herself has sent for me, and her son is now waiting till we join him."

Amazement and disappointment at this intelligence were visible in the faces of them both; Cecilia waited not a single question, but finding she was unable to support Mrs Harrel, who rather suffered herself to be carried than led, she entrusted her between them, and ran forward to enquire of Delvile if his carriage was ready.

She found him with a look of horror that told the tale he had been hearing, listening to one of the waiters; the moment she appeared, he flew to her, and with the utmost emotion exclaimed, "Amiable Miss Beverley! what a dreadful scene have you witnessed! what a cruel task have you nobly performed! such spirit with such softness! so much presence of mind with such feeling!—but you are all excellence! human nature can rise no higher! I believe indeed you are its most perfect ornament!"

Praise such as this, so unexpected, and delivered with such energy, Cecilia heard not without pleasure, even at a moment when her whole mind was occupied by matters foreign to its peculiar interests. She made, however, her enquiry about the carriage, and he told her that he had come in a hackney coach, which was waiting for him at the door.

Mrs Harrel was now brought in, and little was the recompense her assistants received for their aid, when they saw Cecilia so contentedly engaged with young Delvile, whose eyes were rivetted on her face, with an expression of the most lively admiration; each, however, then quitted the other, and hastened to the fair mourner; no time was now lost, Mrs Harrel was supported to the coach, Cecilia followed her, and Delvile, jumping in after them, ordered the man to drive to Portman-square.

Sir Robert and Mr Marriot, confounded though enraged, saw their departure in passive silence; the right of attendance they had so tenaciously denied to each other, here admitted not of dispute; Delvile upon this occasion, appeared as the representative of his father, and his authority seemed the authority of a guardian. Their only consolation was that neither had yielded to the other, and all spirit of altercation or revenge was sunk in their mutual mortification. At the petition of the waiters, from sullen but proud emulation, they paid the expences of the night, and then throwing themselves into their carriages, returned to their respective houses.

CHAPTER XIII

A SOLUTION.

During the ride to town, not merely Cecilia, but Delvile himself attended wholly to Mrs Harrel, whose grief as it became less violent, was more easy to be soothed.

The distress of this eventful night was however not yet over; when they came to Portman-square, Delvile eagerly called to the coachman not to drive up to the house, and anxiously begged Cecilia and Mrs Harrel to sit still, while he went out himself to make some enquiries. They were surprised at the request, yet immediately consented; but before he had quitted them, Davison, who was watching their return, came up to them with information that an execution was then in the house.

Fresh misery was now opened for Mrs Harrel, and fresh horror and perplexity for Cecilia; she had no longer, however, the whole weight either of thought or of conduct upon herself; Delvile in her cares took the most animated interest, and beseeching her to wait a moment and appease her friend, he went himself into the house to learn the state of the affair.

He returned in a few minutes, and seemed in no haste to communicate what he had heard, but entreated them both to go immediately to St James's-square.

Cecilia felt extremely fearful of offending his father by the introduction of Mrs Harrel; yet she had nothing better to propose, and therefore, after a short and distressed argument, she complied.

Delvile then told her that the alarm of his mother, at which he had already hinted, proceeded from a rumour of this very misfortune, to which, though they knew not whether they might give credit, was owing the anxiety which at so late an hour, had induced him to go to Vauxhall in search of her. They gained admittance without any disturbance, as the servant of young Delvile had been ordered to sit up for his master. Cecilia much disliked thus taking possession of the house in the night-time, though Delvile, solicitous to relieve her, desired she would not waste a thought upon the subject, and making his servant shew her the room which had been prepared for her reception, he begged her to compose her spirits, and to comfort her friend, and promised to acquaint his father and mother when they arose with what had happened, that she might be saved all pain from surprise or curiosity when they met.

This service she thankfully accepted, for she dreaded, after the liberty she had taken, to encounter the pride of Mr Delvile without some previous apology, and she feared still more to see his lady without the same preparation, as her frequent breach of appointment might reasonably have offended her, and as her displeasure would affect her more deeply.

It was now near six o'clock, yet the hours seemed as long as they were melancholy till the family arose. They settled to remain quiet till some message was sent to them, but before any arrived, Mrs Harrel, who was seated upon the bed, wearied by fatigue and sorrow, cried herself to sleep like a child.

Cecilia rejoiced in seeing this reprieve from affliction, though her keener sensations unfitted her from partaking of it; much indeed was the uneasiness which kept her awake; the care of Mrs Harrel seemed to devolve upon herself, the reception she might meet from the Delviles was uncertain, and the horrible adventures of the night, refused for a moment to quit her remembrance.

At ten o'clock, a message was brought from Mrs Delvile, to know whether they were ready for breakfast. Mrs Harrel was still asleep, but Cecilia carried her own answer by hastening down stairs.

In her way she was met by young Delvile, whose air upon first approaching her spoke him again prepared to address her with the most distant gravity; but almost the moment he looked at her, he forgot his purpose; her paleness, the heaviness of her eyes, and the fatigue of long watching betrayed by her whole face, again, surprised him into all the tenderness of anxiety, and he enquired after her health not as a compliment of civility, but as a question in which his whole heart was most deeply interested.

Cecilia thanked him for his attention to her friend the night before, and then proceeded to his mother.

Mrs Delvile, coming forward to meet her, removed at once all her fears of displeasure, and banished all necessity of apology, by instantly embracing her, and warmly exclaiming "Charming Miss Beverley! how shall I ever tell you half the admiration with which I have heard of your conduct! The exertion of so much fortitude at a juncture when a weaker mind would have been overpowered by terror, and a heart less under the dominion of well-regulated principles, would have sought only its own relief by flying from distress and confusion, shews such propriety of mind as can only result from the union of good sense with virtue. You are indeed a noble creature! I thought so from the moment I beheld you; I shall think so, I hope, to the last that I live!"

Cecilia, penetrated with joy and gratitude, felt in that instant the amplest recompense for all that she had suffered, and for all that she had lost. Such praise from Mrs Delvile was alone sufficient to make her happy; but when she considered whence it sprung, and that the circumstances with which she was so much struck, must have been related to her by her son, her delight was augmented to an emotion the most pleasing she could experience, from seeing how high she was held in the esteem of those who were highest in her own.

Mrs Delvile then, with the utmost cordiality, began to talk of her affairs, saving her the pain of proposing the change of habitation that now seemed unavoidable, by an immediate invitation to her house, which she made with as much delicacy as if Mr Harrel's had still been open to her, and choice, not necessity, had directed her removal. The whole family, she told her, went into the country in two days, and she hoped that a new scene, with quietness and early hours, would restore both the bloom and sprightliness which her late cares and restlessness had injured. And though she very seriously lamented the rash action of Mr Harrel, she much rejoiced in the acquisition which her own house and happiness would receive from her society.

She next discussed the situation of her widowed friend, and Cecilia produced the packet which had been entrusted to her by her late husband. Mrs Delvile advised her to open it in the presence of Mr Arnott, and begged her to send for any other of her friends she might wish to see or consult, and to claim freely from herself whatever advice or assistance she could bestow.

And then, without waiting for Mr Delvile, she suffered her to swallow a hasty breakfast, and return to Mrs Harrel, whom she had desired the servants to attend, as she concluded that in her present situation she would not chuse to make her appearance.

Cecilia, lightened now from all her cares, more pleased than ever with Mrs Delvile, and enchanted that at last she was settled under her roof, went back with as much ability as inclination to give comfort to Mrs Harrel. She found her but just awaking, and scarce yet conscious where she was, or why not in her own house.

As her powers of recollection returned, she was soothed with the softest compassion by Cecilia, who in pursuance of Mrs Delvile's advice, sent her servant in search of Mr Arnott, and in consequence of her permission, wrote a note of invitation to Mr Monckton.

Mr Arnott, who was already in town, soon arrived; his own man, whom he had left to watch the motions of Mr Harrel, having early in the morning rode to the place of his retreat, with the melancholy tidings of the suicide and execution.

Cecilia instantly went down stairs to him. The meeting was extremely painful to them both. Mr Arnott severely blamed himself for his flight, believing it had hastened the fatal blow, which some further sacrifices might perhaps have eluded; and Cecilia half repented the advice she had given him, though the failure of her own efforts proved the situation of Mr Harrel too desperate for remedy.

He then made the tenderest enquiries about his sister, and entreated her to communicate to him the minutest particulars of the dreadful transaction; after which, she produced the packet, but neither of them had the courage to break the seal; and concluding the contents would be no less than his last will, they determined some third person should be present when they opened it. Cecilia wished much for Mr Monckton, but as his being immediately found was uncertain, and the packet might consist of orders which ought not to be delayed, she proposed, for the sake of expedition, to call in Mr Delvile.

Mr Arnott readily agreed, and she sent to beg a moment's audience with that gentleman.

She was desired to walk into the breakfast-room, where he was sitting with his lady and his son.

Not such was now her reception as when she entered that apartment before; Mr Delvile looked displeased and out of humour, and, making her a stiff bow, while his son brought her a chair, coldly said, "If you are hurried, Miss Beverley, I will attend you directly; if not, I will finish my breakfast, as I shall have but little time the rest of the morning, from the concourse of people upon business, who will crowd upon me till dinner, most of whom will be extremely distressed if I leave town without contriving to see them."

"There is not the least occasion, Sir," answered Cecilia, "that I should trouble you to quit the room I merely came to beg you would have the goodness to be present while Mr Arnott opens a small packet which was last night put into my hands by Mr Harrel."

"And has Mr Arnott," answered he, somewhat sternly, "thought proper to send me such a request?"

"No, Sir," said Cecilia, "the request is mine; and if, as I now fear, it is impertinent, I must entreat you to forget it."

"As far as relates merely to yourself," returned Mr Delvile, "it is another matter; but certainly Mr Arnott can have no possible claim upon my time or attention; and I think it rather extraordinary, that a young man with whom I have no sort of connection or commerce, and whose very name is almost unknown to me, should suppose a person in my style of life so little occupied as to be wholly at his command."

"He had no such idea, Sir," said Cecilia, greatly disconcerted; "the honour of your presence is merely solicited by myself, and simply from the apprehension that some directions may be contained in the papers which, perhaps, ought immediately to be executed."

"I am not, I repeat," said Mr Delvile, more mildly, "displeased at your part of this transaction; your want of experience and knowledge of the world makes you not at all aware of the consequences which may follow my compliance; the papers you speak of may perhaps be of great importance, and hereafter the first witness to their being read may be publickly called upon. You know not the trouble such an affair may occasion, but Mr Arnott ought to be better informed."

Cecilia, making another apology for the error which she had committed, was in no small confusion, quitting the room; but Mr Delvile, perfectly appeased by seeing her distress, stopt her, to say, with much graciousness, "For your sake, Miss Beverley, I am sorry I cannot act in this business; but you see how I am situated! overpowered with affairs of my own, and people who can do nothing without my orders. Besides, should there hereafter be any investigation into the matter, my name might, perhaps, be mentioned, and it would be superfluous to say how ill I should think it used by being brought into such company."

Cecilia then left the rooms secretly vowing that no possible exigence should in future tempt her to apply for assistance to Mr Delvile, which, however ostentatiously offered, was constantly withheld when claimed.

She was beginning to communicate to Mr Arnott her ill success, when young Delvile, with an air of eagerness, followed her into the room. "Pardon me," he cried, "for this intrusion,—but, tell me, is it impossible that in this affair I can represent my father? may not the office you meant for him, devolve upon me? remember how near we are to each other, and honour me for once with supposing us the same!"

Ah who, or what, thought Cecilia, can be so different? She thanked him, with much sweetness, for his offer, but declined accepting it, saying "I will not, now I know the inconveniencies of my request, be so selfish as even to suffer it should be granted."

"You must not deny me," cried he; "where is the packet? why should you lose a moment?"

"Rather ask," answered she, "why I should permit you to lose a moment in a matter that does not concern you? and to risk, perhaps, the loss of many moments hereafter, from a too incautious politeness."

"And what can I risk," cried he, "half so precious as your smallest satisfaction? do you suppose I can flatter myself with a possibility of contributing to it, and yet have the resolution to refuse myself so much pleasure? no, no, the heroic times are over, and self-denial is no longer in fashion!"

"You are very good," said Cecilia; "but indeed after what has passed—"

"No matter for what has passed," interrupted he, "we are now to think of what is to come. I know you too well to doubt your impatience in the execution of a commission which circumstances have rendered sacred; and should any thing either be done or omitted contrary to the directions in your packet, will you not be apt, blameless as you are, to disturb yourself with a thousand fears that you took not proper methods for the discharge of your trust?"

There was something in this earnestness so like his former behaviour, and so far removed from his late reserve, that Cecilia, who perceived it with a pleasure she could hardly disguise, now opposed him no longer, but took up the packet, and broke the seal.

And then, to her no small amazement, instead of the expected will, she found a roll of enormous bills, and a collection of letters from various creditors, threatening the utmost severity of the law if their demands were longer unanswered.

Upon a slip of paper which held these together, was written, in Mr Harrel's hand, To be all paid to-night with a BULLET.

Next appeared two letters of another sort; the first of which was from Sir Robert Floyer, and in these words;

Sir,—As all prospects are now over of the alliance, I hope you will excuse my reminding you of the affair at Brookes's of last Christmas. I have the honour to be, Sir, yours R. FLOYER.

The other was from Mr Marriot.

Sir,—Though I should think £2000 nothing for the smallest hope, I must take the liberty to say I think it a great deal for only ten minutes; you can't have forgot, Sir, the terms of our agreement, but as I find you cannot keep to them, I must beg to be off also on my side, and I am persuaded you are too much a man of honour to take advantage of my over-eagerness in parting with my money without better security. I am, Sir, your most humble servant, A. Marriot.

What a scene of fraud, double-dealing, and iniquity was here laid open! Cecilia, who at first meant to read every thing aloud, found the attempt utterly vain, for so much was she shocked, that she could hardly read on to herself.

Last of all appeared a paper in Mr Harrel's own hand-writing, containing these words.

For Mrs Harrel, Miss Beverley, and Mr Arnott.

I can struggle no longer, the last blow must now be struck! another day robs me of my house and my liberty, and blasts me by the fatal discovery of my double attempts.

This is what I have wished; wholly to be freed, or ruined past all resource, and driven to the long-projected remedy.

A burthen has my existence been these two years, gay as I have appeared; not a night have I gone to bed, but heated and inflamed from a gaming table; not a morning have I awaked, but to be soured with a dun!

I would not lead such a life again, if the slave who works hardest at the oar would change with me.

Had I a son, I would bequeath him a plough; I should then leave him happier than my parents left me.

Idleness has been my destruction; the want of something to do led me into all evil.

A good wife perhaps might have saved me,—mine, I thank her! tried not. Disengaged from me and my affairs, her own pleasures and amusements have occupied her solely. Dreadful will be the catastrophe she will see to-night; let her bring it home, and live better!

If any pity is felt for me, it will be where I have least deserved it! Mr Arnott—Miss Beverley! it will come from you!

To bring myself to this final resolution, hard, I confess, have been my conflicts; it is not that I have feared death, no, I have long wished it, for shame and dread have embittered my days; but something there is within me that causes a deeper horror, that asks my preparation for another world! that demands my authority for quitting this!—what may hereafter—O terrible!—Pray for me, generous Miss Beverley!—kind, gentle Mr Arnott, pray for me!—

Wretch as Mr Harrel appeared, without religion, principle, or honour, this incoherent letter, evidently written in the desperate moment of determined suicide, very much affected both Cecilia and Mr Arnott, and in spite either of abhorrence or resentment, they mutually shed tears over the address to themselves.

Delvile, to whom every part of the affair was new, could only consider these papers as so many specimens of guilt and infamy; he read them, therefore, with astonishment and detestation, and openly congratulated Cecilia upon having escaped the double snares that were spread for her.

While this was passing, Mr Monckton arrived; who felt but little satisfaction from beholding the lady of his heart in confidential discourse with two of his rivals, one of whom had long attacked her by the dangerous flattery of perseverance, and the other, without any attack, had an influence yet more powerful.

Delvile, having performed the office for which he came, concluded, upon the entrance of Mr Monckton, that Cecilia had nothing further to wish from him; for her long acquaintance with that gentleman, his being a married man, and her neighbour in the country, were circumstances well known to him; he merely, therefore, enquired if she would honour him with any commands, and upon her assuring him she had none, he quietly withdrew.

This was no little relief to Mr Monckton, into whose hands Cecilia then put the fatal packet; and while he was reading it, at the desire of Mr Arnott, she went up stairs to prepare Mrs Harrel for his admission.

Mrs Harrel, unused to solitude, and as eager for company when unhappy to console, as when easy to divert her, consented to receive him with pleasure; they both wept at the meeting, and Cecilia, after some words of general comfort, left them together.

She had then a very long and circumstantial conversation with Mr Monckton, who explained whatever had appeared dark in the writings left by Mr Harrel, and who came to her before he saw them, with full knowledge of what they contained.

Mr Harrel had contracted with Sir Robert Floyer a large debt of honour before the arrival in town of Cecilia; and having no power to discharge it, he promised that the prize he expected in his ward should fall to his share, upon condition that the debt was cancelled. Nothing was thought more easy than to arrange this business, for the Baronet was always to be in her way, and the report of the intended alliance was to keep off all other pretenders. Several times, however, her coldness made him think the matter hopeless; and when he received her letter, he would have given up the whole affair; but Mr Harrel, well knowing his inability to satisfy the claims that would follow such a defection, constantly persuaded him the reserve was affected, and that his own pride and want of assiduity occasioned all her discouragement.

But while thus, by amusing the Baronet with false hopes, he kept off his demands, those of others were not less clamorous; his debts increased, his power of paying them diminished; he grew sour and desperate, and in one night lost £3000 beyond what he could produce, or offer any security for.

This, as he said, was what he wished; and now he was, for the present, to extricate himself by doubling stakes and winning, or to force himself into suicide by doubling such a loss. For though, with tolerable ease, he could forget accounts innumerable with his tradesmen, one neglected debt of honour rendered his existence insupportable!

For this last great effort, his difficulty was to raise the £3000 already due, without which the proposal could not be made; and, after various artifices and attempts, he at length contrived a meeting with Mr Marriot, intreated him to lend him £2000 for only two days, and offered his warmest services in his favour with Cecilia.

The rash and impassioned young man, deceived by his accounts into believing that his ward was wholly at his disposal, readily advanced the money, without any other condition than that of leave to visit freely at his house, to the exclusion of Sir Robert Floyer. "The other £1000," continued Mr Monckton, "I know not how he obtained, but he certainly had three. You, I hope, were not so unguarded—"

"Ah, Mr Monckton," said Cecilia, "blame me not too severely! the attacks that were made,—the necessity of otherwise betraying the worthy and half ruined Mr. Arnott—"

"Oh fie," cried he, "to suffer your understanding to be lulled asleep, because the weak-minded Mr Arnott's could not be kept awake! I thought, after such cautions from me, and such experience of your own, you could not again have been thus duped."

"I thought so too," answered she, "but yet when the trial came on,—indeed you know not how I was persecuted."

"Yet you see," returned he, "the utter inutility of the attempt; you see, and I told you beforehand, that nothing could save him."

"True; but had I been firmer in refusal, I might not so well have known it; I might then have upbraided myself with supposing that my compliance would have rescued him."

"You have indeed," cried Mr Monckton, "fallen into most worthless hands, and the Dean was much to blame for naming so lightly a guardian to a fortune such as yours."

"Pardon me," cried Cecilia, "he never entrusted him with my fortune, he committed it wholly to Mr Briggs."

"But if he knew not the various subterfuges by which such a caution might be baffled, he ought to have taken advice of those who were better informed. Mr Briggs, too! what a wretch! mean, low, vulgar, sordid!—the whole city of London, I believe, could not produce such another! how unaccountable to make you the ward of a man whose house you cannot enter without disgust!"

"His house," cried Cecilia, "my uncle never wished me to enter; he believed, and he was right, that my fortune would be safe in his hands; but for myself, he concluded I should always reside at Mr Harrel's." "But does not the city at this time," said Mr Monckton, "abound in families where, while your fortune was in security, you might yourself have lived with propriety? Nothing requires circumspection so minute as the choice of a guardian to a girl of large fortune, and in general one thing only is attended to, an appearance of property. Morals, integrity, character, are either not thought of, or investigated so superficially, that the enquiry were as well wholly omitted." He then continued his relation.

Mr Harrel hastened with his £3000 to the gaming table; one throw of the dice settled the business, he lost, and ought immediately to have doubled the sum. That, however, was never more likely to be in his power; he knew it; he knew, too, the joint claims of Cecilia's deceived admirers, and that his house was again threatened with executions from various quarters;—he went home, loaded his pistols, and took the methods already related to work himself into courage for the deed.

The means by which Mr Monckton had procured these particulars were many and various, and not all such as he could avow; since in the course of his researches, he had tampered with servants and waiters, and scrupled at no methods that led but to discovery.

Nor did his intelligence stop here; he had often, he said, wondered at the patience of Mr Harrel's creditors, but now even that was cleared up by a fresh proof of infamy; he had been himself at the house in Portmansquare, where he was informed that Mr Harrel had kept them quiet, by repeated assurances that his ward, in a short time, meant to lend him money for discharging them all.

Cecilia saw now but too clearly the reason her stay in his house was so important to him; and wondered less at his vehemence upon that subject, though she detested it more.

"Oh how little," cried she, "are the gay and the dissipated to be known upon a short acquaintance! expensive, indeed, and thoughtless and luxurious he appeared to me immediately; but fraudulent, base, designing, capable of every pernicious art of treachery and duplicity,—such, indeed, I expected not to find him, his very flightiness and levity seemed incompatible with such hypocrisy."

"His flightiness," said Mr Monckton, "proceeded not from gaiety of heart, it was merely the effect of effort; and his spirits were as mechanical as his taste for diversion. He had not strong parts, nor were his vices the result of his passions; had oeconomy been as much in fashion as extravagance, he would have been equally eager to practice it; he was a mere time-server, he struggled but to be something, and having neither talents nor sentiment to know what, he looked around him for any pursuit, and seeing distinction was more easily attained in the road to ruin than in any other, he gallopped along it, thoughtless of being thrown when he came to the bottom, and sufficiently gratified in shewing his horsemanship by the way."

And now, all that he had either to hear or to communicate upon this subject being told, he enquired, with a face strongly expressive of his disapprobation, why he found her at Mr Delvile's, and what had become of her resolution to avoid his house?

Cecilia, who, in the hurry of her mind and her affairs, had wholly forgotten that such a resolution had been taken, blushed at the question, and could not, at first, recollect what had urged her to break it; but when he proceeded to mention Mr Briggs, she was no longer distressed; she gave a circumstantial account of her visit to him, related the mean misery in which he lived, and told him the impracticability of her residing in such a house.

Mr Monckton could now in decency make no further opposition, however painful and reluctant was his acquiescence; yet before he quitted her, he gave himself the consolation of considerably obliging her, and softened his chagrin by the sweetness of her acknowledgments.

He enquired how much money in all she had now taken up of the Jew; and hearing it was £9050, he represented to her the additional loss she must suffer by paying an exorbitant interest for so large a sum, and the almost certainty with which she might be assured of very gross imposition; he expatiated, also, upon the injury which her character might receive in the world, were it known that she used such methods to procure money, since the circumstances which had been her inducement would probably either be unnoticed or misrepresented; and when he had awakened in her much uneasiness and regret upon this subject, he offered to pay the Jew without delay, clear her wholly from his power, and quietly receive the money when she came of age from herself.

A proposal so truly friendly made her look upon the regard of Mr Monckton in a higher and nobler point of view than her utmost esteem and reverence had hitherto placed it; yet she declined at first accepting the offer, from an apprehension it might occasion him inconvenience; but when he assured her he had a yet larger sum lying at present useless in a Banker's hands, and promised to receive the same interest for his money he should be paid from the funds, she joyfully listened to him; and it was settled that they should send for the Jew, take his discharge, and utterly dismiss him.

Mr Monckton, however, fearful of appearing too officious in her affairs, wished not to have his part in the transaction published, and advised Cecilia not to reveal the matter to the Delviles. But great as was his [ascendancy] over her mind, her aversion to mystery and hypocrisy were still greater; she would not, therefore, give him this promise, though her own desire to wait some seasonable opportunity for disclosing it, made her consent that their meeting with the Jew should be at the house of Mrs Roberts in Fetter-lane, at twelve o'clock the next morning; where she might also see Mrs Hill and her children before she left town.

They now parted, Cecilia charmed more than ever with her friend, whose kindness, as she suspected not his motives, seemed to spring from the most disinterested generosity.

That, however, was the smallest feature in the character of Mr Monckton, who was entirely a man of the world, shrewd, penetrating, attentive to his interest, and watchful of every advantage to improve it. In the service he now did Cecilia, he was gratified by giving her pleasure, but that was by no means his only gratification; he still hoped her fortune would one day be his own, he was glad to transact any business with her, and happy in making her owe to him an obligation; but his principal inducement was yet stronger; he saw with much alarm the facility of her liberality; and he feared while she continued in correspondence with the Jew, that the easiness with which she could raise money would be a motive with her to continue the practice whenever she was softened by distress, or subdued by entreaty; but he hoped, by totally concluding the negociation, the temptation would be removed; and that the hazard and inconvenience of renewing it, would strengthen her aversion to such an expedient, till, between difficulties and disuse, that dangerous resource would be thought of no more.

Cecilia then returned to Mrs Harrel, whom she found as she had left, weeping in the arms of her brother. They consulted upon what was best to be done, and agreed that she ought instantly to leave town; for which purpose a chaise was ordered directly. They settled also that Mr Arnott, when he had conveyed her to his country house, which was in Suffolk, should hasten back to superintend the funeral, and see if anything could be saved from the creditors for his sister.

Yet this plan, till Cecilia was summoned to dinner, they had not the resolution to put in practice. They were then obliged to be gone, and their parting was very melancholy. Mrs Harrel wept immoderately, and Mr Arnott felt a concern too tender for avowal, though too sincere for concealment. Cecilia, however glad to change her situation, was extremely depressed by their sorrow, and entreated to have frequent accounts of their proceedings, warmly repeating her offers of service, and protestations of faithful regard.

She accompanied them to the chaise, and then went to the dining parlour, where she found Mr and Mrs Delvile, but saw nothing more of their son the whole day.

The next morning after breakfast, Mrs Delvile set out upon some leave-taking visits, and Cecilia went in a chair to Fetter-lane; here, already waiting for her, she met the punctual Mr Monckton, and the disappointed Jew, who most unwillingly was paid off, and relinquished his bonds; and who found in the severe and crafty Mr Monckton, another sort of man to deal with than the necessitous and heedless Mr Harrel.

As soon as he was dismissed, other bonds were drawn and signed, the old ones were destroyed; and Cecilia, to her infinite satisfaction, had no creditor but Mr Monckton. Her bookseller, indeed, was still unpaid, but her debt with him was public, and gave her not any uneasiness.

She now, with the warmest expressions of gratitude, took leave of Mr Monckton, who suffered the most painful struggles in repressing the various apprehensions to which the parting, and her establishment at the Delviles gave rise.

She then enquired briefly into the affairs of Mrs Hill, and having heard a satisfactory account of them, returned to St James's-square.

BOOK VI

CHAPTER I

A DEBATE.

It was still early, and Mrs Delvile was not expected till late. Cecilia, therefore, determined to make a visit to Miss Belfield, to whom she had been denied during the late disorders at Mr Harrel's, and whom she could not endure to mortify by quitting town without seeing, since whatever were her doubts about Delvile, of her she had none.

To Portland-street, therefore, she ordered her chair, deliberating as she went whether it were better to adhere to the reserve she had hitherto maintained, or to satisfy her perplexity at once by an investigation into the truth. And still were these scruples undecided, when, looking in at the windows as she passed them to the door of the house, she perceived Miss Belfield standing in the parlour with a letter in her hand, which she was fervently pressing to her lips.

Struck by this sight, a thousand painful conjectures occurred to her, all representing that the letter was from Delvile, and all explaining to his dishonour the mystery of his late conduct. And far were her suspicions from diminishing, when, upon being shown into the parlour, Miss Belfield, trembling with her eagerness to hide it, hastily forced the letter into her pocket.

Cecilia, surprised, dismayed, alarmed, stopt involuntarily at the door; but Miss Belfield, having secured what was so evidently precious to her, advanced, though not without blushing, and taking her hand, said "How good this is of you, madam, to come to me! when I did not know where to find you, and when I was almost afraid I should have found you no more!"

She then told her, that the first news she had heard the preceding morning, was the violent death of Mr Harrel, which had been related to her, with all its circumstances, by the landlord of their lodgings, who was himself one of his principal creditors, and had immediately been at Portman-square to put in his claims; where he had learnt that all the family had quitted the house, which was entirely occupied by bailiffs. "And I was so sorry," she continued, "that you should meet with any hardships, and not know where to go, and have another home to seek, when I am sure the commonest beggar would never want an habitation, if you had one in your power to give him!—But how sad and melancholy you look! I am afraid this bad action of Mr Harrel has made you quite unhappy? Ah madam! you are too good for this guilty world! your own compassion and benevolence will not suffer you to rest in it!"

Cecilia, touched by this tender mistake of her present uneasiness, embraced her, and with much kindness, answered, "No, sweet Henrietta! it is you who are good, who are innocent, who are guileless!—you, too, I hope are happy!"

"And are not you, madam?" cried Henrietta, fondly returning her caress. "Oh if you are not, who will ever deserve to be! I think I should rather be unhappy myself, than see you so; at least I am sure I ought, for the whole world may be the better for your welfare, and as to me,—who would care what became of me!"

"Ah Henrietta!" cried Cecilia, "do you speak sincerely? do you indeed think yourself so little valued?"

"Why I don't say," answered she, "but that I hope there are some who think a little kindly of me, for if I had not that hope, I should wish to break my heart and die! but what is that to the love and reverence so many have for you?"

"Suppose," said Cecilia, with a forced smile, "I should put your love and reverence to the proof? do you think they would stand it?"

"O yes, indeed I do! and I have wished a thousand and a thousand times that I could but shew you my affection, and let you see that I did not love you because you were a great lady, and high in the world, and full of power to do me service, but because you were so good and so kind, so gentle to the unfortunate, and so sweet to every body!"

"Hold, hold," cried Cecilia, "and let me try if indeed, fairly and truly, you will answer what I mean to ask."

"O yes," cried she warmly, "if it is the dearest secret I have in the world! there is nothing I will not tell you; I will open my whole heart to you, and I shall be proud to think you will let me trust you, for I am sure if you did not care a little for me, you would not take such a trouble."

"You are indeed a sweet creature!" said Cecilia, hesitating whether or not to take advantage of her frankness, "and every time I see you, I love you better. For the world would I not injure you,—and perhaps your confidence—I know not, indeed, if it is fair or right to exact it—" she stopt, extremely perplext, and while Henrietta waited her further enquiries, they were interrupted by the entrance of Mrs Belfield.

"Sure, Child," cried she, to her daughter, "you might have let me know before now who was here, when you knew so well how much I wished an opportunity to see the young lady myself; but here you come down upon pretence to see your brother, and then stay away all the morning, doing nobody knows what." Then, turning to Cecilia, "Ma'am," she continued, "I have been in the greatest concern in the world for the little accident that happened when I saw you before; for to be sure I thought, and indeed nobody will persuade me to the contrary, that it was rather an odd thing for such a young lady as you to come so often after Henny, without so much as thinking of any other reason; especially when, to be sure, there's no more comparison between her and my son, than between anything in the world; however, if it is so, it is so, and I mean to say no more about it, and to be sure he's as contented to think so as if he was as mere an insignificant animal as could be."

"This matter, madam," said Cecilia, "has so long been settled, that I am sorry you should trouble yourself to think of it again."

"O, ma'am, I only mention it by the way of making the proper apology, for as to taking any other notice of it, I have quite left it off; though to be sure what I think I think; but as to my son, he has so got the upper hand of me, that it all goes for nothing, and I might just as well sing to him. Not that I mean to find fault with him neither; so pray, ma'am, don't let what I say be to his prejudice, for I believe all the time, there's nobody like him, neither at this end of the town nor the other; for as to the other, he has more the look of a lord, by half, than of a shopman, and the reason's plain, for that's the sort of company he's always kept, as I daresay a lady such as you must have seen long ago. But for all that, there's some little matters that we mothers fancy we can see into as well as our children; however, if they don't think so, why it answers no purpose to dispute; for as to a better son, to be sure there never was one, and that, as I always say, is the best sign I know for making a good husband."

During this discourse, Henrietta was in the utmost confusion, dreading lest the grossness of her mother should again send off Cecilia in anger; but Cecilia, who perceived her uneasiness, and who was more charmed with her character than ever, from the simplicity of her sincerity, determined to save her that pain, by quietly hearing her harangue, and then quietly departing; though she was much provoked to find from the complaining hints every instant thrown out, that Mrs Belfield was still internally convinced her son's obstinate bashfulness was the only obstacle to his chusing whom he pleased; and that though she no longer dared speak her opinion with openness, she was fully persuaded Cecilia was at his service.

"And for that reason," continued Mrs Belfield, "to be sure any lady that knew her own true advantage, could do nothing better than to take the recommendation of a mother, who must naturally know more of her own children's disposition than can be expected from a stranger; and as to such a son as mine, perhaps there a'n't two such in the world, for he's had a gentleman's education, and turn him which way he will, he'll see never a handsomer person than his own; though, poor dear love, he was always of the thinnest. But the misfortunes he's had to struggle with would make nobody fatter."

Here she was interrupted, and Cecilia not a little surprised, by the entrance of Mr Hobson and Mr Simkins.

"Ladies," cried Mr Hobson, whom she soon found was Mrs Belfield's landlord; "I would not go up stairs without just stopping to let you know a little how the world goes."

Then perceiving and recollecting Cecilia, he exclaimed "I am proud to see you again, ma'am,—Miss, I believe I should say, for I take it you are too young a lady to be entered into matrimony yet."

"Matrimony?" cried Mr Simkins, "no, to be sure, Mr Hobson, how can you be so out of the way? the young lady looks more like to a Miss from a boarding-school, if I might take the liberty for to say so."

"Ay, more's the pity," cried Mrs Belfield, "for as to young ladies waiting and waiting, I don't see the great good of it; especially if a proper match offers; for as to a good husband, I think no lady should be above accepting him, if he's modest and well-behaved, and has been brought up with a genteel education."

"Why as to that, ma'am," said Mr Simkins, "it's another guess matter, for as to the lady's having a proper spouse, if I may be so free, I think as it's no bad thing."

Cecilia now, taking Henrietta's hand, was wishing her good morning; but hearing Mr Hobson say he was just come from Portman-square, her curiosity was excited, and she stayed a little longer.

"Sad work, ma'am," said he; "who'd have thought Mr Harrel asked us all to supper for the mere purpose of such a thing as that! just to serve for a blind, as one may say. But when a man's conscience is foul, what I say is it's ten to one but he makes away with himself. Let every man keep clear of the world, that's my notion, and then he will be in no such hurry to get out of it."

"Why indeed, ma'am," said Mr Simkins, advancing with many bows to Cecilia, "humbly craving pardon for the liberty, I can't pretend for to say I think Mr Harrel did quite the honourable thing by us; for as to his making us drink all that champagne, and the like, it was a sheer take in, so that if I was to speak my mind, I can't say as I esteem it much of a favour."

"Well," said Mrs Belfield, "nothing's to me so surprising as a person's being his own executioner, for as to me, if I was to die for it fifty times, I don't think I could do it."

"So here," resumed Mr Hobson, "we're all defrauded of our dues! nobody's able to get his own, let him have worked for it ever so hard. Sad doings in the square, Miss! all at sixes and sevens; for my part I came off from Vauxhall as soon as the thing had happened, hoping to get the start of the others, or else I should have been proud to wait upon you, ladies, with the particulars; but a man of business never stands upon ceremony, for when money's at stake, that's out of the question. However, I was too late, for the house was seized before ever I could get nigh it."

"I hope, ma'am, if I may be so free," said Mr Simkins, again profoundly bowing, "that you and the other lady did not take it much amiss my not coming back to you, for it was not out of no disrespect, but only I got so squeezed in by the ladies and gentlemen that was looking on, that I could not make my way out, do what I could. But by what I see, I must needs say if one's never in such genteel company, people are always rather of the rudest when one's in a crowd, for if one begs and prays never so, there's no making 'em conformable."

"Pray," said Cecilia, "is it likely any thing will remain for Mrs Harrel?"

"Remain, ma'am?" repeated Mr Hobson, "Yes, a matter of a hundred bills without a receipt to 'em! To be sure, ma'am, I don't want to affront you, that was his intimate acquaintance, more especially as you've done nothing disrespectful by me, which is more than I can say for Mrs Harrel, who seemed downright ashamed of me, and of Mr Simkins too, though all things considered, it would have been as well for her not to have been quite so high. But of that in its proper season!"

"Fie, Mr Hobson fie," cried the supple Mr Simkins, "how can you be so hard? for my share, I must needs own I think the poor lady's to be pitied; for it must have been but a melancholy sight to her, to see her spouse cut off so in the flower of his youth, as one may say; and you ought to scorn to take exceptions at a lady's proudness when she's in so much trouble. To be sure, I can't say myself as she was over-complaisant to make us welcome; but I hope I am above being so unpitiful as for to owe her a grudge for it now she's so down in the mouth."

"Let everybody be civil!" cried Mr Hobson, "that's my notion; and then I shall be as much above being unpitiful as anybody else."

"Mrs Harrel," said Cecilia, "was then too unhappy, and is now, surely, too unfortunate, to make it possible any resentment should be harboured against her."

"You speak, ma'am, like a lady of sense," returned Mr Hobson, "and, indeed, that's the character I hear of you; but for all that, ma'am, every body's willing to stand up for their own friends, for which reason, ma'am, to be sure you'll be making the best of it, both for the Relict, and the late gentleman himself; but, ma'am, if I was to make bold to speak my mind in a fair manner, what I should say would be this; a man here to go shooting himself with all his debts unpaid, is a mere piece of scandal, ma'am! I beg pardon, but what I say is, the truth's the truth, and I can't call it by no other nomination."

Cecilia now, finding she had not any chance of pacifying him, rang for her servant and chair.

Mr Simkins then, affecting to lower his voice, said reproachfully to his friend "Indeed, Mr Hobson, to speak ingenusly, I must needs say I don't think it over and above pelite in you to be so hard upon the young lady's acquaintance that was, now he's defunct. To be sure I can't pretend for to deny but he behaved rather comical; for not paying of nobody, nor so much as making one a little compliment, or the like, though he made no bones of taking all one's goods, and always chused to have the prime of every thing, why it's what I can't pretend to stand up for. But that's neither here nor there, for if he had behaved as bad again, poor Miss could not tell how to help it; and I dares to say she had no more hand in it than nobody at all."

"No, to be sure," cried Mrs Belfield, "what should she have to do with it? Do you suppose a young lady of her fortune would want to take advantage of a person in trade? I am sure it would be both a shame and a sin if she did, for if she has not money enough, I wonder who has. And for my part, I think when a young lady has such a fine fortune as that, the only thing she has to do, is to be thinking of making a good use of it, by dividing it, as one may say, with a good husband. For as to keeping it all for herself, I dare say she's a lady of too much generosity; and as to only marrying somebody that's got as much of his own, why it is not half so much a favour; and if the young lady would take my advice, she'd marry for love, for as to lucre, she's enough in all conscience."

"As to all that," said Mr Hobson, "it makes no alteration in my argument; I am speaking to the purpose, and not for the matter of complaisance; and therefore I'm bold to say Mr Harrel's action had nothing of the gentleman in it. A man has a right to his own life, you'll tell me; but what of that? that's no argument at all, for it does not give him a bit the more right to my property; and a man's running in debt, and spending other people's substances, for no reason in the world but just because he can blow out his own brains when he's done,—though it's a thing neither lawful nor religious to do,—why it's acting quite out of character, and a great hardship to trade into the bargain."

"I heartily wish it had been otherwise," said Cecilia; "but I still hope, if any thing can be done for Mrs Harrel, you will not object to such a proposal."

"Ma'am, as I said before," returned Mr Hobson, "I see you're a lady of sense, and for that I honour you; but as to any thing being done, it's what I call a distinct thing. What's mine is mine, and what's another man's is his; that's my way of arguing; but then if he takes what's mine, where's the law to hinder my taking what's his? This is what I call talking to the purpose. Now as to a man's cutting his throat, or the like of that, for blowing out his own brains may be called the self-same thing, what are his creditors the better for that? nothing at all, but so much the worse it's a false notion to respect it, for there's no respect in it; it's contrary to law, and a prejudice against religion."

"I agree entirely in your opinion," said Cecilia, "but still Mrs Harrel"—

"I know your argument, ma'am," interrupted Mr Hobson; "Mrs Harrel i'n't the worse for her husband's being shot through the head, because she was no accessory to the same, and for that reason, it's a hardship she should lose all her substance; this, ma'am, is what I say, speaking to your side of the argument. But now, ma'am, please to take notice what I argue upon the reply; what have we creditors to do with a man's family? Suppose I am a cabinet-maker? When I send in my chairs, do I ask who is to sit upon them? No; it's all one to me whether it's the gentleman's progeny or his friends, I must be paid for the chairs the same, use them who may. That's the law, ma'am, and no man need be ashamed to abide by it."

The truth of this speech palliating its sententious absurdity, made Cecilia give up her faint attempt to soften him; and her chair being ready, she arose to take leave.

"Lack-a-day, ma'am," cried Mrs Belfield, "I hope you won't go yet, for I expect my son home soon, and I've a heap of things to talk to you about besides, only Mr Hobson having so much to say stopt my mouth. But I should take it as a great favour, ma'am, if you would come some afternoon and drink a dish of tea with me, for then we should have time to say all our say. And I'm sure, ma'am, if you would only let one of your footmen just take a run to let me know when you'd come, my son would be very proud to give you the meeting; and the servants can't have much else to do at your house, for where there's such a heap of 'em, they commonly think of nothing all day long but standing and gaping at one another."

"I am going out of town to-morrow," said Cecilia, "and therefore cannot have the pleasure of calling upon Miss Belfield again."

She then slightly courtsied, and left the room.

The gentle Henrietta, her eyes swimming in tears, followed her to her chair; but she followed her not alone, Mrs Belfield also attended, repining very loudly at the unlucky absence of her son; and the cringing Mr Simkins, creeping after her and bowing, said in a low voice, "I humbly crave pardon, ma'am, for the liberty, but I hope you won't think as I have any share in Mr Hobson's behaving so rude, for I must needs say, I don't think it over genteel in no shape." And Mr Hobson himself, bent upon having one more sentence heard, called out, even after she was seated in her chair, "All I say, ma'am, is this; let every man be honest; that's what I argue, and that's my notion of things."

Cecilia still reached home before Mrs Delvile; but most uneasy were her sensations, and most unquiet was her heart; the letter she had seen in the hands of Henrietta seemed to corroborate all her former suspicions, since if it came not from one infinitely dear to her she would not have shewn such fondness for it, and if that one was not dear to her in secret, she would not have concealed it.

Where then was the hope that any but Delvile could have written it? in secret she could not cherish two, and that Delvile was cherished most fondly, the artlessness of her character unfitted her for disguising.

And why should he write to her? what was his pretence? That he loved her she could now less than ever believe, since his late conduct to herself, though perplexing and inconsistent, evinced at least a partiality incompatible with a passion for another. What then, could she infer, but that he had seduced her affections, and ruined her peace, for the idle and cruel gratification of temporary vanity?

"And if such," cried she, "is the depravity of this accomplished hypocrite, if such is the littleness of soul that a manner so noble disguises, shall be next, urged, perhaps, rather by prudence than preference, make me the object of his pursuit, and the food of his vain-glory? And shall I, warned and instructed as I am, be as easy a prey and as wretched a dupe? No, I will be better satisfied with his conduct, before I venture to trust him, and since I am richer than Henrietta and less likely to be deserted, when won, I will be more on my guard to know why I am addressed, and vindicate the rights of innocence, if I find she has been thus deluded, by forgetting his talents in his treachery, and renouncing him for ever!"

Such were the reflections and surmises that dampt all the long-sought pleasure of her change of residence, and made her habitation in St James's-square no happier than it had been at Mr Harrel's!

She dined again with only Mr and Mrs Delvile, and did not see their son all day; which, in her present uncertainty what to think of him, was an absence she scarcely regretted.

When the servants retired, Mr Delvile told her that he had that morning received two visits upon her account, both from admirers, who each pretended to having had leave to wait upon her from Mr Harrel.

He then named Sir Robert Floyer and Mr Marriot.

"I believe, indeed," said Cecilia, "that neither of them were treated perfectly well; to me, however, their own behaviour has by no means been strictly honourable. I have always, when referred to, been very explicit; and what other methods they were pleased to take, I cannot wonder should fail."

"I told them," said Mr Delvile, "that, since you were now under my roof, I could not refuse to receive their proposals, especially as there would be no impropriety in your alliance with either of them but I told them, at the same time, that I could by no means think of pressing their suit, as that was an office which, however well it might do for Mr Harrel, would be totally improper and unbecoming for me."

"Certainly;" said Cecilia, "and permit me, Sir, to entreat that, should they again apply to you, they may be wholly discouraged from repeating their visits, and assured that far from having trifled with them hitherto, the resolutions I have declared will never be varied."

"I am happy," said Mrs Delvile, "to see so much spirit and discernment where arts of all sorts will be practised to ensnare and delude. Fortune and independence were never so securely lodged as in Miss Beverley, and I doubt not but her choice, whenever it is decided, will reflect as much honour upon her heart, as her difficulty in making it does upon her understanding."

Mr Delvile then enquired whether she had fixed upon any person to choose as a guardian in the place of Mr Harrel. No, she said, nor should she, unless it were absolutely necessary.

"I believe, indeed," said Mrs Delvile, "your affairs will not much miss him! Since I have heard of the excess of his extravagance, I have extremely rejoiced in the uncommon prudence and sagacity of his fair ward, who, in such dangerous hands, with less penetration and sound sense, might have been drawn into a thousand difficulties, and perhaps defrauded of half her fortune."

Cecilia received but little joy from this most unseasonable compliment, which, with many of the same sort that were frequently, though accidentally made, intimidated her from the confession she had planned and finding nothing but censure was likely to follow the discovery, she at length determined to give it up wholly, unless any connection should take place which might render necessary its avowal. Yet something she could not but murmur, that an action so detrimental to her own interest, and which, at the time, appeared indispensable to her benevolence, should now be considered as a mark of such folly and imprudence that she did not dare own it.

CHAPTER II

A RAILING.

The next morning the family purposed setting off as soon as breakfast was over; young Delvile, however, waited not so long; the fineness of the weather tempted him, he said, to travel on horse-back, and therefore he had risen very early, and was already gone. Cecilia could not but wonder, yet did not repine.

Just as breakfast was over, and Mr and Mrs Delvile and Cecilia were preparing to depart, to their no little surprise, the door was opened, and, out of breath with haste and with heat, in stumpt Mr Briggs! "So," cried he to Cecilia, "what's all this? hay?—where are you going?—a coach at the door! horses to every wheel! Servants fine as lords! what's in the wind now? think to chouse me out of my belongings?"

"I thought, Sir," said Cecilia, who instantly understood him, though Mr and Mrs Delvile stared at him in utter astonishment, "I had explained before I left you that I should not return."

"Didn't, didn't!" answered he, angrily; "waited for you three days, dressed a breast o' mutton o' purpose; got in a lobster, and two crabs; all spoilt by keeping; stink already; weather quite muggy, forced to souse 'em in vinegar; one expense brings on another; never begin the like agen."

"I am very sorry, indeed," said Cecilia, much disconcerted, "if there has been any mistake through my neglect; but I had hoped I was understood, and I have been so much occupied—"

"Ay, ay," interrupted he, "fine work! rare doings! a merry Vauxhalling, with pistols at all your noddles! thought as much! thought he'd tip the perch; saw he wasn't stanch; knew he'd go by his company,—a set of jackanapes! all blacklegs! nobody warm among 'em; fellows with a month's good living upon their backs, and not sixpence for the hangman in their pockets!"

Mrs Delvile now, with a look of arch congratulation at Cecilia as the object of this agreeable visit, finding it not likely to be immediately concluded, returned to her chair; but Mr Delvile, leaning sternly upon his cane, moved not from the spot where he stood at his entrance, but surveyed him from head to foot, with the most astonished contempt at his undaunted vulgarity.

"Well I'd all your cash myself; seized that, else!—run out the constable for you, next, and made you blow out your brains for company. Mind what I say, never give your mind to a gold lace hat! many a one wears it don't know five farthings from twopence. A good man always wears a bob wig; make that your rule. Ever see Master Harrel wear such a thing? No, I'll warrant! better if he had; kept his head on his own shoulders. And now, pray, how does he cut up? what has he left behind him? a twey-case, I suppose, and a bit of a hat won't go on a man's head!"

Cecilia, perceiving, with great confusion, that Mr Delvile, though evidently provoked by this intrusion, would not deign to speak, that Mr Briggs might be regarded as belonging wholly to herself, hastily said "I will not, Sir, as your time is precious, detain you here, but, as soon as it is in my power, I will wait upon you in the city."

Mr Briggs, however, without listening to her, thought proper to continue his harangue.

"Invited me once to his house; sent me a card, half of it printed like a book! t'other half a scrawl could not read; pretended to give a supper; all a mere bam; went without my dinner, and got nothing to eat; all glass and shew; victuals painted all manner of colours; lighted up like a pastry-cook on twelfth-day; wanted something solid, and got a great lump of sweetmeat; found it as cold as a stone, all froze in my mouth like ice; made me jump again, and brought the tears in my eyes; forced to spit it out; believe it was nothing but a snowball, just set up for show, and covered over with a little sugar. Pretty way to spend money! Stuffing, and piping, and hopping! never could rest till every farthing was gone; nothing left but his own fool's pate, and even that he could not hold together."

"At present, Sir," said Cecilia, "we are all going out of town; the carriage is waiting at the door, and therefore—"

"No such thing," cried he; "Sha'n't go; come for you myself; take you to my own house. Got every thing ready, been to the broker's, bought a nice blanket, hardly a brack in it. Pick up a table soon; one in my eye."

"I am sorry you have so totally mistaken me, Sir; for I am now going into the country with Mr and Mrs Delvile."

"Won't consent, won't consent! what will you go there for? hear of nothing but dead dukes; as well visit an old tomb."

Here Mr Delvile, who felt himself insulted in a manner he could least support, after looking at him very disdainfully, turned to Cecilia, and said "Miss Beverley, if this person wishes for a longer conference with you, I am sorry you did not appoint a more seasonable hour for your interview."

"Ay, ay," cried the impenetrable Mr Briggs; "want to hurry her off! see that! But 't won't do; a'n't to be nicked; chuse to come in for my thirds; won't be gulled, sha'n't have more than your share."

"Sir!" cried Mr Delvile, with a look meant to be nothing less than petrific.

"What!" cried he, with an arch leer; "all above it, hay? warrant your Spanish Don never thinks of such a thing! don't believe 'em my duck! great cry and little wool; no more of the ready than other folks; mere puff and go one."

"This is language, Sir," said Mr Delvile, "so utterly incomprehensible, that I presume you do not even intend it should be understood; otherwise, I should very little scruple to inform you, that no man of the name of Delvile brooks the smallest insinuation of dishonour."

"Don't he?" returned Mr Briggs, with a grin; "why how will he help it? will the old grandees jump up out of their graves to frighten us?"

"What old grandees, Sir? to whom are you pleased to allude?"

"Why all them old grandfathers and aunts you brag of; a set of poor souls you won't let rest in their coffins; mere clay and dirt! fine things to be proud of! a parcel of old mouldy rubbish quite departed this life! raking up bones and dust, nobody knows for what! ought to be ashamed; who cares for dead carcases? nothing but [carrion]. My little Tom's worth forty of 'em!"

"I can so ill make out, Miss Beverley," said the astonished Mr Delvile, "what this person is pleased to dive at, that I cannot pretend to enter into any sort of conversation with him; you will therefore be so good as to let me know when he has finished his discourse, and you are at leisure to set off."

And then, with a very stately air, he was quitting the room; but was soon stopt, upon Mr Briggs calling out "Ay, ay, Don Duke, poke in the old charnel houses by yourself, none of your defunct for me! didn't care if they were all hung in a string. Who's the better for 'em?'

"Pray, Sir," cried Mr Delvile, turning round, "to whom were you pleased to address that speech?"

"To one Don Puffendorff," replied Mr Briggs; "know ever such a person, hay?"

"Don who? Sir!" said Mr Delvile, stalking nearer to him, "I must trouble you to say that name over again."

"Suppose don't chuse it? how then?"

"I am to blame," said Mr Delvile, scornfully waving his hand with a repulsive motion, "to suffer myself to be irritated so unworthily; and I am sorry, in my own house, to be compelled to hint that the sooner I have it to myself, the better I shall be contented with it."

"Ay, ay, want to get me off; want to have her to yourself! won't be so soon choused; who's the better man? hay? which do you think is warmest? and all got by myself; obliged to never a grandee for a penny; what do you say to that? will you cast an account with me?"

"Very extraordinary this!" cried Mr Delvile; "the most extraordinary circumstance of the kind I ever met with! a person to enter my house in order to talk in this incomprehensible manner! a person, too, I hardly know by sight!"

"Never mind, old Don," cried Briggs, with a facetious nod, "Know me better another time!"

"Old who, Sir!—what!"

"Come to a fair reckoning," continued Mr Briggs; "suppose you were in my case, and had never a farthing but of your own getting; where would you be then? What would become of your fine coach and horses? you might stump your feet off before you'd ever get into one. Where would be all this fine crockery work for your breakfast? you might pop your head under a pump, or drink out of your own paw; what would you do for that fine jemmy tye? Where would you get a gold head to your stick?—You might dig long enough in them cold vaults before any of your old grandfathers would pop out to give you one."

Mr Delvile, feeling more enraged than he thought suited his dignity, restrained himself from making any further answer, but going up to the bell, rang it with great violence.

"And as to ringing a bell," continued Mr Briggs, "you'd never know what it was in your life, unless could make interest to be a dust-man."

"A dust-man!"—repeated Mr Delvile, unable to command his silence longer, "I protest"—and biting his lips, he stopt short.

"Ay, love it, don't you? suits your taste; why not one dust as well as another? Dust in a cart good as dust of a charnel-house; don't smell half so bad."

A servant now entering, Mr Delvile called out "Is everything ready?"

"Yes, Sir."

He then begged Mrs Delvile to go into the coach, and telling Cecilia to follow when at leisure, left the room.

"I will come immediately, Sir," said Cecilia; "Mr Briggs, I am sorry to leave you, and much concerned you have had this trouble; but I can detain Mr Delvile no longer."

And then away she ran, notwithstanding he repeatedly charged her to stay. He followed them, however, to the coach, with bitter revilings that every body was to make more of his ward than himself, and with the most virulent complaints of his losses from the blanket, the breast of mutton, the crabs and the lobster!

Nothing, however, more was said to him; Cecilia, as if she had not heard him, only bowed her head, and the coach driving off, they soon lost sight of him.

This incident by no means rendered the journey pleasant, or Mr Delvile gracious; his own dignity, that constant object of his thoughts and his cares, had received a wound from this attack which he had not the sense to despise; and the vulgarity and impudence of Mr Briggs, which ought to have made his familiarity and boldness equally contemptible and ridiculous, served only with a man whose pride out-ran his understanding, to render them doubly mortifying and stinging. He could talk, therefore, of nothing the whole way that they went, but the extreme impropriety of which the Dean of had been guilty, in exposing him to scenes and situations so much beneath his rank, by leaguing him with a person so coarse and disgraceful.

They slept one night upon the road, and arrived the next day at Delvile Castle.

CHAPTER III

AN ANTIQUE MANSION.

Delvile Castle was situated in a large and woody park, and surrounded by a moat. A drawbridge which fronted the entrance was every night, by order of Mr Delvile, with the same care as if still necessary for the preservation of the family, regularly drawn up. Some fortifications still remained entire, and vestiges were every where to be traced of more; no taste was shown in the disposition of the grounds, no openings were contrived through the wood for distant views or beautiful objects; the mansion-house was ancient, large and magnificent, but constructed with as little attention to convenience and comfort, as to airiness and elegance; it was dark, heavy and monastic, equally in want of repair and of improvement. The grandeur of its former inhabitants was every where visible, but the decay into which it was falling rendered such remains mere objects for meditation and melancholy; while the evident struggle to support some appearance of its ancient dignity, made the dwelling and all in its vicinity wear an aspect of constraint and austerity. Festivity, joy and pleasure, seemed foreign to the purposes of its construction; silence, solemnity and contemplation were adapted to it only.

Mrs Delvile, however, took all possible care to make the apartments and situation of Cecilia commodious and pleasant, and to banish by her kindness and animation the gloom and formality which her mansion inspired. Nor were her efforts ungratefully received; Cecilia, charmed by every mark of attention from a woman she so highly admired, returned her solicitude by encreasing affection, and repaid all her care by the revival of her spirits. She was happy, indeed, to have quitted the disorderly house of Mr Harrel, where terror, so continually awakened, was only to be lulled by the grossest imposition; and though her mind, depressed by what was passed, and in suspence with what was to come, was by no means in a state for uninterrupted enjoyment, yet to find herself placed, at last, without effort or impropriety, in the very mansion she had so long considered as her road to happiness, rendered her, notwithstanding her remaining sources of inquietude, more contented than she had yet felt herself since her departure from Suffolk.

Even the imperious Mr Delvile was more supportable here than in London; secure in his own castle, he looked around him with a pride of power and of possession which softened while it swelled him. His superiority was undisputed, his will was without controul. He was not, as in the great capital of the kingdom, surrounded by competitors; no rivalry disturbed his peace, no equality mortified his greatness; all he saw were either vassals of his power, or guests bending to his pleasure; he abated therefore, considerably, the stern gloom of his haughtiness, and soothed his proud mind by the courtesy of condescension.

Little, however, was the opportunity Cecilia found, for evincing that spirit and forbearance she had planned in relation to Delvile; he breakfasted by himself every morning, rode or walked out alone till driven home by the heat of the day, and spent the rest of his time till dinner in his own study. When he then appeared, his conversation was always general, and his attention not more engaged by Cecilia than by his mother. Left by them with his father, sometimes he appeared again at tea-time, but more commonly he rode or strolled out to some neighbouring family, and it was always uncertain whether he was again seen before dinner the next day.

By this conduct, reserve on her part was rendered totally unnecessary; she could give no discouragement where she met with no assiduity; she had no occasion to fly where she was never pursued.

Strange, however, she thought such behaviour, and utterly impossible to be the effect of accident; his desire to avoid her seemed scrupulous and pointed, and however to the world it might wear the appearance of chance, to her watchful anxiety a thousand circumstances marked it for design. She found that his friends at home had never seen so little of him, complaints were continually made of his frequent absences, and much surprise was expressed at his new manner of life, and what might be the occupations which so strangely engrossed his time.

Had her heart not interfered in this matter, she might now have been perfectly at rest, since she was spared the renunciation she had projected, and since, without either mental exertion or personal trouble, the affair seemed totally dropt, and Delvile, far from manifesting any design of conquest, shunned all occasions of gallantry, and sedulously avoided even common conversation with her. If he saw her preparing to walk out in an evening, he was certain to stay at home; if his mother was with her, and invited him to join them, he was sure to be ready with some other engagement; and if by accident he met her in the park, he merely stopt to speak of the weather, bowed, and hurried on.

How to reconcile a coldness so extraordinary with a fervour so animated as that which he had lately shewn, was indeed not easy; sometimes she fancied he had entangled not only the poor Henrietta but himself, at other times she believed him merely capricious; but that he studied to avoid her she was convinced invariably, and such a conviction was alone sufficient to determine her upon forwarding his purpose. And, when her first surprise was over, and first chagrin abated, her own pride came to her aid, and she resolved to use every method in her power to conquer a partiality so un gratefully bestowed. She rejoiced that in no instance she had ever betrayed it, and she saw that his own behaviour prevented all suspicion of it in the family. Yet, in the midst of her mortification and displeasure, she found some consolation in seeing that those mercenary views of which she had once been led to accuse him, were farthest from his thoughts, and that whatever was the state of his mind, she had no artifice to apprehend, nor design to guard against. All therefore that remained was to imitate his example, be civil and formal, shun all interviews that were not public, and decline all discourse but what good breeding occasionally made necessary.

By these means their meetings became more rare than ever, and of shorter duration, for if one by any accident was detained, the other retired; till, by their mutual diligence, they soon only saw each other at dinner; and though neither of them knew the motives or the intentions of the other, the best concerted agreement could not more effectually have separated them.

This task to Cecilia was at first extremely painful; but time and constancy of mind soon lessened its difficulty. She amused herself with walking and reading, she commissioned Mr Monckton to send her a Piano Forte of Merlin's, she was fond of fine work, and she found in the conversation of Mrs Delvile a never-failing resource against languor and sadness. Leaving therefore to himself her mysterious son, she wisely resolved to find other employment for her thoughts, than conjectures with which she could not be satisfied, and doubts that might never be explained.

Very few families visited at the castle, and fewer still had their visits returned. The arrogance of Mr Delvile had offended all the neighbouring gentry, who could easily be better entertained than by receiving instructions of their own inferiority, which however readily they might allow, was by no means so pleasant a subject as to recompense them for hearing no other. And if Mr Delvile was shunned through hatred, his lady no less was avoided through fear; high-spirited and fastidious, she was easily wearied and disgusted, she bore neither with frailty nor folly—those two principal ingredients in human nature! She required, to obtain her favour, the union of virtue and abilities with elegance, which meeting but rarely, she was rarely disposed to be pleased; and disdaining to conceal either contempt or aversion, she inspired in return nothing but dread or resentment; making thus, by a want of that lenity which is the milk of human kindness, and the bond of society, enemies the most numerous and illiberal by those very talents which, more meekly borne, would have rendered her not merely admired, but adored!

In proportion, however, as she was thus at war with the world in general, the chosen few who were honoured with her favour, she loved with a zeal all her own; her heart, liberal, open, and but too daringly sincere, was fervent in affection, and enthusiastic in admiration; the friends who were dear to her, she was devoted to serve, she magnified their virtues till she thought them of an higher race of beings, she inflamed her generosity with ideas of what she owed to them, till her life seemed too small a sacrifice to be refused for their service.

Such was the love which already she felt for Cecilia; her countenance had struck, her manners had charmed her, her understanding was displayed by the quick intelligence of her eyes, and every action and every notion spoke her mind the seat of elegance. In secret she sometimes regretted that she was not higher born, but that regret always vanished when she saw and conversed with her.

Her own youth had been passed in all the severity of affliction; she had been married to Mr Delvile by her relations, without any consultation of her heart or her will. Her strong mind disdained useless complaints, yet her discontent, however private, was deep. Ardent in her disposition, and naturally violent in her passions, her feelings were extremely acute, and to curb them by reason and principle had been the chief and hard study of her life. The effort had calmed, though it had not made her happy. To love Mr Delvile she felt was impossible; proud without merit, and imperious without capacity, she saw with bitterness the inferiority of his faculties, and she found in his temper no qualities to endear or attract; yet she respected his birth and his family, of which her own was a branch, and whatever was her misery from the connection, she steadily behaved to him with the strictest propriety.

Her son, however, when she was blessed with his presence, had a power over her mind that mitigated all her sorrows, and almost lulled even her wishes to sleep; she rather idolised than loved him, yet her fondness flowed not from relationship, but from his worth and his character, his talents and his disposition. She saw in him, indeed, all her own virtues and excellencies, with a toleration for the imperfections of others to which she was wholly a stranger. Whatever was great or good she expected him to perform; occasion alone she thought wanting to manifest him the first of human beings.

Nor here was Mr Delvile himself less sanguine in his hopes; his son was not only the first object of his affection, but the chief idol of his pride, and he did not merely cherish but reverence him as his successor, the only support of his ancient name and family, without whose life and health the whole race would be extinct. He consulted him in all his affairs, never mentioned him but with distinction, and expected the whole world to bow down before him.

Delvile in his behaviour to his father imitated the conduct of his mother, who opposed him in nothing when his pleasure was made known, but who forbore to enquire into his opinion except in cases of necessity. Their minds, indeed, were totally dissimilar; and Delvile well knew that if he submitted to his directions, he must demand such respect as the world would refuse with indignation, and scarcely speak to a man whose genealogy was not known to him.

But though duty and gratitude were the only ties that bound him to his father, he loved his mother not merely with filial affection, but with the purest esteem and highest reverence; he knew, too, that while without him her existence would be a burthen, her tenderness was no effusion of weak partiality, but founded on the strongest assurances of his worth; and however to maternal indulgence its origin might be owing, the rectitude of his own conduct could alone save it from diminution.

Such was the house in which Cecilia was now settled, and with which she lived almost to the exclusion of the sight of any other; for though she had now been three weeks at the castle, she had only at church seen any family but the Delviles.

Nor did any thing in the course of that time occur to her, but the reception of a melancholy letter from Mrs Harrel, filled with complaints of her retirement and misery; and another, from Mr Arnott, with an account of the funeral, the difficulties he had had to encounter with the creditors, who had even seized the dead body, and the numerous expences in which he had been involved, by petitions he could not withstand, from the meaner and more clamorous of those whom his late brother-in-law had left unpaid. He concluded with a pathetic prayer for her happiness, and a declaration that his own was lost for ever, since now he was even deprived of her sight. Cecilia wrote an affectionate answer to Mrs Harrel, promising, when fully at liberty, that she would herself fetch her to her own house in Suffolk; but she could only send her compliments to Mr Arnott, though her compassion urged a kinder message; as she feared even a shadow of encouragement to so serious, yet hopeless a passion.

CHAPTER IV

A RATTLE.

At this time, the house was much enlivened by a visit from Lady Honoria Pemberton, who came to spend a month with Mrs Delvile.

Cecilia had now but little leisure, for Lady Honoria would hardly rest a moment away from her; she insisted upon walking with her, sitting with her, working with her, and singing with her; whatever she did, she chose to do also; wherever she went, she was bent upon accompanying her; and Mrs Delvile, who wished her well, though she had no patience with her foibles, encouraged this intimacy from the hope it might do her service.

It was not, however, that Lady Honoria had conceived any regard for Cecilia; on the contrary, had she been told she should see her no more, she would have heard it with the same composure as if she had been told she should meet with her daily; she had no motive for pursuing her but that she had nothing else to do, and no fondness for her society but, what resulted from aversion to solitude.

Lady Honoria had received a fashionable education, in which her proficiency had been equal to what fashion made requisite; she sung a little; played the harpsichord a little, painted a little, worked a little, and danced a great deal. She had quick parts and high spirits, though her mind was uncultivated, and she was totally void of judgment or discretion; she was careless of giving offence, and indifferent to all that was thought of her; the delight of her life was to create wonder by her rattle, and whether that wonder was to her advantage or discredit, she did not for a moment trouble herself to consider.

A character of so much levity with so little heart had no great chance of raising esteem or regard in Cecilia, who at almost any other period of her life would have been wearied of her importunate attendance; but at present, the unsettled state of her own mind made her glad to give it any employment, and the sprightliness of Lady Honoria served therefore to amuse her. Yet she could not forbear being hurt by finding that the behaviour of Delvile was so exactly the same to them both, that any common observer would with difficulty have pronounced which he preferred.

One morning about a week after her ladyship's arrival at the castle, she came running into Cecilia's room, saying she had very good news for her.

"A charming opening!" cried Cecilia, "pray tell it me."

"Why my Lord Derford is coming!"

"O what a melancholy dearth of incident," cried Cecilia, "if this is your best intelligence!"

"Why it's better than nothing; better than going to sleep over a family party; and I vow I have sometimes such difficulty to keep awake, that I am frightened to death lest I should be taken with a sudden nap, and affront them all. Now pray speak the truth without squeamishness, don't you find it very terrible?"

"No, I find nothing very terrible with Mrs Delvile."

"O, I like Mrs Delvile, too, of all things, for I believe she's the cleverest woman in the world; but then I know she does not like me, so there's no being very fond of her. Besides, really, if I admired her as much again, I should be, dreadfully tired of seeing nothing else. She never stirs out, you know, and has no company at home, which is an extremely tiresome plan, for it only serves to make us all doubly sick of one another; though you must know it's one great reason why my father likes I should come; for he has some very old-fashioned notions, though I take a great deal of pains to make him get the better of them. But I am always excessively rejoiced when the visit has been paid, for I am obliged to come every year. I don't mean now, indeed, because your being here makes it vastly more tolerable."

"You do me much honour," cried Cecilia, laughing.

"But really, when my Lord Derford comes, it can't possibly be quite so bad, for at least there will be something else to look at; and you must know my eyes tire extremely of always seeing the same objects. And we can ask him, too, for a little news, and that will put Mrs Delvile in a passion, which will help to give us a little spirit; though I know we shall not get the smallest intelligence from him, for he knows nothing in the world that's going forward. And, indeed, that's no great matter, for if he did, he would not know how to tell it, he's so excessively silly. However, I shall ask him all sort of things, for the less he can answer, the more it will plague him; and I like to plague a fool amazingly, because he can never plague one again.—Though really I ought to beg your pardon, for he is one of your admirers."

"Oh pray make no stranger of me! you have my free consent to say whatever you please of him."

"I assure you, then, I like my old Lord Ernolf the best of the two, for he has a thousand times more sense than his son, and upon my word I don't think he is much uglier. But I wonder vastly you would not marry him, for all that, for you might have done exactly what you pleased with him, which, altogether, would have been no inconvenient circumstance."

"When I want a pupil," answered Cecilia, "I shall think that an admirable recommendation; but were I to marry, I would rather find a tutor, of the two."

"I am sure I should not," cried Lady Honoria, carelessly, "for one has enough to do with tutors before hand, and the best thing I know of marrying is to get rid of them. I fancy you think so too, only it's a pretty speech to make. Oh how my sister Euphrasia would adore you!—Pray are you always as grave as you are now?"

"No,—yes,—indeed I hardly know."

"I fancy it's this dismal place that hurts your spirits. I remember when I saw you in St James's-square I thought you very lively. But really these thick walls are enough to inspire the vapours if one never had them before."

"I don't think they have had a very bad effect upon your ladyship!"

"O yes they have; if Euphrasia was here she would hardly know me. And the extreme want of taste and entertainment in all the family is quite melancholy; for even if by chance one has the good fortune to hear any intelligence, Mrs Delvile will hardly let it be repeated, for fear it should happen to be untrue, as if that could possibly signify! I am sure I had as lieve the things were false as not, for they tell as well one way as the other, if she would but have patience to hear them. But she's extremely severe, you know, as almost all those very clever women are; so that she keeps a kind of restraint upon me whether I will or no. However, that's nothing compared to her caro sposo, for he is utterly insufferable; so solemn, and so dull! so stately and so tiresome! Mortimer, too, gets worse and worse; O 'tis a sad tribe! I dare say he will soon grow quite as horrible as his father. Don't you think so?"

"Why indeed,—no,—I don't think there's much resemblance," said Cecilia, with some hesitation.

"He is the most altered creature," continued her ladyship, "I ever saw in my life. Once I thought him the most agreeable young man in the world; but if you observe, that's all over now, and he is getting just as stupid and dismal as the rest of them. I wish you had been here last summer; I assure you, you would quite have fallen in love with him."

"Should I?" said Cecilia, with a conscious smile.

"Yes, for he was quite delightful; all spirit and gaiety, but now, if it was not for you, I really think I should pretend to lose my way, and instead of going over that old draw-bridge, throw myself into the moat. I wish Euphrasia was here. It's just the right place for her. She'll fancy herself in a monastery as soon as she comes, and nothing will make her half so happy, for she is always wishing to be a Nun, poor little simpleton.

"Is there any chance that Lady Euphrasia may come?"

"O no, she can't at present, because it would not be proper; but I mean if ever she is married to Mortimer."

"Married to him!" repeated Cecilia, in the utmost consternation.

"I believe, my dear," cried Lady Honoria, looking at her very archly, "you intend to be married to him yourself?"

"Me? no, indeed!"

"You look very guilty, though," cried she laughing, "and indeed when you came hither, every body said that the whole affair was arranged."

"For shame, Lady Honoria!" said Cecilia, again changing colour, "I am sure this must be your own fancy,—invention,—"

"No, I assure you; I heard it at several places; and every body said how charmingly your fortune would build up all these old fortifications; but some people said they knew Mr Harrel had sold you to Mr Marriot, and that if you married Mortimer, there would be a lawsuit that would take away half your estate; and others said you had promised your hand to Sir Robert Floyer, and repented when you heard of his mortgages, and he gave it out every where that he would fight any man that pretended to you; and then again some said that you were all the time privately married to Mr Arnott, but did not dare own it, because he was so afraid of fighting with Sir Robert."

"O Lady Honoria!" cried Cecilia, half laughing, "what wild inventions are these! and all I hope, your own?"

"No, indeed, they were current over the whole town. But don't take any notice of what I told you about Euphrasia, for perhaps, it may never happen."

"Perhaps," said Cecilia, reviving by believing it all fiction, "it has never been in agitation?"

"O yes; it is negociating at this very moment, I believe, among the higher powers; only Mr Delvile does not yet know whether Euphrasia has fortune enough for what he wants."

Ah, thought Cecilia, how do I rejoice that my independent situation exempts me from being disposed of for life, by thus being set up to sale!

"They thought of me, once, for Mortimer," continued Lady Honoria, "but I'm vastly glad that's over, for I never should have survived being shut up in this place; it's much fitter for Euphrasia. To tell you the truth, I believe they could not make out money enough; but Euphrasia has a fortune of her own, besides what we shall have together, for Grandmama left her every thing that was in her own power."

"Is Lady Euphrasia your elder sister?"

"O no, poor little thing, she's two years younger. Grandmama brought her up, and` she has seen nothing at all of the world, for she has never been presented yet, so she is not come out, you know; but she's to come out next year. However, she once saw Mortimer, but she did not like him at all."

"Not like him!" cried Cecilia, greatly surprised.

"No, she thought him too gay,—Oh dear, I wish she could see him now! I am sure I hope she would find him sad enough! she is the most formal little grave thing you ever beheld; she'll preach to you sometimes for half an hour together. Grandmama taught her nothing in the world but to say her prayers, so that almost every other word you say, she thinks is quite wicked."

The conversation was now interrupted by their separating to dress for dinner. It left Cecilia in much perplexity; she knew not what wholly to credit, or wholly to disbelieve; but her chief concern arose from the unfortunate change of countenance which Lady Honoria had been so quick in observing.

The next time she was alone with Mrs Delvile, "Miss Beverley," she said, "has your little rattling tormentor acquainted you who is coming?"

"Lord Derford, do you mean, ma'am?"

"Yes, with his father; shall you dislike to see them?"

"Not if, as I hope, they come merely to wait upon you and Mr Delvile."

"Mr Delvile and myself," answered she smiling, "will certainly have the honour of receiving them."

"Lord Ernolf," said Cecilia, "can never suppose his visit will make any change in me; I have been very explicit with him, and he seemed equally rational and well bred in forbearing any importunity upon the subject."

"It has however been much believed in town," said Mrs Delvile, "that you were strangely shackled by Mr Harrel, and therefore his lordship may probably hope that a change in your situation may be followed by a change in his favour."

"I shall be sorry if he does," said Cecilia, "for he will then find himself much deceived."

"You are right, very right," cried Mrs Delvile, "to be difficult in your choice, and to take time for looking around you before you make any. I have forborn all questions upon this subject, lest you should find any reluctance in answering them; but I am now too deeply interested in your welfare to be contented in total ignorance of your designs; will you, then, suffer me to make a few enquiries?"

Cecilia gave a ready, but blushing assent.

"Tell me, then, of the many admirers who have graced your train, which there is you have distinguished with any intention of future preference?"

"Not one, madam!"

"And, out of so many, is there not one that, hereafter, you mean to distinguish?"

"Ah madam!" cried Cecilia, shaking her head, "many as they may seem, I have little reason to be proud of them; there is one only who, had my fortune been smaller, would, I believe, ever have thought of me, and there is one only, who, were it now diminished, would ever think of me more."

"This sincerity," cried Mrs Delvile, "is just what I expected from you. There is, then, one?"

"I believe there is,—and the worthy Mr Arnott is the man; I am much indeed deceived, if his partiality for me is not truly disinterested, and I almost wish"—

"What, my love?"

"That I could return it more gratefully!"

"And do you not?"

"No!—I cannot! I esteem him, I have the truest regard for his character, and were I now by any fatal necessity, compelled to belong to any one of those who have been pleased to address me, I should not hesitate a moment in shewing him my gratitude; but yet, for some time at least, such a proof of it would render me very miserable."

"You may perhaps think so now," returned Mrs Delvile; "but with sentiments so strongly in his favour, you will probably be led hereafter to pity—and accept him."

"No, indeed, madam; I pretend not, I own, to open my whole heart to you;—I know not that you would have patience, for so uninteresting a detail; but though there are some things I venture not to mention, there is nothing, believe me, in which I will deceive you."

"I do believe you," cried Mrs Delvile, embracing her; "and the more readily because, not merely among your avowed admirers, but among the whole race of men, I scarce know one to whom I should think you worthily consigned!"

Ah! thought Cecilia, that scarce! who may it mean to except?

"To shew you," she continued, "that I will deserve your confidence in future, I will refrain from distressing you by any further questions at present; you will not, I think, act materially without consulting me, and for your thoughts—it were tyranny, not friendship, to investigate them more narrowly."

Cecilia's gratitude for this delicacy, would instantly have induced her to tell every secret of her soul, had she not apprehended such a confession would have seemed soliciting her interest and assistance, in the only affair in which she would have disdained even to receive them.

She thanked her, therefore, for her kindness, and the conversation was dropt; she much wished to have known whether these enquiries sprung simply from friendly curiosity, or whether she was desirous from any nearer motive to be satisfied with respect to her freedom or engagements. This, however, she had no method of discovering, and was therefore compelled to wait quietly till time should make it clear.

CHAPTER V

A STORM.

One evening about this time, which was the latter end of July, Lady Honoria and Cecilia deferred walking out till very late, and then found it so pleasant, that they had strolled into the Park two miles from the house, when they were met by young Delvile; who, however, only reminded them how far they had to return, and walked on.

"He grows quite intolerable!" cried Lady Honoria, when he was gone; "it's really a melancholy thing to see a young man behave so like an old Monk. I dare say in another week he won't take off his hat to us; and, in about a fortnight, I suppose he'll shut himself up in one of those little round towers, and shave his head, and live upon roots, and howl if any body comes near him. I really half wonder he does not think it too dissipated to let Fidel run after him so. A thousand to one but he shoots him some day for giving a sudden bark when he's in one of these gloomy fits. Something, however, must certainly be the matter with him. Perhaps he is in love."

"Can nothing be the matter with him but that?" cried Cecilia.

"Nay, I don't know; but I am sure if he is, his Mistress has not much occasion to be jealous of you or me, for never, I think, were two poor Damsels so neglected!"

The utmost art of malice could not have furnished speech more truly mortifying to Cecilia than this thoughtless and accidental sally of Lady Honoria's; particularly, however, upon her guard, from the raillery she had already endured, she answered, with apparent indifference, "he is meditating, perhaps, upon Lady Euphrasia."

"O no," cried Lady Honoria, "for he did not take any notice of her when he saw her; I am sure if he marries her, it will only be because he cannot help it."

"Poor Lady Euphrasia!"

"O no, not at all; he'll make her two or three fine speeches, and then she'll be perfectly contented especially if he looks as dismally at her as he does at us! and that probably he will do the more readily for not liking to look at her at all. But she's such a romantic little thing, she'll never suspect him."

Here they were somewhat alarmed by a sudden darkness in the air, which was presently succeeded by a thunder storm; they instantly turned back, and began running home, when a violent shower of rain obliged them to take shelter under a large tree; where in two minutes they were joined by Delvile, who came to offer his assistance in hurrying them home; and finding the thunder and lightning continue, begged them to move on, in defiance of the rain, as their present situation exposed them to more danger than a wet hat and cloak, which might be changed in a moment.

Cecilia readily assented; but Lady Honoria, extremely frightened, protested she would not stir till the storm was over. It was in vain he represented her mistake in supposing herself in a place of security; she clung to the tree, screamed at every flash of lightning, and all her gay spirits were lost in her apprehensions.

Delvile then earnestly proposed to Cecilia conducting her home by herself, and returning again to Lady Honoria; but she thought it wrong to quit her companion, and hardly right to accept his assistance separately. They waited, therefore, some time all together; but the storm increasing with great violence, the thunder growing louder, and the lightning becoming stronger, Delvile grew impatient even to anger at Lady Honoria's resistance, and warmly expostulated upon its folly and danger. But the present was no season for lessons in philosophy; prejudices she had never been taught to surmount made her think herself in a place of safety, and she was now too much terrified to give argument fair play.

Finding her thus impracticable, Delvile eagerly said to Cecilia, "Come then, Miss Beverley, let us wait no longer; I will see you home, and then return to Lady Honoria."

"By no means," cried she, "my life is not more precious than either of yours, and therefore it may run the same risk."

"It is more precious," cried he with vehemence, "than the air I breathe!" and seizing her hand, he drew it under his arm, and, without waiting her consent, almost forced her away with him, saying as they ran, "How could a thousand Lady Honoria's recompense the world for the loss of one Miss

Beverley? we may, indeed, find many thousand such as Lady Honoria, but such as Miss Beverley—where shall we ever find another?"

Cecilia, surprised, yet gratified, could not speak, for the speed with which they ran almost took away her breath; and before they were near home, slackening her pace, and panting, she confessed her strength was exhausted, and that she could go so fast no further.

"Let us then stop and rest," cried he; "but why will you not lean upon me? surely this is no time for scruples, and for idle and unnecessary scruples, Miss Beverley can never find a time."

Cecilia then, urged equally by shame at his speech and by weakness from fatigue, leant upon his arm but she soon repented her condescension; for Delvile, with an emotion he seemed to find wholly irrepressible, passionately exclaimed "sweet lovely burthen! O why not thus for ever!"

The strength of Cecilia was now instantly restored, and she hastily withdrew from his hold; he suffered her to disengage herself, but said in a faultering voice, "pardon me, Cecilia!—Madam!—Miss Beverley, I mean!—"

Cecilia, without making any answer, walked on by herself, as quick a pace as she was able; and Delvile, not venturing to oppose her, silently followed.

They had gone but a few steps, before there came a violent shower of hail; and the wind, which was very high, being immediately in their faces, Cecilia was so pelted and incommoded, that she was frequently obliged to stop, in defiance of her utmost efforts to force herself forward. Delvile then approaching her, proposed that she should again stand under a tree, as the thunder and lightning for the present seemed over, and wait there till the fury of the hail was past; and Cecilia, though never before so little disposed to oblige him, was so much distressed by the violence of the wind and hail, that she was forced to comply.

Every instant now seemed an age; yet neither hail nor wind abated; mean time they were both silent, and both, though with different feelings, equally comfortless.

Delvile, however, who took care to place himself on the side whence the wind blew hardest, perceived, in spite of his endeavours to save her, some hail-stones lodged upon her thin summer cloak; he then took off his own hat, and, though he ventured not to let it touch her, held it in such a manner as to shelter her better.

Cecilia now could no longer be either silent or unmoved, but turning to him with much emotion, said, "Why will you do this, Mr Delvile?"

"What would I not do," answered he, "to obtain forgiveness from Miss Beverley?"

"Well, well,—pray put on your hat."

"Do you command it?"

"No, certainly!—but I wish it."

"Ah!" cried he, instantly putting it on, "whose are the commands that would have half the weight with your wishes?"

And then, after another pause, he added, "do you forgive me?"

Cecilia, ashamed of the cause of their dissension, and softened by the seriousness of his manner, answered very readily, "yes, yes,—why will you make me remember such nonsense?"

"All sweetness," cried he warmly, and snatching her hand, "is Miss Beverley!—O that I had power—that it were not utterly impossible—that the cruelty of my situation—"

"I find," cried she, greatly agitated, and forcibly drawing away her hand, "you will teach me, for another time, the folly of fearing bad weather!"

And she hurried from beneath the tree; and Delvile perceiving one of the servants approach with an umbrella, went forward to take it from him, and directed him to hasten instantly to Lady Honoria.

Then returning to Cecilia, he would have held it over her head, but with an air of displeasure, she took it into her own hand.

"Will you not let me carry it for you?" he cried.

"No, Sir, there is not any occasion."

They then proceeded silently on.

The storm was now soon over; but it grew very dark, and as they had quitted the path while they ran, in order to get home by a shorter cut, the walk was so bad from the height of the grass, and the unevenness of the ground, that Cecilia had the utmost difficulty to make her way; yet she resolutely refused any assistance from Delvile, who walked anxiously by her side, and seemed equally fearful upon his own account and upon hers, to trust himself with being importunate.

At length they came to a place which Cecilia in vain tried to pass; Delvile then grew more urgent to help her; firm, however, in declining all aid, she preferred going a considerable way round to another part of the park which led to the house. Delvile, angry as well as mortified, proposed to assist her no more, but followed without saying a word.

Cecilia, though she felt not all the resentment she displayed, still thought it necessary to support it, as she was much provoked with the perpetual inconsistency of his behaviour, and deemed it wholly improper to suffer, without discouragement, occasional sallies of tenderness from one who, in his general conduct, behaved with the most scrupulous reserve.

They now arrived at the castle; but entering by a back way, came to a small and narrow passage which obstructed the entrance of the umbrella; Delvile once more, and almost involuntarily, offered to help her; but, letting down the spring, she coldly said she had no further use for it.

He then went forward to open a small gate which led by another long passage into the hall; but hearing the servants advance, he held it for an instant in his hand, while, in a tone of voice the most dejected, he said "I am grieved to find you thus offended; but were it possible you could know half the wretchedness of my heart, the generosity of your own would make you regret this severity!" and then, opening the gate, he bowed, and went another way.

Cecilia was now in the midst of servants; but so much shocked and astonished by the unexpected speech of Delvile, which instantly changed all her anger into sorrow, that she scarce knew what they said to her, nor what she replied; though they all with one voice enquired what was become of Lady Honoria, and which way they should run to seek her.

Mrs Delvile then came also, and she was obliged to recollect herself. She immediately proposed her going to bed, and drinking white wine whey to prevent taking cold; cold, indeed, she feared not; yet she agreed to the proposal, for she was confounded and dismayed by what had passed, and utterly unable to hold any conversation.

Her perplexity and distress were, however, all attributed to fatigue and fright; and Mrs Delvile, having assisted in hurrying her to bed, went to perform the same office for Lady Honoria, who arrived at that time.

Left at length by herself, she revolved in her mind the adventure of the evening, and the whole behaviour of Delvile since first she was acquainted with him. That he loved her with tenderness, with fondness loved her, seemed no longer to admit of any doubt, for however distant and cold he appeared, when acting with circumspection and design, the moment he was off his guard from surprise, terror, accident of any sort, the moment that he was betrayed into acting from nature and inclination, he was constantly certain to discover a regard the most animated and flattering.

This regard, however, was not more evident than his desire to conceal and to conquer it; he seemed to dread even her sight, and to have imposed upon himself the most rigid forbearance of all conversation or intercourse with her.

Whence could this arise? what strange and unfathomable cause could render necessary a conduct so mysterious? he knew not, indeed, that she herself wished it changed, but he could not be ignorant that his chance with almost any woman would at least be worth trying.

Was the obstacle which thus discouraged him the condition imposed by her uncle's will of giving her own name to the man she married? this she herself thought was an unpleasant circumstance, but yet so common for an heiress, that it could hardly out-weigh the many advantages of such a connection.

Henrietta again occurred to her; the letter she had seen in her hands was still unexplained; yet her entire conviction that Henrietta was not loved by him, joined to a certainty that affection alone could ever make him think of her, lessened upon this subject her suspicions every moment.

Lady Euphrasia Pemberton, at last, rested most upon her mind, and she thought it probable some actual treaty was negociating with the Duke of Derwent.

Mrs Delvile she had every reason to believe was her friend, though she was scrupulously delicate in avoiding either raillery or observation upon the subject of her son, whom she rarely mentioned, and never but upon occasions in which Cecilia could have no possible interest.

The Father, therefore, notwithstanding all Mr Monckton had represented to the contrary, appeared to be the real obstacle; his pride might readily object to her birth, which though not contemptible, was merely decent, and which, if traced beyond her grandfather, lost all title even to that epithet.

"If this, however," she cried, "is at last his situation, how much have I been to blame in censuring his conduct! for while to me he has appeared capricious, he has, in fact, acted wholly from necessity; if his father insists upon his forming another connection, has he not been honourable, prudent and just, in flying an object that made him think of disobedience, and endeavouring to keep her ignorant of a partiality it is his duty to curb?"

All, therefore, that remained for her to do or to resolve, was to guard her own secret with more assiduous care than ever, and since she found that their union was by himself thought impossible, to keep from his knowledge that the regret was not all his own.

CHAPTER VI

A MYSTERY.

For two days, in consequence of violent colds caught during the storm, Lady Honoria Pemberton and Cecilia were confined to their rooms. Cecilia, glad by solitude and reflection to compose her spirits and settle her plan of conduct, would willingly have still prolonged her retirement, but the abatement of her cold affording her no pretence, she was obliged on the third day to make her appearance.

Lady Honoria, though less recovered, as she had been more a sufferer, was impatient of any restraint, and would take no denial to quitting her room at the same time; at dinner, therefore, all the family met at usual.

Mr Delvile, with his accustomed solemnity of civility, made various enquiries and congratulations upon their danger and their security, carefully in both, addressing himself first to Lady Honoria, and then with more stateliness in his kindness, to Cecilia. His lady, who had frequently visited them both, had nothing new to hear.

Delvile did not come in till they were all seated, when, hastily saying he was glad to see both the ladies so well again, he instantly employed himself in carving, with the agitation of a man who feared trusting himself to sit idle.

Little, however, as he said, Cecilia was much struck by the melancholy tone of his voice, and the moment she raised her eyes, she observed that his countenance was equally sad.

"Mortimer," cried Mr Delvile, "I am sure you are not well; I cannot imagine why you will not have some advice."

"Were I to send for a physician, Sir," cried Delvile, with affected chearfulness, "he would find it much more difficult to imagine what advice to give me."

"Permit me however, Mr Mortimer," cried Lady Honoria, "to return you my humble thanks for the honour of your assistance in the thunder storm! I am afraid you made yourself ill by attending me!"

"Your ladyship," returned Delvile, colouring very high, yet pretending to laugh; "made so great a coward of me, that I ran away from shame at my own inferiority of courage."

"Were you, then, with Lady Honoria during the storm?" cried Mrs Delvile.

"No, Madam!" cried Lady Honoria very quick; "but he was so good as to leave me during the storm."

"Mortimer," said Mr Delvile, "is this possible?"

"O Lady Honoria was such a Heroine," answered Delvile, "that she wholly disdained receiving any assistance; her valour was so much more undaunted than mine, that she ventured to brave the lightning under an oak tree!"

"Now, dear Mrs Delvile," exclaimed Lady Honoria, "think what a simpleton he would have made of me! he wanted to persuade me that in the open air I should be less exposed to danger than under the shelter of a thick tree!"

"Lady Honoria," replied Mrs Delvile, with a sarcastic smile, "the next tale of scandal you oblige me to hear, I will insist for your punishment that you shall read one of Mr Newbury's little books! there are twenty of them that will explain this matter to you, and such reading will at least employ your time as usefully as such tales!"

"Well, ma'am," said Lady Honoria, "I don't know whether you are laughing at me or not, but really I concluded Mr Mortimer only chose to amuse himself in a tête-à-tête with Miss Beverley."

"He was not with Miss Beverley," cried Mrs Delvile with quickness; "she was alone,—I saw her myself the moment she came in."

"Yes, ma'am,—but not then,-he was gone;"—said Cecilia, endeavouring, but not very successfully, to speak with composure.

"I had the honour," cried Delvile, making, with equal success, the same attempt, "to wait upon Miss Beverley to the little gate; and I was then returning to Lady Honoria when I met her ladyship just coming in."

"Very extraordinary, Mortimer," said Mr Delvile, staring, "to attend Lady Honoria the last!"

"Don't be angry in earnest, Sir," cried Lady Honoria, gaily, "for I did not mean to turn tell-tale."

Here the subject was dropt; greatly to the joy both of Delvile and Cecilia, who mutually exerted themselves in talking upon what next was started, in order to prevent its being recurred to again.

That fear, however, over, Delvile said little more; sadness hung heavily on his mind; he was absent, disturbed, uneasy; yet he endeavoured no longer to avoid Cecilia; on the contrary, when she arose to quit the room, he looked evidently disappointed.

The ladies' colds kept them at home all the evening, and Delvile, for the first time since their arrival at the castle, joined them at tea; nor when it was over, did he as usual retire; he loitered, pretended to be caught by a new pamphlet, and looked as anxiously eager to speak with Cecilia, as he had hitherto appeared to shun her.

With new emotion and fresh distress Cecilia perceived this change; what he might have to say she could not conjecture, but all that foreran his communication convinced her it was nothing she could wish; and much as she had desired some explanation of his designs, when the long-expected moment seemed arriving, prognostications the most cruel of the event, repressed her impatience, and deadened her curiosity. She earnestly lamented her unfortunate residence in his house, where the adoration of every inhabitant, from his father to the lowest servant, had impressed her with the strongest belief of his general worthiness, and greatly, though imperceptibly, encreased her regard for him, since she had now not a doubt remaining but that some cruel, some fatal obstacle, prohibited their union.

To collect fortitude to hear it with composure, was now her whole study; but though, when alone, she thought any discovery preferable to suspence, all her courage failed her when Delvile appeared, and if she could not detain Lady Honoria, she involuntarily followed her.

Thus passed four or five days; during which the health of Delvile seemed to suffer with his mind, and though he refused to acknowledge he was ill, it was evident to every body that he was far from well.

Mr Delvile frequently urged him to consent to have some advice; but he always revived, though with forced and transitory spirits, at the mention of a physician, and the proposal ended in nothing.

Mrs Delvile, too, at length grew alarmed; her enquiries were more penetrating and pointed, but they were not more successful; every attack of this sort was followed by immediate gaiety, which, however constrained, served, for the time, to change the subject. Mrs Delvile, however, was not soon to be deceived; she watched her son incessantly, and seemed to feel an inquietude scarce less than his own.

Cecilia's distress was now augmented every moment, and the difficulty to conceal it grew every hour more painful; she felt herself the cause of the dejection of the son, and that thought made her feel guilty in the presence of the mother; the explanation she expected threatened her with new misery, and the courage to endure it she tried in vain to acquire; her heart was most cruelly oppressed, apprehension and suspence never left it for an instant; rest abandoned her at night, and chearfulness by day.

At this time the two lords, Ernolf and Derford, arrived; and Cecilia, who at first had lamented their design, now rejoiced in their presence, since they divided the attention of Mrs Delvile, which she began to fear was not wholly directed to her son, and since they saved her from having the whole force of Lady Honoria's high spirits and gay rattle to herself.

Their immediate observations upon the ill looks of Delvile, startled both Cecilia and the mother even more than their own fears, which they had hoped were rather the result of apprehension than of reason. Cecilia now severely reproached herself with having deferred the conference he was evidently seeking, not doubting but she had contributed to his indisposition by denying him the relief he might expect from concluding the affair.

Melancholy as was this idea, it was yet a motive to overpower her reluctance, and determine her no longer to shun what it seemed necessary to endure.

Deep reasoners, however, when they are also nice casuists, frequently resolve with a tardiness which renders their resolutions of no effect; this was the case with Cecilia; the same morning that she came down stairs prepared to meet with firmness the blow which she believed awaited her, Delvile, who, since the arrival of the two lords, had always appeared at the general breakfast, acknowledged in answer to his mother's earnest enquiries, that he had a cold and head-ache; and had he, at the same time, acknowledged a pleurisy and fever, the alarm instantly spread in the family could not have been greater; Mr Delvile, furiously ringing the bell, ordered a man and horse to go that moment to Dr Lyster, the physician to the family, and not to return without him if he was himself alive; and Mrs Delvile, not less distressed, though more quiet, fixed her eyes upon her son, with an expression of anxiety that shewed her whole happiness was bound in his recovery.

Delvile endeavoured to laugh away their fears, assuring them he should be well the next day, and representing in ridiculous terms the perplexity of Dr Lyster to contrive some prescription for him.

Cecilia's behaviour, guided by prudence and modesty, was steady and composed; she believed his illness and his uneasiness were the same, and she hoped the resolution she had taken would bring relief to them both while the terrors of Mr and Mrs Delvile seemed so greatly beyond the occasion, that her own were rather lessened than increased by them.

Dr Lyster soon arrived; he was a humane and excellent physician, and a man of sound judgment.

Delvile, gaily, shaking hands with him, said "I believe, Dr Lyster, you little expected to meet a patient, who, were he as skilful, would be as able to do business as yourself."

"What, with such a hand as this?" cried the Doctor; "come, come, you must not teach me my own profession. When I attend a patient, I come to tell how he is myself, not to be told."

"He is, then ill!" cried Mrs Delvile; "oh Mortimer, why have you thus deceived us!"

"What is his disorder?" cried Mr Delvile; "let us call in more help; who shall we send for, doctor?"

And again he rang the bell.

"What now?" said Dr Lyster, coolly; "must a man be dying if he is not in perfect health? we want nobody else; I hope I can prescribe for a cold without demanding a consultation?"

"But are you sure it is merely a cold?" cried Mr Delvile; "may not some dreadful malady"—

"Pray, Sir, have patience," interrupted the doctor; "Mr Mortimer and I will have some discourse together presently; mean time, let us all sit down, and behave like Christians; I never talk of my art before company. 'Tis hard you won't let me be a gentleman at large for two minutes!"

Lady Honoria and Cecilia would then have risen, but neither Dr Lyster nor Delvile would permit them to go; and a conversation tolerably lively took place, after which, the party in general separating, the doctor accompanied Delvile to his own apartment.

Cecilia then went up stairs, where she most impatiently waited some intelligence; none, however, arriving, in about half an hour she returned to the parlour; she found it empty, but was soon joined by Lady Honoria and Lord Ernolf.

Lady Honoria, happy in having something going forward, and not much concerning herself whether it were good or evil, was as eager to communicate what she had gathered, as Cecilia was to hear it.

"Well, my dear," she cried, "so I don't find at last but that all this prodigious illness will be laid to your account."

"To my account?" cried Cecilia, "how is that possible?"

"Why this tender chicken caught cold in the storm last week, and not being put to bed by its mama, and nursed with white-wine whey, the poor thing has got a fever."

"He is a fine young man," said Lord Ernolf; "I should be sorry any harm happened to him."

"He was a fine young man, my lord," cried Lady Honoria, "but he is grown intolerably stupid lately; however, it's all the fault of his father and mother. Was ever any thing half so ridiculous as their behaviour this morning? it was with the utmost difficulty I forbore laughing in their faces; and really, I believe if I was to meet with such an unfortunate accident with Mr Delvile, it would turn him to marble at once! indeed he is little better now, but such an affront as that would never let him move from the spot where he received it."

"I forgive him, however," returned Lord Ernolf, "for his anxiety about his son, since he is the last of so ancient a family."

"That is his great misfortune, my lord," answered Lady Honoria, "because it is the very reason they make such a puppet of him. If there were but a few more little masters to dandle and fondle, I'll answer for it this precious Mortimer would soon be left to himself; and then, really, I believe he would be a good tolerable sort of young man. Don't you think he would, Miss Beverley?"

"O yes!" said Cecilia, "I believe—I think so!"

"Nay, nay, I did not ask if you thought him tolerable now, so no need to be frightened."

Here they were interrupted by the entrance of Dr Lyster.

"Well, Sir," cried Lady Honoria, "and when am I to go into mourning for my cousin Mortimer?"

"Why very soon," answered he, "unless you take better care of him. He has confessed to me that after being out in the storm last Wednesday, he sat in his wet cloaths all the evening."

"Dear," cried Lady Honoria, "and what would that do to him? I have no notion of a man's always wanting a cambric handkerchief about his throat."

"Perhaps your ladyship had rather make him apply it to his eyes?" cried the doctor; "however, sitting inactive in wet cloaths would destroy a stouter man than Mr Delvile; but he forgot it, he says! which of you two young ladies could not have given as good reason?"

"Your most obedient," said Lady Honoria, "and why should not a lady give as good a reason as a gentleman?"

"I don't know," answered he, drily, "but from want of practice, I believe."

"O worse and worse!" cried Lady Honoria; "you shall never be my physician; if I was to be attended by you, you'd make me sick instead of well."

"All the better," answered he, "for then I must have the honour of attending you till I made you well instead of sick." And with a good-humoured smile, he left them; and Lord Derford, at the same time, coming into the room, Cecilia contrived to stroll out into the park.

The account to which she had been listening redoubled her uneasiness; she was conscious that whatever was the indisposition of Delvile, and whether it was mental or bodily, she was herself its occasion; through her he had been negligent, she had rendered him forgetful, and in consulting her own fears in preference to his peace, she had avoided an explanation, though he had vigilantly sought one. She knew not, he told her, half the wretchedness of his heart.—Alas! thought she, he little conjectures the state of mine!

Lady Honoria suffered her not to be long alone; in about half an hour she ran after her, gaily calling out, "O Miss Beverley, you have lost the delightfullest diversion in the world! I have just had the most ridiculous scene with my Lord Derford that you ever heard in your life! I asked him what put it in his head to be in love with you,—and he had the simplicity to answer, quite seriously, his father!"

"He was very right," said Cecilia, "if the desire of uniting two estates is to be denominated being in love; for that, most certainly, was put into his head by his father."

"O but you have not heard half. I told him, then, that, as a friend, in confidence I must acquaint him, I believed you intended to marry Mortimer—"

"Good heaven, Lady Honoria!"

"O, you shall hear the reason; because, as I assured him, it was proper he should immediately call him to account."

"Are you mad, Lady Honoria?"

"For you know, said I, Miss Beverley has had one duel fought for her already, and a lady who has once had that compliment paid her, always expects it from every new admirer; and I really believe your not observing that form is the true cause of her coldness to you."

"Is it possible you can have talked so wildly?"

"Yes, and what is much better, he believed every word I said!"

"Much better?—No, indeed, it is much worse! and if, in fact, he is so uncommonly weak, I shall really be but little indebted to your ladyship for giving him such notions."

"O I would not but have done it for the world! for I never laughed so immoderately in my life. He began assuring me he was not afraid, for he said he had practised fencing more than any thing; so I made him promise to send a challenge to Mortimer as soon as he is well enough to come down again; for Dr Lyster has ordered him to keep his room."

Cecilia, smothering her concern for this last piece of intelligence by pretending to feel it merely for the former, expostulated with Lady Honoria upon so mischievous a frolic, and earnestly entreated her to go back and contradict it all.

"No, no, not for the world!" cried she; "he has not the least spirit, and I dare say he would not fight to save the whole nation from destruction; but I'll make him believe that it's necessary, in order to give him something to think of, for really his poor head is so vacant, that I am sure if one might but play upon it with sticks, it would sound just like a drum."

Cecilia, finding it vain to combat with her fantasies, was at length obliged to submit.

The rest of the day she passed very unpleasantly; Delvile appeared not; his father was restless and disturbed, and his mother, though attentive to her guests, and, for their sakes rallying her spirits, was visibly ill disposed to think or to talk but of her son.

One diversion, however, Cecilia found for herself; Delvile had a favourite spaniel, which, when he walked followed him, and when he rode, ran by his horse; this dog, who was not admitted into the house, she now took under her own care; and spent almost the whole day out of doors, chiefly for the satisfaction of making him her companion.

The next morning, when Dr Lyster came again, she kept in the way, in order to hear his opinion; and was sitting with Lady Honoria in the parlour, when he entered it to write a prescription.

Mrs Delvile, in a few moments, followed him, and with a face and voice of the tenderest maternal apprehensions, said "Doctor, one thing entrust me with immediately; I can neither bear imposition nor suspense;—you know what I would say!—tell me if I have any thing to fear, that my preparations may be adequate!"

"Nothing, I believe, in the world."

"You believe!" repeated Mrs Delvile, starting; "Oh doctor!"

"Why you would not have me say I am certain, would you? these are no times for Popery and infallibility; however, I assure you I think him perfectly safe. He has done a foolish and idle trick, but no man is wise always. We must get rid of his fever, and then if his cold remains, with any cough, he may make a little excursion to Bristol."

"To Bristol! nay then,—I understand you too well!"

"No, no, you don't understand me at all; I don't send him to Bristol because he is in a bad way, but merely because I mean to put him in a good one."

"Let him, then, go immediately; why should he increase the danger by waiting a moment? I will order—"

"Hold, hold! I know what to order myself! 'Tis a strange thing people will always teach me my own duty! why should I make a man travel such weather as this in a fever? do you think I want to confine him in a mad-house, or be confined in one myself?"

"Certainly you know best—but still if there is any danger—"

"No, no, there is not! only we don't chuse there should be any. And how will he entertain himself better than by going to Bristol? I send him merely on a jaunt of pleasure; and I am sure he will be safer there than shut up in a house with two such young ladies as these."

And then he made off. Mrs Delvile, too anxious for conversation, left the room, and Cecilia, too conscious for silence, forced herself into discourse with Lady Honoria.

Three days she passed in this uncertainty what she had to expect; blaming those fears which had deferred an explanation, and tormented by Lady Honoria, whose raillery and levity now grew very unseasonable. Fidel, the favourite spaniel, was almost her only consolation, and she pleased herself not inconsiderably by making a friend of the faithful animal.

CHAPTER VII

AN ANECDOTE.

On the fourth day the house wore a better aspect; Delvile's fever was gone, and Dr Lyster permitted him to leave his room; a cough, however, remained, and his journey to Bristol was settled to take place in three days. Cecilia, knowing he was now expected down stairs, hastened out of the parlour the moment she had finished her breakfast; for affected by his illness, and hurt at the approaching separation, she dreaded the first meeting, and wished to fortify her mind for bearing it with propriety.

In a very few minutes, Lady Honoria, running after her, entreated that she would come down; "for Mortimer," she cried, "is in the parlour, and the poor child is made so much of by its papa and mama, that I wish they don't half kill him by their ridiculous fondness. It is amazing to me he is so patient with them, for if they teized me half as much, I should be ready to jump up and shake them. But I wish you would come down, for I assure you it's a comical scene."

"Your ladyship is soon diverted! but what is there so comical in the anxiety of parents for an only son?"

"Lord, they don't care a straw for him all the time! it's merely that he may live to keep up this old castle, which I hope in my heart he will pull down the moment they are dead! But do pray come; it will really give you spirits to see them all. The father keeps ringing the bell to order half a hundred pair of boots for him, and all the greatcoats in the county; and the mother sits and looks as if a hearse and mourning coach were already coming over the drawbridge; but the most diverting object among them is my Lord Derford! O, it is really too entertaining to see him! there he sits, thinking the whole time of his challenge! I intend to employ him all this afternoon in practising to shoot at a mark."

And then again she pressed her to join the group, and Cecilia, fearing her opposition might seem strange, consented.

Delvile arose at her entrance, and, with tolerable steadiness, she congratulated him on his recovery; and then, taking her usual seat, employed herself in embroidering a screen. She joined too, occasionally, in the conversation, and observed, not without surprise, that Delvile seemed much less dejected than before his confinement.

Soon after, he ordered his horse, and, accompanied by Lord Derford, rode out. Mr Delvile then took Lord Ernolf to shew him some intended improvements in another part of the castle, and Lady Honoria walked away in search of any entertainment she could find.

Mrs Delvile, in better spirits than she had been for many days, sent for her own work, and sitting by Cecilia, conversed with her again as in former times; mixing instruction with entertainment, and general satire with particular kindness, in a manner at once so lively and so flattering, that Cecilia herself reviving, found but little difficulty in bearing her part in the conversation.

And thus, with some gaiety, and tolerable ease, was spent the greatest part of the morning; but just as they were talking of changing their dress for dinner, Lady Honoria with an air of the utmost exultation, came flying into the room. "Well, ma'am," she cried, "I have some news now that I must tell you, because it will make you believe me another time though I know it will put you in a passion."

"That's sweetly designed, at least!" said Mrs Delvile, laughing; "however, I'll trust you, for my passions will not, just now, be irritated by straws."

"Why, ma'am, don't you remember I told you when you were in town that Mr Mortimer kept a mistress—"

"Yes!" cried Mrs Delvile, disdainfully, "and you may remember, Lady Honoria, I told you—"

"O, you would not believe a word of it! but it's all true, I assure you! and now he has brought her down here; he sent for her about three weeks ago, and he has boarded her at a cottage, about half a mile from the Park-gate."

Cecilia, to whom Henrietta Belfield was instantly present, changed colour repeatedly, and turned so extremely sick, she could with difficulty keep her seat. She forced herself, however, to continue her work, though she knew so little what she was about, that she put her needle in and out of the same place without ceasing.

Meanwhile Mrs Delvile, with a countenance of the utmost indignation, exclaimed, "Lady Honoria, if you think a tale of scandal such as this reflects no disgrace upon its relater, you must pardon me for entreating you to find an auditor more of the same opinion than myself."

"Nay, ma'am, since you are so angry, I'll tell you the whole affair, for this is but half of it. He has a child here, too,—I vow I long to see it!—and he is so fond of it that he spends half his time in nursing it;—and that, I suppose, is the thing that takes him out so much; and I fancy, too, that's what has made him grow so grave, for may be he thinks it would not be pretty to be very frisky, now he's a papa."

Not only Cecilia, but Mrs Delvile herself was now overpowered, and she sat for some time wholly silent and confounded; Lady Honoria then, turning to Cecilia exclaimed, "Bless me, Miss Beverley, what are you about! why that flower is the most ridiculous thing I ever saw! you have spoilt your whole work."

Cecilia, in the utmost confusion, though pretending to laugh, then began to unpick it; and Mrs Delvile, recovering, more calmly, though not less angrily, said "And has this tale the honour of being invented solely by your ladyship, or had it any other assistant?"

"O no, I assure you, it's no invention of mine; I had it from very good authority upon my word. But only look at Miss Beverley! would not one think I had said that she had a child herself? She looks as pale as death. My dear, I am sure you can't be well?"

"I beg your pardon," cried Cecilia, forcing a smile, though extremely provoked with her; "I never was better."

And then, with the hope of appearing unconcerned, she raised her head; but meeting the eyes of Mrs Delvile fixed upon her face with a look of penetrating observation, abashed and guilty, she again dropt it, and resumed her work.

"Well, my dear," said Lady Honoria, "I am sure there is no occasion to send for Dr Lyster to you, for you recover yourself in a moment; you have the finest colour now I ever saw; has not she, Mrs Delvile? did you ever see anybody blush so becomingly?"

"I wish, Lady Honoria," said Mrs Delvile, with severity, "it were possible to see you blush!"

"O but I never do! not but what it's pretty enough too; but I don't know how it is, it never happens. Now Euphrasia can blush from morning to night. I can't think how she contrives it. Miss Beverley, too, plays at it vastly well; she's red and white, and white and red half a dozen times in a minute. Especially," looking at her archly, and lowering her voice, "if you talk to her of Mortimer!"

"No, indeed! no such thing!" cried Cecilia with some resentment, and again looking up; but glancing her eyes towards Mrs Delvile, and again meeting hers, filled with the strongest expression of enquiring solicitude, unable to sustain their inquisition, and shocked to find herself thus watchfully observed, she returned in hasty confusion to her employment.

"Well, my dear," cried Lady Honoria, again, "but what are you about now? do you intend to unpick the whole screen?"

"How can she tell what she is doing," said Mrs Delvile, with quickness, "if you torment her thus incessantly? I will take you away from her, that she may have a little peace. You shall do me the honour to attend my toilette, and acquaint me with some further particulars of this extraordinary discovery."

Mrs Delvile then left the room, but Lady Honoria, before she followed her, said in a low voice "Pity me, Miss Beverley, if you have the least good-nature! I am now going to hear a lecture of two hours long!"

Cecilia, left to herself was in a perturbation almost insupportable; Delvile's mysterious conduct seemed the result of some entanglement of vice; Henrietta Belfield, the artless Henrietta Belfield, she feared had been abused, and her own ill-fated partiality, which now more than ever she wished unknown even to herself, was evidently betrayed where most the dignity of her mind made her desire it to be concealed!

In this state of shame, regret and resentment, which made her forget to change her dress, or her place, she was suddenly surprised by Delvile.

Starting and colouring, she busied herself with collecting her work, that she might hurry out of the room. Delvile, though silent himself, endeavoured to assist her; but when she would have gone, he attempted to stop her, saying "Miss Beverley, for three minutes only."

"No, sir," cried she, indignantly, "not for an instant!" and leaving him utterly astonished, she hastened to her own apartment.

She was then sorry she had been so precipitate; nothing had been clearly proved against him; no authority was so likely to be fallacious as that of Lady Honoria; neither was he under any engagement to herself that could give her any right to manifest such displeasure. These reflections, however, came too late, and the quick feelings of her agitated mind were too rapid to wait the dictates of cool reason. At dinner she attended wholly to Lord Ernolf, whose assiduous politeness, profiting by the humour, saved her the painful effort of forcing conversation, or the guilty consciousness of giving way to silence, and enabled her to preserve her general tenor between taciturnity and loquaciousness. Mrs Delvile she did not once dare look at; but her son, she saw, seemed greatly hurt; yet it was proudly, not sorrowfully, and therefore she saw it with less uneasiness.

During the rest of the day, which was passed in general society, Mrs Delvile, though much occupied, frequently leaving the room, and sending for Lady Honoria, was more soft, kind and gentle with Cecilia than ever, looking at her with the utmost tenderness, often taking her hand, and speaking to her with even unusual sweetness. Cecilia with mingled sadness and pleasure observed this encreasing regard, which she could not but attribute to the discovery made through Lady Honoria's mischievous intelligence, and which, while it rejoiced her with the belief of her approbation, added fresh force to her regret in considering it was fruitless. Delvile, mean-time, evidently offended himself, conversed only with the gentlemen, and went very early into his own room.

When they were all retiring, Mrs Delvile, following Cecilia, dismissed her maid to talk with her alone.

"I am not, I hope, often," she cried, "solicitous or importunate to speak about my son; his character, I believe, wants no vindication; clear and unsullied, it has always been its own support; yet the aspersion cast upon it this morning by Lady Honoria, I think myself bound to explain, not partially as his mother, but simply as his friend."

Cecilia, who knew not whither such an explanation might lead, nor wherefore it was made, heard this opening with much emotion, but gave neither to that nor to what followed any interruption.

Mrs Delvile then continued; she had taken the trouble, she said, to sift the whole affair, in order to shame Lady Honoria by a pointed conviction of what she had invented, and to trace from the foundation the circumstances whence her surmises or report had sprung.

Delvile, it seems, about a fortnight before the present time, in one of his morning walks, had observed a gipsey sitting by the side of the high road, who seemed extremely ill, and who had a very beautiful child tied to her back.

Struck with the baby, he stopt to enquire to whom it belonged; to herself, she said, and begged his charity with the most pitiable cries of distress; telling him that she was travelling to join some of her fraternity, who were in a body near Bath, but was so ill with an ague and fever that she feared she should die on the road.

Delvile desired her to go to the next cottage, and promised to pay for her board there till she was better. He then spoke to the man and his wife who owned it to take them in, who, glad to oblige his Honour, instantly consented, and he had since called twice to see in what manner they went on.

"How simple," continued Mrs Delvile, "is a matter of fact in itself, and how complex when embellished! This tale has been told by the cottagers to our servants; it has travelled, probably gaining something from every mouth, to Lady Honoria's maid, and, having reached her ladyship, was swelled in a moment into all we heard! I think, however, that, for some time at least, her levity will be rather less daring. I have not, in this affair, at all spared her; I made her hear from Mortimer himself the little story as it happened; I then carried her to the cottage, where we had the whole matter confirmed; and I afterwards insisted upon being told myself by her maid all she had related to her lady, that she might thus be unanswerably convicted of inventing whatever she omitted. I have occasioned her some confusion, and, for the moment, a little resentment; but she is so volatile that neither will last; and though, with regard to my own family, I may perhaps have rendered her more cautious, I fear, with regard to the world in general, she is utterly incorrigible, because it has neither pleasure nor advantage to offer, that can compensate for the deprivation of relating one staring story, or ridiculous anecdote."

And then, wishing her good night, she added, "I make not any apology for this detail, which you owe, not, believe me, to a mother's folly, but, if I [know] myself at all, to a love of truth and justice. Mortimer, independent of all connection with me, cannot but to every body appear of a character which may be deemed even exemplary; calumny, therefore, falling upon such a subject, injures not only himself but society, since it weakens all confidence in virtue, and strengthens the scepticism of depravity."

She then left her.

"Ah!" thought Cecilia, "to me, at least, this solicitude for his fame needs no apology! humane and generous Delvile! never, again, will I a moment doubt your worthiness!" And then, cherishing that darling idea, she forgot all her cares and apprehensions, her quarrel, her suspicions, and the approaching separation, and, recompensed for every thing by this refutation of his guilt, she hastened to bed, and composed herself to rest.

CHAPTER VIII

A CONFERENCE.

Early the next morning Cecilia had a visit from Lady Honoria, who came to tell her story her own way, and laugh at the anxiety of Mrs Delvile, and the trouble she had taken; "for, after all," continued she, "what did the whole matter signify? and how could I possibly help the mistake? when I heard of his paying for a woman's board, what was so natural as to suppose she must be his mistress? especially as there was a child in the case. O how I wish you had been with us! you never saw such a ridiculous sight in your life; away we went in the chaise full drive to the cottage, frightening all the people almost into fits; out came the poor woman, away ran the poor man,—both of them thought the end of the world at hand! The gipsey was best off, for she went to her old business, and began begging. I assure you, I believe she would be very pretty if she was not so ill, and so I dare say Mortimer thought too, or I fancy he would not have taken such care of her."

"Fie, fie, Lady Honoria! will nothing bring conviction to you?"

"Nay, you know, there's no harm in that, for why should not pretty people live as well as ugly ones? There's no occasion to leave nothing in the world but frights. I looked hard at the baby, to see if it was like Mortimer, but I could not make it out; those young things are like nothing. I tried if it would talk, for I wanted sadly to make it call Mrs Delvile grandmama; however, the little urchin could say nothing to be understood. O what a rage would Mrs Delvile have been in! I suppose this whole castle would hardly have been thought heavy enough to crush such an insolent brat, though it were to have fallen upon it all at a blow!"

Thus rattled this light-hearted lady till the family was assembled to breakfast; and then Cecilia, softened towards Delvile by newly-excited admiration, as well as by the absence which would separate them the following day, intended, by every little courteous office in her power, to make her peace with him before his departure; but she observed, with much chagrin, that Mrs Delvile never ceased to watch her, which, added to an air of pride in the coldness of Delvile, that he had never before assumed, discouraged her from making the attempt, and compelled her to seem quiet and unconcerned.

As soon as breakfast was over, the gentlemen all rode or walked out; and when the ladies were by themselves, Lady Honoria suddenly exclaimed, "Mrs Delvile, I can't imagine for what reason you send Mr Mortimer to Bristol."

"For a reason, Lady Honoria, that with all your wildness, I should be very sorry you should know better by experience."

"Why then, ma'am; had we not better make a party, and all go? Miss Beverley, should you like to join it? I am afraid it would be vastly disagreeable to you."

Cecilia, now again was red and white, and white and red a dozen times in a minute; and Mrs Delvile, rising and taking her hand, expressively said, "Miss Beverley, you have a thousand times too much sensibility for this mad-cap of a companion. I believe I shall punish her by taking you away from her all this morning; will you come and sit with me in the dressing-room?"

Cecilia assented without daring to look at her, and followed in trembling, up stairs. Something of importance, she fancied, would ensue, her secret she saw was revealed, and therefore she could form no conjecture but that Delvile would be the subject of their discourse yet whether to explain his behaviour, or plead his cause, whether to express her separate approbation, or communicate some intelligence from himself, she had neither time, opportunity nor clue to unravel. All that was undoubted seemed the affection of Mrs Delvile, all that, on her own part, could be resolved, was to suppress her partiality till she knew if it might properly be avowed.

Mrs Delvile, who saw her perturbation, led immediately to subjects of indifference, and talked upon them so long, and with so much ease, that Cecilia, recovering her composure, began to think she had been mistaken, and that nothing was intended but a tranquil conversation.

As soon, however, as she had quieted her apprehensions, she sat silent herself, with a look that Cecilia easily construed into thoughtful perplexity in what manner she should introduce what she meant to communicate.

This pause was succeeded by her speaking of Lady Honoria; "how wild, how careless, how incorrigible she is! she lost her mother early; and the Duke, who idolizes her, and who, marrying very late, is already an old man, she rules entirely; with him, and a supple governess, who has neither courage to oppose her, nor heart to wish well but to her own interest, she has lived almost wholly. Lately, indeed, she has come more into the world, but without even a desire of improvement, and with no view and no thought but to gratify her idle humour by laughing at whatever goes forward."

"She certainly neither wants parts nor discernment," said Cecilia; "and, when my mind is not occupied by other matters, I find her conversation entertaining and agreeable."

"Yes," said Mrs Delvile, "but that light sort of wit which attacks, with equal alacrity, what is serious or what is gay, is twenty times offensive, to once that it is exhilarating; since it shews that while its only aim is self-diversion, it has the most insolent negligence with respect to any pain it gives to others. The rank of Lady Honoria, though it has not rendered her proud, nor even made her conscious she has any dignity to support, has yet given her a saucy indifference whom she pleases or hurts, that borders upon what in a woman is of all things the most odious, a daring defiance of the world and its opinions."

Cecilia, never less disposed to enter upon her defence, made but little answer; and, soon after, Mrs Delvile added, "I heartily wish she were properly established; and yet, according to the pernicious manners and maxims of the present age, she is perhaps more secure from misconduct while single, than she will be when married. Her father, I fear, will leave her too much to herself, and in that case I scarce know what may become of her; she has neither judgment nor principle to direct her choice, and therefore, in all probability, the same whim which one day will guide it, will the next lead her to repent it."

Again they were both silent; and then Mrs Delvile, gravely, yet with energy exclaimed, "How few are there, how very few, who marry at once upon principles rational, and feelings pleasant! interest and inclination are eternally at strife, and where either is wholly sacrificed, the other is inadequate to happiness. Yet how rarely do they divide the attention! the young are rash, and the aged are mercenary; their deliberations are never in concert, their views are scarce ever blended; one vanquishes, and the other submits; neither party temporizes, and commonly each is unhappy."

"The time," she continued, "is now arrived when reflections of this sort cannot too seriously occupy me; the errors I have observed in others, I would fain avoid committing; yet such is the blindness of self-love, that perhaps, even at the moment I censure them, I am falling, without consciousness, into the same! nothing, however, shall through negligence be wrong; for where is the son who merits care and attention, if Mortimer from his parents deserves not to meet them?"

The expectations of Cecilia were now again awakened, and awakened with fresh terrors lest Mrs Delvile, from compassion, meant to offer her services; vigorously, therefore, she determined to exert herself, and rather give up Mortimer and all thoughts of him for ever, than submit to receive assistance in persuading him to the union.

"Mr Delvile," she continued, "is most earnest and impatient that some alliance should take place without further delay; and for myself, could I see him with propriety and with happiness disposed of, what a weight of anxiety would be removed from my heart!"

Cecilia now made an effort to speak, attempting to say "Certainly, it is a matter of great consequence;" but so low was her voice, and so confused her manner, that Mrs Delvile, though attentively listening, heard not a word. She forbore, however, to make her repeat what she said, and went on herself as if speaking in answer.

"Not only his own, but the peace of his whole family will depend upon his election, since he is the last of his race. This castle and estate, and another in the north, were entailed upon him by the late Lord Delvile, his grandfather, who, disobliged by his eldest son, the present lord, left every thing he had power to dispose of to his second son, Mr Delvile, and at his death, to his grandson, Mortimer. And even the present lord, though always at variance with his brother, is fond of his nephew, and has declared him his heir. I, also, have one sister, who is rich, who has no children, and who has made the same declaration. Yet though with such high expectations, he must not connect himself imprudently; for his paternal estate wants repair, and he is well entitled with a wife to expect what it requires."

Most true! thought Cecilia, yet ashamed of her recent failure, she applied herself to her work, and would not again try to speak.

"He is amiable, accomplished, well educated, and well born; far may we look, and not meet with his equal; no woman need disdain, and few women would refuse him."

Cecilia blushed her concurrence; yet could well at that moment have spared hearing the eulogy.

"Yet how difficult," she continued, "to find a proper alliance! there are many who have some recommendations, but who is there wholly unexceptionable?"

This question seemed unanswerable; nor could Cecilia devise what it meant.

"Girls of high family have but seldom large fortunes, since the heads of their house commonly require their whole wealth for the support of their own dignity; while on the other hand, girls of large fortune are frequently ignorant, insolent, or low born; kept up by their friends lest they should fall a prey to adventurers, they have no acquaintance with the world, and little enlargement from education; their instructions are limited to a few merely youthful accomplishments; the first notion they imbibe is of their own importance, the first lesson they are taught is the value of riches, and even from their cradles, their little minds are narrowed, and their self-sufficiency is excited, by cautions to beware of fortune-hunters, and assurances that the whole world will be at their feet. Among such should we seek a companion for Mortimer? surely not. Formed for domestic happiness, and delighting in elegant society, his mind would disdain an alliance in which its affections had no share."

Cecilia colouring and trembling, thought now the moment of her trial was approaching, and half mortified and half frightened prepared herself to sustain it with firmness.

"I venture, therefore, my dear Miss Beverley, to speak to you upon this subject as a friend who will have patience to hear my perplexities; you see upon what they hang,—where the birth is such as Mortimer Delvile may claim, the fortune generally fails; and where the fortune is adequate to his expectations, the birth yet more frequently would disgrace us."

Cecilia, astonished by this speech, and quite off her guard from momentary surprize, involuntarily raised her head to look at Mrs Delvile, in whose countenance she observed the most anxious concern, though her manner of speaking had seemed placid and composed.

"Once," she continued, without appearing to remark the emotion of her auditor, "Mr Delvile thought of uniting him with his cousin Lady Honoria; but he never could endure the proposal; and who shall blame his repugnance? her sister, indeed, Lady Euphrasia, is much preferable, her education has been better, and her fortune is much more considerable. At present, however, Mortimer seems greatly averse to her, and who has a right to be difficult, if we deny it to him?"

Wonder, uncertainty, expectation and suspense now all attacked Cecilia, and all harassed her with redoubled violence; why she was called to this conference she knew not; the approbation she had thought so certain, she doubted, and the proposal of assistance she had apprehended, she ceased to think would be offered some fearful mystery, some cruel obscurity, still clouded all her prospects, and not merely obstructed her view of the future, but made what was immediately before her gloomy and indistinct.

The state of her mind seemed read by Mrs Delvile, who examined her with eyes of such penetrating keenness, that they rather made discoveries than enquiries. She was silent some time, and looked irresolute how to proceed; but at length, she arose, and taking Cecilia by the hand, who almost drew it back from her dread of what would follow, she said "I will torment you no more, my sweet young friend, with perplexities which you cannot relieve; this only I will say, and then drop the subject for ever; when my solicitude for Mortimer is removed, and he is established to the satisfaction of us all, no care will remain in the heart of his mother, half so fervent, so anxious and so sincere as the disposal of my amiable Cecilia, for whose welfare and happiness my wishes are even maternal."

She then kissed her glowing cheek, and perceiving her almost stupified with astonishment, spared her any effort to speak, by hastily leaving her in possession of her room.

Undeceived in her expectations and chilled in her hopes, the heart of Cecilia no longer struggled to sustain its dignity, or conceal its tenderness; the conflict was at an end, Mrs Delvile had been open, though her son was mysterious; but, in removing her doubts, she had bereft her of her peace. She now found her own mistake in building upon her approbation; she saw nothing was less in her intentions, and that even when most ardent in affectionate regard, she separated her interest from that of her son as if their union was a matter of utter impossibility. "Yet why," cried Cecilia, "oh why is it deemed so! that she loves me, she is ever eager to proclaim, that my fortune would be, peculiarly useful, she makes not a secret, and that I, at least, should start no insuperable objections, she has, alas! but too obviously discovered! Has she doubts of her son?—no, she has too much discernment; the father, then, the haughty, impracticable father, has destined him for some woman of rank, and will listen to no other alliance."

This notion somewhat soothed her in the disappointment she suffered; yet to know herself betrayed to Mrs Delvile, and to see no other consequence ensue but that of exciting a tender compassion, which led her to discourage, from benevolence, hopes too high to be indulged, was a mortification so severe, that it caused her a deeper depression of spirits than any occurrence of her life had yet occasioned.

"What Henrietta Belfield is to me," she cried, "I am to Mrs Delvile! but what in her is amiable and artless, in me is disgraceful and unworthy. And this is the situation which so long I have desired! This is the change of habitation which I thought would make me so happy! oh who can chuse, who can judge for himself? who can point out the road to his own felicity, or decide upon the spot where his peace will be ensured!"

Still, however, she had something to do, some spirit to exert, and some fortitude to manifest; Mortimer, she was certain, suspected not his own power; his mother, she knew, was both too good and too wise to reveal it to him, and she determined, by caution and firmness upon his leave-taking and departure, to retrieve, if possible, that credit with Mrs Delvile, which she feared her betrayed susceptibility had weakened.

As soon, therefore, as she recovered from her consternation, she quitted Mrs Delvile's apartment, and seeking Lady Honoria herself, determined not to spend even a moment alone, till Mortimer was gone; lest the sadness of her reflections should overpower her resolution, and give a melancholy to her air and manner which he might attribute, with but too much justice, to concern upon his own account.

CHAPTER IX

AN ATTACK.

At dinner, with the assistance of Lord Ernolf, who was most happy to give it, Cecilia seemed tolerably easy. Lord Derford, too, encouraged by his father, endeavoured to engage some share of her attention; but he totally failed; her mind was superior to little arts of coquetry, and her pride had too much dignity to evaporate in pique; she determined, therefore, at this time, as at all others, to be consistent in shewing him he had no chance of her favour.

At tea, when they were again assembled, Mortimer's journey was the only subject of discourse, and it was agreed that he should set out very early in the morning, and, as the weather was extremely hot, not travel at all in the middle of the day.

Lady Honoria then, in a whisper to Cecilia, said, "I suppose, Miss Beverley, you will rise with the lark to-morrow morning? for your health, I mean. Early rising, you know, is vastly good for you."

Cecilia, affecting not to understand her, said she should rise, she supposed, at her usual time.

"I'll tell Mortimer, however," returned her ladyship, "to look up at your window before he goes off; for if he will play Romeo, you, I dare say, will play Juliet, and this old castle is quite the thing for the musty family of the Capulets; I dare say Shakespeare thought of it when he wrote of them."

"Say to him what you please for yourself," cried Cecilia, "but let me entreat you to say nothing for me."

"And my Lord Derford," continued she, "will make an excessive pretty Paris, for he is vastly in love, though he has got nothing to say; but what shall we do for a Mercutio? we may find five hundred whining Romeos to one gay and charming Mercutio. Besides, Mrs Delvile, to do her justice, is really too good for the old Nurse, though Mr Delvile himself may serve for all the Capulets and all the Montagues at once, for he has pride enough for both their houses, and twenty more besides. By the way, if I don't take care, I shall have this Romeo run away before I have made my little dainty country Paris pick a quarrel with him."

She then walked up to one of the windows, and motioning Lord Derford to follow her, Cecilia heard her say to him, "Well, my lord, have you writ your letter? and have you sent it? Miss Beverley, I assure you, will be charmed beyond measure by such a piece of gallantry."

"No, ma'am," answered the simple young lord, "I have not sent it yet, for I have only writ a foul copy."

"O my lord," cried she, "that is the very thing you ought to send! a foul copy of a challenge is always better than a fair one, for it looks written with more agitation. I am vastly glad you mentioned that."

Cecilia then, rising and joining them, said, "What mischief is Lady Honoria about now? we must all be upon our guards, my lord, for she has a spirit of diversion that will not spare us."

"Pray why do you interfere?" cried Lady Honoria, and then, in a lower voice, she added, "what do you apprehend? do you suppose Mortimer cannot manage such a poor little ideot as this?"

"I don't suppose any thing about the matter!"

"Well, then, don't interrupt my operations. Lord Derford, Miss Beverley has been whispering me, that if you put this scheme in execution, she shall find you, ever after, irresistible."

"Lord Derford, I hope," said Cecilia, laughing, "is too well acquainted with your ladyship to be in any danger of credulity."

"Vastly well!" cried she, "I see you are determined to provoke me, so if you spoil my schemes, I will spoil yours, and tell a certain gentleman your tender terrors for his safety."

Cecilia now, extremely alarmed, most earnestly entreated her to be quiet; but the discovery of her fright only excited her ladyship's laughter, and, with a look the most mischievously wicked, she called out "Pray Mr Mortimer, come hither!"

Mortimer instantly obeyed; and Cecilia at the same moment would with pleasure have endured almost any punishment to have been twenty miles off.

"I have something," continued her ladyship, "of the utmost consequence to communicate to you. We have been settling an admirable plan for you; will you promise to be guided by us if I tell it you?"

"O certainly!" cried he; "to doubt that would disgrace us all round."

"Well, then,—Miss Beverley, have you any objection to my proceeding?" "None at all!" answered Cecilia, who had the understanding to know that the greatest excitement to ridicule is opposition.

"Well, then, I must tell you," she continued, "it is the advice of us all, that as soon as you come to the possession of your estate, you make some capital alterations in this antient castle."

Cecilia, greatly relieved, could with gratitude have embraced her; and Mortimer, very certain that such rattle was all her own, promised the utmost submission to her orders, and begged her further directions, declaring that he could not, at least, desire a fairer architect.

"What we mean," said she, "may be effected with the utmost ease; it is only to take out these old windows, and fix some thick iron grates in their place, and so turn the castle into a gaol for the county."

Mortimer laughed heartily at this proposition; but his father, unfortunately hearing it, sternly advanced, and with great austerity said, "If I thought my son capable of putting such an insult upon his ancestors, whatever may be the value I feel for him, I would banish him my presence for ever."

"Dear Sir," cried Lady Honoria, "how would his ancestors ever know it?"

"How?—why—that is a very extraordinary question, Lady Honoria!"

"Besides, Sir, I dare say the sheriff, or the mayor and corporation, or some of those sort of people, would give him money enough, for the use of it, to run him up a mighty pretty neat little box somewhere near Richmond."

"A box!" exclaimed he indignantly; "a neat little box for the heir of an estate such as this!"

"I only mean," cried she, giddily, "that he might have some place a little more pleasant to live in, for really that old moat and draw-bridge are enough to vapour him to death; I cannot for my life imagine any use they are of; unless, indeed, to frighten away the deer, for nothing else offer to come over. But, if you were to turn the house into a gaol—"

"A gaol?" cried Mr Delvile, still more angrily, "your ladyship must pardon me if I entreat you not to mention that word again when you are pleased to speak of Delvile Castle."

"Dear Sir, why not?"

"Because it is a term that, in itself, from a young lady, has a sound peculiarly improper; and which, applied to any gentleman's antient family seat,—a thing, Lady Honoria, always respectable, however lightly spoken of!—has an effect the least agreeable that can be devised; for it implies an idea either that the family, or the mansion, is going into decay."

"Well, Sir, you know, with regard to the mansion, it is certainly very true, for all that other side, by the old tower, looks as if it would fall upon one's head every time one is forced to pass it."

"I protest, Lady Honoria," said Mr Delvile, "that old tower, of which you are pleased to speak so slightingly, is the most honourable testimony to the antiquity of the castle of any now remaining, and I would not part with it for all the new boxes, as you style them, in the kingdom."

"I am sure I am very glad of it, Sir, for I dare say nobody would give even one of them for it."

"Pardon me, Lady Honoria, you are greatly mistaken; they would give a thousand; such a thing, belonging to a man from his own ancestors, is invaluable."

"Why, dear Sir, what in the world could they do with it? unless, indeed, they were to let some man paint it for an opera scene."

"A worthy use indeed!" cried Mr Delvile, more and more affronted; "and pray does your ladyship talk thus to my Lord Duke?"

"O yes; and he never minds it at all."

"It were strange if he did!" cried Mrs Delvile; "my only astonishment is that anybody can be found who does mind it."

"Why now, Mrs Delvile," she answered, "pray be sincere; can you possibly think this Gothic ugly old place at all comparable to any of the new villas about town?"

"Gothic ugly old place!" repeated Mr Delvile, in utter amazement at her dauntless flightiness; "your ladyship really does my humble dwelling too much honour!"

"Lord, I beg a thousand pardons!" cried she, "I really did not think of what I was saying. Come, dear Miss Beverley, and walk out with me, for I am too much shocked to stay a moment longer."

And then, taking Cecilia by the arm, she hurried her into the park, through a door which led thither from the parlour.

"For heaven's sake, Lady Honoria," said Cecilia, "could you find no better entertainment for Mr Delvile than ridiculing his own house?"

"O," cried she, laughing, "did you never hear us quarrel before? why when I was here last summer, I used to affront him ten times a day."

"And was that a regular ceremony?"

"No, really, I did not do it purposely; but it so happened; either by talking of the castle, or the tower, or the draw-bridge, or the fortifications; or wishing they were all employed to fill up that odious moat; or something of that sort; for you know a small matter will put him out of humour."

"And do you call it so small a matter to wish a man's whole habitation annihilated?"

"Lord, I don't wish anything about it! I only say so to provoke him."

"And what strange pleasure can that give you?"

"O the greatest in the world! I take much delight in seeing anybody in a passion. It makes them look so excessively ugly!"

"And is that the way you like every body should look, Lady Honoria?"

"O my dear, if you mean me, I never was in a passion twice in my life; for as soon as ever I have provoked the people, I always run away. But sometimes I am in a dreadful fright lest they should see me laugh, for they make such horrid grimaces it is hardly possible to look at them. When my father has been angry with me, I have sometimes been obliged to pretend I was crying, by way of excuse for putting my handkerchief to my face; for really he looks so excessively hideous, you would suppose he was making mouths, like the children, merely to frighten one."

"Amazing!" exclaimed Cecilia, "your ladyship can, indeed, never want diversion, to find it in the anger of your father. But does it give you no other sensation? are you not afraid?"

"O never! O what can he do to me, you know? he can only storm a little, and swear a little, for he always swears when he is angry; and perhaps order me to my own room; and ten to one but that happens to be the very thing I want; for we never quarrel but when we are alone, and then it's so dull, I am always wishing to run away."

"And can you take no other method of leaving him?"

"Why I think none so easily; and it can do him no harm, you know; I often tell him, when we make friends, that if it were not for a postilion and his daughter, he would be quite out of practice in scolding and swearing; for whenever he is upon the road he does nothing else; though why he is in such a hurry, nobody can divine, for go whither he will he has nothing to do."

Thus ran on this flighty lady, happy in high animal spirits, and careless who was otherwise, till, at some distance, they perceived Lord Derford, who was approaching to join them.

"Miss Beverley," cried she, "here comes your adorer; I shall therefore only walk on till we arrive at that large oak, and then make him prostrate himself at your feet, and leave you together."

"Your ladyship is extremely good! but I am glad to be apprized of your intention, as it will enable me to save you that trouble."

She then turned quick back, and passing Lord Derford, who still walked on towards Lady Honoria, she returned to the house; but, upon entering the parlour, found all the company dispersed, Delvile alone excepted, who was walking about the room, with his tablets in his hand, in which he had been writing.

From a mixture of shame and surprize, Cecilia, at the sight of him, was involuntarily retreating; but, hastening to the door, he called out in a reproachful tone, "Will you not even enter the same room with me?"

"O yes," cried she, returning; "I was only afraid I disturbed you."

"No, madam," answered he, gravely; "you are the only person who could not disturb me, since my employment was making memorandums for a letter to yourself; with which, however, I did not desire to importune you, but that you have denied me the honour of even a five minutes' audience."

Cecilia, in the utmost confusion at this attack, knew not whether to stand still or proceed; but, as he presently continued his speech, she found she had no choice but to stay.

"I should be sorry to quit this place, especially as the length of my absence is extremely uncertain, while I have the unhappiness to be under your displeasure, without making some little attempt to apologize for the behaviour which incurred it. Must I, then, finish my letter, or will you at last deign to hear me?"

"My displeasure, Sir," said Cecilia, "died with its occasion; I beg, therefore, that it may rest no longer in your remembrance."

"I meant not, madam, to infer, that the subject or indeed that the object merited your deliberate attention; I simply wish to explain what may have appeared mysterious in my conduct, and for what may have seemed still more censurable, to beg your pardon."

Cecilia now, recovered from her first apprehensions, and calmed, because piqued, by the calmness with which he spoke himself, made no opposition to his request, but suffering him to shut both the door leading into the garden, and that which led into the hall, she seated herself at one of the windows, determined to listen with intrepidity to this long expected explanation.

The preparations, however, which he made to obviate being overheard, added to the steadiness with which Cecilia waited his further proceedings, soon robbed him of the courage with which he began the assault, and evidently gave him a wish of retreating himself.

At length, after much hesitation, he said "This indulgence, madam, deserves my most grateful acknowledgments; it is, indeed, what I had little right, and still less reason, after the severity I have met with from you, to expect."

And here, at the very mention of severity, his courage, called upon by his pride, instantly returned, and he went on with the same spirit he had begun.

"That severity, however, I mean not to lament; on the contrary, in a situation such as mine, it was perhaps the first blessing I could receive; I have found from it, indeed, more advantage and relief than from all that philosophy, reflection or fortitude could offer. It has shewn me the vanity of bewailing the barrier, placed by fate to my wishes, since it has shewn me that another, less inevitable, but equally insuperable, would have opposed them. I have determined, therefore, after a struggle I must confess the most painful, to deny myself the dangerous solace of your society, and endeavour, by joining dissipation to reason, to forget the too great pleasure which hitherto it has afforded me."

"Easy, Sir," cried Cecilia, "will be your task; I can only wish the re-establishment of your health may be found no more difficult."

"Ah, madam," cried he, with a reproachful smile, "he jests at scars who never felt a wound!—but this is a strain in which I have no right to talk, and I will neither offend your delicacy, nor my own integrity, by endeavouring to work upon the generosity of your disposition in order to excite your compassion. Not such was the motive with which I begged this audience; but merely a desire, before I tear myself away, to open to you my heart, without palliation or reserve."

He paused a few moments; and Cecilia finding her suspicions just that this interview was meant to be final, considered that her trial, however severe, would be short, and called forth all her resolution to sustain it with spirit.

"Long before I had the honour of your acquaintance," he continued, "your character and your accomplishments were known to me; Mr Biddulph of Suffolk, who was my first friend at Oxford, and with whom my intimacy is still undiminished, was early sensible of your excellencies; we corresponded, and his letters were filled with your praises. He confessed to me, that his admiration had been unfortunate;—alas! I might now make the same confession to him!"

Mr Biddulph, among many of the neighbouring gentlemen, had made proposals to the Dean for Cecilia, which, at her desire, were rejected.

"When Mr Harrel saw masks in Portman-square, my curiosity to behold a lady so adored, and so cruel, led me thither; your dress made you easily distinguished.—Ah Miss Beverley! I venture not to mention what I then felt for my friend! I will only say that something which I felt for myself, warned me instantly to avoid you, since the clause in your uncle's will was already well known to me."

Now, then, at last, thought Cecilia, all perplexity is over!—the change of name is the obstacle; he inherits all the pride of his family,—and therefore to that family will I unrepining leave him!

"This warning," he continued, "I should not have disregarded, had I not, at the Opera, been deceived into a belief you were engaged; I then wished no longer to shun you; bound in honour to forbear all efforts at supplanting a man, to whom I thought you almost united, I considered you already as married, and eagerly as I sought your society, I sought it not with more pleasure than innocence. Yet even then, to be candid, I found in myself a restlessness about your affairs that kept me in eternal perturbation; but I flattered myself it was mere curiosity, and only excited by the perpetual change of opinion to which occasion gave rise, concerning which was the happy man."

"I am sorry," said Cecilia, coolly, "there was any such mistake."

"I will not, madam, fatigue you," he returned, "by tracing the progress of my unfortunate admiration; will endeavour to be more brief, for I see you are already wearied." He stopt a moment, hoping for some little encouragement; but Cecilia, in no humour to give it, assumed an air of unconcern, and sat wholly quiet.

"I knew not," he then went on, with a look of extreme mortification, "the warmth with which I honoured your virtues, till you deigned to plead to me for Mr Belfield,—but let me not recollect the feelings of that moment!—yet were they nothing,—cold, languid, lifeless to what I afterwards experienced, when you undeceived me finally with respect to your situation, and informed me the report concerning Sir Robert Floyer was equally erroneous with that which concerned Belfield! O what was the agitation of my whole soul at that instant!—to know you disengaged,—to see you before me,—by the disorder of my whole frame to discover the mistake I had cherished—"

Cecilia then, half rising, yet again seating herself, looked extremely impatient to be gone.

"Pardon me, madam," he cried; "I will have done, and trace my feelings and my sufferings no longer, but hasten, for my own sake as well as yours, to the reason why I have spoken at all. From the hour that my ill-destined passion was fully known to myself, I weighed all the consequences of indulging it, and found, added to the extreme hazard of success, an impropriety even in the attempt. My honour in the honour of my family is bound; what to that would seem wrong, in me would be unjustifiable; yet where inducements so numerous were opposed by one single objection!—where virtue, beauty, education and family were all unexceptionable,—Oh cruel clause! barbarous and repulsive clause! that forbids my aspiring to the first of women, but by an action that with my own family would degrade me for ever!"

He stopt, overpowered by his own emotion, and Cecilia arose. "I see, madam," he cried, "your eagerness to be gone, and however at this moment I may lament it, I shall recollect it hereafter with advantage. But to conclude; I determined to avoid you, and, by avoiding, to endeavour to forget you; I determined, also, that no human being, and yourself least of all, should know, should even suspect the situation of my mind; and though upon various occasions, my prudence and forbearance have suddenly yielded to surprise and to passion, the surrender has been short, and almost, I believe, unnoticed.

"This silence and this avoidance I sustained with decent constancy, till during the storm, in an ill-fated moment, I saw, or thought I saw you in some danger, and then, all caution off guard, all resolution surprised, every passion awake, and tenderness triumphant—"

"Why, Sir," cried Cecilia, angrily, "and for what purpose all this?"

"Alas, I know not!" said he, with a deep sigh, "I thought myself better qualified for this conference, and meant to be firm and concise. I have told my story ill, but as your own understanding will point out the cause, your own benevolence will perhaps urge some excuse.

"Too certain, since that unfortunate accident, that all disguise was vain, and convinced by your displeasure of the impropriety of which I had been guilty, I determined, as the only apology I could offer, to open to you my whole heart, and then fly you perhaps for ever.

"This, madam, incoherently indeed, yet with sincerity, I have now done; my sufferings and my conflicts I do not mention, for I dare not! O were I to paint to you the bitter struggles of a mind all at war with itself,—Duty, spirit, and fortitude, combating love, happiness and inclination,—each conquering alternately, and alternately each vanquished,—I could endure it no longer, I resolved by one effort to finish the strife, and to undergo an instant of even exquisite torture, in preference to a continuance of such lingering misery!"

"The restoration of your health, Sir, and since you fancy it has been injured, of your happiness," said Cecilia, "will, I hope, be as speedy, as I doubt not they are certain."

"Since I fancy it has been injured!" repeated he; "what a phrase, after an avowal such as mine! But why should I wish to convince you of my sincerity, when to you it cannot be more indifferent, than to myself it is unfortunate! I have now only to entreat your pardon for the robbery I have committed upon your time, and to repeat my acknowledgments that you have endeavoured to hear me with patience."

"If you honour me, Sir, with some portion of your esteem," said the offended Cecilia, "these acknowledgments, perhaps, should be mine; suppose them, however made, for I have a letter to write, and can therefore stay no longer."

"Nor do I presume, madam," cried he proudly, "to detain you; hitherto you may frequently have thought me mysterious, sometimes strange and capricious, and perhaps almost always, unmeaning; to clear myself from these imputations, by a candid confession of the motives which have governed me, is all that I wished. Once, also—I hope but once,—you thought me impertinent,—there, indeed, I less dare vindicate myself—"

"There is no occasion, Sir," interrupted she, walking towards the door, "for further vindication in any thing; I am perfectly satisfied, and if my good wishes are worth your acceptance, assure yourself you possess them."

"Barbarous, and insulting!" cried he, half to himself; and then, with a quick motion hastening to open the door for her, "Go, madam," he added, almost breathless with conflicting emotions, "go, and be your happiness unalterable as your inflexibility!"

Cecilia was turning back to answer this reproach, but the sight of Lady Honoria, who was entering at the other door, deterred her, and she went on.

When she came to her own room, she walked about it some time in a state so unsettled, between anger and disappointment, sorrow and pride, that she scarce knew to which emotion to give way, and felt almost bursting with each.

"The die," she cried, "is at last thrown; and this affair is concluded for ever! Delvile himself is content to relinquish me; no father has commanded, no mother has interfered, he has required no admonition, full well enabled to act for himself by the powerful instigation of hereditary arrogance! Yet my family, he says,—unexpected condescension! my family and every other circumstance is unexceptionable; how feeble, then, is that regard which yields to one only objection! how potent that haughtiness which to nothing will give way! Well, let him keep his name! since so wondrous its properties, so all-sufficient its preservation, what vanity, what presumption in me, to suppose myself an equivalent for its loss!"

Thus, deeply offended, her spirits were supported by resentment, and not only while in company, but when alone, she found herself scarce averse to the approaching separation, and enabled to endure it without repining.

CHAPTER X

A RETREAT.

The next morning Cecilia arose late, not only to avoid the raillery of Lady Honoria, but to escape seeing the departure of Delvile; she knew that the spirit with which she had left him, made him, at present, think her wholly insensible, and she was at least happy to be spared the mortification of a discovery, since she found him thus content, without even solicitation, to resign her.

Before she was dressed, Lady Honoria ran into her room, "A new scheme of politics!" she cried; "our great statesman intends to leave us; he can't trust his baby out of his sight, so he is going to nurse him while upon the road himself. Poor pretty dear Mortimer! what a puppet do they make of him! I have a vast inclination to get a pap-boat myself, and make him a present of it."

Cecilia then enquired further particulars, and heard that Mr Delvile purposed accompanying his son to Bristol, whose journey, therefore, was postponed for a few hours to give time for new preparations.

Mr Delvile, who, upon this occasion, thought himself overwhelmed with business, because, before his departure, he had some directions to give to his domestics, chose to breakfast in his own apartment; Mrs Delvile, also, wishing for some private conversation with her son, invited him to partake of hers in her dressing-room, sending an apology to her guests, and begging they would order their breakfasts when they pleased.

Mr Delvile, scrupulous in ceremony, had made sundry apologies to Lord Ernolf for leaving him; but his real anxiety for his son overpowering his artificial character, the excuses he gave to that nobleman were such as could not possibly offend; and the views of his lordship himself in his visit, being nothing interrupted, so long as Cecilia continued at the castle, he readily engaged, as a proof that he was not affronted, to remain with Mrs Delvile till his return.

Cecilia, therefore, had her breakfast with the two lords and Lady Honoria; and when it was over, Lord Ernolf proposed to his son riding the first stage with the two Mr Delviles on horseback. This was agreed upon, and they left the room; and then Lady Honoria, full of frolic and gaiety, seized one of the napkins, and protested she would send it to Mortimer for a slabbering-bib; she therefore made it up in a parcel, and wrote upon the inside of the paper with which she enveloped it, "A pin-a fore for Master Mortimer Delvile, lest he should daub his pappy when he is feeding him." Eager to have this properly conveyed, she then ran out, to give it in charge to her own man, who was to present him with it as he got into the chaise.

She had but just quitted the room, when the door of it was again opened, and by Mortimer himself, booted, and equipped for his journey.

"Miss Beverley here! and alone!" cried he, with a look, and in a voice, which shewed that all the pride of the preceding evening was sunk into the deepest dejection; "and does she not fly as I approach her? can she patiently bear in her sight one so strange, so fiery, so inconsistent? But she is too wise to resent the ravings of a madman;—and who, under the influence of a passion at once hopeless and violent, can boast, but at intervals, full possession of his reason?"

Cecilia, utterly astonished by a gentleness so humble, looked at him in silent surprise; he advanced to her mournfully, and added, "I am ashamed, indeed, of the bitterness of spirit with which I last night provoked your displeasure, when I should have supplicated your lenity; but though I was prepared for your coldness, I could not endure it, and though your indifference was almost friendly, it made me little less than frantic; so strangely may justice be blinded by passion, and every faculty of reason be warped by selfishness!"

"You have no apology to make, Sir," cried Cecilia, "since, believe me, I require none."

"You may well," returned he, half-smiling, "dispense with my apologies, since under the sanction of that word, I obtained your hearing yesterday. But, believe me, you will now find me far more reasonable; a whole night's reflections—reflections which no repose interrupted!—have brought me to my senses. Even lunatics, you know, have lucid moments!"

"Do you intend, Sir, to set off soon?"

"I believe so; I wait only for my father. But why is Miss Beverley so impatient? I shall not soon return; that, at least, is certain, and, for a few instants delay, may surely offer some palliation;—See! if I am not ready to again accuse you of severity!—I must run, I find, or all my boasted reformation will end but in fresh offence, fresh disgrace, and fresh contrition! Adieu, madam!—and may all prosperity attend you! That will be ever my darling wish, however long my absence, however distant the climates which may part us!" He was then hurrying away, but Cecilia, from an impulse of surprise too sudden to be restrained, exclaimed "The climates?—do you, then, mean to leave England?"

"Yes," cried he, with quickness, "for why should I remain in it? a few weeks only could I fill up in any tour so near home, and hither in a few weeks to return would be folly and madness; in an absence so brief, what thought but that of the approaching meeting would occupy me? and what, at that meeting, should I feel, but joy the most dangerous, and delight which I dare not think of!—every conflict renewed, every struggle re-felt, again all this scene would require to be acted, again I must tear myself away, and every tumultuous passion now beating in my heart would be revived, and, if possible, be revived with added misery!—No!—neither my temper nor my constitution will endure such another shock, one parting shall suffice, and the fortitude with which I will lengthen my self-exile, shall atone to myself for the weakness which makes it requisite!"

And then, with a vehemence that seemed fearful of the smallest delay, he was again, and yet more hastily going, when Cecilia, with much emotion, called out, "Two moments, Sir!"

"Two thousand! two million!" cried he, impetuously, and returning, with a look of the most earnest surprise, he added, "What is it Miss Beverley will condescend to command?"

"Nothing," cried she, recovering her presence of mind, "but to beg you will by no means, upon my account, quit your country and your friends, since another asylum can be found for myself, and since I would much sooner part from Mrs Delvile, greatly and sincerely as I reverence her, than be instrumental to robbing her, even for a month, of her son."

"Generous and humane is the consideration," cried he; "but who half so generous, so humane as Miss Beverley? so soft to all others, so noble in herself? Can my mother have a wish, when I leave her with you? No; she is sensible of your worth, she adores you, almost as I adore you myself! you are now under her protection, you seem, indeed, born for each other; let me not, then, deprive her of so honourable a charge—Oh, why must he, who sees in such colours the excellencies of both, who admires with such fervour the perfections you unite, be torn with this violence from the objects he reveres, even though half his life he would sacrifice, to spend in their society what remained!"—

"Well, then, Sir," said Cecilia, who now felt her courage decline, and the softness of sorrow steal fast upon her spirits, "if you will not give up your scheme, let me no longer detain you."

"Will you not wish me a good journey?"

"Yes,—very sincerely."

"And will you pardon the unguarded errors which have offended you?"

"I will think of them, Sir, no more."

"Farewell, then, most amiable of women, and may every blessing you deserve light on your head! I leave to you my mother, certain of your sympathetic affection for a character so resembling your own. When you, madam, leave her, may the happy successor in your favour—" He paused, his voice faultered, Cecilia, too, turned away from him, and, uttering a deep sigh, he caught her hand, and pressing it to his lips, exclaimed, "O great be your felicity, in whatever way you receive it!—pure as your virtues, and warm as your benevolence!—Oh too lovely Miss Beverley!—why, why must I quit you!"

Cecilia, though she trusted not her voice to reprove him, forced away her hand, and then, in the utmost perturbation, he rushed out of the room.

This scene for Cecilia, was the most unfortunate that could have happened; the gentleness of Delvile was alone sufficient to melt her, since her pride had no subsistence when not fed by his own; and while his mildness had blunted her displeasure, his anguish had penetrated her heart. Lost in thought and in sadness, she continued fixed to her seat; and looking at the door through which he had passed, as if, with himself, he had shut out all for which she existed.

This pensive dejection was not long uninterrupted; Lady Honoria came running back, with intelligence, in what manner she had disposed of her napkin, and Cecilia in listening, endeavoured to find some diversion; but her ladyship, though volatile not undiscerning, soon perceived that her attention was constrained, and looking at her with much archness, said, "I believe, my dear, I must find another napkin for you! not, how ever, for your mouth, but for your eyes! Has Mortimer been in to take leave of you?"

"Take leave of me?—No,—is he gone?"

"O no, Pappy has a world of business to settle first; he won't be ready these two hours. But don't look so sorrowful, for I'll run and bring Mortimer to console you."

Away she flew, and Cecilia, who had no power to prevent her, finding her spirits unequal either to another parting, or to the raillery of Lady Honoria, should Mortimer, for his own sake, avoid it, took refuge in flight, and seizing an umbrella, escaped into the park; where, to perplex any pursuers, instead of chusing her usual walk, she directed her steps to a thick and unfrequented wood, and never rested till she was more than two miles from the house. Fidel, however, who now always accompanied her, ran by her side, and, when she thought herself sufficiently distant and private to be safe, she sat down under a tree, and caressing her faithful favourite, soothed her own tenderness by lamenting that he had lost his master; and, having now no part to act, and no dignity to support, no observation to fear, and no inference to guard against, she gave vent to her long smothered emotions, by weeping without caution or restraint.

She had met with an object whose character answered all her wishes for him with whom she should entrust her fortune, and whose turn of mind, so similar to her own, promised her the highest domestic felicity; to this object her affections had involuntarily bent, they were seconded by esteem, and unchecked by any suspicion of impropriety in her choice; she had found too, in return, that his heart was all her own; her birth, indeed, was inferior, but it was not disgraceful; her disposition, education and temper seemed equal to his fondest wishes; yet, at the very time when their union appeared most likely, when they mixed with the same society, and dwelt under the same roof, when the father to one, was the guardian to the other, and interest seemed to invite their alliance even more than affection, the young man himself, without counsel or command, could tear himself from her presence by an effort all his own, forbear to seek her heart, and almost charge her not to grant it, and determining upon voluntary exile, quit his country and his connections with no view, and for no reason, but merely that he might avoid the sight of her he loved!

Though the motive for this conduct was now no longer unknown to her, she neither thought it satisfactory nor necessary; yet, while she censured his flight, she bewailed his loss, and though his inducement was repugnant to her opinion, his command over his passions she admired and applauded.

CHAPTER XI

A WORRY.

Cecilia continued in this private spot, happy at least to be alone, till she was summoned by the dinner bell to return home.

As soon as she entered the parlour, where every body was assembled before her, she observed, by the countenance of Mrs Delvile, that she had passed the morning as sadly as herself.

"Miss Beverley," cried Lady Honoria, before she was seated, "I insist upon your taking my place to-day."

"Why so, madam?"

"Because I cannot suffer you to sit by a window with such a terrible cold."

"Your ladyship is very good, but indeed I have not any cold at all."

"O my dear, I must beg your pardon there; your eyes are quite bloodshot; Mrs Delvile, Lord Ernolf, are not her eyes quite red?—Lord, and so I protest are her cheeks! now do pray look in the glass, I assure you you will hardly know yourself."

Mrs Delvile, who regarded her with the utmost kindness, affected to understand Lady Honoria's speech literally, both to lessen her apparent confusion, and the suspicious surmises of Lord Ernolf; she therefore said, "you have indeed a bad cold, my love; but shade your eyes with your hat, and after dinner you shall bathe them in rose water, which will soon take off the inflammation."

Cecilia, perceiving her intention, for which she felt the utmost gratitude, no longer denied her cold, nor refused the offer of Lady Honoria; who, delighting in mischief, whencesoever it proceeded, presently added, "This cold is a judgment upon you for leaving me alone all this morning; but I suppose you chose a tête-à-tête with your favourite, without the intrusion of any third person."

Here every body stared, and Cecilia very seriously declared she had been quite alone.

"Is it possible you can so forget yourself?" cried Lady Honoria; "had you not your dearly beloved with you?"

Cecilia, who now comprehended that she meant Fidel, coloured more deeply than ever, but attempted to laugh, and began eating her dinner.

"Here seems some matter of much intricacy," cried Lord Ernolf, "but, to me, wholly unintelligible."

"And to me also," cried Mrs Delvile, "but I am content to let it remain so; for the mysteries of Lady Honoria are so frequent, that they deaden curiosity."

"Dear madam, that is very unnatural," cried Lady Honoria, "for I am sure you must long to know who I mean."

"I do, at least," said Lord Ernolf.

"Why then, my lord, you must know, Miss Beverley has two companions, and I am one, and Fidel is the other; but Fidel was with her all this morning, and she would not admit me to the conference. I suppose she had something private to say to him of his master's journey."

"What rattle is this?" cried Mrs Delvile; "Fidel is gone with my son, is he not?" turning to the servants.

"No, madam, Mr Mortimer did not enquire for him."

"That's very strange," said she, "I never knew him quit home without him before."

"Dear ma'am, if he had taken him," cried Lady Honoria, "what could poor Miss Beverley have done? for she has no friend here but him and me, and really he's so much the greater favourite, that it is well if I do not poison him some day for very spite."

Cecilia had no resource but in forcing a laugh, and Mrs Delvile, who evidently felt for her, contrived soon to change the subject; yet not before Lord Ernolf, with infinite chagrin, was certain by all that passed of the hopeless state of affairs for his son.

The rest of the day, and every hour of the two days following, Cecilia passed in the most comfortless constraint, fearful of being a moment alone, lest the heaviness of her heart should seek relief in tears, which consolation, melancholy as it was, she found too dangerous for indulgence; yet the gaiety of Lady Honoria lost all power of entertainment, and even the kindness of Mrs Delvile, now she imputed it to compassion, gave her more mortification than pleasure.

On the third·day, letters arrived from Bristol; but they brought with them nothing of comfort, for though Mortimer wrote gaily, his father sent word that his fever seemed threatening to return.

Mrs Delvile was now in the extremest anxiety; and the task of Cecilia in appearing chearful and unconcerned, became more and more difficult to perform. Lord Ernolf's efforts to oblige her grew as hopeless to himself, as they were irksome to her; and Lady Honoria alone, of the whole house, could either find or make the smallest diversion. But while Lord Derford remained, she had still an object for ridicule, and while Cecilia could colour and be confused, she had still a subject for mischief.

Thus passed a week, during which the news from Bristol being every day less and less pleasant, Mrs Delvile shewed an earnest desire to make a journey thither herself, and proposed, half laughing and half seriously, that the whole party should accompany her.

Lady Honoria's time, however, was already expired, and her father intended to send for her in a few days.

Mrs Delvile, who knew that such a charge would occupy all her time, willingly deferred setting out till her ladyship should be gone, but wrote word to Bristol that she should shortly be there, attended by the two lords, who insisted upon escorting her.

Cecilia now was in a state of the utmost distress; her stay at the castle she knew kept Delvile at a distance; to accompany his mother to Bristol, was forcing herself into his sight, which equally from prudence and pride she wished to avoid; and even Mrs Delvile evidently desired her absence, since whenever the journey was talked of, she preferably addressed herself to any one else who was present.

All she could devise to relieve herself from a situation so painful, was begging permission to make a visit without delay to her old friend Mrs Charlton in Suffolk.

This resolution taken, she put it into immediate execution, and seeking Mrs Delvile, enquired if she might venture to make a petition to her?

"Undoubtedly," answered she; "but let it not be very disagreeable, since I feel already that I can refuse you nothing."

"I have an old friend, ma'am," she then cried, speaking fast, and in much haste to have done, "who I have not for many months seen, and, as my health does not require a Bristol journey,—if you would honour me with mentioning my request to Mr Delvile, I think I might take the present opportunity of making Mrs Charlton a visit."

Mrs Delvile looked at her some time without speaking, and then, fervently embracing her, "sweet Cecilia!" she cried, "yes, you are all that I thought you! good, wise, discreet, tender, and noble at once!—how to part with you, indeed, I know not,—but you shall do as you please, for that I am sure will be right, and therefore I will make no opposition."

Cecilia blushed and thanked her, yet saw but too plainly that all the motives of her scheme were clearly comprehended. She hastened, therefore, to write to Mrs Charlton, and prepare for her reception.

Mr Delvile, though with his usual formality, sent his permission; and Mortimer at the same time, begged his mother would bring with her Fidel, whom he had unluckily forgotten.

Lady Honoria, who was present when Mrs Delvile mentioned this commission, said in a whisper to Cecilia, "Miss Beverley, don't let him go."

"Why not?"

"O, you had a great deal better take him slyly into Suffolk."

"I would as soon," answered Cecilia, "take with me the side-board of plate, for I should scarcely think it more a robbery."

"Oh, I beg your pardon, I am sure they might all take such a theft for an honour; and if I was going to Bristol, I would bid Mortimer send him to you immediately. However, if you wish it, I will write to him. He's my cousin, you know, so there will be no great impropriety in it."

Cecilia thanked her for so courteous an offer, but entreated that she might by no means draw her into such a condescension.

She then made immediate preparations for her journey into Suffolk, which she saw gave equal surprize and chagrin to Lord Ernolf, upon whose affairs Mrs Delvile herself now desired to speak with her.

"Tell me, Miss Beverley," she cried, "briefly and positively your opinion of Lord Derford?"

"I think of him so little, madam," she answered, "that I cannot say of him much; he appears, however, to be inoffensive; but, indeed, were I never to see him again, he is one of those I should forget I had ever seen at all."

"That is so exactly the case with myself also," cried Mrs Delvile, "that to plead for him, I find utterly impossible, though my Lord Ernolf has strongly requested me; but to press such an alliance, I should think an indignity to your understanding."

Cecilia was much gratified by this speech; but she soon after added, "There is one reason, indeed, which would render such a connection desirable, though that is only one."

"What is it, madam?"

"His title."

"And why so? I am sure I have no ambition of that sort."

"No, my love," said Mrs Delvile, smiling, "I mean not by way of gratification to your pride, but to his; since a title, by taking place of a family name, would obviate the only objection that any man could form to an alliance with Miss Beverley."

Cecilia, who too well understood her, suppressed a sigh, and changed the subject of conversation.

One day was sufficient for all the preparations she required, and, as she meant to set out very early the next morning, she took leave of Lady Honoria, and the Lords Ernolf and Derford, when they separated for the night; but Mrs Delvile followed her to her room.

She expressed her concern at losing her in the warmest and most flattering terms, yet said nothing of her coming back, nor of the length of her stay; she desired, however, to hear from her frequently, and assured her that out of her own immediate family, there was nobody in the world she so tenderly valued.

She continued with her till it grew so late that they were almost necessarily parted; and then rising to be gone, "See," she cried, "with what reluctance I quit you! no interest but so dear a one as that which calls me away, should induce me, with my own consent, to bear your absence scarcely an hour; but the world is full of mortifications, and to endure, or to sink under them, makes all the distinction between the noble or the weak-minded. To you this may be said with safety; to most young women it would pass for a reflection."

"You are very good," said Cecilia, smothering the emotions to which this speech gave rise, "and if indeed you honour me with an opinion so flattering, I will endeavour, if it is possibly in my power, not to forfeit it."

"Ah, my love!" cried Mrs Delvile warmly, "if upon my opinion of you alone depended our residence with each other, when should we ever part, and how live a moment asunder? But what title have I to monopolize two such blessings? the mother of Mortimer Delvile should at nothing repine; the mother of Cecilia Beverley had alone equal reason to be proud."

"You are determined, madam," said Cecilia, forcing a smile, "that I shall be worthy, by giving me the sweetest of motives, that of deserving such praise." And then, in a faint voice, she desired her respects to Mr Delvile, and added, "you will find, I hope, every body at Bristol better than you expect."

"I hope so," returned she; "and that you too, will find your Mrs Charlton well, happy, and good as you left her; but suffer her not to drive me from your remembrance, and never fancy that because she has known you longer, she loves you more; my acquaintance with you, though short, has been critical, and she must hear from you a world of anecdotes, before she can have reason to love you as much."

"Ah, madam," cried Cecilia, tears starting into her eyes, "let us part now!—where will be that strength of mind you expect from me, if I listen to you any longer!"

"You are right, my love," answered Mrs Delvile, "since all tenderness enfeebles fortitude." Then affectionately embracing her, "Adieu," she cried, "sweetest Cecilia, amiable and most excellent creature, adieu!—you, carry with you my highest approbation, my love, my esteem, my fondest wishes!—and shall I—yes, generous girl! I will add my warmest gratitude!"

This last word she spoke almost in a whisper, again kissed her, and hastened out of the room.

Cecilia, surprised and affected, gratified and depressed, remained almost motionless, and could not, for a great length of time, either ring for her maid, or persuade herself to go to rest. She saw throughout the whole behaviour of Mrs Delvile, a warmth of regard which, though strongly opposed by family pride, made her almost miserable to promote the very union she thought necessary to discountenance; she saw, too, that it was with the utmost difficulty she preserved the steadiness of her opposition, and that she had a conflict perpetual with herself, to forbear openly acknowledging the contrariety of her wishes, and the perplexity of her distress; but chiefly she was struck with her expressive use of the word gratitude. "Wherefore should she be grateful," thought Cecilia, "what have I done, or had power to do? infinitely, indeed, is she deceived, if she supposes that her son has acted by my directions; my influence with him is nothing, and he could not be more his own master, were he utterly indifferent to me. To conceal my own disappointment has, been all I have attempted; and perhaps she may think of me thus highly, from supposing that the firmness of her son is owing to my caution and reserve; ah, she knows him not!—were my heart at this moment laid open to him,—were all its weakness, its partiality, its ill-fated admiration displayed, he would but double his vigilance to avoid and forget me, and find the task all the easier by his abatement of esteem. Oh strange infatuation of unconquerable prejudice! his very life will he sacrifice in preference to his name, and while the conflict of his mind threatens to level him with the dust, he disdains to unite himself where one wish is unsatisfied!"

These reflections, and the uncertainty if she should ever in Delvile Castle sleep again, disturbed her the whole night, and made all calling in the morning unnecessary; she arose at five o'clock, dressed herself with the utmost heaviness of heart, and in going through a long gallery which led to the staircase, as she passed the door of Mortimer's chamber, the thought of his ill health, his intended long journey, and the probability that she might never see him more, so deeply impressed and saddened her, that scarcely could she force herself to proceed, without stopping to weep and to pray for him; she was surrounded, however, by servants, and compelled therefore to hasten to the chaise; she flung herself in, and, leaning back, drew her hat over her eyes, and thought, as the carriage drove off, her last hope of earthly happiness extinguished.

BOOK VII

CHAPTER I

A RENOVATION.

Cecilia was accompanied by her maid in the chaise, and her own servant and one of Mrs Delvile's attended her on horseback.

The quietness of her dejection was soon interrupted by a loud cry among the men of "home! home! home!" She then looked out of one of the windows, and perceived Fidel, running after the carriage, and barking at the servants, who were all endeavouring to send him back.

Touched by this proof of the animal's gratitude for her attention to him, and conscious she had herself occasioned his master's leaving him, the scheme of Lady Honoria occurred to her, and she almost wished to put it in execution, but this was the thought of a moment, and motioning him with her hand to go back, she desired Mrs Delvile's man to return with him immediately, and commit him to the care of somebody in the castle.

This little incident, however trifling, was the most important of her journey, for she arrived at the house of Mrs Charlton without meeting any other.

The sight of that lady gave her a sensation of pleasure to which she had long been a stranger, pleasure pure, unmixed, unaffected and unrestrained; it revived all her early affection, and with it, something resembling at least her early tranquility; again she was in the house where it had once been undisturbed, again she enjoyed the society which was once all she had wished, and again saw the same scene, the same faces, and same prospects she had beheld while her heart was all devoted to her friends.

Mrs Charlton, though old and infirm, preserved an understanding, which, whenever unbiassed by her affections, was sure to direct her unerringly; but the extreme softness of her temper frequently misled her judgment, by making it, at the pleasure either of misfortune or of artifice, always yield to compassion, and pliant to entreaty. Where her counsel and opinion were demanded, they were certain to reflect honour on her capacity and discernment; but where her assistance or her pity were supplicated, her purse and her tears were immediately bestowed, and in her zeal to alleviate distress she forgot if the object were deserving her solicitude, and stopt not to consider propriety or discretion, if happiness, however momentary, were in her power to grant.

This generous foible was, however, kept somewhat in subjection by the watchfulness of two grand-daughters, who, fearing the injury they might themselves receive from it, failed not to point out both its inconvenience and its danger.

These ladies were daughters of a deceased and only son of Mrs Charlton; they were single, and lived with their grand-mother, whose fortune, which was considerable, they expected to share between them, and they waited with eagerness for the moment of appropriation; narrow-minded and rapacious, they wished to monopolize whatever she possessed, and thought themselves aggrieved by her smallest donations. Their chief employment was to keep from her all objects of distress, and in this though they could not succeed, they at least confined her liberality to such as resembled themselves; since neither the spirited could brook, nor the delicate support the checks and rebuffs from the granddaughters, which followed the gifts of Mrs Charlton. Cecilia, of all her acquaintance, was the only one whose intimacy they encouraged, for they knew her fortune made her superior to any mercenary views, and they received from her themselves more civilities than they paid.

Mrs Charlton loved Cecilia with an excess of fondness, that not only took place of the love she bore her other friends, but to which even her regard for the Miss Charltons was inferior and feeble. Cecilia when a child had reverenced her as a mother, and, grateful for her tenderness and care, had afterwards cherished her as a friend. The revival of this early connection delighted them both, it was balm to the wounded mind of Cecilia, it was renovation to the existence of Mrs Charlton.

Early the next morning she wrote a card to Mr Monckton and Lady Margaret, acquainting them with her return into Suffolk, and desiring to know when she might pay her respects to her Ladyship. She received from the old lady a verbal answer, when she pleased, but Mr Monckton came instantly himself to Mrs Charlton's.

His astonishment, his rapture at this unexpected incident were almost boundless; he thought it a sudden turn of fortune in his own favour, and concluded, now she had escaped the danger of Delvile Castle, the road was short and certain that led to his own security.

Her satisfaction in the meeting was as sincere, though not so animated as his own; but this similarity in their feelings was of short duration, for when he enquired into what had passed at the castle, with the reasons of her quitting it, the pain she felt in giving even a cursory and evasive account, was opposed on his part by the warmest delight in hearing it; he could not obtain from her the particulars of what had happened, but the reluctance with which she spoke, the air of mortification with which she heard his questions, and the evident displeasure which was mingled in her chagrin, when he forced her to mention Delvile, were all proofs the most indisputable and satisfactory, that they had either parted without any explanation, or with one by which Cecilia had been hurt and offended.

He now readily concluded that since the fiery trial he had most apprehended was over; and she had quitted in anger the asylum she had sought in extacy, Delvile himself did not covet the alliance, which, since they were separated, was never likely to take place. He had therefore little difficulty in promising all success to himself.

She was once more upon the spot where she had regarded him as the first of men, he knew that during her absence no one had settled in the neighbourhood who had any pretensions to dispute with him that pre-eminence, he should again have access to her, at pleasure, and so sanguine grew his hopes, that he almost began to rejoice even in the partiality to Delvile that had hitherto been his terror, from believing it would give her for a time, that sullen distaste of all other connections, to which those who at once are delicate and fervent are commonly led by early disappointment. His whole solicitude therefore now was to preserve her esteem, to seek her confidence, and to regain whatever by absence might be lost of the [ascendancy] over her mind which her respect for his knowledge and capacity had for many years given him. Fortune at this time seemed to prosper all his views, and, by a stroke the most sudden and unexpected, to render more rational his hopes and his plans than he had himself been able to effect by the utmost craft of worldly wisdom.

The day following Cecilia, in Mrs Charlton's chaise, waited upon Lady Margaret. She was received by Miss Bennet, her companion, with the most fawning courtesy; but when conducted to the lady of the house, she saw herself so evidently unwelcome, that she even regretted the civility which had prompted her visit.

She found with her nobody but Mr Morrice, who was the only young man that could persuade himself to endure her company in the absence of her husband, but who, in common with most young men who are assiduous in their attendance upon old ladies, doubted not but he ensured himself a handsome legacy for his trouble.

Almost the first speech which her ladyship made, was "So you are not married yet, I find; if Mr Monckton had been a real friend, he would have taken care to have seen for some establishment for you."

"I was by no means," cried Cecilia, with spirit, "either in so much haste or distress as to require from Mr Monckton any such exertion of his friendship."

"Ma'am," cried Morrice, "what a terrible night we had of it at Vauxhall! poor Harrel! I was really excessively sorry for him. I had not courage to see you or Mrs Harrel after it. But as soon as I heard you were in St James's-square, I tried to wait upon you; for really going to Mr Harrel's again would have been quite too dismal. I would rather have run a mile by the side of a race-horse."

"There is no occasion for any apology," said Cecilia, "for I was very little disposed either to see or think of visitors."

"So I thought, ma'am;" answered he, with quickness, "and really that made me the less alert in finding you out. However, ma'am, next winter I shall be excessively happy to make up for the deficiency; besides, I shall be much obliged to you to introduce me to Mr Delvile, for I have a great desire to be acquainted with him."

Mr Delvile, thought Cecilia, would be but too proud to hear it! However, she merely answered that she had no present prospect of spending any time at Mr. Delvile's next winter.

"True, ma'am, true," cried he, "now I recollect, you become your own mistress between this and then; and so I suppose you will naturally chuse a house of your own, which will be much more eligible."

"I don't think that," said Lady Margaret, "I never saw anything eligible come of young women's having houses of their own; she will do a much better thing to marry, and have some proper person to take care of her."

"Nothing more right, ma'am!" returned he; "a young lady in a house by herself must be subject to a thousand dangers. What sort of place, ma'am, has Mr Delvile got in the country? I hear he has a good deal of ground there, and a large house."

"It is an old castle, Sir, and situated in a park."

"That must be terribly forlorn; I dare say, ma'am, you were very happy to return into Suffolk."

"I did not find it forlorn; I was very well satisfied with it."

"Why, indeed, upon second thoughts, I don't much wonder; an old castle in a large park must make a very romantic appearance; something noble in it, I dare say."

"Aye," cried Lady Margaret, "they said you were to become mistress of it, and marry Mr Delvile's son and I cannot, for my own part, see any objection to it."

"I am told of so many strange reports," said Cecilia, "and all, to myself so unaccountable, that I begin now to hear of them without much wonder."

"That's a charming young man, I believe," said Morrice; "I had the pleasure once or twice of meeting him at poor Harrel's, and he seemed mighty agreeable. Is not he so, ma'am?"

"Yes,—I believe so."

"Nay, I don't mean to speak of him as any thing very extraordinary," cried Morrice, imagining her hesitation proceeded from dislike, "I merely meant as the world goes,—in a common sort of a way."

Here they were joined by Mr Monckton and some gentlemen who were on a visit at his house; for his anxiety was not of a sort to lead him to solitude, nor his disposition to make him deny himself any kind of enjoyment which he had power to attain. A general conversation ensued, which lasted till Cecilia ended her visit; Mr Monckton then took her hand to lead her to the chaise, but told her, in their way out, of some alterations in his grounds, which he desired to shew her; his view of detaining her was to gather what she thought of her reception, and whether she had yet any suspicions of the jealousy of Lady Margaret; well knowing, from the delicacy of her character, that if once she became acquainted with it, she would scrupulously avoid all intercourse with him, from the fear of encreasing her uneasiness.

He began, therefore, with talking of the pleasure which Lady Margaret took in the plantations, and of his hope that Cecilia would often favour her by visiting them, without waiting to have her visits returned, as she was entitled by her infirmities to particular indulgencies. He was continuing in this strain, receiving from Cecilia hardly any answer, when suddenly from behind a thick laurel bush, jumpt up Mr Morrice; who had run out of the house by a shorter cut, and planted himself there to surprise them.

"So ho!" cried he with a loud laugh, "I have caught you! This will be a fine anecdote for Lady Margaret; I vow I'll tell her."

Mr Monckton, never off his guard, readily answered "Aye, prithee do, Morrice; but don't omit to relate also what we said of yourself."

"Of me?" cried he, with some eagerness; "why you never mentioned me."

"O that won't pass, I assure you; we shall tell another tale at table by and by; and bring the old proverb of the ill luck of listeners upon you in its full force."

"Well, I'll be hanged if I know what you mean!"

"Why you won't pretend you did not hear Miss Beverley say you were the truest Ouran Outang, or man-monkey, she ever knew?"

"No, indeed, that I did not!

"No?—Nor how much she admired your dexterity in escaping being horse-whipt three times a day for your incurable impudence?"

"Not a word on't! Horse-whipt!—Miss Beverley, pray did you say any such thing?"

"Ay," cried Monckton, again, "and not only horse-whipt, but horse-ponded, for she thought when, one had heated, the other might cool you; and then you might be fitted again for your native woods, for she insists upon it you was brought from Africa, and are not yet half tamed."

"O Lord!" cried Morrice, amazed, "I should not have suspected Miss Beverley would have talked so!"

"And do you suspect she did now?" cried Cecilia.

"Pho, pho," cried Monckton, coolly, "why he heard it himself the whole time! and so shall all our party by and bye, if I can but remember to mention it."

Cecilia then returned to the chaise, leaving Mr Monckton to settle the matter with his credulous guest as he pleased; for supposing he was merely gratifying a love of sport, or taking this method of checking the general forwardness of the young man, she forbore any interference that might mar his intention. But Mr Monckton loved not to be rallied concerning Cecilia, though he was indifferent to all that could be said to him of any other woman; he meant, therefore, to intimidate Morrice from renewing the subject; and he succeeded to his wish; poor Morrice, whose watching and whose speech were the mere blunders of chance, made without the slightest suspicion of Mr Monckton's designs, now apprehended some scheme to render himself ridiculous, and though he did not believe Cecilia had made use of such expressions, he fancied Mr Monckton meant to turn the laugh against him, and determined, therefore, to say nothing that might remind him of what had passed.

Mr Monckton had at this time admitted him to his house merely from an expectation of finding more amusement in his blundering and giddiness, than he was capable, during his anxiety concerning Cecilia, of receiving from conversation of an higher sort. The character of Morrice was, indeed, particularly adapted for the entertainment of a large house in the country; eager for sport, and always ready for enterprize; willing to oblige, yet tormented with no delicacy about offending; the first to promote mischief for any other, and the last to be offended when exposed to it himself; gay, thoughtless, and volatile,-a happy composition of levity and good-humour.

Cecilia, however, to quitting the house, determined not to visit it again very speedily; for she was extremely disgusted with Lady Margaret, though she suspected no particular motives of enmity, against which she was guarded alike by her own unsuspicious innocence, and by an high esteem of Mr Monckton, which she firmly believed he returned with equal honesty of undesigning friendship.

Her next excursion was to visit Mrs Harrel; she found that unhappy lady a prey to all the misery of unoccupied solitude; torn from whatever had, to her, made existence seem valuable, her mind was as listless as her person was inactive, and she was at a loss how to employ even a moment of the day; she had now neither a party to form, nor an entertainment to plan, company to arrange, nor dress to consider; and these, with visits and public places, had filled all her time since her marriage, which, as it had happened very early in her life, had merely taken place of girlish amusements, masters and governesses.

This helplessness of insipidity, however, though naturally the effect of a mind devoid of all genuine resources, was dignified by herself with the appellation of sorrow; nor was this merely a screen to the world; unused to investigate her feelings or examine her heart, the general compassion she met for the loss of her husband, persuaded her that indeed she lamented his destiny; though had no change in her life been caused by his suicide, she would scarcely, when the first shock was over, have thought of it again.

She received Cecilia with great pleasure; and with still greater, heard the renewal of her promises to fit up a room for her in her house, as soon as she came of age; a period which now was hardly a month distant. Far greater, however, as well as infinitely purer, was the joy which her presence bestowed upon Mr Arnott; she saw it herself with a sensation of regret, not only at the constant passion which occasioned it, but even at her own inability to participate in or reward it for with him an alliance would meet with no opposition; his character was amiable, his situation in life unexceptionable; he loved her with the tenderest affection, and no pride, she well knew, would interfere to overpower it; yet, in return, to grant him her love, she felt as utterly impossible as to refuse him her esteem; and the superior attractions of Delvile, of which neither displeasure nor mortification could rob him, shut up her heart, for the present, more firmly than ever, as Mr Monckton had well imagined, to all other assailants. Yet she by no means weakly gave way to repining or regret; her suspence was at an end, her hopes and her fears were subsided into certainty; Delvile, in quitting her, had acquainted her that he had left her for ever, and even, though not, indeed, with much steadiness, had prayed for her happiness in union with some other; she held it therefore as essential to her character as to her peace, to manifest equal fortitude in subduing her partiality; she forbore to hint to Mrs Charlton what had passed, that the subject might never be started; allowed herself no time for dangerous recollection; strolled in her old walks, and renewed her old acquaintance, and by a vigorous exertion of active wisdom, doubted not compleating, before long, the subjection of her unfortunate tenderness. Nor was her task so difficult as she had feared; resolution, in such cases, may act the office of time, and anticipate by reason and self-denial, what that, much less nobly, effects through forgetfulness and inconstancy.

CHAPTER II

A VISIT.

One week only, however, had yet tried the perseverance of Cecilia, when, while she was working with Mrs Charlton in her dressing-room, her maid hastily entered it, and with a smile that seemed announcing welcome news, said, "Lord, ma'am, here's Fidel!" and, at the same moment, she was followed by the dog, who jumpt upon Cecilia in a transport of delight.

"Good heaven," cried she, all amazement, "who has brought him? whence does he come?"

"A country man brought him, ma'am; but he only put him in, and would not stay a minute."

"But whom did he enquire for?—who saw him?—what did he say?"

"He saw Ralph, ma'am."

Ralph, then, was instantly called; and these questions being repeated, he said, "Ma'am, it was a man I never saw before; but he only bid me take care to deliver the dog into your own hands, and said you would have a letter about him soon, and then went away; I wanted him to stay till I came up stairs, but he was off at once."

Cecilia, quite confounded by this account, could make neither comment nor answer; but, as soon as the servants had left the room, Mrs Charlton entreated to know to whom the dog had belonged, convinced by her extreme agitation, that something interesting and uncommon must relate to him.

This was no time for disguise; astonishment and confusion bereft Cecilia of all power to attempt it; and, after a very few evasions, she briefly communicated her situation with respect to Delvile, his leaving her, his motives, and his mother's evident concurrence; for these were all so connected with her knowledge of Fidel, that she led to them unavoidably in telling what she knew of him.

Very little penetration was requisite, to gather from her manner all that was united in her narrative of her own feelings and disappointment in the course of this affair; and Mrs Charlton, who had hitherto believed the whole world at her disposal, and that she continued single from no reason but her own difficulty of choice, was utterly amazed to find that any man existed who could withstand the united allurements of so much beauty, sweetness, and fortune. She felt herself sometimes inclined to hate, and at other times to pity him; yet concluded that her own extreme coldness was the real cause of his flight, and warmly blamed a reserve which had thus ruined her happiness.

Cecilia was in the extremest perplexity and distress to conjecture the meaning of so unaccountable a present, and so strange a message. Delvile, she knew, had desired the dog might follow him to Bristol; his mother, always pleased to oblige him, would now less than ever neglect any opportunity; she could not, therefore, doubt that she had sent or taken him thither, and thence, according to all appearances, he must now come. But was it likely Delvile would take such a liberty? Was it probable, when so lately he had almost exhorted her to forget him, he would even wish to present her with such a remembrance of himself? And what was the letter she was bid to expect? Whence and from what was it to come?

All was inexplicable! the only thing she could surmise, with any semblance of probability, was that the whole was some frolic of Lady Honoria Pemberton, who had persuaded Delvile to send her the dog, and perhaps assured him she had herself requested to have him.

Provoked by this suggestion, her first thought was instantly having him conveyed to the castle; but uncertain what the whole affair meant, and hoping some explanation in the letter she was promised, she determined to wait till it came, or at least till she heard from Mrs Delvile, before she took any measures herself in the business. Mutual accounts of their safe arrivals at Bristol and in Suffolk, had already passed between them, and she expected very soon to have further intelligence; though she was now, by the whole behaviour of Mrs Delvile, convinced she wished not again to have her an inmate of her house, and that the rest of her minority might pass, without opposition; in the house of Mrs Charlton.

Day after day, however, passed, and yet she heard nothing more; a week, a fortnight elapsed, and still no letter came. She now concluded the promise was a deception, and repented that she had waited a moment with any such expectation. Her peace, during this time, was greatly disturbed; this present made her fear she was thought meanly of by Mr Delvile; the silence of his mother gave her apprehensions for his health, and her own irresolution how to act, kept her in perpetual inquietude. She tried in vain to behave as if this incident had not happened; her mind was uneasy, and the same actions produced not the same effects; when she now worked or read, the sight of Fidel by her side distracted her attention; when she walked, it was the same, for Fidel always followed her; and though, in visiting her old acquaintance, she forbore to let him accompany her, she was secretly planning the whole time the contents of some letter, which she expected to meet with, on returning to Mrs Charlton's.

Those gentlemen in the country who, during the life-time of the Dean, had paid their addresses to Cecilia, again waited upon her at Mrs Charlton's, and renewed their proposals. They had now, however, still less chance of success, and their dismission was brief and decisive.

Among these came Mr Biddulph; and to him Cecilia was involuntarily most civil, because she knew him to be the friend of Delvile. Yet his conversation encreased the uneasiness of her suspence; for after speaking of the family in general which she had left, he enquired more particularly concerning Delvile, and then added, "I am, indeed, greatly grieved to find, by all the accounts I receive of him, that he is now in a very bad state of health."

This speech gave her fresh subject for apprehension; and in proportion as the silence of Mrs Delvile grew more alarming, her regard for her favourite Fidel became more partial. The affectionate animal seemed to mourn the loss of his master, and while sometimes she indulged herself in fancifully telling him her fears, she imagined she read in his countenance the faithfullest sympathy.

One week of her minority was now all that remained, and she was soon wholly occupied in preparations for coming of age. She purposed taking possession of a large house that had belonged to her uncle, which was situated only three miles from that of Mrs Charlton; and she employed herself in giving orders for fitting it up, and in hearing complaints, and promising indulgencies, to various of her tenants.

At this time, while she was at breakfast one morning, a letter arrived from Mrs Delvile. She apologised for not writing sooner, but added that various family occurrences, which had robbed her of all leisure, might easily be imagined, when she acquainted her that Mortimer had determined upon again going abroad.... They were all, she said, returned to Delvile Castle, but mentioned nothing either of the health of her son, or of her own regret, and filled up the rest of her letter, with general news and expressions of kindness; though, in a postscript, was inserted, "We have lost our poor Fidel."

Cecilia was still meditating upon this letter, by which her perplexity how to act was rather encreased than diminished, when, to her great surprise, Lady Honoria Pemberton was announced. She hastily begged one of the Miss Charltons to convey Fidel out of sight, from a dread of her raillery, should she, at last, be unconcerned in the transaction, and then went to receive her.

Lady Honoria, who was with her governess, gave a brief history of her quitting Delvile Castle, and said she was now going with her father to visit a noble family in Norfolk; but she had obtained his permission to leave him at the inn where they had slept, in order to make a short excursion to Bury, for the pleasure of seeing Miss Beverley.

"And therefore," she continued, "I can stay but half an hour; so you must give me some account of yourself as fast as possible."

"What account does your ladyship require?"

"Why, who you live with here, and who are your companions, and what you do with yourself."

"Why, I live with Mrs Charlton; and for companions, I have at least a score; here are her two grand-daughters, and Mrs and Miss—."

"Pho, pho," interrupted Lady Honoria, "but I don't mean such hum-drum companions as those; you'll tell me next, I suppose, of the parson and his wife and three daughters, with all their cousins and aunts; I hate those sort of people. What I desire to hear of is, who are your particular favourites; and whether you take long walks here, as you used to do at the Castle, and who you have to accompany you?" And then, looking at her very archly, she added, "A pretty little dog, now, I should think, would be vastly agreeable in such a place as this.—Ah, Miss Beverley! you have not left off that trick of colouring, I see!"

"If I colour now," said Cecilia, fully convinced of the justness of her suspicions, "I think it must be for your ladyship, not myself; for, if I am not much mistaken, either in person, or by proxy, a blush from Lady Honoria Pemberton would not, just now, be wholly out of season."

"Lord," cried she, "how like that is to a speech of Mrs Delvile's! She has taught you exactly her manner of talking. But do you know I am informed you have got Fidel with you here? O fie, Miss Beverley! What will papa and mamma say, when they find you have taken away poor little master's plaything?"

"And O fie, Lady Honoria! what shall I say, when I find you guilty of this mischievous frolic! I must beg, however, since you have gone thus far, that you will proceed a little farther, and send back the dog to the person from whom you received him."

"No, not I! manage him all your own way; if you chuse to accept dogs from gentlemen, you know, it is your affair, and not mine."

"If you really will not return him yourself, you must at least pardon me should you hear that I do in your ladyship's name."

Lady Honoria for some time only laughed and rallied, without coming to any explanation; but when she had exhausted all the sport she could make, she frankly owned that she had herself ordered the dog to be privately stolen, and then sent a man with him to Mrs Charlton's.

"But you know," she continued, "I really owed you a spite for being so ill-natured as to run away after sending me to call Mortimer to comfort and take leave of you."

"Do you dream, Lady Honoria? when did I send you?"

"Why you know you looked as if you wished it, and that was the same thing. But really it made me appear excessively silly, when I had forced him to come back with me, and told him you were waiting for him,—to see nothing of you at all, and not be able to find or trace you. He took it all for my own invention."

"And was it not your own invention?"

"Why that's nothing to the purpose; I wanted him to believe you sent me, for I knew else he would not come."

"Your ladyship was a great deal too good!"

"Why now suppose I had brought you together, what possible harm could have happened from it? It would merely have given each of you some notion of a fever and ague; for first you would both have been hot, and then you would both have been cold, and then you would both have turned red, and then you would both have turned white, and then you would both have pretended to simper at the trick; and then there would have been an end of it."

"This is a very easy way of settling it all," cried Cecilia laughing; "however, you must be content to abide by your own theft, for you cannot in conscience expect I should take it upon myself."

"You are terribly ungrateful, I see," said her ladyship, "for all the trouble and contrivance and expence I have been at merely to oblige you, while the whole time, poor Mortimer, I dare say, has had his sweet Pet advertised in all the newspapers, and cried in every market-town in the kingdom. By the way, if you do send him back, I would advise you to let your man demand the reward that has been offered for him, which may serve in part of payment for his travelling expenses."

Cecilia could only shake her head, and recollect Mrs Delvile's expression, that her levity was incorrigible.

"O if you had seen," she continued, "how sheepish Mortimer looked when I told him you were dying to see him before he set off! he coloured so!—just as you do now!—but I think you're vastly alike."

"I fear, then," cried Cecilia, not very angry at this speech, "there is but little chance your ladyship should like either of us."

"O yes, I do! I like odd people of all things."

"Odd people? and in what are we so very odd?"

"O, in a thousand things. You're so good, you know, and so grave, and so squeamish."

"Squeamish? how?"

"Why, you know, you never laugh at the old folks, and never fly at your servants, nor smoke people before their faces, and are so civil to the old fograms, you would make one imagine you liked nobody so well. By the way, I could do no good with my little Lord Derford; he pretended to find out I was only laughing at him, and so he minded nothing I told him. I dare say, however, his father made the detection, for I am sure he had not wit enough to discover it himself."

Cecilia then, very seriously began to entreat that she would return the dog herself, and confess her frolic, remonstrating in strong terms upon the mischievous tendency and consequences of such inconsiderate flights.

"Well," cried she, rising, "this is all vastly true; but I have no time to hear any more of it just now; besides, it's only forestalling my next lecture from Mrs Delvile, for you talk so much alike, that it is really very perplexing to me to remember which is which."

She then hurried away, protesting she had already outstayed her father's patience, and declaring the delay of another minute would occasion half a dozen expresses to know whether she was gone towards Scotland or Flanders.

This visit, however, was both pleasant and consolatory to Cecilia; who was now relieved from her suspence, and revived in her spirits by the intelligence that Delvile had no share in sending her a present, which, from him, would have been humiliating and impertinent. She regretted, indeed, that she had not instantly returned it to the castle, which she was now convinced was the measure she ought to have pursued; but to make all possible reparation, she determined that her own servant should set out with him the next morning to Bristol, and take a letter to Mrs Delvile to explain what had happened, since to conceal it from any delicacy to Lady Honoria, would be to expose herself to suspicions the most mortifying, for which that gay and careless young lady would never thank her.

She gave orders, therefore, to her servant to get ready for the journey.

When she communicated these little transactions to Mrs Charlton, that kind-hearted old lady, who knew her fondness for Fidel, advised her not yet to part with him, but merely to acquaint Mrs Delvile where he was, and what Lady Honoria had done, and, by leaving to herself the care of settling his restoration, to give her, at least, an opportunity of offering him to her acceptance.

Cecilia, however, would listen to no such proposal; she saw the firmness of Delvile in his resolution to avoid her, and knew that policy, as well as propriety, made it necessary she should part with what she could only retain to remind her of one whom she now most wished to forget.

CHAPTER III

AN INCIDENT.

The spirits of Cecilia, however, internally failed her; she considered her separation from Delvile to be now, in all probability, for life, since she saw that no struggle either of interest, inclination, or health, could bend him from his purpose; his mother, too, seemed to regard his name and his existence as equally valuable, and the scruples of his father she was certain would be still more insurmountable. Her own pride, excited by theirs, made her, indeed, with more anger than sorrow, see this general consent to abandon her; but pride and anger both failed when she considered the situation of his health; sorrow, there, took the lead, and admitted no partner; it represented him to her not only as lost to herself, but to the world; and so sad grew her reflections, and so heavy her heart, that, to avoid from Mrs Charlton observations which pained her, she stole into a summer-house in the garden the moment she had done tea, declining any companion but her affectionate Fidel.

Her tenderness and her sorrow found here a romantic consolation, in complaining to him of the absence of his master, his voluntary exile, and her fears for his health; calling upon him to participate in her sorrow, and lamenting that even this little relief would soon be denied her; and that in losing Fidel no vestige of Mortimer, but in her own breast, would remain; "Go, then, dear Fidel," she cried, "carry back to your master all that nourishes his remembrance! Bid him not love you the less for having some time belonged to Cecilia; but never may his proud heart be fed with the vain glory of knowing how fondly for his sake she has cherished you! Go, dear Fidel, guard him by night, and follow him by day; serve him with zeal, and love him with fidelity;—oh that his health were invincible as his pride!—there, alone, is he vulnerable—"

Here Fidel, with a loud barking, suddenly sprang away from her, and, as she turned her eyes towards the door to see what had thus startled him, she beheld standing there, as if immoveable, young Delvile himself!

Her astonishment at this sight almost bereft her of her understanding; it appeared to her supernatural, and she rather believed it was his ghost than himself. Fixed in mute wonder, she stood still though terrified, her eyes almost bursting from their sockets to be satisfied if what they saw was real.

Delvile, too, was some time speechless; he looked not at her, indeed, with any doubt of her existence, but as if what he had heard was to him as amazing as to her what she saw. At length, however, tormented by the dog, who jumpt up to him, licked his hands, and by his rapturous joy forced himself into notice, he was moved to return his caresses, saying, "Yes, dear Fidel! you have a claim indeed to my attention, and with the fondest gratitude will I cherish you ever!"

At the sound of his voice, Cecilia again began to breathe; and Delvile having quieted the dog, now entered the summer-house, saying, as he advanced, "Is this possible!—am I not in a dream?—Good God! is it indeed possible!"

The consternation of doubt and astonishment which had seized every faculty of Cecilia, now changed into certainty that Delvile indeed was present, all her recollection returned as she listened, to this question, and the wild rambling of fancy with which she had incautiously indulged her sorrow, rushing suddenly upon her mind, she felt herself wholly overpowered by consciousness and shame, and sunk, almost fainting, upon a window-seat.

Delvile instantly flew to her, penetrated with gratitude, and filled with wonder and delight, which, however internally combated by sensations less pleasant, were too potent for controul, and he poured forth at her feet the most passionate acknowledgments.

Cecilia, surprised, affected, and trembling with a thousand emotions, endeavoured to break from him and rise; but, eagerly detaining her, "No, loveliest Miss Beverley," he cried, "not thus must we now part! this moment only have I discovered what a treasure I was leaving; and, but for Fidel, I had quitted it in ignorance for ever."

"Indeed," cried Cecilia, in the extremest agitation, "indeed you may believe me Fidel is here quite by accident.—Lady Honoria took him away,—I knew nothing of the matter,—she stole him, she sent him, she did every thing herself."

"O kind Lady Honoria!" cried Delvile, more and more delighted, "how shall I ever thank her!—And did she also tell you to caress and to cherish him?—to talk to him of his master—"

"O heaven!" interrupted Cecilia, in an agony of mortification and shame, "to what has my unguarded folly reduced me!" Then again endeavouring to break from him, "Leave me, Mr Delvile," she cried, "leave me, or let me pass!—never can I see you more!—never bear you again in my sight!"

"Come, dear Fidel!" cried he, still detaining her, "come and plead for your master! come and ask in his name who now has a proud heart, whose pride now is invincible!"

"Oh go!" cried Cecilia, looking away from him while she spoke, "repeat not those hateful words, if you wish me not to detest myself eternally!"

"Ever-lovely Miss Beverley," cried he, more seriously, "why this resentment? why all this causeless distress? Has not my heart long since been known to you? have you not witnessed its sufferings, and been assured of its tenderness? why, then, this untimely reserve? this unabating coldness? Oh why try to rob me of the felicity you have inadvertently given me! and to sour the happiness of a moment that recompenses such exquisite misery!"

"Oh Mr Delvile!" cried she, impatiently, though half softened, "was this honourable or right? to steal upon me thus privately—to listen to me thus secretly—"

"You blame me," cried he, "too soon; your own friend, Mrs Charlton, permitted me to come hither in search of you;—then, indeed, when I heard the sound of your voice—when I heard that voice talk of Fidel—of his master—"

"Oh stop, stop!" cried she; "I cannot support the recollection! there is no punishment, indeed, which my own indiscretion does not merit,—but I shall have sufficient in the bitterness of self-reproach!"

"Why will you talk thus, my beloved Miss Beverley? what have you done,—what, let me ask, have I done, that such infinite disgrace and depression should follow this little sensibility to a passion so fervent? Does it not render you more dear to me than ever? does it not add new life, new vigour, to the devotion by which I am bound to you?"

"No, no," cried the mortified Cecilia, who from the moment she found herself betrayed, believed herself to be lost, "far other is the effect it will have! and the same mad folly by which I am ruined in my own esteem, will ruin me in yours!—I cannot endure to think of it!—why will you persist in detaining me?—You have filled me with anguish and mortification,—you have taught me the bitterest of lessons, that of hating and contemning myself!"

"Good heaven," cried he, much hurt, "what strange apprehensions thus terrify you? are you with me less safe than with yourself? is it my honour you doubt? is it my integrity you fear? Surely I cannot be so little known to you; and to make protestations now, would but give a new alarm to a delicacy already too agitated.—Else would I tell you that more sacred than my life will I hold what I have heard, that the words just now graven on my heart, shall remain there to eternity unseen; and that higher than ever, not only in my love, but my esteem, is the beautiful speaker."—

"Ah no!" cried Cecilia, with a sigh, "that, at least, is impossible, for lower than ever is she sunk from deserving it!"

"No," cried he, with fervour, "she is raised, she is exalted! I find her more excellent and perfect than I had even dared believe her; I discover new virtues in the spring of every action; I see what I took for indifference, was dignity; I perceive what I imagined the most rigid insensibility, was nobleness, was propriety, was true greatness of mind!"

Cecilia was somewhat appeased by this speech; and, after a little hesitation, she said, with a half smile, "Must I thank you for this good-nature in seeking to reconcile me with myself?—or shall I quarrel with you for flattery, in giving me praise you can so little think I merit?"

"Ah!" cried he, "were I to praise as I think of you! were my language permitted to accord with my opinion of your worth, you would not then simply call me a flatterer, you would tell me I was an idolater, and fear at least for my principles, if not for my understanding."

"I shall have but little right, however," said Cecilia, again rising, "to arraign your understanding while I act as if bereft of my own. Now, at least, let me pass; indeed you will greatly displease me by any further opposition."

"Will you suffer me, then, to see you early to-morrow morning?"

"No, Sir; nor the next morning, nor the morning after that! This meeting has been wrong, another would be worse; in this I have accusation enough for folly,—in another the charge would be far more heavy."

"Does Miss Beverley, then," cried he gravely, "think me capable of desiring to see her for mere selfish gratification? of intending to trifle either with her time or her feelings? no; the conference I desire will be important and decisive. This night I shall devote solely to deliberation; to-morrow shall be given to action. Without some thinking I dare venture at no plan;—I presume not to communicate to you the various interests that divide me, but the result of them all I can take no denial to your hearing."

Cecilia, who felt when thus stated the justice of his request, now opposed it no longer, but insisted upon his instantly departing.

"True," cried he, "I must go!—the longer I stay, the more I am fascinated, and the weaker are those reasoning powers of which I now want the strongest exertion." He then repeated his professions of eternal regard, besought her not to regret the happiness she had given him, and after disobeying her injunctions of going till she was seriously displeased, he only stayed to obtain her pardon, and permission to be early the next morning, and then, though still slowly and reluctantly, he left her.

Scarce was Cecilia again alone, but the whole of what had passed seemed a vision of her imagination. That Delvile should be at Bury, that he should visit her at Mrs Charlton's, surprise her by herself, and discover her most secret thoughts, appeared so strange and so incredible, that, occupied rather by wonder than, thinking, she continued almost motionless in the place where he had left her, till Mrs Charlton sent to request that she would return to the house. She then enquired if any body was with her, and being answered in the negative, obeyed the summons.

Mrs Charlton, with a smile of much meaning, hoped she had had a pleasant walk; but Cecilia seriously remonstrated on the dangerous imprudence she had committed in suffering her to be so unguardedly surprised. Mrs Charlton, however, more anxious for her future and solid happiness, than for her present apprehensions and delicacy, repented not the step she had taken; and when she gathered from Cecilia the substance of what had past, unmindful of the expostulations which accompanied it, she thought with exultation that the sudden meeting she had permitted, would now, by making known to each their mutual affection, determine them to defer no longer a union upon which their mutual peace of mind so much depended. And Cecilia, finding she had been thus betrayed designedly, not inadvertently, could hardly reproach her zeal, though she lamented its indiscretion.

She then asked by what means he had obtained admission, and made himself known; and heard that he had enquired at the door for Miss Beverley, and, having sent in his name, was shewn into the parlour, where Mrs Charlton, much pleased with his appearance, had suddenly conceived the little plan which she had executed, of contriving a surprise for Cecilia, from which she rationally expected the very consequences that ensued, though the immediate means she had not conjectured.

The account was still unsatisfactory to Cecilia, who could frame to herself no possible reason for a visit so extraordinary, and so totally inconsistent with his declarations and resolutions.

This, however, was a matter of but little moment, compared with the other subjects to which the interview had given rise; Delvile, upon whom so long, though secretly, her dearest hopes of happiness had rested, was now become acquainted with his power, and knew himself the master of her destiny; he had quitted her avowedly to decide what it should be, since his present subject of deliberation included her fate in his own; the next morning he was to call, and acquaint her with his decree, not doubting her concurrence which ever way be resolved.

A subjection so undue, and which she could not but consider as disgraceful, both shocked and afflicted her; and the reflection that the man who of all men she preferred, was acquainted with her preference, yet hesitated whether to accept or abandon her, mortified and provoked her, alternately, occupied her thoughts the whole night, and kept her from peace and from rest.

CHAPTER IV

A PROPOSITION.

Early the next morning, Delvile again made his appearance. Cecilia, who was at breakfast with Mrs and Miss Charltons, received him with the most painful confusion, and he was evidently himself in a state of the utmost perturbation. Mrs Charlton made a pretence almost immediately for sending away both her grand-daughters, and then, without taking the trouble of devising one for herself, arose and followed them, though Cecilia made sundry signs of solicitation that she would stay.

Finding herself now alone with him, she hastily, and without knowing what she said, cried, "How is Mrs Delvile, Sir? Is she still at Bristol?"

"At Bristol? no; have you never heard she is returned to Delvile Castle?"

"O, true!—I meant Delvile Castle,—but I hope she found some benefit from the waters?"

"She had not, I believe, any occasion to try them."

Cecilia, ashamed of these two following mistakes, coloured high; but ventured not again to speak; and Delvile, who seemed big with something he feared to utter, arose, and walked for a few instants about the room; after which, exclaiming aloud "How vain is every plan which passes the present hour!" He advanced to Cecilia, who pretended to be looking at some work, and seating himself next her, "when we parted yesterday," he cried, "I presumed to say one night alone should be given to deliberation,—and to-day, this very day to action!—but I forgot that though in deliberating I had only myself to consult, in acting I was not so independent; and that when my own doubts were satisfied, and my own resolutions taken, other doubts and other resolutions must be considered, by which my purposed proceedings might be retarded, might perhaps be wholly prevented!"

He paused, but Cecilia, unable to conjecture to what he was leading, made not any answer.

"Upon you, madam," he continued, "all that is good or evil of my future life, as far as relates to its happiness or misery, will, from this very hour, almost solely depend; yet much as I rely upon your goodness, and superior as I know you to trifling or affectation, what I now come to propose—to petition—to entreat—I cannot summon courage to mention, from a dread of alarming you!"

What next, thought Cecilia, trembling at this introduction, is preparing for me! does he mean to ask me to solicit Mrs Delvile's consent! or from myself must he receive commands that we should never meet more!

"Is Miss Beverley," cried he, "determined not to, speak to me? Is she bent upon silence only to intimidate me? Indeed if she knew how greatly I respect her, she would honour me with more confidence."

"When, Sir," cried she, "do you mean to make your tour?"

"Never!" cried he, with fervour, "unless banished by you, never!—no, loveliest Miss Beverley, I can now quit you no more! Fortune, beauty, worth and sweetness I had power to relinquish, and severe as was the task, I compelled myself to perform it,—but when to these I find joined so attractive a softness,—a pity for my sufferings so unexpectedly gentle no! sweetest Miss Beverley, I can quit you no more!" And then, seizing her hand, with yet greater energy, he went on, "I here," he cried, "offer you my vows, I here own you sole arbitress of my fate! I give you not merely the possession of my heart,—that, indeed, I had no power to withhold from you,—but I give you the direction of my conduct, I entreat you to become my counsellor and guide. Will Miss Beverley accept such an office? Will she deign to listen to such a prayer?"

"Yes," cried Cecilia, involuntarily delighted to find that such was the result of his night's deliberation, "I am most ready to give you my counsel; which I now do,—that you set off for the Continent to-morrow morning."

"O how malicious!" cried he, half laughing, "yet not so immediately do I even request your counsel; something must first be done to qualify you for giving it; penetration, skill and understanding, however amply you possess them, are not sufficient to fit you for the charge; something still more is requisite, you must be invested with fuller powers, you must have a right less disputable, and a title, that not alone, inclination, not even judgment alone must sanctify, but which law must enforce, and rites the most solemn support!"

"I think, then," said Cecilia, deeply blushing, "I must be content to forbear giving any counsel at all, if the qualifications for it are so difficult of acquirement."

"Resent not my presumption," cried he, "my beloved Miss Beverley, but let the severity of my recent sufferings palliate my present temerity; for where affliction has been deep and serious, causeless and unnecessary misery will find little encouragement; and mine has been serious indeed! Sweetly, then, permit me, in proportion to its bitterness, to rejoice in the soft reverse which now flatters me with its approach."

Cecilia, abashed and uneasy, uncertain of what was to follow, and unwilling to speak till more assured, paused, and then abruptly exclaimed "I am afraid Mrs Charlton is waiting for me," and would have hurried away; but Delvile, almost forcibly preventing her, compelled her to stay; and, after a short conversation, on his side the most impassioned, and on hers the most confused, obtained from her, what, indeed, after the surprise of the preceding evening she could but ill deny, a frank confirmation of his power over her heart, and an ingenuous, though reluctant acknowledgment, how long he had possessed it.

This confession, made, as affairs now stood, wholly in opposition to her judgment, was torn from her by an impetuous urgency which she had not presence of mind to resist, and with which Delvile, when particularly animated, had long been accustomed to overpower all opposition. The joy with which he heard it, though but little mixed with wonder, was as violent as the eagerness with which he had sought it; yet it was not of long duration, a sudden, and most painful recollection presently quelled it, and even in the midst of his rapturous acknowledgment, seemed to strike him to the heart.

Cecilia, soon perceiving both in his countenance and manner an alteration that shocked her, bitterly repented an avowal she could never recall, and looked aghast with expectation and dread.

Delvile, who with quickness saw a change of expression in her of which in himself he was unconscious, exclaimed, with much emotion, "O how transient is human felicity! How rapidly fly those rare and exquisite moments in which it is perfect! Ah! sweetest Miss Beverley, what words shall I find to soften what I have now to reveal! to tell you that, after goodness, candour, generosity such as yours, a request, a supplication remains yet to be uttered that banishes me, if refused, from your presence for ever!"

Cecilia, extremely dismayed, desired to know what it was; an evident dread of offending her kept him some time from proceeding, but at length, after repeatedly expressing his fears of her disapprobation, and a repugnance even on his own part to the very measure he was obliged to urge, he acknowledged that all his hopes of being ever united to her, rested upon obtaining her consent to an immediate and secret marriage.

Cecilia, thunderstruck by this declaration, remained for a few instants too much confounded to speak; but when he was beginning an explanatory apology, she started up, and glowing with indignation, said, "I had flattered myself, Sir, that both my character and my conduct, independent of my situation in life, would have exempted me at all times from a proposal which I shall ever think myself degraded by having heard."

And then she was again going, but Delvile still preventing her, said "I knew too well how much you would be alarmed, and such was my dread of your displeasure that it had power even to embitter the happiness I sought with so much earnestness, and to render your condescension insufficient to ensure it. Yet wonder not at my scheme; wild as it may appear, it is the result of deliberation, and censurable as it may seem, it springs not from unworthy motives."

"Whatever may be your motives with respect to yourself, Sir," said Cecilia, "with respect to me they must certainly be disgraceful; I will not, therefore, listen to them."

"You wrong me cruelly," cried he, with warmth, "and a moment's reflection must tell you that however distinct may be our honour or our disgrace in every other instance, in that by which we should be united, they must inevitably be the same; and far sooner would I voluntarily relinquish you, than be myself accessory to tainting that delicacy of which the unsullied purity has been the chief source of my admiration."

"Why, then," cried Cecilia, reproachfully, "have you mentioned to me such a project?"

"Circumstances the most singular, and necessity the most unavoidable," he answered, "should alone have ever tempted me to form it. No longer ago than yesterday morning, I believed myself incapable of even wishing it; but extraordinary situations call for extraordinary resolutions, and in private as well as public life, palliate, at least, extraordinary actions. Alas! the proposal which so much offends you is my final resource! it is the sole barrier between myself and perpetual misery!—the only expedient in my power to save me from eternally parting from you!—for I am compelled now cruelly to confess, that my family, I am certain, will never consent to our union!"

"Neither, then, Sir," cried Cecilia, with great spirit, "will I! The disdain I may meet with I pretend not to retort, but wilfully to encounter, were meanly to deserve it. I will enter into no family in opposition to its wishes, I will consent to no alliance that may expose me to indignity. Nothing is so contagious as contempt!—The example of your friends might work powerfully upon yourself, and who shall dare assure me you would not catch the infection?"

"I dare assure you!" cried he; "hasty you may perhaps think me, and somewhat impetuous I cannot deny myself; but believe me not of so wretched a character as to be capable, in any affair of moment, of fickleness or caprice."

"But what, Sir, is my security to the contrary? Have you not this moment avowed that but yesterday you held in abhorrence the very plan that to-day you propose? And may you not to-morrow resume again the same opinion?"

"Cruel Miss Beverley! how unjust is this inference! If yesterday I disapproved what to-day I recommend, a little recollection must surely tell you why; and that not my opinion, but my situation is changed."

The conscious Cecilia here turned away her head; too certain he alluded to the discovery of her partiality.

"Have you not yourself," he continued, "witnessed the steadiness of my mind? Have you not beheld me fly, when I had power to pursue, and avoid, when I had opportunity to seek you? After witnessing my constancy upon such trying occasions, is it equitable, is it right to suspect me of wavering?"

"But what," cried she, "was the constancy which brought you into Suffolk?—When all occasion was over for our meeting any more, when you told me you were going abroad, and took leave of me for ever,—where, then, was your steadiness in this unnecessary journey?"

"Have a care," cried he, half smiling, and taking a letter from his pocket, "have a care, upon this point, how you provoke me to spew my justification!"

"Ah!" cried Cecilia, blushing, "'tis some trick of Lady Honoria!"

"No, upon my honour. The authority is less doubtful; I believe I should hardly else have regarded it."

Cecilia, much alarmed, held out her hand for the letter; and looking first at the end was much astonished to see the name of Biddulph. She then cast her eye over the beginning, and when she saw her own name, read the following paragraph.

"Miss Beverley, as you doubtless know, is returned into Suffolk; every body here saw her with the utmost surprize; from the moment I had heard of her residence in Delvile Castle, I had given her up for lost; but, upon her unexpected appearance among us again, I was weak enough once more to make trial of her heart. I soon found, however, that the pain of a second rejection you might have spared me, and that though she had quitted Delvile Castle, she had not for nothing entered it; at the sound of your name, she blushes; at the mention of your illness, she turns pale; and the dog you have given her, which I recollected immediately, is her darling companion. Oh happy Delvile! yet so lovely a conquest you abandon.—"

Cecilia could read no more; the letter dropt from her hand; to find herself thus by her own emotions betrayed, made her instantly conclude she was universally discovered; and turning sick at the supposition, all her spirit forsook her, and she burst into tears.

"Good heaven," cried Delvile, extremely shocked, "what has thus affected you? Can the jealous surmises of an apprehensive rival—"

"Do not talk to me," interrupted she, impatiently, "and do not detain me,—I am extremely disturbed,—I wish to be alone,—I beg, I even entreat you would leave me."

"I will go, I will obey you in every thing!" cried he, eagerly, "tell me but when I may return, and when you will suffer me to explain to you all the motives of my proposal?"

"Never, never!" cried she, with earnestness, "I am sufficiently lowered already, but never will I intrude myself into a family that disdains me!"

"Disdains? No, you are revered in it! who could disdain you! That fatal clause alone—"

"Well, well, pray leave me; indeed I cannot hear you; I am unfit for argument, and all reasoning now is nothing less than cruelty."

"I am gone," cried he, "this moment! I would not even wish to take advantage of your agitation in order to work upon your sensibility. My desire is not to surprize, but to reconcile you to my plan. What is it I seek in Miss Beverley? An Heiress? No, as such she has seen I could resist her; nor yet the light trifler of a spring or two, neglected when no longer a novelty; no, no!—it is a companion for ever, it is a solace for every care, it is a bosom friend through every period of life that I seek in Miss Beverley! Her esteem, therefore, to me is as precious as her affection, for how can I hope her friendship in the winter of my days, if their brighter and gayer season is darkened by doubts of my integrity? All shall be clear and explicit; no latent cause of uneasiness shall disturb our future quiet; we will now be sincere, that hereafter we may be easy; and sweetly in unclouded felicity, time shall glide away imperceptibly, and we will make an interest with each other in the gaiety of youth, to bear with the infirmities of age, and alleviate them by kindness and sympathy. And then shall my soothing Cecilia—"

"O say no more!" interrupted she, softened in her own despite by a plan so consonant to her wishes, "what language is this! how improper for you to use, or me to hear!"

She then very earnestly insisted upon his going; and after a thousand times taking leave and returning, promising obedience, yet pursuing his own way, he at length said if she would consent to receive a letter from him, he would endeavour to commit what he had to communicate to paper, since their mutual agitation made him unable to explain himself with clearness, and rather hurt his cause than assisted it, by leaving all his arguments unfinished and obscure.

Another dispute now arose; Cecilia protesting she would receive no letter, and hear nothing upon the subject; and Delvile impetuously declaring he would submit to no award without being first heard. At length he conquered, and at length he departed.

Cecilia then felt her whole heart sink within her at the unhappiness of her situation. She considered herself now condemned to refuse Delvile herself, as the only condition upon which he even solicited her favour, neither the strictness of her principles, nor the delicacy of her mind, would suffer her to accept. Her displeasure at the proposal had been wholly unaffected, and she regarded it as an injury to her character ever to have received it; yet that Delvile's pride of heart should give way to his passion, that he should love her with so much fondness as to relinquish for her the ambitious schemes of his family, and even that darling name which so lately seemed annexed to his existence, were circumstances to which she was not insensible, and proofs of tenderness and regard which she had thought incompatible with the general spirit of his disposition. Yet however by these she was gratified, she resolved never to comply with so humiliating a measure, but to wait the consent of his friends, or renounce him for ever.

CHAPTER V

A LETTER.

As soon as Mrs Charlton was acquainted with the departure of young Delvile, she returned to Cecilia, impatient to be informed what had passed. The narration she heard both hurt and astonished her; that Cecilia, the Heiress of such a fortune, the possessor of so much beauty, descended of a worthy family, and formed and educated to grace a noble one, should be rejected by people to whom her wealth would be most useful, and only in secret have their alliance proposed to her, she deemed an indignity that called for nothing but resentment, and approved and enforced the resolution of her young friend to resist all solicitations which Mr and Mrs Delvile did not second themselves.

About, two hours after Delvile was gone, his letter arrived. Cecilia opened it with trepidation, and read as follows.

To Miss Beverley.

September 20, 1779.

What could be the apprehensions, the suspicions of Miss Beverley when so earnestly she prohibited my writing? From a temper so unguarded as mine could she fear any subtlety of doctrine? Is my character so little known to her that she can think me capable of craft or duplicity? Had I even the desire, I have neither the address nor the patience to practice them; no, loveliest Miss Beverley, though sometimes by vehemence I may incautiously offend, by sophistry, believe me, I never shall injure; my ambition, as I have told you, is to convince, not beguile, and my arguments shall be simple as my professions shall be sincere.

Yet how again may I venture to mention a proposal which so lately almost before you had heard you rejected? Suffer me, however, to assure you it resulted neither from insensibility to your delicacy, nor to my own duty; I made it, on the contrary, with that reluctance and timidity which were given me by an apprehension that both seemed to be offended by it;—but alas! already I have said what with grief I must repeat, I have no resource, no alternative, between receiving the honour of your hand in secret or foregoing you for ever.

You will wonder, you may well wonder at such a declaration; and again that severe renunciation with which you wounded me, will tremble on your lips,—Oh there let it stop! nor let the air again be agitated with sounds so discordant!

In that cruel and heart-breaking moment when I tore myself from you at Delvile Castle, I confessed to you the reason of my flight, and I determined to see you no more. I named not to you, then, my family, the potency of my own objections against daring to solicit your favour rendering theirs immaterial; my own are now wholly removed, but theirs remain in full force.

My father, descended of a race which though decaying in wealth, is unsubdued in pride, considers himself as the guardian of the honour of his house, to which he holds the name of his ancestors inseparably annexed; my mother, born of the same family, and bred to the same ideas, has strengthened this opinion by giving it the sanction of her own.

Such being their sentiments; you will not, madam, be surprised that their only son, the sole inheritor of their fortune, and sole object of their expectations, should early have admitted the same. Indeed almost the first lesson I was taught was that of reverencing the family from which I am descended, and the name to which I am born. I was bid consider myself as its only remaining support, and sedulously instructed neither to act nor think but with a view to its aggrandizement and dignity.

Thus, unchecked by ourselves, and uncontrouled by the world, this haughty self-importance acquired by time a strength, and by mutual encouragement a firmness, which Miss Beverley alone could possibly, I believe, have shaken! What, therefore, was my secret alarm, when first I was conscious of the force of her attractions, and found my mind wholly occupied with admiration of her excellencies! All that pride could demand, and all to which ambition could aspire, all that happiness could covet, or the most scrupulous delicacy exact, in her I found united; and while my heart was enslaved by her charms, my understanding exulted in its fetters. Yet to forfeit my name, to give up for-ever a family which upon me rested its latest expectations,—Honour, I thought forbad it, propriety and manly spirit revolted at the sacrifice. The renunciation of my birth-right seemed a desertion of the post in which I was stationed; I forbore, therefore, even in my wishes, to solicit your favour, and vigorously determined to fly you as dangerous to my peace, because unattainable without dishonour.

Such was the intended regulation of my conduct at the time I received Biddulph's letter; in three days I was to leave England; my father, with much persuasion, had consented to my departure; my mother, who penetrated into my motives, had never opposed it; but how great was the change wrought upon my mind by reading that letter! my steadiness forsook me, my resolution wavered; yet I thought him deceived, and attributed his suspicions to jealousy; but still, Fidel I knew was missing—and to hear he was your darling companion—was it possible to quit England in a state of such uncertainty? to be harassed in distant climates with conjectures I might then never satisfy? No; I told my friends I must visit Biddulph before I left the kingdom, and promising to return to them in three or four days, I hastily set out for Suffolk, and rested not till I arrived at Mrs Charlton's.

What a scene there awaited me! to behold the loved mistress of my heart, the opposed, yet resistless object of my fondest admiration, caressing an animal she knew to be mine, mourning over him his master's ill health, and sweetly recommending to him fidelity,—Ah! forgive the retrospection, I will dwell on it no longer. Little, indeed, had I imagined with what softness the dignity of Miss Beverley was blended, though always conscious that her virtues, her attractions, and her excellencies, would reflect lustre upon the highest station to which human grandeur could raise her, and would still be more exalted than her rank, though that were the most eminent upon earth.—And had there been a thousand, and ten thousand obstacles to oppose my addressing her, vigorously and undauntedly would I have combated with them all, in preference to yielding to this single objection!

Let not the frankness of this declaration irritate you, but rather let it serve to convince you of the sincerity of what follows; various as are the calamities of life which may render me miserable, YOU only, among even its chosen felicities, have power to make me happy. Fame, honours, wealth, ambition, were insufficient without you; all chance of internal peace, and every softer hope is now centered in your favour, and to lose you, from whatever cause, ensures me wretchedness unmitigated. With respect therefore to myself, the die is finally cast, and the conflict between bosom felicity and family pride is deliberately over. This name which so vainly I have cherished and so painfully supported, I now find inadequate to recompense me for the sacrifice which its preservation requires. I part with it, I own, with regret that the surrender is necessary; yet is it rather an imaginary than an actual evil, and though a deep wound to pride, no offence to morality.

Thus have I laid open to you my whole heart, confessed my perplexities, acknowledged my vain-glory, and exposed with equal sincerity the sources of my doubts, and the motives of my decision; but now, indeed, how to proceed I know not; the difficulties which are yet to encounter I fear to enumerate, and the petition I have to urge I have scarce courage to mention.

My family, mistaking ambition for honour, and rank for dignity, have long planned a splendid connection for me, to which though my invariable repugnance has stopt any advances, their wishes and their views immovably adhere. I am but too certain they will now listen to no other. I dread, therefore, to make a trial where I despair of success, I know not how to risk a prayer with those who may silence me by a command.

In a situation so desperate, what then remains? Must I make an application with a certainty of rejection, and then mock all authority by acting in defiance of it? Or, harder task yet! relinquish my dearest hopes when no longer persuaded of their impropriety? Ah! sweetest Miss Beverley, end the struggle at once! My happiness, my peace, are wholly in your power, for the moment of our union secures them for life.

It may seem to you strange that I should thus purpose to brave the friends whom I venture not to entreat; but from my knowledge of their characters and sentiments I am certain I have no other resource. Their favourite principles were too early imbibed to be now at this late season eradicated. Slaves that we all are to habits, and dupes to appearances, jealous guardians of our pride, to which our comfort is sacrificed, and even our virtue made subservient, what conviction can be offered by reason, to notions that exist but by prejudice? They have been cherished too long for rhetorick to remove them, they can only be expelled by all-powerful Necessity. Life is, indeed, too brief, and success too precarious, to trust, in any case where happiness is concerned, the extirpation of deep-rooted and darling opinions, to the slow-working influence of argument and disquisition.

Yet bigotted as they are to rank and family, they adore Miss Beverley, and though their consent to the forfeiture of their name might forever be denied, when once they beheld her the head and ornament of their house, her elegance and accomplishments joined to the splendour of her fortune, would speedily make them forget the plans which now wholly absorb them. Their sense of honour is in nothing inferior to their sense of high birth; your condescension, therefore, would be felt by them in its fullest force, and though, during their first surprize, they might be irritated against their son, they would make it the study of their lives that the lady who for him had done so much, should never, through their means, repine for herself.

With regard to settlements, the privacy of our union would not affect them; one Confident we must unavoidably trust, and I would deposit in the hands of whatever person you would name, a bond by which I would engage myself to settle both your fortune and my own, according to the arbitration of our mutual friends. The time for secrecy though painful would be short, and even from the altar, if you desired it, I would hasten to Delvile Castle. Not one of my friends should you see till they waited upon you themselves to solicit your presence at their house, till our residence elsewhere was fixed.

Oh loveliest Cecilia, from a dream Of happiness so sweet awaken me not! from a plan Of felicity so attractive turn not away! If one part of it is unpleasant, reject not therefore all; and since without some drawback no earthly bliss is attainable, do not, by a refinement too scrupulous for the short period of our existence, deny yourself that delight which your benevolence will afford you, in snatching from the pangs of unavailing regret and misery, the gratefullest of men in the humblest and most devoted of your servants, MORTIMER DELVILE.

Cecilia read and re-read this letter, but with a perturbation of mind that made her little able to weigh its contents. Paragraph by paragraph her sentiments varied, and her determination was changed; the earnestness of his supplication now softened her into compliance, the acknowledged pride of his family now irritated her into resentment, and the confession of his own regret now sickened her into despondence. She meant in an immediate answer, to have written a final dismission; but though proof against his entreaties, because not convinced by his arguments, there was something in the conclusion of his letter that staggered her resolution.

Those scruples and that refinement against which he warned her, she herself thought might be overstrained, and to gratify unnecessary punctilio, the short period of existence be rendered causelessly unhappy. He had truly said that their union would be no offence to morality, and with respect merely to pride, why should that be spared? He knew he possessed her heart, she had long been certain of his, her character had early gained the affection of his mother, and the essential service which an income such as hers must do the family, would soon be felt too powerfully to make her connection with it regretted.

These reflections were so pleasant she knew not how to discard them; and the consciousness that her secret was betrayed not only to himself, but to Mr Biddulph, Lord Ernolf, Lady Honoria Pemberton, and Mrs Delvile, gave them additional force, by making it probable she was yet more widely suspected. But still her delicacy and her principles revolted against a conduct of which the secrecy seemed to imply the impropriety. "How shall I meet Mrs Delvile," cried she, "after an action so clandestine? How, after praise such as she has bestowed upon me, bear the severity of her eye, when she thinks I have seduced from her the obedience of her son! A son who is the sole solace and first hope of her existence, whose virtues make all her happiness, and whose filial piety is her only glory!—And well may she glory in a son such as Delvile! Nobly has he exerted himself in situations the most difficult, his family and his ideas of honour he has preferred to his peace and health, he has fulfilled with spirit and integrity the various, the conflicting duties of life. Even now, perhaps, in his present application, he may merely think himself bound by knowing me no longer free, and his generous sensibility to the weakness he has discovered, without any of the conviction to which he pretends, may have occasioned this proposal!"

A suggestion so mortifying again changed her determination; and the tears of Henrietta Belfield, with the letter which she had surprized in her hand recurring to her memory, all her thoughts turned once more upon rejecting him for-ever.

In this fluctuating state of mind she found writing impracticable; while uncertain what to wish, to decide was impossible. She disdained coquetry, she was superior to trifling, the candour and openness of Delvile had merited all her sincerity, and therefore while any doubt remained, with herself, she held it unworthy her character to tell him she had none.

Mrs Charlton, upon reading the letter, became again the advocate of Delvile; the frankness with which he had stated his difficulties assured her of his probity, and by explaining his former conduct, satisfied her with the rectitude of his future intentions. "Do not, therefore, my dear child," cried she, "become the parent of your own misery by refusing him; he deserves you alike from his principles and his affection, and the task would both be long and melancholy to disengage him from your heart. I see not, however, the least occasion for the disgrace of a private marriage; I know not any family to which you would not be an honour, and those who feel not your merit, are little worth pleasing. Let Mr Delvile, therefore, apply openly to his friends, and if they refuse their consent, be their prejudices their reward. You are freed from all obligations where caprice only can raise objections, and you may then, in the face of the world, vindicate your choice."

The wishes of Cecilia accorded with this advice, though the general tenour of Delvile's letter gave her little reason to expect he would follow it.

CHAPTER VI

A DISCUSSION.

The day past away, and Cecilia had yet written no answer; the evening came, and her resolution was still unfixed. Delvile, at length, was again announced; and though she dreaded trusting herself to his entreaties, the necessity of hastening some decision deterred her from refusing to see him.

Mrs Charlton was with her when he entered the room; he attempted at first some general conversation, though the anxiety of his mind was strongly pictured upon his face. Cecilia endeavoured also to talk upon common topics, though her evident embarrassment spoke the absence of her thoughts.

Delvile at length, unable any longer to bear suspence, turned to Mrs Charlton, and said, "You are probably acquainted, madam, with the purport of the letter I had the honour of sending to Miss Beverley this morning?"

"Yes, Sir," answered the old lady, "and you need desire little more than that her opinion of it may be as favourable as mine."

Delvile bowed and thanked her; and looking at Cecilia, to whom he ventured not to speak, he perceived in her countenance a mixture of dejection and confusion, that told him whatever might be her opinion, it had by no means encreased her happiness.

"But why, Sir," said Mrs Charlton, "should you be thus sure of the disapprobation of your friends? had you not better hear what they have to say?"

"I know, madam, what they have to say," returned he; "for their language and their principles have been invariable from my birth; to apply to them, therefore, for a concession which I am certain they will not grant, were only a cruel device to lay all my misery to their account."

"And if they are so perverse, they deserve from you nothing better," said Mrs Charlton; "speak to them, however; you will then have done your duty; and if they are obstinately unjust, you will have acquired a right to act for yourself."

"To mock their authority," answered Delvile, "would be more offensive than to oppose it; to solicit their approbation, and then act in defiance of it, might justly provoke their indignation.—No; if at last I am reduced to appeal to them, by their decision I must abide."

To this Mrs Charlton could make no answer, and in a few minutes she left the room.

"And is such, also," said Delvile, "the opinion of Miss Beverley? has she doomed me to be wretched, and does she wish that doom to be signed by my nearest friends!"

"If your friends, Sir," said Cecilia, "are so undoubtedly inflexible, it were madness, upon any plan, to risk their displeasure."

"To entreaty," he answered, "they will be inflexible, but not to forgiveness. My father, though haughty, dearly, even passionately loves me; my mother, though high-spirited, is just, noble, and generous. She is, indeed, the most exalted of women, and her power over my mind I am unaccustomed to resist. Miss Beverley alone seems born to be her daughter—"

"No, no," interrupted Cecilia, "as her daughter she rejects me!"

"She loves, she adores you!" cried he warmly; "and were I not certain she feels your excellencies as they ought to be felt, my veneration for you both should even yet spare you my present supplication. But you would become, I am certain, the first blessing of her life; in you she would behold all the felicity of her son,—his restoration to health, to his country, to his friends!"

"O Sir," cried Cecilia, with emotion, "how deep a trench of real misery do you sink, in order to raise this pile of fancied happiness! But I will not be responsible for your offending such a mother; scarcely can you honour her yourself more than I do; and I here declare most solemnly—"

"O stop!" interrupted Delvile, "and resolve not till you have heard me. Would you, were she no more, were my father also no more, would you yet persist in refusing me?"

"Why should you ask me?" said Cecilia, blushing; "you would then be your own agent, and perhaps—"

She hesitated, and Delvile vehemently exclaimed, "Oh make me not a monster! force me not to desire the death of the very beings by whom I live! weaken not the bonds of affection by which they are endeared to me, and compel me not to wish them no more as the sole barriers to my happiness!"

"Heaven forbid!" cried Cecilia, "could I believe you so impious, I should suffer little indeed in desiring your eternal absence."

"Why then only upon their extinction must I rest my hope of your favour?"

Cecilia, staggered and distressed by this question, could make no answer. Delvile, perceiving her embarrassment, redoubled his urgency; and before she had power to recollect herself, she had almost consented to his plan, when Henrietta Belfield rushing into her memory, she hastily exclaimed, "One doubt there is, which I know not how to mention, but ought to have cleared up;—you are acquainted with—you remember Miss Belfield?"

"Certainly; but what of Miss Belfield that can raise a doubt in the mind of Miss Beverley?"

Cecilia coloured, and was silent.

"Is it possible," continued he, "you could ever for an instant suppose—but I cannot even name a supposition so foreign to all possibility."

"She is surely very amiable?"

"Yes," answered he, "she is innocent, gentle, and engaging; and I heartily wish she were in a better situation."

"Did you ever occasionally, or by any accident, correspond with her?"

"Never in my life."

"And were not your visits to the brother sometimes—"

"Have a care," interrupted he, laughing, "lest I reverse the question, and ask if your visits to the sister were not sometimes for the brother! But what does this mean? Could Miss Beverley imagine that after knowing her, the charms of Miss Belfield could put me in any danger?"

Cecilia, bound in delicacy and friendship not to betray the tender and trusting Henrietta, and internally satisfied of his innocence by his frankness, evaded any answer; and would now have done with the subject; but Delvile, eager wholly to exculpate himself, though by no means displeased at an enquiry which shewed so much interest in his affections, continued his explanation.

"Miss Belfield has, I grant, an attraction in the simplicity of her manners which charms by its singularity; her heart, too, seems all purity, and her temper all softness. I have not, you find, been blind to her merit; on the contrary, I have both admired and pitied her. But far indeed is she removed from all chance of rivalry in my heart! A character such as hers for a while is irresistibly alluring; but when its novelty is over, simplicity uninformed becomes wearisome, and softness without dignity is too indiscriminate to give delight. We sigh for entertainment, when cloyed by mere sweetness; and heavily drags on the load of life when the companion of our social hours wants spirit, intelligence, and cultivation. With Miss Beverley all these—"

"Talk not of all these," cried Cecilia, "when one single obstacle has power to render them valueless."

"But now," cried he, "that obstacle is surmounted."

"Surmounted only for a moment! for even in your letter this morning you confess the regret with which it fills you."

"And why should I deceive you? Why pretend to think with pleasure, or even with indifference, of an obstacle which has had thus long the power to make me miserable? But where is happiness without allay? Is perfect bliss the condition of humanity? Oh if we refuse to taste it till in its last state of refinement, how shall the cup of evil be ever from our lips?"

"How indeed!" said Cecilia, with a sigh; "the regret, I believe, will remain eternally upon your mind, and she, perhaps, who should cause, might soon be taught to partake of it."

"O Miss Beverley! how have I merited this severity? Did I make my proposals lightly? Did I suffer my eagerness to conquer my reason? Have I not, on the contrary, been steady and considerate? neither biassed by passion nor betrayed by tenderness?"

"And yet in what," said Cecilia, "consists this boasted steadiness? I perceived it indeed, at Delvile Castle, but here—"

"The pride of heart which supported me there," cried he, "will support me no longer; what sustained my firmness, but your apparent severity? What enabled me to fly you, but your invariable coldness? The rigour with which I trampled upon my feelings I thought fortitude and spirit,—but I knew not then the pitying sympathy of Cecilia!"

"O that you knew it not yet!" cried she, blushing; "before that fatal accident you thought of me, I believe, in a manner far more honourable."

"Impossible! differently, I thought of you, but never, better, never so well as now. I then represented you all lovely in beauty, all perfect in goodness and virtue; but it was virtue in its highest majesty, not, as now, blended with the softest sensibility."

"Alas!" said Cecilia, "how the portrait is faded!"

"No, it is but more from the life; it is the sublimity of an angel, mingled with all that is attractive in woman. But who is the friend we may venture to trust? To whom may I give my bond? And from whom may I receive a treasure which for the rest of my life will constitute all its felicity?"

"Where can I," cried Cecilia, "find a friend, who, in this critical moment will instruct me how to act!"

"You will find one," answered he, "in your own bosom; ask but yourself this plain question; will any virtue be offended by your honouring me with your hand?"

"Yes; duty will be offended, since it is contrary to the will of your parents."

"But is there no time for emancipation? Am not I of an age to chuse for myself the partner of my life? Will not you in a few days be the uncontrolled mistress of your actions? Are we not both independent? Your ample fortune all your own, and the estates of my father so entailed they must unavoidably be mine?"

"And are these," said Cecilia, "considerations to set us free from our duty?"

"No, but they are circumstances to relieve us from slavery. Let me not offend you if I am still more explicit. When no law, human or divine, can be injured by our union, when one motive of pride is all that can be opposed to a thousand motives of convenience and happiness, why should we both be made unhappy, merely lest that pride should lose its gratification?"

This question, which so often and so angrily she had revolved in her own mind, again silenced her; and Delvile, with the eagerness of approaching success, redoubled his solicitations.

"Be mine," he cried, "sweetest Cecilia, and all will go well. To refer me to my friends is, effectually, to banish me for ever. Spare me, then, the unavailing task; and save me from the resistless entreaties of a mother, whose every desire I have held sacred, whose wish has been my law, and whose commands I have implicitly, invariably obeyed! Oh generously save me from the dreadful alternative of wounding her maternal heart by a peremptory refusal, or of torturing my own with pangs to which it is unequal by an extorted obedience!"

"Alas!" cried Cecilia, "how utterly impossible I can relieve you!"

"And why? once mine, irrevocably mine—."

"No, that would but irritate,—and irritate past hope of pardon."

"Indeed you are mistaken; to your merit they are far from insensible, and your fortune is just what they wish. Trust me, therefore, when I assure you that their displeasure, which both respect and justice will guard them from ever shewing you, will soon die wholly away. I speak not merely from my hopes; in judging my own friends, I consider human nature in general. Inevitable evils are ever best supported. It is suspence, it is hope that make the food of misery; certainty is always endured, because known to be past amendment, and felt to give defiance to struggling."

"And can you," cried Cecilia, "with reasoning so desperate be satisfied?

"In a situation so extraordinary as ours," answered he, "there is no other. The voice of the world at large will be all in our favour. Our union neither injures our fortunes, nor taints our morality; with the character of each the other is satisfied, and both must be alike exculpated from mercenary views of interest, or romantic contempt of poverty; what right have we, then, to repine at an objection which, however potent, is single? Surely none. Oh if wholly unchecked were the happiness I now have in view, if no foul storm sometimes lowered over the prospect, and for the moment obscured its brightness, how could my heart find room for joy so superlative? The whole world might rise against me as the first man in it who had nothing left to wish!"

Cecilia, whose own hopes aided this reasoning, found not much to oppose to it; and with little more of entreaty, and still less of argument, Delvile at length obtained her consent to his plan. Fearfully, indeed, and with unfeigned reluctance she gave it, but it was the only alternative with a separation for-ever, to which she held not the necessity adequate to the pain.

The thanks of Delvile were as vehement as had been his entreaties, which yet, however, were not at an end; the concession she had made was imperfect, unless its performance were immediate, and he now endeavoured to prevail with her to be his before the expiration of a week.

Here, however, his task ceased to be difficult; Cecilia, as ingenuous by nature as she was honourable from principle, having once brought her mind to consent to his proposal, sought not by studied difficulties to enhance the value of her compliance; the great point resolved upon, she held all else of too little importance for a contest.

Mrs Charlton was now called in, and acquainted with the result of their conference. Her approbation by no means followed the scheme of privacy; yet she was too much rejoiced in seeing her young friend near the period of her long suspence and uneasiness, to oppose any plan which might forward their termination.

Delvile then again begged to know what male confidant might be entrusted with their project.

Mr Monckton immediately occurred to Cecilia, though the certainty of his ill-will to the cause made all application to him disagreeable; but his long and steady friendship for her, his readiness to counsel and assist her, and the promises she had occasionally made, not to act without his advice, all concurred to persuade her that in a matter of such importance, she owed to him her confidence, and should be culpable to proceed without it. Upon him, therefore, she fixed; yet finding in herself a repugnance insuperable to acquainting him with her situation, she agreed that Delvile, who instantly proposed to be her messenger, should open to him the affair, and prepare him for their meeting.

Delvile then, rapid in thought and fertile in expedients, with a celerity and vigour which bore down all objections, arranged the whole conduct of the business. To avoid suspicion, he determined instantly to quit her, and, as soon as he had executed his commission with Mr Monckton, to hasten to London, that the necessary preparations for their marriage might be made with dispatch and secrecy. He purposed, also, to find out Mr Belfield; that he might draw up the bond with which he meant to entrust Mr Monckton. This measure Cecilia would have opposed, but he refused to listen to her. Mrs Charlton herself, though her age and infirmities had long confined her to her own house, gratified Cecilia upon this critical occasion with consenting to accompany her to the altar. Mr Monckton was depended upon for giving her away, and a church in London was the place appointed for the performance of the ceremony. In three days the principal difficulties to the union would be removed by Cecilia's coming of age, and in five days it was agreed that they should actually meet in town. The moment they were married Delvile promised to set off for the castle, while in another chaise, Cecilia returned to Mrs Charlton's. This settled, he conjured her to be punctual, and earnestly recommending himself to her fidelity and affection, he bid her adieu.

CHAPTER VII

A RETROSPECTION.

Left now to herself, sensations unfelt before filled the heart of Cecilia. All that had passed for a while appeared a dream; her ideas were indistinct, her memory was confused, her faculties seemed all out of order, and she had but an imperfect consciousness either of the transaction in which she had just been engaged, or of the promise she had bound herself to fulfil; even truth from imagination she scarcely could separate; all was darkness and doubt, inquietude and disorder!

But when at length her recollection more clearly returned, and her situation appeared to her such as it really was, divested alike of false terrors or delusive expectations, she found herself still further removed from tranquility.

Hitherto, though no stranger to sorrow, which the sickness and early loss of her friends had first taught her to feel, and which the subsequent anxiety of her own heart had since instructed her to bear, she had yet invariably possessed the consolation of self-approving reflections; but the step she was now about to take, all her principles opposed; it terrified her as undutiful, it shocked her as clandestine, and scarce was Delvile out of sight, before she regretted her consent to it as the loss of her self-esteem, and believed, even if a reconciliation took place, the remembrance of a wilful fault would still follow her, blemish in her own eyes the character she had hoped to support, and be a constant allay to her happiness, by telling her how unworthily she had obtained it.

Where frailty has never been voluntary, nor error stubborn, where the pride of early integrity is unsubdued, and the first purity of innocence is inviolate, how fearfully delicate, how "tremblingly alive," is the conscience of man! strange, that what in its first state is so tender, can in its last become so callous!

Compared with the general lot of human misery, Cecilia had suffered nothing; but compared with the exaltation of ideal happiness, she had suffered much; willingly, however, would she again have borne all that had distressed her, experienced the same painful suspence, endured the same melancholy parting, and gone through the same cruel task of combating inclination with reason, to have relieved her virtuous mind from the new-born and intolerable terror of conscientious reproaches.

The equity of her notions permitted her not from the earnestness of Delvile's entreaties to draw any palliation for her consent to his proposal; she was conscious that but for her own too great facility those entreaties would have been ineffectual, since she well knew how little from any other of her admirers they would have availed.

But chiefly her affliction and repentance hung upon Mrs Delvile, whom she loved, reverenced and honoured, whom she dreaded to offend, and whom she well knew expected from her even exemplary virtue. Her praises, her partiality, her confidence in her character, which hitherto had been her pride, she now only recollected with shame and with sadness. The terror of the first interview never ceased to be present to her; she shrunk even in imagination from her wrath-darting eye, she felt stung by pointed satire, and subdued by cold contempt.

Yet to disappoint Delvile so late, by forfeiting a promise so positively accorded; to trifle with a man who to her had been uniformly candid, to waver when her word was engaged, and retract when he thought himself secure,—honour, justice and shame told her the time was now past.

"And yet is not this," cried she, "placing nominal before actual evil? Is it not studying appearance at the expence of reality? If agreeing to wrong is criminal, is not performing it worse? If repentance for ill actions calls for mercy, has not repentance for ill intentions a yet higher claim?—And what reproaches from Delvile can be so bitter as my own? What separation, what sorrow, what possible calamity can hang upon my mind with such heaviness, as the sense of committing voluntary evil?"

This thought so much affected her, that, conquering all regret either for Delvile or herself, she resolved to write to him instantly, and acquaint him of the alteration in her sentiments.

This, however, after having so deeply engaged herself, was by no means easy; and many letters were begun, but not one of them was finished, when a sudden recollection obliged her to give over the attempt,—for she knew not whither to direct to him.

In the haste with which their plan had been formed and settled, it had never once occurred to them that any, occasion for writing was likely to happen. Delvile, indeed, knew that her address would still be the same; and with regard to his own, as his journey to London was to be secret, he purposed not having any fixed habitation. On the day of their marriage, and not before, they had appointed to meet at the house of Mrs Roberts, in Fetter-Lane, whence they were instantly to proceed to the church.

She might still, indeed, enclose a letter for him in one to Mrs Hill, to be delivered to him on the destined morning when he called to claim her; but to fail him at the last moment, when Mr Belfield would have drawn up the bond, when a licence was procured, the clergyman waiting to perform the ceremony, and Delvile without a suspicion but that the next moment would unite them for ever, seemed extending prudence into treachery, and power into tyranny. Delvile had done nothing to merit such treatment, he had practised no deceit, he had been guilty of no perfidy, he had opened to her his whole heart, and after shewing it without any disguise, the option had been all her own to accept or refuse him.

A ray of joy now broke its way through the gloom of her apprehensions. "Ah!" cried she, "I have not, then, any means to recede! an unprovoked breach of promise at the very moment destined for its performance, would but vary the mode of acting wrong, without approaching nearer to acting right!"

This idea for a while not merely calmed but delighted her; to be the wife of Delvile seemed now a matter of necessity, and she soothed herself with believing that to struggle against it were vain.

The next morning during breakfast Mr Monckton arrived.

Not greater, though winged with joy, had been the expedition of Delvile to open to him his plan, than was his own, though only goaded by desperation, to make some effort with Cecilia for rendering it abortive. Nor could all his self-denial, the command which he held over his passions, nor the rigour with which his feelings were made subservient to his interest, in this sudden hour of trial, avail to preserve his equanimity. The refinements of hypocrisy, and the arts of insinuation, offered advantages too distant, and exacted attentions too subtle, for a moment so alarming; those arts and those attentions he had already for many years practised, with an address the most masterly, and a diligence the most indefatigable; success had of late seemed to follow his toils; the encreasing infirmities of his wife, the disappointment and retirement of Cecilia, uniting to promise him a conclusion equally speedy and happy; when now, by a sudden and unexpected stroke, the sweet solace of his future cares, the long-projected recompence of his past sufferings, was to be snatched from him for ever, and by one who, compared with himself, was but the acquaintance of a day.

Almost wholly off his guard from the surprise and horror of this apprehension, he entered the room with such an air of haste and perturbation, that Mrs Charlton and her grand-daughters demanded what was the matter.

"I am come," he answered abruptly, yet endeavouring to recollect himself, "to speak with Miss Beverley upon business of some importance."

"My dear, then," said Mrs Charlton, "you had better go with Mr Monckton into your dressing-room."

Cecilia, deeply blushing, arose and led the way; slowly, however, she proceeded, though urged by Mr Monckton to make speed. Certain of his disapprobation, and but doubtfully relieved from her own, she dreaded a conference which on his side, she foresaw, would be all exhortation and reproof, and on hers all timidity and shame.

"Good God," cried he, "Miss Beverley, what is this you have done? bound yourself to marry a man who despises, who scorns, who refuses to own you!"

Shocked by this opening, she started, but could make no answer.

"See you not," he continued, "the indignity which is offered you? Does the loose, the flimsy veil with which it is covered, hide it from your understanding, or disguise it from your delicacy?"

"I thought not,—I meant not," said she, more and more confounded, "to submit to any indignity, though my pride, in an exigence so peculiar, may give way, for a while, to convenience."

"To convenience?" repeated he, "to contempt, to derision, to insolence!"—

"O Mr Monckton!" interrupted Cecilia, "make not use of such expressions! they are too cruel for me to hear, and if I thought they were just, would make me miserable for life!"

"You are deceived, grossly deceived," replied he, "if you doubt their truth for a moment; they are not, indeed, even decently concealed from you; they are glaring as the day, and wilful blindness can alone obscure them."

"I am sorry, Sir," said Cecilia, whose confusion, at a charge so rough, began now to give way to anger, "if this is your opinion; and I am sorry, too, for the liberty I have taken in troubling you upon such a subject."

An apology so full of displeasure instantly taught Mr Monckton the error he was committing, and checking, therefore, the violence of those emotions to which his sudden and desperate disappointment gave rise, and which betrayed him into reproaches so unskilful, he endeavoured to recover his accustomed equanimity, and assuming an air of friendly openness, said, "Let me not offend you, my dear Miss Beverley, by a freedom which results merely from a solicitude to serve you, and which the length and intimacy of our acquaintance had, I hoped, long since authorised. I know not how to see you on the brink of destruction without speaking, yet, if you are averse to my sincerity, I will curb it, and have done."

"No, do not have done," cried she, much softened; "your sincerity does me nothing but honour, and hitherto, I am sure, it has done me nothing but good. Perhaps I deserve your utmost censure; I feared it, indeed, before you came, and ought, therefore, to have better prepared myself for meeting with it."

This speech completed Mr Monckton's self-victory; it shewed him not only the impropriety of his turbulence, but gave him room to hope that a mildness more crafty would have better success.

"You cannot but be certain," he answered, "that my zeal proceeds wholly from a desire to be of use to you; my knowledge of the world might possibly, I thought, assist your inexperience, and the disinterestedness of my regard, might enable me to see and to point out the dangers to which you are exposed, from artifice and duplicity in those who have other purposes to answer than what simply belong to your welfare."

"Neither artifice nor duplicity," cried Cecilia, jealous for the honour of Delvile, "have been practised against me. Argument, and not persuasion, determined me, and if I have done wrong—those who prompted me have erred as unwittingly as myself."

"You are too generous to perceive the difference, or you would find nothing less alike. If, however, my plainness will not offend you, before it is quite too late, I will point out to you a few of the evils,—for there are some I cannot even mention, which at this instant do not merely threaten, but await you."

Cecilia started at this terrifying offer, and afraid to accept, yet ashamed to refuse, hung back irresolute.

"I see," said Mr Monckton, after a pause of some continuance, "your determination admits no appeal. The consequence must, indeed, be all your own, but I am greatly grieved to find how little you are aware of its seriousness. Hereafter you will wish, perhaps, that the friend of your earliest youth had been permitted to advise you; at present you only think him officious and impertinent, and therefore he can do nothing you will be so likely to approve as quitting you. I wish you, then, greater happiness than seems prepared to follow you, and a counsellor more prosperous in offering his assistance."

He would then have taken his leave; but Cecilia called out, "Oh, Mr Monckton! do you then give me up?"

"Not unless you wish it."

"Alas, I know not what to wish! except, indeed, the restoration of that security from self-blame, which till yesterday, even in the midst of disappointment, quieted and consoled me."

"Are you, then, sensible you have gone wrong, yet resolute not to turn back?"

"Could I tell, could I see," cried she, with energy, "which way I ought to turn, not a moment would I hesitate how to act! my heart should have no power, my happiness no choice,—I would recover my own esteem by any sacrifice that could be made!"

"What, then, can possibly be your doubt? To be as you were yesterday what is wanting but your own inclination?"

"Every thing is wanting; right, honour, firmness, all by which the just are bound, and all which the conscientious hold sacred!"

"These scruples are merely romantic; your own good sense, had it fairer play, would contemn them; but it is warped at present by prejudice and prepossession."

"No, indeed!" cried she, colouring at the charge, "I may have entered too precipitately into an engagement I ought to have avoided, but it is weakness of judgment, not of heart, that disables me from retrieving my error."

"Yet you will neither hear whither it may lead you, nor which way you may escape from it?"

"Yes, Sir," cried she, trembling, "I am now ready to hear both."

"Briefly, then, I will tell you. It will lead you into a family of which every individual will disdain you; it will make you inmate of a house of which no other inmate will associate with you; you will be insulted as an inferior, and reproached as an intruder; your birth will be a subject of ridicule, and your whole race only named with derision; and while the elders of the proud castle treat you with open contempt, the man for whom you suffer will not dare to support you."

"Impossible! impossible!" cried Cecilia, with the most angry emotion; "this whole representation is exaggerated, and the latter part is utterly without foundation."

"The latter part," said Mr Monckton, "is of all other least disputable; the man who now dares not own, will then never venture to defend you. On the contrary, to make peace for himself, he will be the first to neglect you. The ruined estates of his ancestors will be repaired by your fortune, while the name which you carry into his family will be constantly resented as an injury; you will thus be plundered though you are scorned, and told to consider yourself honoured that they condescend to make use of you! nor here rests the evil of a forced connection with so much arrogance,—even your children, should you have any, will be educated to despise you!"

"Dreadful and horrible!" cried Cecilia;—"I can hear no more,—Oh, Mr Monckton, what a prospect have you opened to my view!"

"Fly from it, then, while it is yet in your power,—when two paths are before you, chuse not that which leads to destruction; send instantly after Delvile, and tell him you have recovered your senses."

"I would long since have sent,—I wanted not a representation such as this,—but I know not how to direct to him, nor whither he is gone."

"All art and baseness to prevent your recantation!"

"No, Sir, no," cried she, with quickness; "whatever may be the truth of your painting in general, all that concerns—"

Ashamed of the vindication she intended, which yet in her own mind was firm and animated, she stopt, and left the sentence unfinished.

"In what place were you to meet?" said Mr Monckton; "you can at least send to him there."

"We were only to have met," answered she, in much confusion, "at the last moment,—and that would be too late—it would be too—I could not, without some previous notice, break a promise which I gave without any restriction."

"Is this your only objection?"

"It is; but it is one which I cannot conquer."

"Then you would give up this ill-boding connection, but from notions of delicacy with regard to the time?"

"Indeed I meant it, before you came."

"I, then, will obviate this objection; give me but the commission, either verbally or in writing, and I will undertake to find him out, and deliver it before night."

Cecilia, little expecting this offer, turned extremely pale, and after pausing some moments, said in a faultering voice, "What, then, Sir, is your advice, in what manner—"

"I will say to him all that is necessary; trust the matter with me."

"No,—he deserves, at least, an apology from myself,—though how to make it—"

She stopt, she hesitated, she went out of the room for pen and ink, she returned without them, and the agitation of her mind every instant encreasing, she begged him, in a faint voice, to excuse her while she consulted with Mrs Charlton, and promising to wait upon him again, was hurrying away.

Mr Monckton, however, saw too great danger in so much emotion to trust her out of his sight; he told her, therefore, that she would only encrease her perplexity, without reaping any advantage, by an application to Mrs Charlton, and that if she was really sincere in wishing to recede, there was not a moment to be lost, and Delvile should immediately be pursued.

Cecilia, sensible of the truth of this speech, and once more recollecting the unaffected earnestness with which but an hour or two before, she had herself desired to renounce this engagement, now summoned her utmost courage to her aid, and, after a short, but painful struggle, determined to act consistently with her professions and her character, and, by one great and final effort, to conclude all her doubts, and try to silence even her regret, by completing the triumph of fortitude over inclination.

She called, therefore, for pen and ink, and without venturing herself from the room, wrote the following letter.

To Mortimer Delvile, Esq.

Accuse me not of caprice, and pardon my irresolution, when you find me shrinking with terror from the promise I have made, and no longer either able or willing to perform it. The reproaches of your family I should very ill endure; but the reproaches of my own heart for an action I can neither approve nor defend, would be still more oppressive. With such a weight upon the mind length of life would be burthensome; with a sensation of guilt early death would be terrific! These being my notions of the engagement into which we have entered, you cannot wonder, and you have still less reason to repine, that I dare not fulfil it. Alas! where would be your chance of happiness with one who in the very act of becoming yours would forfeit her own!

I blush at this tardy recantation, and I grieve at the disappointment it may occasion you; but I have yielded to the exhortations of an inward monitor, who is never to be neglected with impunity. Consult him yourself, and I shall need no other advocate. Adieu, and may all felicity attend you! if to hear of the almost total privation of mine, will mitigate the resentment with which you will probably read this letter, it may be mitigated but too easily! Yet my consent to a clandestine action shall never be repeated; and though I confess to you I am not happy, I solemnly declare my resolution is unalterable. A little reflection will tell you I am right, though a great deal of lenity may scarce suffice to make you pardon my being right no sooner. C. B.

This letter, which with trembling haste, resulting from a fear of her own steadiness, she folded and sealed, Mr Monckton, from the same apprehension yet more eagerly received, and scarce waiting to bid her good morning, mounted his horse, and pursued his way to London.

Cecilia returned to Mrs Charlton to acquaint her with what had passed; and notwithstanding the sorrow she felt in apparently injuring the man whom, in the whole world she most wished to oblige, she yet found a satisfaction in the sacrifice she had made, that recompensed her for much of her sufferings, and soothed her into something like tranquility; the true power of virtue she had scarce experienced before, for she found it a resource against the cruellest dejection, and a supporter in the bitterest disappointment.

CHAPTER VIII

AN EMBARRASSMENT.

The day passed on without any intelligence; the next day, also, passed in the same manner, and on the third, which was her birthday, Cecilia became of age.

The preparations which had long been making among her tenants to celebrate this event, Cecilia appeared to take some share, and endeavoured to find some pleasure in. She gave a public dinner to all who were willing to partake of it, she promised redress to those who complained of hard usage, she pardoned many debts, and distributed money, food, and clothing to the poor. These benevolent occupations made time seem less heavy, and while they freed her from solitude, diverted her suspense. She still, however, continued at the house of Mrs Charlton, the workmen having disappointed her in finishing her own.

But, in defiance of her utmost exertion, towards the evening of this day the uneasiness of her uncertainty grew almost intolerable. The next morning she had promised Delvile to set out for London, and he expected the morning after to claim her for his wife; yet Mr Monckton neither sent nor came, and she knew not if her letter was delivered, or if still he was unprepared for the disappointment by which he was awaited. A secret regret for the unhappiness she must occasion him, which silently yet powerfully reproached her, stole fast upon her mind, and poisoned its tranquility; for though her opinion was invariable in holding his proposal to be wrong, she thought too highly of his character to believe he would have made it but from a mistaken notion it was right. She painted him, therefore, to herself, as glowing with indignation, accusing her of inconsistency, and perhaps suspecting her of coquetry, and imputing her change of conduct to motives the most trifling and narrow, till with resentment and disdain, he drove her wholly from his thoughts.

In a few minutes, however, the picture was reversed; Delvile no more appeared storming nor unreasonable; his face wore an aspect of sorrow, and his brow was clouded with disappointment; he forbore to reproach her, but the look which her imagination delineated was more piercing than words of severest import.

These images pursued and tormented her, drew tears from her eyes, and loaded her heart with anguish. Yet, when she recollected that her conduct had had in view an higher motive than pleasing Delvile, she felt that it ought to offer her an higher satisfaction; she tried, therefore, to revive her spirits, by reflecting upon her integrity, and refused all indulgence to this enervating sadness, beyond what the weakness of human nature demands, as some relief to its sufferings upon every fresh attack of misery.

A conduct such as this was the best antidote against affliction, whose arrows are never with so little difficulty repelled, as when they light upon a conscience which no self-reproach has laid bare to their malignancy.

Before six o'clock the next morning, her maid came to her bedside with the following letter, which she told; her had been brought by an express.

To Miss Beverley.

May this letter, with one only from Delvile Castle, be the last that Miss Beverley may ever receive!

Yet sweet to me as is that hope, I write in the utmost uneasiness; I have just heard that a gentleman, whom, by the description that is given of him, I imagine is Mr Monckton, has been in search of me with a letter which he was anxious to deliver immediately.

Perhaps this letter is from Miss Beverley, perhaps it contains directions which ought instantly to be followed; could I divine what they are, with what eagerness would I study to anticipate their execution! It will not, I hope, be too late to receive them on Saturday, when her power over my actions will be confirmed, and when every wish she will communicate, shall be gratefully, joyfully, and with delight fulfilled.

I have sought Belfield in vain; he has left Lord Vannelt, and no one knows whither he is gone. I have been obliged, therefore, to trust a stranger to draw up the bond; but he is a man of good character, and the time of secrecy will be too short to put his discretion in much danger. To-morrow, Friday, I shall spend solely in endeavouring to discover. Mr Monckton; I have leisure sufficient for the search, since so prosperous has been my diligence, that every thing is prepared!

I have seen some lodgings in Pall-Mall, which I think are commodious and will suit you; send a servant, therefore, before you to secure them. If upon your arrival I should venture to meet you there, be not, I beseech you, offended or alarmed; I shall take every possible precaution neither to be known nor seen, and I will stay with you only three minutes. The messenger who carries this is ignorant from whom it comes, for I fear his repeating my name among your servants, and he could scarce return to me with an answer before you will yourself be in town. Yes, loveliest Cecilia! at the very moment you receive this letter, the chaise will, I flatter myself, be at the door, which is to bring to me a treasure that will enrich every future hour of my life! And oh as to me it will be exhaustless, may but its sweet dispenser experience some share of the happiness she bestows, and then what, save her own purity, will be so perfect, so unsullied, as the felicity of her! M.D.

The perturbation of Cecilia upon reading this letter was unspeakable; Mr Monckton, she found, had been wholly unsuccessful, all her heroism had answered no purpose, and the transaction was as backward as before she had exerted it.

She was, now, therefore, called upon to think and act entirely for herself. Her opinion was still the same, nor did her resolution waver, yet how to put it in execution she could not discern. To write to him was impossible, since she was ignorant where he was to be found; to disappoint him at the last moment she could not resolve, since such a conduct appeared to her unfeeling and unjustifiable; for a few instants she thought of having him waited for at night in London, with a letter; but the danger of entrusting any one with such a commission, and the uncertainty of finding him, should he disguise himself, made the success of this scheme too precarious for trial.

One expedient alone occurred to her, which, though she felt to be hazardous, she believed was without an alternative; this was no other than hastening to London herself, consenting to the interview he had proposed in Pall-Mall, and then, by strongly stating her objections, and confessing the grief they occasioned her, to pique at once his generosity and his pride upon releasing her himself from the engagement into which he had entered.

She had no time to deliberate; her plan, therefore, was decided almost as soon as formed, and every moment being precious, she was obliged to awaken Mrs Charlton, and communicate to her at once the letter from Delvile, and the new resolution she had taken.

Mrs Charlton, having no object in view but the happiness of her young friend, with a facility that looked not for objections, and scarce saw them when presented, agreed to the expedition, and kindly consented to accompany her to London; for Cecilia, however concerned to hurry and fatigue her, was too anxious for the sanction of her presence to hesitate in soliciting it.

A chaise, therefore, was ordered; and with posthorses for speed, and two servants on horseback, the moment Mrs Charlton was ready, they set out on their journey.

Scarce had they proceeded two miles on their way, when they were met by Mr Monckton, who was hastening to their house.

Amazed and alarmed at a sight so unexpected, he stopt the chaise to enquire whither they were going.

Cecilia, without answering, asked if her letter had yet been received?

"I could not," said Mr Monckton, "deliver it to a man who was not to be found; I was at this moment coming to acquaint how vainly I had sought him; but still that your journey is unnecessary unless voluntary, since I have left it at the house where you told me you should meet to-morrow morning, and where he must then unavoidably receive it."

"Indeed, Sir," cried Cecilia, "to-morrow morning will be too late,—in conscience, in justice, and even in decency too late! I must, therefore, go to town; yet I go not, believe me, in opposition to your injunctions, but to enable myself, without treachery or dishonour, to fulfil them."

Mr Monckton, aghast and confounded, made not any answer, till Cecilia gave orders to the postilion to drive on; he then hastily called to stop him, and began the warmest expostulations; but Cecilia, firm when she believed herself right, though wavering when fearful she was wrong, told him it was now too late to change her plan, and repeating her orders to the postilion, left him to his own reflections; grieved herself to reject his counsel, yet too intently occupied by her own affairs and designs, to think long of any other.

CHAPTER IX

A TORMENT.

At—they stopt for dinner; Mrs Charlton being too much fatigued to go on without some rest, though the haste of Cecilia to meet Delvile time enough for new arranging their affairs, made her regret every moment that was spent upon the road.

Their meal was not long, and they were returning to their chaise, when they were suddenly encountered by Mr Morrice, who was just alighted from his horse.

He congratulated himself upon the happiness of meeting them with the air of a man who nothing doubted that happiness being mutual; then hastening to speak of the Grove, "I could hardly," he cried, "get away; my friend Monckton won't know what to do without me, for Lady Margaret, poor old soul, is in a shocking bad way indeed; there's hardly any staying in the room with her; her breathing is just like the grunting of a hog. She can't possibly last long, for she's quite upon her last legs, and tumbles about so when she walks alone, one would swear she was drunk."

"If you take infirmity," said Mrs Charlton, who was now helped into the chaise, "for intoxication, you must suppose no old person sober."

"Vastly well said, ma'am," cried he; "I really forgot your being an old lady yourself, or I should not have made the observation. However, as to poor Lady Margaret, she may do as well as ever by and bye, for she has an excellent constitution, and I suppose she has been hardly any better than she is now these forty years, for I remember when I was quite a boy hearing her called a limping old puddle."

"Well, we'll discuss this matter, if you please," said Cecilia, "some other time." And ordered the postilion to drive on. But before they came to their next stage, Morrice having changed his horse, joined them, and rode on by their side, begging them to observe what haste he had made on purpose to have the pleasure of escorting them.

This forwardness was very offensive to Mrs Charlton, whose years and character had long procured her more deference and respect; but Cecilia, anxious only to hasten her journey, was indifferent to every thing, save what retarded it.

At the same Inn they both again changed horses, and he still continued riding with them, and occasionally talking, till they were within twenty miles of London, when a disturbance upon the road exciting his curiosity, he hastily rode away from them to enquire into its cause.

Upon coming up to the place whence it proceeded, they saw a party of gentlemen on horseback surrounding a chaise which had been just overturned; and while the confusion in the road obliged the postilion to stop Cecilia heard a lady's voice exclaiming, "I declare I dare say I am killed!" and instantly recollecting Miss Larolles, the fear of discovery and delay made her desire the man to drive on with all speed. He was preparing to obey her, but Morrice, galloping after them, called out, "Miss Beverley, one of the ladies that has been overturned, is an acquaintance of yours. I used to see her with you at Mrs Harrel's."

"Did you?" said Cecilia, much disconcerted, "I hope she is not hurt?'

"No, not at all; but the lady with her is bruised to death; won't you come and see her?"

"I am too much in haste at present,—and I can do them no good; but Mrs Charlton I am sure will spare her servant, if he can be of any use."

"O but the young lady wants to speak to you; she is coming up to the chaise as fast as ever she can."

"And how should she know me?" cried Cecilia, with much surprise; "I am sure she could not see me."

"O, I told her,", answered Morrice, with a nod of self-approbation for what he had done, "I told her it was you, for I knew I could soon overtake you."

Displeasure at this officiousness was unavailing, for looking out of the window, she perceived Miss Larolles, followed by half her party, not three paces from the chaise.

"O my dear creature," she called out, "what a terrible accident! I assure you I am so monstrously frightened you've no idea. It's the luckiest thing in the world that you were going this way. Never any thing happened so excessively provoking; you've no notion what a fall we've had. It's horrid shocking, I assure you. How have you been all this time? You can't conceive how glad I am to see you."

"And to which will Miss Beverley answer first," cried a voice which announced Mr Gosport, "the joy or the sorrow? For so adroitly are they blended, that a common auditor could with difficulty decide, whether condolence, or congratulation should have the precedency."

"How can you be so excessive horrid," cried Miss Larolles, "to talk of congratulation, when one's in such a shocking panic that one does not know if one's dead or alive!"

"Dead, then, for any wager," returned he, "if we may judge by your stillness."

"I desire, now, you won't begin joking," cried she, "for I assure you it's an excessive serious affair. I was never so rejoiced in my life as when I found I was not killed. I've been so squeezed you've no notion. I thought for a full hour I had broke both my arms."

"And my heart at the same time," said Mr Gosport; "I hope you did not imagine that the least fragile of the three?"

"All our hearts, give me leave to add," said Captain Aresby—just then advancing, "all our hearts must have been abimés, by the indisposition of Miss Larolles, had not their doom been fortunately revoked by the sight of Miss Beverley."

"Well, this is excessive odd,", cried Miss Larolles, "that every body should run away so from poor Mrs Mears; she'll be so affronted you've no idea. I thought, Captain Aresby, you would have stayed to take care of her."

"I'll run and see how she is myself," cried Morrice, and away he gallopped.

"Really, ma'am," said the Captain, "I am quite au desespoir to have failed in any of my devoirs; but I make it a principle to be a mere looker on upon these occasions, lest I should be so unhappy as to commit any faux pas by too much empressement."

"An admirable caution!" said Mr Gosport, "and, to so ardent a temper, a necessary check!"

Cecilia, whom the surprise and vexation of so unseasonable a meeting, when she particularly wished to have escaped all notice, had hitherto kept in painful silence, began now to recover some presence of mind; and making her compliments to Miss Larolles and Mr Gosport, with a slight bow to the Captain, she apologized for hurrying away, but told them she had an engagement in London which could not be deferred, and was then giving orders to the postilion to drive on, when Morrice returning full speed, called out "The poor lady's so bad she is not able to stir a step; she can't put a foot to the ground, and she says she's quite black and blue; so I told her I was sure Miss Beverley would not refuse to make room for her in her chaise, till the other can be put to rights; and she says she shall take it as a great favour. Here, postilion, a little more to the right! come, ladies and gentlemen, get out of the way." This impertinence, however extraordinary, Cecilia could not oppose; for Mrs Charlton, ever compassionate and complying where there was any appearance of distress, instantly seconded the proposal; the chaise, therefore, was turned back, and she was obliged to offer a place in it to Mrs Mears, who, though more frightened than hurt, readily accepted it, notwithstanding, to make way for her without incommoding Mrs Charlton, she was forced to get out herself.

She failed not, however, to desire that all possible expedition might be used in refitting the other chaise for their reception; and all the gentlemen but one, dismounted their horses, in order to assist, or seem to assist in getting it ready.

This only unconcerned spectator in the midst of the apparent general bustle, was Mr Meadows; who viewed all that passed without troubling himself to interfere, and with an air of the most evident carelessness whether matters went well or went ill.

Miss Larolles, now returning to the scene of action, suddenly screamed out, "O dear, where's my little dog! I never thought of him, I declare! I love him better than any thing in the world. I would not have him hurt for a hundred thousand pounds. Lord, where is he?"

"Crushed or suffocated in the overturn, no doubt," said Mr Gosport; "but as you must have been his executioner, what softer death could he die? If you will yourself inflict the punishment, I will submit to the same fate."

"Lord, how you love to plague one!" cried she and then enquired among the servants what was become of her dog. The poor little animal, forgotten by its mistress, and disregarded by all others, was now discovered by its yelping; and soon found to have been the most material sufferer by the overturn, one of its fore legs being broken.

Could screams or lamentations, reproaches to the servants, or complaints against the Destinies, have abated his pain, or made a callus of the fracture, but short would have been the duration of his misery; for neither words were saved, nor lungs were spared, the very air was rent with cries, and all present were upbraided as if accomplices in the disaster.

The postilion, at length, interrupted this vociferation with news that the chaise was again fit for use; and Cecilia, eager to be gone, finding him little regarded, repeated what he said to Miss Larolles.

"The chaise?" cried she, "why you don't suppose I'll ever get into that horrid chaise any more? I do assure you I would not upon any account."

"Not get into it?" said Cecilia, "for what purpose, then, have we all waited till it was ready?"

"O, I declare I would not go in it for forty thousand worlds. I would rather walk to an inn, if it's a hundred and fifty miles off."

"But as it happens," said Mr Gosport, "to be only seven miles, I fancy you will condescend to ride."

"Seven miles! Lord, how shocking! you frighten me so you have no idea. Poor Mrs Mears! She'll have to go quite alone. I dare say the chaise will be down fifty times by the way. Ten to one but she breaks her neck! only conceive how horrid! I assure you I am excessive glad I am out of it."

"Very friendly, indeed!" said Mr Gosport. "Mrs Mears, then, may break her bones at her leisure!"

Mrs Mears, however, when applied to, professed an equal aversion to the carriage in which she had been so unfortunate, and declared she would rather walk than return to it, though one of her ankles was already so swelled that she could hardly stand.

"Why then the best way, ladies," cried Morrice, with the look of a man happy in vanquishing all difficulties, "will be for Mrs Charlton, and that poor lady with the bruises, to go together in that sound chaise, and then for us gentlemen to escort this young lady and Miss Beverley on foot, till we all come to the next inn. Miss Beverley, I know, is an excellent walker, for I have heard Mr Monckton say so."

Cecilia, though in the utmost consternation at a proposal, which must so long retard a journey she had so many reasons to wish hastened, knew not how either in decency or humanity to oppose it; and the fear of raising suspicion, from a consciousness how much there was to suspect, forced her to curb her impatience, and reduced her even to repeat the offer which Morrice had made, though she could scarce look at him for anger at his unseasonable forwardness.

No voice dissenting, the troop began to be formed. The foot consisted of the two young ladies, and Mr Gosport, who alighted to walk with Cecilia; the cavalry, of Mr Meadows, the Captain, and Morrice, who walked their horses a foot pace, while the rest of the party rode on with the chaise, as attendants upon Mrs Mears.

Just before they set off, Mr Meadows, riding negligently up to the carriage, exerted himself so far as to say to Mrs Mears, "Are you hurt, ma'am?" and, at the same instant, seeming to recollect Cecilia, he turned about, and yawning while he touched his hat, said, "O, how d'ye do, ma'am?" and then, without waiting an answer to either of his questions, flapped it over his eyes, and joined the cavalcade, though without appearing to have any consciousness that he belonged to it.

Cecilia would most gladly have used the rejected chaise herself, but could not make such a proposal to Mrs Charlton, who was past the age and the courage for even any appearance of enterprize. Upon enquiry, however, she had the satisfaction to hear that the distance to the next stage was but two miles, though multiplied to seven by the malice of Mr Gosport.

Miss Larolles carried her little dog in her arms, declaring she would never more trust him a moment away from her. She acquainted Cecilia that she had been for some time upon a visit to Mrs Mears, who, with the rest of the party, had taken her to see—house and gardens, where they had made an early dinner, from which they were just returning home when the chaise broke down.

She then proceeded, with her usual volubility, to relate the little nothings that had passed since the winter, flying from subject to subject, with no meaning but to be heard, and no wish but to talk, ever rapid in speech, though minute in detail. This loquacity met not with any interruption, save now and then a sarcastic remark, from Mr Gosport; for Cecilia was too much occupied by her own affairs, to answer or listen to such uninteresting discourse.

Her silence, however, was at length forcibly broken; Mr Gosport, taking advantage of the first moment Miss Larolles stopt for breath, said, "Pray what carries you to town, Miss Beverley, at this time of the year?"

Cecilia, whose thoughts had been wholly employed upon what would pass at her approaching meeting with Delvile, was so entirely unprepared for this question, that she could make to it no manner of answer, till Mr Gosport, in a tone of some surprise, repeated it, and then, not without hesitation, she said, "I have some business, Sir, in London,—pray how long have you been in the country?"

"Business, have you?" cried he, struck by her evasion; "and pray what can you and business have in common?"

"More than you may imagine," answered she, with greater steadiness; "and perhaps before long I may even have enough to teach me the enjoyment of leisure."

"Why you don't pretend to play my Lady Notable, and become your own steward?"

"And what can I do better?"

"What? Why seek one ready made to take the trouble off your hands. There are such creatures to be found, I promise you; beasts of burthen, who will freely undertake the management of your estate, for no other reward than the trifling one of possessing it. Can you no where meet with such an animal?"

"I don't know," answered she, laughing, "I have not been looking out."

"And have none such made application to you?"

"Why no,—I believe not."

"Fie, fie! no register-office keeper has been pestered with more claimants. You know they assault you by dozens."

"You must pardon me, indeed, I know not any such thing."

"You know, then, why they do not, and that is much the same."

"I may conjecture why, at least; the place, I suppose, is not worth the service."

"No, no; the place, they conclude, is already seized, and the fee—simple of the estate is the heart of the owner. Is it not so?"

"The heart of the owner," answered she, a little confused, "may, indeed, be simple, but not, perhaps, so easily seized as you imagine."

"Have you, then, wisely saved it from a storm, by a generous surrender? you have been, indeed, in an excellent school for the study both of attack and defence; Delvile-Castle is a fortress which, even in ruins, proves its strength by its antiquity; and it teaches, also, an admirable lesson, by displaying the dangerous, the infallible power of time, which defies all might, and undermines all strength; which breaks down every barrier, and shews nothing endurable but itself." Then looking at her with an arch earnestness, "I think," he added, "you made a long visit there; did this observation never occur to you? did you never perceive, never feel, rather, the insidious properties of time?"

"Yes, certainly," answered she, alarmed at the very mention of Delvile Castle, yet affecting to understand literally what was said metaphorically, "the havoc of time upon the place could not fail striking me."

"And was its havoc," said he, yet more archly, "merely external? is all within safe? sound and firm? and did the length of your residence shew its power by no new mischief?"

"Doubtless, not," answered she, with the same pretended ignorance, "the place is not in so desperate a condition as to exhibit any visible marks of decay in the course of three or four months."

"And, do you not know," cried he, "that the place to which I allude may receive a mischief in as many minutes which double the number of years cannot rectify? The internal parts of a building are not less vulnerable to accident than its outside; and though the evil may more easily be concealed, it will with greater difficulty be remedied. Many a fair structure have I seen, which, like that now before me" (looking with much significance at Cecilia), "has to the eye seemed perfect in all its parts, and unhurt either by time or casualty, while within, some lurking evil, some latent injury, has secretly worked its way into the very heart of the edifice, where it has consumed its strength, and laid waste its powers, till, sinking deeper and deeper, it has sapped its very foundation, before the superstructure has exhibited any token of danger. Is such an accident among the things you hold to be possible?"

"Your language," said she, colouring very high, "is so florid, that I must own it renders your meaning rather obscure."

"Shall I illustrate it by an example? Suppose, during your abode in Delvile Castle?"

"No, no," interrupted she, with involuntary quickness, "why should I trouble you to make illustrations?"

"O pray, my dear creature," cried Miss Larolles, "how is Mrs Harrel? I was never so sorry for any body in my life. I quite forgot to ask after her."

"Ay, poor Harrel!" cried Morrice, "he was a great loss to his friends. I had just begun to have a regard for him; we were growing extremely intimate. Poor fellow! he really gave most excellent dinners."

"Harrel?" suddenly exclaimed Mr Meadows, who seemed just then to first hear what was going forward, "who was he?"

"O, as good-natured a fellow as ever I knew in my life," answered Morrice; "he was never out of humour; he was drinking and singing and dancing to the very last moment. Don't you remember him, Sir, that night at Vauxhall?"

Mr Meadows made not any answer, but rode languidly on.

Morrice, ever more flippant than sagacious, called out, "I really believe the gentleman's deaf! he won't so much as say umph, and hay, now; but I'll give him such a hallow in his ears, as shall make him hear me, whether he will or no. Sir! I say!" bawling aloud, "have you forgot that night at Vauxhall?"

Mr Meadows, starting at being thus shouted at, looked towards Morrice with some surprise, and said, "Were you so obliging, Sir, as to speak to me?"

"Lord, yes, Sir," said Morrice, amazed; "I thought you had asked something about Mr Harrel, so I just made an answer to it;—that's all."

"Sir, you are very good," returned he, slightly bowing, and then looking another way, as if thoroughly satisfied with what had passed.

"But I say, Sir," resumed Morrice, "don't you remember how Mr Harrel"—

"Mr who, Sir?"

"Mr Harrel, Sir; was not you just now asking me who he was?"

"O, ay, true," cried Meadows, in a tone of extreme weariness, "I am much obliged to you. Pray give my respects to him." And, touching his hat, he was riding away; but the astonished Morrice called out, "Your respects to him? why lord! Sir, don't you know he's dead?"

"Dead?—who, Sir?"

"Why Mr Harrel, Sir."

"Harrel?—O, very true," cried Meadows, with a face of sudden recollection; "he shot himself, I think, or was knocked down, or something of that sort. I remember it perfectly."

"O pray," cried Miss Larolles, "don't let's talk about it, it's the cruellest thing I ever knew in my life. I assure you I was so shocked, I thought I should never have got the better of it. I remember the next night at Ranelagh I could talk of nothing else. I dare say I told it to 500 people. I assure you I was tired to death; only conceive how distressing!"

"An excellent method," cried Mr Gosport, "to drive it out of your own head, by driving it into the heads of your neighbours! But were you not afraid, by such an ebullition of pathos, to burst as many hearts as you had auditors?"

"O I assure you," cried she, "every body was so excessive shocked you've no notion; one heard of nothing else; all the world was raving mad about it."

"Really yes," cried the Captain; "the subject was obsedé upon one partout. There was scarce any breathing for it; it poured from all directions; I must confess I was aneanti with it to a degree."

"But the most shocking thing in nature," cried Miss Larolles, "was going to the sale. I never missed a single day. One used to meet the whole world there, and every body was so sorry you can't conceive. It was quite horrid. I assure you I never suffered so much before; it made me so unhappy you can't imagine."

"That I am most ready to grant," said Mr Gosport, "be the powers of imagination ever so eccentric."

"Sir Robert Floyer and Mr Marriot," continued Miss Larolles, "have behaved so ill you've no idea, for they have done nothing ever since but say how monstrously Mr Harrel had cheated them, and how they lost such immense sums by him;—only conceive how ill-natured!"

"And they complain," cried Morrice, "that old Mr Delvile used them worse; for that when they had been defrauded of all that money on purpose to pay their addresses to Miss Beverley, he would never let them see her, but all of a sudden took her off into the country, on purpose to marry her to his own son."

The cheeks of Cecilia now glowed with the deepest blushes; but finding by a general silence that she was expected to make some answer, she said, with what unconcern she could assume, "They were very much mistaken; Mr Delvile had no such view."

"Indeed?" cried Mr Gosport, again perceiving her change of countenance; "and is it possible you have actually escaped a siege, while every body concluded you taken by assault? Pray where is young Delvile at present?"

"I don't—I can't tell, Sir."

"Is it long since you have seen him?"

"It is two months," answered she, with yet more hesitation, "since I was at Delvile Castle."

"O, but," cried Morrice, "did not you see him while he was in Suffolk? I believe, indeed, he is there now, for it was only yesterday I heard of his coming down, by a gentleman who called upon Lady Margaret, and told us he had seen a stranger, a day or two ago, at Mrs Charlton's door, and when he asked who he was, they told him his name was Delvile, and said he was on a visit at Mr Biddulph's."

Cecilia was quite confounded by this speech; to have it known that Delvile had visited her, was in itself alarming, but to have her own equivocation thus glaringly exposed, was infinitely more dangerous. The just suspicions to which it must give rise filled her with dread, and the palpable evasion in which she had been discovered, overwhelmed, her with confusion.

"So you had forgotten," said Mr Gosport, looking at her with much archness, "that you had seen him within the two months? but no wonder; for where is the lady who having so many admirers, can be at the trouble to remember which of them she saw last? or who, being so accustomed to adulation, can hold it worth while to enquire whence it comes? A thousand Mr Delviles are to Miss Beverley but as one; used from them all to the same tale, she regards them not individually as lovers, but collectively as men; and to gather, even from herself, which she is most inclined to favour, she must probably desire, like Portia in the Merchant of Venice, that their names may be run over one by one, before she can distinctly tell which is which."

The gallant gaiety of this speech was some relief to Cecilia, who was beginning a laughing reply, when Morrice called out, "That man looks as if he was upon the scout." And, raising her eyes, she perceived a man on horseback, who, though much muffled up, his hat flapped, and a handkerchief held to his mouth and chin, she instantly, by his air and figure, recognized to be Delvile.

In much consternation at this sight, she forgot what she meant to say, and dropping her eyes, walked silently on. Mr Gosport, attentive to her motions, looked from her to the horseman, and after a short examination, said, "I think I have seen that man before; have you, Miss Beverley?"

"Me?—no,"—answered she, "I believe not,—I hardly indeed, see him now."

"I have, I am pretty sure," said Morrice; "and if I could see his face, I dare say I should recollect him."

"He seems very willing to know if he can recollect any of us," said Mr Gosport, "and, if I am not mistaken, he sees much better than he is seen."

He was now come up to them, and though a glance sufficed to discover the object of his search, the sight of the party with which she was surrounded made him not dare stop or speak to her, and therefore, clapping spurs to his horse, he galloped past them.

"See," cried Morrice, looking after him, "how he turns round to examine us! I wonder who he is."

"Perhaps some highwayman!" cried Miss Larolles; "I assure you I am in a prodigious fright; I should hate to be robbed so you can't think."

"I was going to make much the same conjecture," said Mr Gosport, "and, if I am not greatly deceived, that man is a robber of no common sort. What think you, Miss Beverley, can you discern a thief in disguise?"

"No, indeed; I pretend to no such extraordinary knowledge."

"That's true; for all that you pretend to is extraordinary ignorance."

"I have a good mind," said Morrice, "to ride after him, and see what he is about."

"What for?" exclaimed Cecilia, greatly alarmed "there can certainly be no occasion!"

"No, pray don't," cried Miss Larolles, "for I assure you if he should come back to rob us, I should die upon the spot. Nothing could be so disagreeable I should scream so, you've no idea."

Morrice then gave up the proposal, and they walked quietly on; but Cecilia was extremely disturbed by this accident; she readily conjectured that, impatient for her arrival, Delvile had ridden that way, to see what had retarded her, and she was sensible that nothing could be so desirable as an immediate explanation of the motive of her journey. Such a meeting, therefore, had she been alone, was just what she could have wished, though, thus unluckily encompassed, it only added to her anxiety.

Involuntarily, however, she quickened her pace, through her eagerness to be relieved from so troublesome a party; but Miss Larolles, who was in no such haste, protested she could not keep up with her; saying, "You don't consider that I have got this sweet little dog to carry, and he is such a shocking plague to me you've no notion. Only conceive what a weight he is!"

"Pray, ma'am," cried Morrice, "let me take him for you; I'll be very careful of him, I promise you; and you need not be afraid to trust me, for I understand more about dogs than about any thing."

Miss Larolles, after many fond caresses, being really weary, consented, and Morrice placed the little animal before him on horseback; but while this matter was adjusting, and Miss Larolles was giving directions how she would have it held, Morrice exclaimed, "Look, look! that man is coming back! He is certainly watching us. There! now he's going off again!—I suppose he saw me remarking him."

"I dare say he's laying in wait to rob us," said Miss Larolles; "so when we turn off the high road, to go to Mrs Mears, I suppose he'll come galloping after us. It's excessive horrid, I assure you."

"'Tis a petrifying thing," said the captain, "that one must always be degouté by some wretched being or other of this sort; but pray be not deranged, I will ride after him, if you please, and do mon possible to get rid of him."

"Indeed I wish you would," answered Miss Larolles, "for I assure you he has put such shocking notions into my head, it's quite disagreeable."

"I shall make it a principle," said the captain, "to have the honour of obeying you." And was riding off, when Cecilia, in great agitation, called out "Why should you go, Sir?—he is not in our way,—pray let him alone,—for what purpose should you pursue him?"

"I hope," said Mr Gosport, "for the purpose of making him join our company, to some part of which I fancy he would be no very intolerable addition."

This speech again silenced Cecilia, who perceived, with the utmost confusion, that both Delvile and herself were undoubtedly suspected by Mr Gosport, if not already actually betrayed to him. She was obliged, therefore, to let the matter take its course, though quite sick with apprehension lest a full discovery should follow the projected pursuit.

The Captain, who wanted not courage, however deeply in vanity and affectation he had buried common sense, stood suspended, upon the request of Cecilia, that he would not go, and, with a shrug of distress, said, "Give me leave to own I am parfaitment in a state the most accablant in the world; nothing could give me greater pleasure than to profit of the occasion to accommodate either of these ladies; but as they proceed upon different principles, I am indecidé to a degree which way to turn myself!"

"Put it to the vote, then," said Morrice; "the two ladies have both spoke; now, then, for the gentlemen. Come, Sir," to Mr Gosport, "what say you?"

"O, fetch the culprit back, by all means," answered he; "and then let us all insist upon his opening his cause, by telling us in what he has offended us; for there is no part of his business, I believe, with which we are less acquainted."

"Well," said Morrice, "I'm for asking him a few questions too; so is the Captain; so every body has spoke but you, Sir," addressing himself to Mr Meadows, "So now, Sir, let's hear your opinion."

Mr Meadows, appearing wholly inattentive, rode on.

"Why, Sir, I say!" cried Morrice, louder, "we are all waiting for your vote. Pray what is the gentleman's name? it's deuced hard to make him hear one."

"His name is Meadows," said Miss Larolles, in a low voice, "and I assure you sometimes he won't hear people by the hour together. He's so excessive absent you've no notion. One day he made me so mad, that I could not help crying; and Mr Sawyer was standing by the whole time! and I assure you I believe he laughed at me. Only conceive how distressing!"

"May be," said Morrice, "it's out of bashfulness perhaps he thinks we shall cut him up."

"Bashfulness," repeated Miss Larolles; "Lord, you don't conceive the thing at all. Why he's at the very head of the ton. There's nothing in the world so fashionable as taking no notice of things, and never seeing people, and saying nothing at all, and never hearing a word, and not knowing one's own acquaintance. All the ton people do so, and I assure you as to Mr Meadows, he's so excessively courted by every body, that if he does but say a syllable, he thinks it such an immense favour, you've no idea."

This account, however little alluring in itself, of his celebrity, was yet sufficient to make Morrice covet his further acquaintance; for Morrice was ever attentive to turn his pleasure to his profit, and never negligent of his interest, but when ignorant how to pursue it. He returned, therefore, to the charge, though by no means with the same freedom he had begun it, and lowering his voice to a tone of respect and submission, he said, "Pray, Sir, may we take the liberty to ask your advice, whether we shall go on, or take a turn back?"

Mr Meadows made not any answer; but when Morrice was going to repeat his question, without appearing even to know that he was near him, he abruptly said to Miss Larolles, "Pray what is become of Mrs Mears? I don't see her amongst us."

"Lord, Mr Meadows," exclaimed she, "how can you be so odd? Don't you remember she went on in a chaise to the inn?"

"O, ay, true," cried he; "I protest I had quite forgot it; I beg your pardon, indeed. Yes, I recollect now,—she fell off her horse."

"Her horse? Why you know she was in her chaise."

"Her chaise, was it?—ay, true, so it was. Poor thing!—I am glad she was not hurt."

"Not hurt? Why she's so excessively bruised, she can't stir a step! Only conceive what a memory you've got!"

"I am most extremely sorry for her indeed," cried he, again stretching himself and yawning; "poor soul!—I hope she won't die. Do you think she will!"

"Die!" repeated Miss Larolles, with a scream, "Lord, how shocking! You are really enough to frighten one to hear you."

"But, Sir," said Morrice, "I wish you would be so kind as to give us your vote; the man will else be gone so far, we sha'n't be able to overtake him.—Though I do really believe that is the very fellow coming back to peep at us again!"

"I am ennuyé to a degree," cried the Captain; "he is certainly set upon us as a spy, and I must really beg leave to enquire of him upon what principle he incommodes us."—And instantly he rode after him.

"And so will I too," cried Morrice, following.

Miss Larolles screamed after him to give her first her little dog; but with a schoolboy's eagerness to be foremost, he galloped on without heeding her.

The uneasiness of Cecilia now encreased every moment; the discovery of Delvile seemed unavoidable, and his impatient and indiscreet watchfulness must have rendered the motives of his disguise but too glaring. All she had left to hope was arriving at the inn before the detection was announced, and at least saving herself the cruel mortification of hearing the raillery which would follow it.

Even this, however, was not allowed her; Miss Larolles, whom she had no means to quit, hardly stirred another step, from her anxiety for her dog, and the earnestness of her curiosity about the stranger. She loitered, stopt now to talk, and now to listen, and was scarce moved a yard from the spot where she had been left, when the Captain and Morrice returned.

"We could not for our lives overtake the fellow," said Morrice; "he was well mounted, I promise you, and I'll warrant he knows what he's about, for he turned off so short at a place where there were two narrow lanes, that we could not make out which way he went."

Cecilia, relieved and delighted by this unexpected escape, now recovered her composure, and was content to saunter on without repining.

"But though we could not seize his person," said the Captain, "we have debarrassed ourselves tout à fait from his pursuit; I hope, therefore, Miss Larolles will make a revoke of her apprehensions."

The answer to this was nothing but a loud scream, with an exclamation, "Lord, where's my dog?"

"Your dog!" cried Morrice, looking aghast, "good stars! I never thought of him!"

"How excessive barbarous!" cried Miss Larolles, "you've killed him, I dare say. Only think how shocking! I had rather have seen any body served so in the world. I shall never forgive it, I assure you."

"Lord, ma'am," said Morrice, "how can you suppose I've killed him? Poor, pretty creature, I'm sure I liked him prodigiously. I can't think for my life where he can be; but I have a notion he must have dropt down some where while I happened to be on the full gallop. I'll go look [for] him, however, for we went at such a rate that I never missed him."

Away again rode Morrice.

"I am abimé to the greatest degree," said the Captain, "that the poor little sweet fellow should be lost if I had thought him in any danger, I would have made it a principle to have had a regard to his person myself. Will you give me leave, ma'am, to have the honour of seeking him partout?"

"O, I wish you would with all my heart; for I assure you if I don't find him, I shall think it so excessive distressing you can't conceive."

The Captain touched his hat, and was gone.

These repeated impediments almost robbed Cecilia of all patience; yet her total inability of resistance obliged her to submit, and compelled her to go, stop, or turn, according to their own motions.

"Now if Mr Meadows had the least good-nature in the world," said Miss Larolles, "he would offer to help us; but he's so excessive odd, that I believe if we were all of us to fall down and break our necks, he would be so absent he would hardly take the trouble to ask us how we did."

"Why in so desperate a case," said Mr Gosport, "the trouble would be rather superfluous. However, don't repine that one of the cavaliers stays with us by way of guard, lest your friend the spy should take us by surprize while our troop is dispersed."

"O Lord," cried Miss Larolles, "now you put it in my head, I dare say that wretch has got my dog! only think how horrid!"

"I saw plainly," said Mr Gosport, looking significantly at Cecilia, "that he was feloniously inclined, though I must confess I took him not for a dog-stealer."

Miss Larolles then, running up to Mr Meadows, called out, "I have a prodigious immense favour to ask of you, Mr Meadows."

"Ma'am!" cried Mr Meadows, with his usual start.

"It's only to know, whether if that horrid creature should come back, you could not just ride up to him and shoot him, before he gets to us? Now will you promise me to do it?"

"You are vastly good," said he, with a vacant smile; "what a charming evening! Do you love the country?"

"Yes, vastly; only I'm so monstrously tired, I can hardly stir a step. Do you like it?"

"The country? O no! I detest it! Dusty hedges, and chirping sparrows! 'Tis amazing to me any body can exist upon such terms."

"I assure you," cried Miss Larolles, "I'm quite of your opinion. I hate the country so you've no notion. I wish with all my heart it was all under ground. I declare, when I first go into it for the summer, I cry so you can't think. I like nothing but London.—Don't you?"

"London!" repeated Mr Meadows, "O melancholy! the sink of all vice and depravity. Streets without light! Houses without air! Neighbourhood without society! Talkers without listeners!—'Tis astonishing any rational being can endure to be so miserably immured."

"Lord, Mr Meadows," cried she, angrily, "I believe you would have one live no where!"

"True, very true, ma'am," said he, yawning, "one really lives no where; one does but vegetate, and wish it all at an end. Don't you find it so, ma'am?"

"Me? no indeed; I assure you I like living of all things. Whenever I'm ill, I'm in such a fright you've no idea. I always think I'm going to die, and it puts me so out of spirits you can't think. Does not it you, too?"

Here Mr Meadows, looking another way, began to whistle.

"Lord," cried Miss Larolles, "how excessive distressing! to ask one questions, and then never hear what one answers!"

Here the Captain returned alone; and Miss Larolles, flying to meet him, demanded where was her dog?

"I have the malbeur to assure you," answered he, "that I never was more aneanti in my life! the pretty little fellow has broke another leg!"

Miss Larolles, in a passion of grief, then declared she was certain that Morrice had maimed him thus on purpose, and desired to know where the vile wretch was?

"He was so much discomposed at the incident," replied the Captain, "that he rode instantly another way. I took up the pretty fellow therefore myself, and have done mon possible not to derange him."

The unfortunate little animal was then delivered to Miss Larolles; and after much lamentation, they at length continued their walk; and, without further adventure, arrived at the inn.

Frances Burney – A Short Biography

Frances Burney was born on June 13th, 1752 in Lynn Regis (now King's Lynn).

Her mother, Esther, was described as of "warmth and intelligence," the daughter of a French refugee, she had been brought up a Catholic.

Frances's father, Charles Burney, was a noted musician, musicologist and composer as well as being a man of letters.

In 1760 the family moved to Poland Street, In London's Soho, giving them an entrée to a wider circle of the cultural elite.

A difficult situation arose in 1766 when Charles Burney eloped to marry for a second time. Elizabeth Allen, was the wealthy widow of a King's Lynn wine merchant and already the mother of three children.

The two families were now merged into one and tensions were always simmering as Elizabeth established her rules in an overbearing way, always with the threat of anger near to the surface.

Her father had always favoured her sisters Esther and Susanna over Frances. By the age of 8 Frances had still not learned the alphabet and couldn't read. Her sisters were sent to be educated in Paris whilst Frances educated herself, reading from the family library, which she then devoured as her ambitions began to take hold. She now also began her own 'scribblings'.

In 1762, her mother, Esther, died and it was a loss that Frances was to feel deeply for the rest of her life.

However, there was one family friend who had spotted Frances's talents. He was Samuel Crisp. He encouraged Frances to write, mainly by requesting frequent journal-letters from her that recounted the family goings-on and also that of her social circle in London.

Frances was fifteen by the time her father eventually remarried in 1767. Pressure was also being exerted for her to give up writing; it was "unladylike" and "might vex Mrs. Allen."

Feeling that she had been improper, she burnt her first manuscript, The History of Caroline Evelyn, which she had written in secret. However, Frances did keep an account of the emotions that led up to this in her diaries which she thereafter continued to write, a practice she kept faith with for 72 years.

Frances was a talented storyteller with a strong sense of character, she often wrote these "journal-diaries" as correspondence to her family and friends, recounting events from her life and her observations upon them. Her diary contains the extensive reading in her father's library, as well the visits and behaviour of the various important arts personalities who came to their home. Frances and her sister Susanna were particularly close, and it was to her that Frances would correspond throughout her adult life, in the form of such journal-letters.

In 1775 Frances received a proposal from Thomas Barlow, whom she had met only once before, and which she recounts amusingly in her journals.

By 1778 Frances Burney was ready to be acknowledged as an author. The publication that year of Evelina or the History of a Young Lady's Entrance into the World, was published anonymously in 1778, without her father's knowledge or permission, by Thomas Lowndes, who, after reading the first volume, agreed to publish it upon receipt of the finished work.

This was a time when having a novel published by a young woman was almost unthinkable. In fact, she had her brother pose as its author. Unfortunately, he was also the negotiator and despite its critical success and praise from such luminaries as Edmund Burke and Dr Johnson she received only twenty guineas.

Its comic depictions of English society and realistic use of accents among the working class brought it to the attention of her father who was at first surprised and then supportive that his daughter had published a novel and enhanced the family's standing. With the books rare use of a female teenage protagonist Frances was already pushing the boundaries of the novel.

It also brought Frances an invitation to the home of patron of the arts Hester Thrale. Here she met Dr Johnson, who would remain her friend and correspondent throughout the period of her visits, from 1779 to 1783. Mrs Thrale wrote to Dr Burney on July 22nd, stating that: "Mr. Johnson returned home full of the Prayes of the Book I had lent him, and protesting that there were passages in it which might do honour to Richardson: we talk of it for ever, and he feels ardent after the dénouement; he could not get rid of the Rogue, he said." Dr Johnson's best compliments were eagerly transcribed in Frances's diary.

Sojourns at Streatham could occupy months at a time, and on several occasions the guests, including Frances, made trips to Brighton and Bath. As with other notable events, these experiences were faithfully recorded.

In 1779, encouraged by the public's warm reception of comic material in Evelina, and with offers of help from Arthur Murphy and Richard Brinsley Sheridan, Frances began to write a dramatic comedy called The Witlings. The play satirised London society, including the literary world and its pretensions.

It was not published at the time as her father and Samuel Crisp thought it would offend some of the public by seeming to mock the Bluestockings, and also their reservations about the propriety of a woman writing comedy. The play is the story of Celia and Beaufort, lovers kept apart by their families due to "economic insufficiency".

In 1781 Samuel Crisp died. Much of her subsequent work, Cecilia, or Memoirs of an Heiress, was written after much discussion with Crisp. The novel was published the following year. Her advance was now £250 and the first edition ran to 2000 copies, the first of several printings that year alone.

The narrative of Cecilia tells of Cecilia Beverley, whose inheritance from her uncle comes on the condition that she marries but keeps the family name.

In 1784 one of her greatest supporters, and her frequent correspondent, Dr Johnson, died. Her promising relationship with a clergyman, George Owen Cambridge, was also over. Frances was 33 years old but she had made a great deal of her life already.

In 1785, thanks to her association with Mary Granville Delany, a woman influential in both literary and royal circles, Frances travelled to the court of King George III and Queen Charlotte. There she was offered the post of "Keeper of the Robes", and a salary of £200 per annum. Frances hesitated. She had no wish to be separated from her family, nor to anything that would restrict her time in writing. But, unmarried at 34, she felt obliged to accept and thought that improved social status and income might allow her greater freedom to write.

She developed a warm relationship with the queen and princesses that lasted into her later years, yet her worries were prophetic: the position exhausted her and left her little, if any, time to write.

She was unhappy and her feelings were amplified by a poor relationship with her colleague, Elizabeth Schwellenburg, co-Keeper of the Robes.

But despite writing little in the way of novels she still kept at her journals recounting life at court and the various political and social events.

By 1790, frustrated at her lack of writing, her further failed relationships, and with her health failing she asked to be released from service. The request was granted.

She returned to her father's house in Chelsea, but continued to receive a yearly pension of £100. She maintained a friendship with the royal family and received letters from the princesses until her death.

Between 1790–91 Frances wrote four blank-verse tragedies: Hubert de Vere, The Siege of Pevensey, Elberta and Edwy and Elgiva. Only the last was performed but met with public failure and played for only one night.

The French Revolution which had begun in 1789 brought support from many English literates for the ideals of equality and social justice. It was now that Frances became acquainted with a group of French exiles known as "Constitutionalists", who had fled France and were living at Juniper Hall, near Mickleham, where Frances's sister Susanna lived.

Frances quickly became attached to General Alexandre D'Arblay, an artillery officer who had been adjutant-general to Lafayette, a hero of the French Revolution.

Frances's father disapproved because of Alexandre's poverty, his Catholicism, and his ambiguous social status as an émigré. In spite of these objections they were married on July 28th, 1793.

On December 18th, 1794, Frances gave birth to their only child, a son, Alexander.

The impoverished couple were saved from poverty in 1796 by the publication of her next novel Camilla, or a Picture of Youth, a story of frustrated love and impoverishment. She made £1000 on the novel and sold the copyright for another £1000. This was enough to enable them to build a house in Westhumble; Camilla Cottage. Their life was now happy on all fronts.

Sadly, the news that her sister Susanna and her family were moving to Ireland that year caused her, and her father, some consternation, as did her sister Charlotte's remarriage in 1798 to the pamphleteer Ralph Broome.

Between 1797–1801 Frances wrote three further comedies; Love and Fashion, A Busy Day and The Woman Hater. All were unpublished during her lifetime.

The illness and death of Susanna in 1800 brought an end to their lifelong correspondence. Frances was devastated and only resumed her journal writing at the request of her husband, for the benefit of their son.

In 1801 D'Arblay was offered service with the government of Napoleon in France, and in 1802 Frances and her son followed him to Paris, where they expected to remain for a year. The outbreak of the war between France and England meant their stay extended for ten years. Although the conditions of their time left her isolated from her family, Frances was supportive of her husband's decision to move.

In August 1810 Frances developed pains in her breast. Her husband suspected breast cancer. Through her royal network of acquaintances, she was treated by leading physicians and, a year later, on September 30th, 1811, she underwent a mastectomy performed by "7 men in black". The operation was performed by M. Dubois, the accoucheur (midwife or obstetrician) to the Empress Marie Louise, Duchess of Parma, and widely considered the best doctor in France. Frances was later able to write about the operation in detail, since she was conscious through most of it, anesthetics not yet being in use.

Frances survived, even though she was still in recovery and not back to full health, returned to England in 1812 to visit her ailing father and also to avoid young Alexander's conscription into the French army

In 1814, Frances published her fourth novel, The Wanderer or, Female Difficulties, a few days before her father's death. A story of love and misalliance set in the French Revolution", it criticises the English treatment of foreigners during the war.

Frances made £1500 from the first run, but it did not go into a second English printing, although it met her immediate financial needs.

In 1815 Napoleon escaped from Elba. D'Arblay was then serving with the King's Guard, and he became involved in the military actions that followed. Frances joined her wounded husband at Trèves, and together they returned to Bath, England. Frances wrote an account of this and of her Paris years in her Waterloo Journal, written between 1818 and 1832. D'Arblay was rewarded with promotion to lieutenant-general but died shortly afterwards, in 1818, of cancer.

Frances now moved to London to be nearer to her son, a fellow at Christ's College. In honour of her father she gathered and in 1832 published, in three volumes, the Memoirs of Doctor Burney. The memoirs overly praised her father's accomplishments and character. Always protective of her father and the family's reputation, she deliberately destroyed evidence of facts that were painful or unflattering.

She now lived almost in retirement, outliving her son, Alexander, who died in 1837, and her sister, Charlotte, who died in 1838.

Frances continued to receive many visits from younger members of the Burney family, who gathered to listen to her fascinating accounts and her talents for imitating the people she described. She continued to write in her journals but alas her canon of novels and plays received no further additions.

Frances Burney died on January 6th, 1840.

She was buried with her son and her husband in Walcot cemetery in Bath.

There is a Royal Society of Arts blue plaque to record her period of residence at 11 Bolton Street, Mayfair.

Fiction

The History of Caroline Evelyn, (manuscript destroyed by author, 1767.)
Evelina: or, The History of a Young Lady's Entrance into the World. 1778.
Cecilia: or, Memoirs of an Heiress. 1782.
Camilla: or, A Picture of Youth. 1796.
The Wanderer: or, Female Difficulties. 1814.

Non Fiction

Brief Reflections Relative to the French Emigrant Clergy. 1793.
Memoirs of Doctor Burney. 1832.

Journals & Letters

The Early Diary of Frances Burney 1768–1778. 2 volumes. 1889.
The Diary and Letters of Madame D'Arblay. 1904.
The Diary of Fanny Burney.
Dr. Johnson & Fanny Burney by Fanny Burney.
The Early Journals and Letters of Fanny Burney, 1768–1786. 5 volumes.
The Court Journals and Letters of Frances Burney. 4 volumes. (to date).
The Journals and Letters of Fanny Burney (Madame D'Arblay) 1791–1840. 12 volumes.

Plays

The Witlings, 1779 (satirical comedy).
Edwy and Elgiva, 1790 (verse tragedy). Produced at Drury Lane, 21 March 1795.
Hubert de Vere, 1788–91 (verse tragedy).
The Siege of Pevensey, 1788–91 (verse tragedy).
Elberta, (fragment) 1788–91 (verse tragedy).
Love and Fashion, 1799 (satirical comedy).
The Woman Hater, 1800–1801 (satirical comedy).
A Busy Day, 1800–1801 (satirical comedy).

www.ingramcontent.com/pod-product-compliance
Lightning Source LLC
Chambersburg PA
CBHW061207170626
46809CB00003B/1275